I'M NOT YOUR SWEET BABBOO!

Other *Peanuts* Kids' Collections

Snoopy: Cowabunga

Charlie Brown and Friends

Charlie Brown: Pow!

Woodstock: Master of Disguise

Snoopy: Contact!

Snoopy: Party Animal

Charlie Brown: Here We Go Again

Snoopy to the Rescue

Snoopy: What's Wrong With Dog Lips?

I'M NOT YOUR SWEET BABBOO!

A PEANUTS™ Collection

CHARLES M. SCHULZ

Andrews McMeel
PUBLISHING®

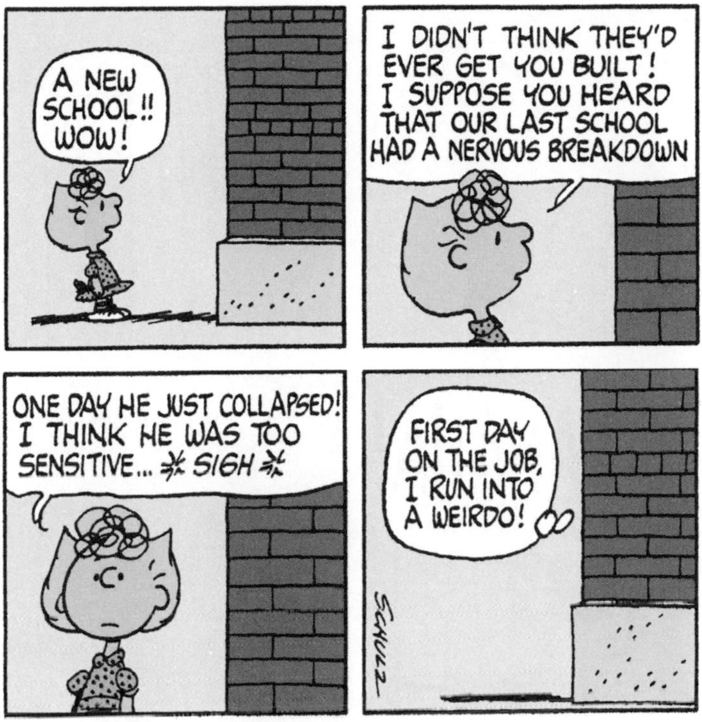
A NEW SCHOOL!! WOW!
I DIDN'T THINK THEY'D EVER GET YOU BUILT! I SUPPOSE YOU HEARD THAT OUR LAST SCHOOL HAD A NERVOUS BREAKDOWN
ONE DAY HE JUST COLLAPSED! I THINK HE WAS TOO SENSITIVE... *SIGH*
FIRST DAY ON THE JOB, I RUN INTO A WEIRDO!
SCHULZ

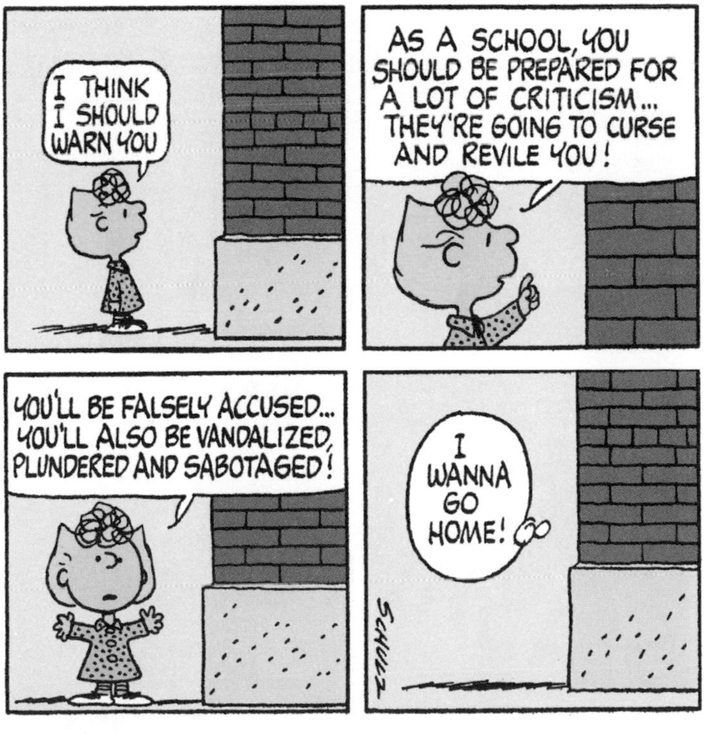
I THINK I SHOULD WARN YOU
AS A SCHOOL, YOU SHOULD BE PREPARED FOR A LOT OF CRITICISM... THEY'RE GOING TO CURSE AND REVILE YOU!
YOU'LL BE FALSELY ACCUSED... YOU'LL ALSO BE VANDALIZED, PLUNDERED AND SABOTAGED!
I WANNA GO HOME!
SCHULZ

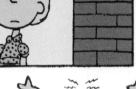

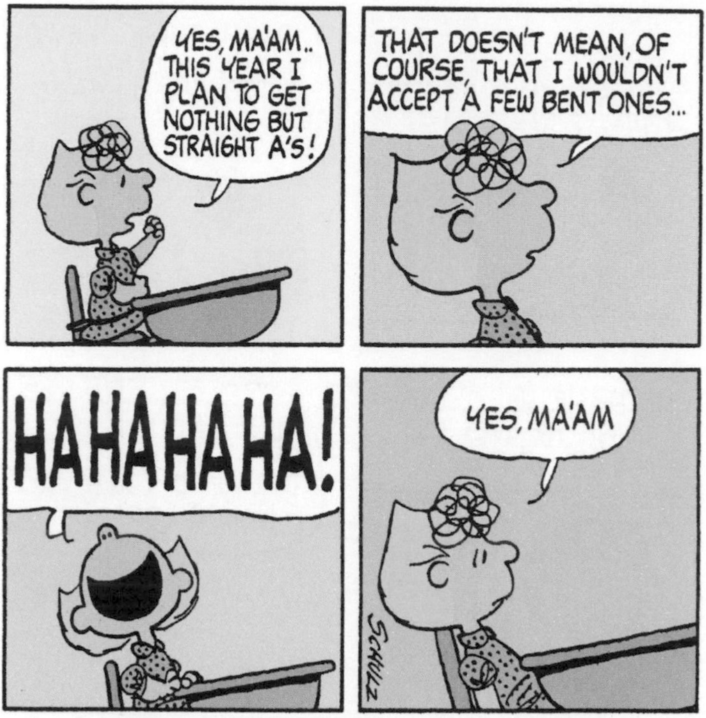
YES, MA'AM.. THIS YEAR I PLAN TO GET NOTHING BUT STRAIGHT A'S!
THAT DOESN'T MEAN, OF COURSE, THAT I WOULDN'T ACCEPT A FEW BENT ONES...
HAHAHAHA!
YES, MA'AM
SCHULZ

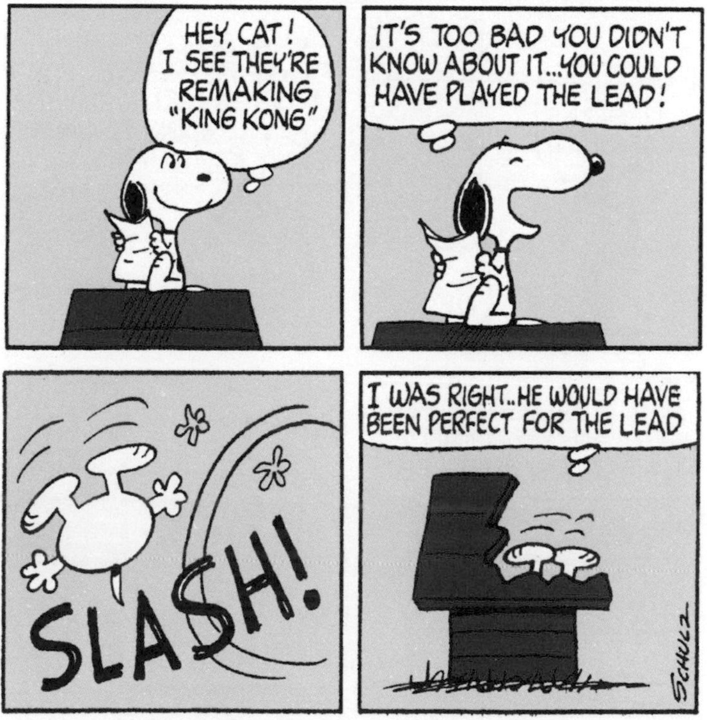
HEY, CAT! I SEE THEY'RE REMAKING "KING KONG"
IT'S TOO BAD YOU DIDN'T KNOW ABOUT IT...YOU COULD HAVE PLAYED THE LEAD!
SLASH!
I WAS RIGHT..HE WOULD HAVE BEEN PERFECT FOR THE LEAD
SCHULZ

I FEEL LIKE GOING TO THE PARK...LET'S TAKE A VOTE ON IT...
THEY DON'T HAVE ANYTHING TO EAT THERE?! STOMACHS NEVER WANT TO GO ANY PLACE WHERE YOU DON'T EAT!
?
THE NOSE NEVER KNOWS! HOW ABOUT THE EARS? ALL RIGHT, EARS, PAY ATTENTION..
THAT'S THE TROUBLE WITH EARS...THEY NEVER LISTEN...DO YOU WANT TO GO TO THE PARK, OR DON'T YOU?
"IF THERE'S A BAND PLAYING!" HOW DO I KNOW IF THERE'S GOING TO BE A BAND PLAYING?
THERE'S NO USE IN EVEN ASKING THE FEET... FEET ALWAYS WANT TO STAY HOME...
I DON'T CARE WHAT ANY OF YOU SAY...WE'RE GOING TO THE PARK! I'M STILL IN CHARGE!
IT NEVER FAILS..THEY ALL COMPLAIN ABOUT GOING, BUT AFTER WE GET HERE, THEY ALL HAVE A GOOD TIME!
SCHULZ

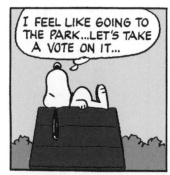

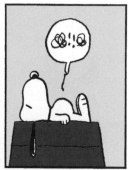

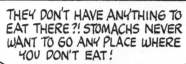

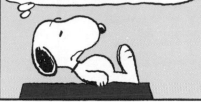

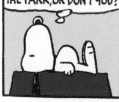

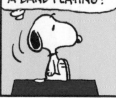

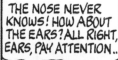

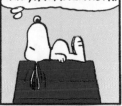

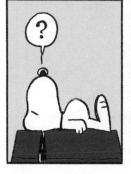

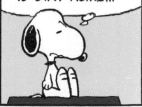

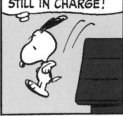

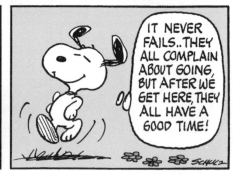

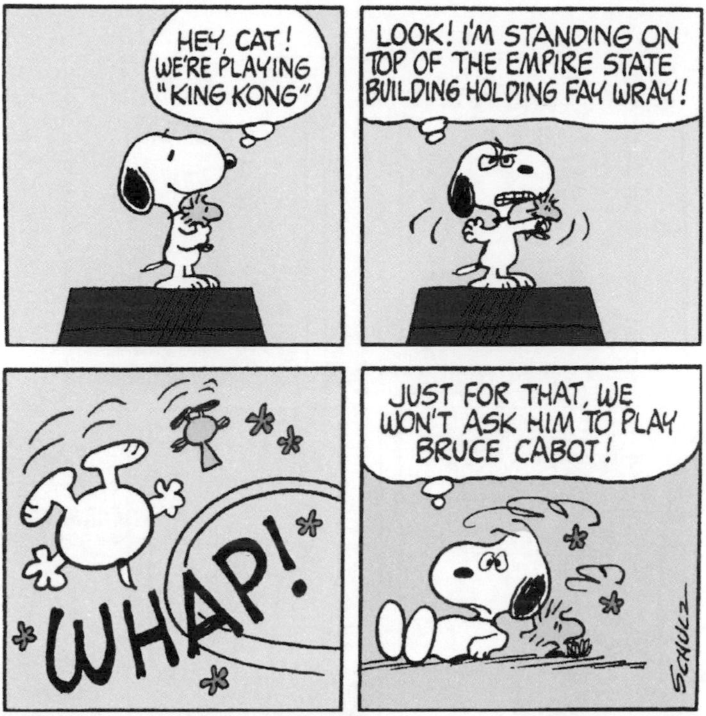
HEY, CAT! WE'RE PLAYING "KING KONG"
LOOK! I'M STANDING ON TOP OF THE EMPIRE STATE BUILDING HOLDING FAY WRAY!
WHAP!
JUST FOR THAT, WE WON'T ASK HIM TO PLAY BRUCE CABOT!
SCHULZ

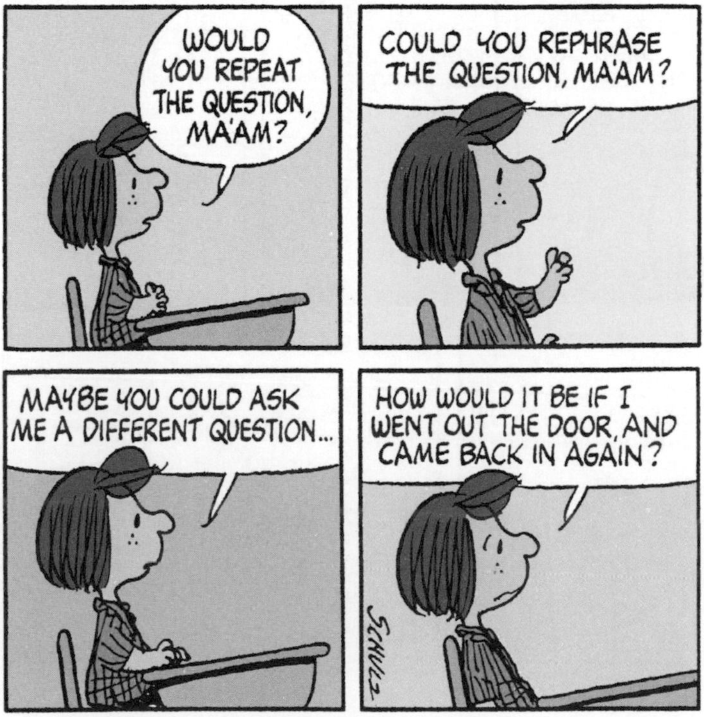
WOULD YOU REPEAT THE QUESTION, MA'AM?
COULD YOU REPHRASE THE QUESTION, MA'AM?
MAYBE YOU COULD ASK ME A DIFFERENT QUESTION...
HOW WOULD IT BE IF I WENT OUT THE DOOR, AND CAME BACK IN AGAIN?
SCHULZ

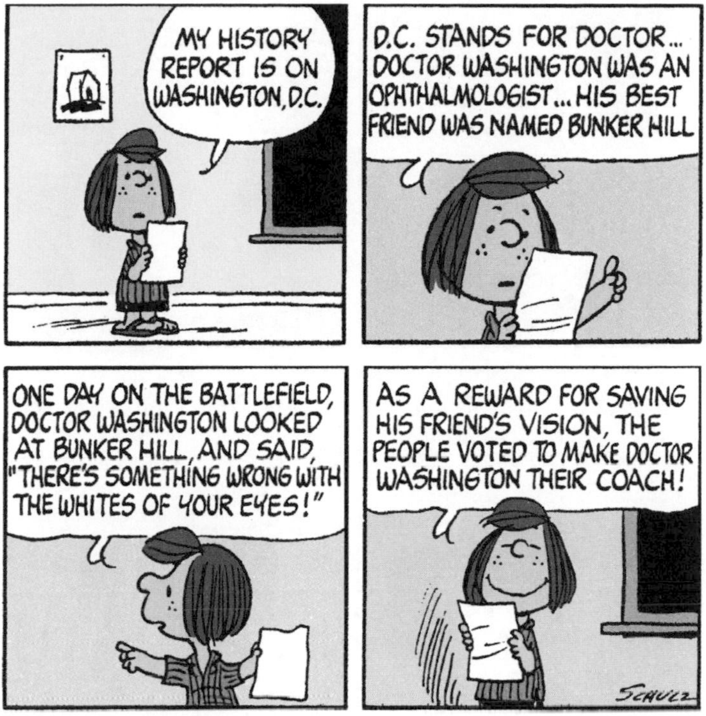
MY HISTORY REPORT IS ON WASHINGTON, D.C.
D.C. STANDS FOR DOCTOR... DOCTOR WASHINGTON WAS AN OPHTHALMOLOGIST... HIS BEST FRIEND WAS NAMED BUNKER HILL
ONE DAY ON THE BATTLEFIELD, DOCTOR WASHINGTON LOOKED AT BUNKER HILL, AND SAID, "THERE'S SOMETHING WRONG WITH THE WHITES OF YOUR EYES!"
AS A REWARD FOR SAVING HIS FRIEND'S VISION, THE PEOPLE VOTED TO MAKE DOCTOR WASHINGTON THEIR COACH!
SCHULZ

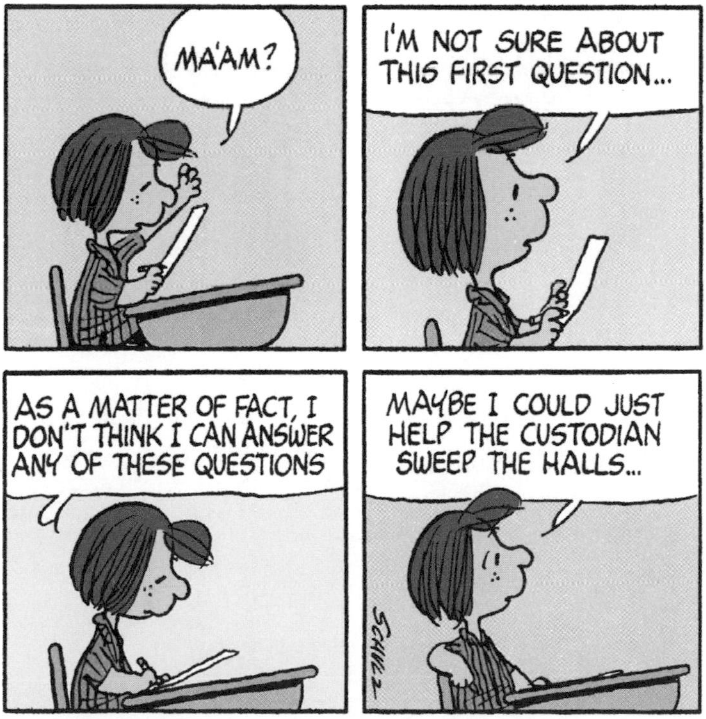
MA'AM?
I'M NOT SURE ABOUT THIS FIRST QUESTION...
AS A MATTER OF FACT, I DON'T THINK I CAN ANSWER ANY OF THESE QUESTIONS
MAYBE I COULD JUST HELP THE CUSTODIAN SWEEP THE HALLS...
SCHULZ

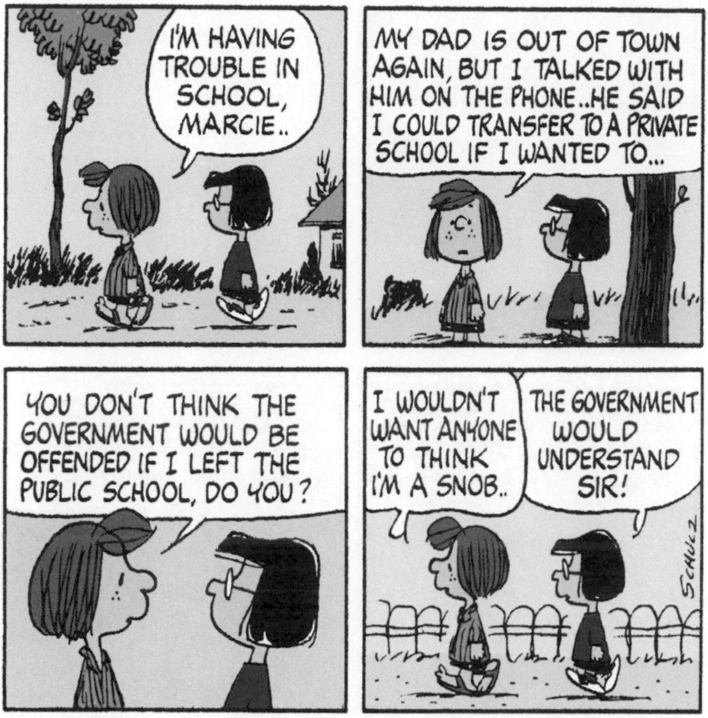
I'M HAVING TROUBLE IN SCHOOL, MARCIE..
MY DAD IS OUT OF TOWN AGAIN, BUT I TALKED WITH HIM ON THE PHONE..HE SAID I COULD TRANSFER TO A PRIVATE SCHOOL IF I WANTED TO...
YOU DON'T THINK THE GOVERNMENT WOULD BE OFFENDED IF I LEFT THE PUBLIC SCHOOL, DO YOU?
I WOULDN'T WANT ANYONE TO THINK I'M A SNOB..
THE GOVERNMENT WOULD UNDERSTAND SIR!
SCHULZ

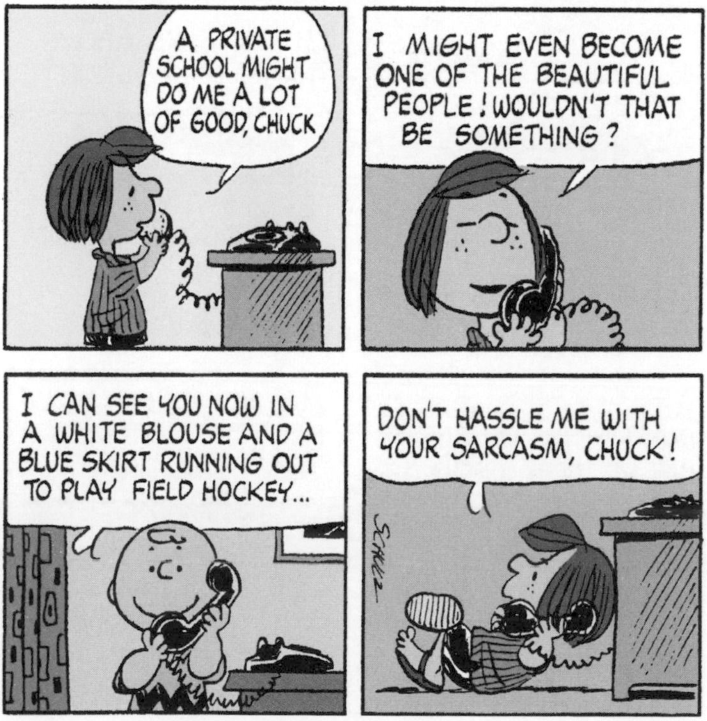
A PRIVATE SCHOOL MIGHT DO ME A LOT OF GOOD, CHUCK
I MIGHT EVEN BECOME ONE OF THE BEAUTIFUL PEOPLE! WOULDN'T THAT BE SOMETHING?
I CAN SEE YOU NOW IN A WHITE BLOUSE AND A BLUE SKIRT RUNNING OUT TO PLAY FIELD HOCKEY...
DON'T HASSLE ME WITH YOUR SARCASM, CHUCK!
SCHULZ

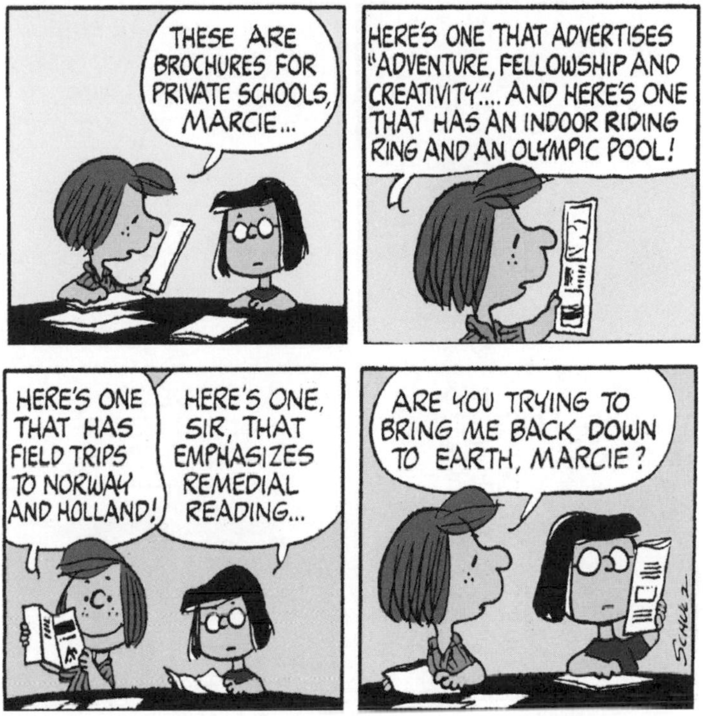
THESE ARE BROCHURES FOR PRIVATE SCHOOLS, MARCIE...
HERE'S ONE THAT ADVERTISES "ADVENTURE, FELLOWSHIP AND CREATIVITY"!... AND HERE'S ONE THAT HAS AN INDOOR RIDING RING AND AN OLYMPIC POOL!
HERE'S ONE THAT HAS FIELD TRIPS TO NORWAY AND HOLLAND!
HERE'S ONE, SIR, THAT EMPHASIZES REMEDIAL READING...
ARE YOU TRYING TO BRING ME BACK DOWN TO EARTH, MARCIE?
SCHULZ

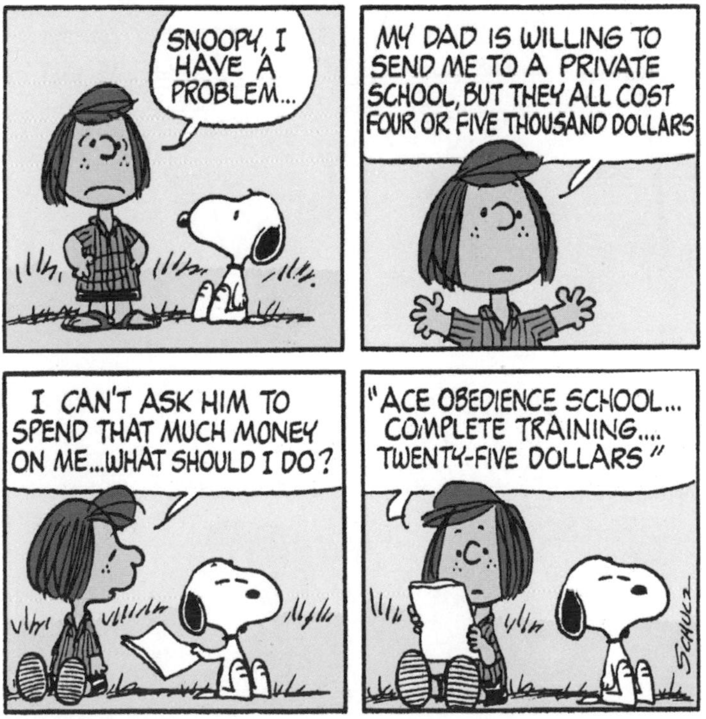
SNOOPY, I HAVE A PROBLEM...
MY DAD IS WILLING TO SEND ME TO A PRIVATE SCHOOL, BUT THEY ALL COST FOUR OR FIVE THOUSAND DOLLARS
I CAN'T ASK HIM TO SPEND THAT MUCH MONEY ON ME...WHAT SHOULD I DO?
"ACE OBEDIENCE SCHOOL... COMPLETE TRAINING.... TWENTY-FIVE DOLLARS"
SCHULZ

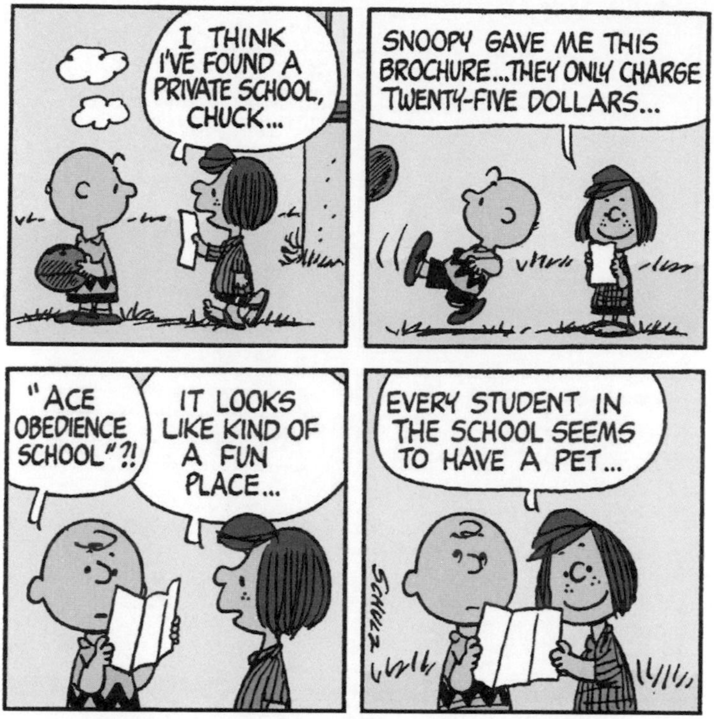
I THINK I'VE FOUND A PRIVATE SCHOOL, CHUCK...
SNOOPY GAVE ME THIS BROCHURE...THEY ONLY CHARGE TWENTY-FIVE DOLLARS...
"ACE OBEDIENCE SCHOOL"?!
IT LOOKS LIKE KIND OF A FUN PLACE...
EVERY STUDENT IN THE SCHOOL SEEMS TO HAVE A PET...
SCHULZ

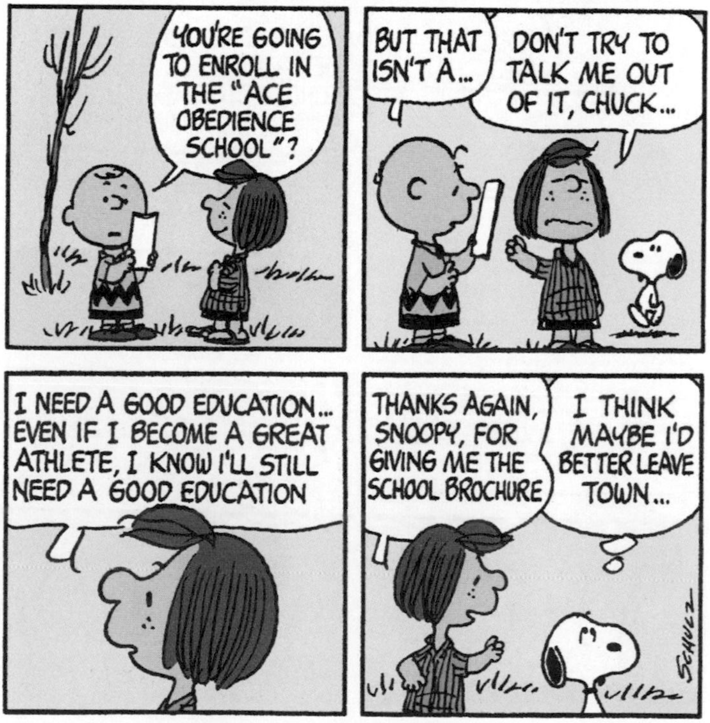
YOU'RE GOING TO ENROLL IN THE "ACE OBEDIENCE SCHOOL"?
BUT THAT ISN'T A...
DON'T TRY TO TALK ME OUT OF IT, CHUCK...
I NEED A GOOD EDUCATION... EVEN IF I BECOME A GREAT ATHLETE, I KNOW I'LL STILL NEED A GOOD EDUCATION
THANKS AGAIN, SNOOPY, FOR GIVING ME THE SCHOOL BROCHURE
I THINK MAYBE I'D BETTER LEAVE TOWN...
SCHULZ

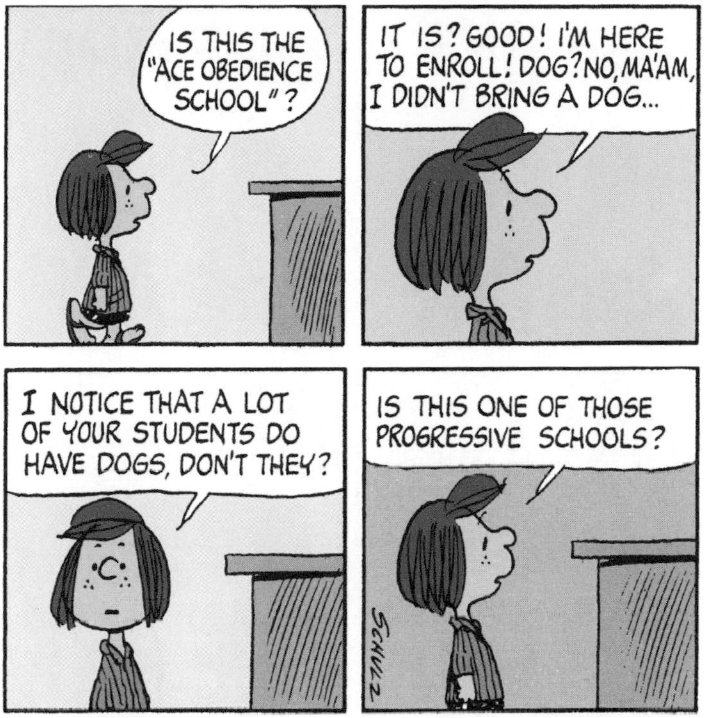
IS THIS THE "ACE OBEDIENCE SCHOOL"?
IT IS? GOOD! I'M HERE TO ENROLL! DOG? NO, MA'AM, I DIDN'T BRING A DOG...
I NOTICE THAT A LOT OF YOUR STUDENTS DO HAVE DOGS, DON'T THEY?
IS THIS ONE OF THOSE PROGRESSIVE SCHOOLS?
SCHULZ

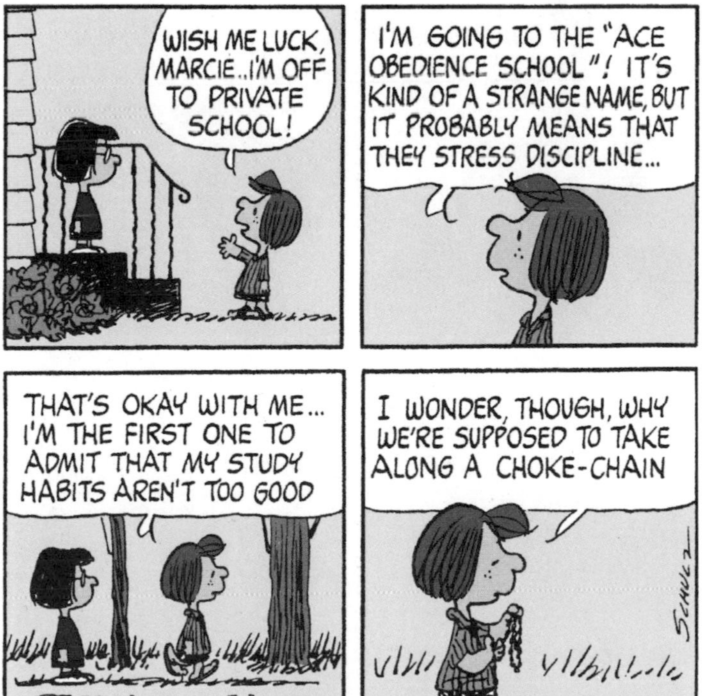
WISH ME LUCK, MARCIE..I'M OFF TO PRIVATE SCHOOL!
I'M GOING TO THE "ACE OBEDIENCE SCHOOL"! IT'S KIND OF A STRANGE NAME, BUT IT PROBABLY MEANS THAT THEY STRESS DISCIPLINE...
THAT'S OKAY WITH ME... I'M THE FIRST ONE TO ADMIT THAT MY STUDY HABITS AREN'T TOO GOOD
I WONDER, THOUGH, WHY WE'RE SUPPOSED TO TAKE ALONG A CHOKE-CHAIN
SCHULZ

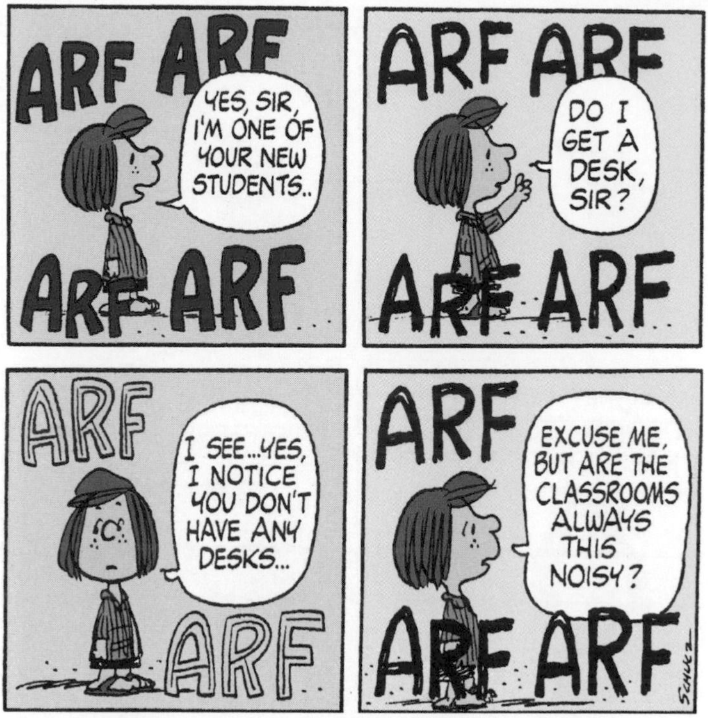
ARF ARF
YES, SIR, I'M ONE OF YOUR NEW STUDENTS..
ARF ARF
ARF ARF
DO I GET A DESK, SIR?
ARF ARF
ARF
I SEE...YES, I NOTICE YOU DON'T HAVE ANY DESKS...
ARF
ARF
EXCUSE ME, BUT ARE THE CLASSROOMS ALWAYS THIS NOISY?
ARF ARF
SCHULZ

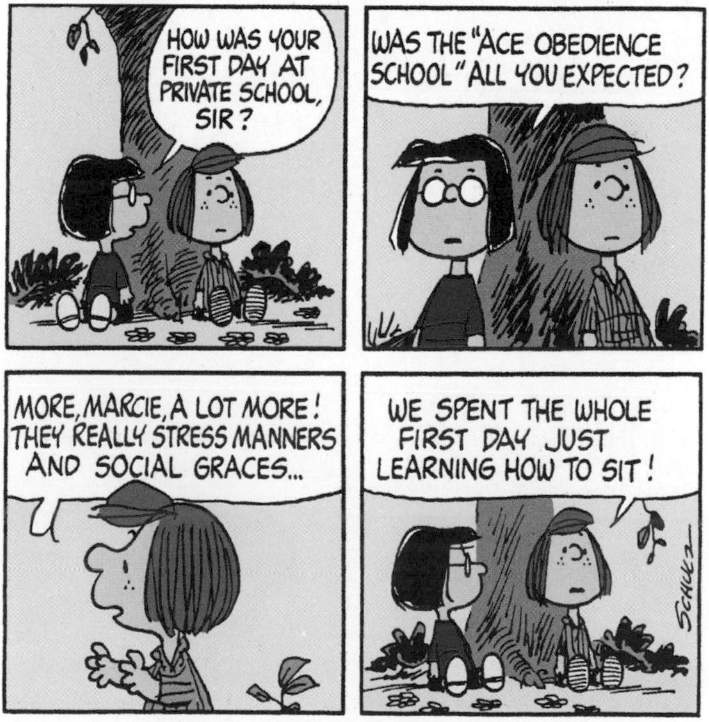
HOW WAS YOUR FIRST DAY AT PRIVATE SCHOOL, SIR?
WAS THE "ACE OBEDIENCE SCHOOL" ALL YOU EXPECTED?
MORE, MARCIE, A LOT MORE! THEY REALLY STRESS MANNERS AND SOCIAL GRACES...
WE SPENT THE WHOLE FIRST DAY JUST LEARNING HOW TO SIT!
SCHULZ

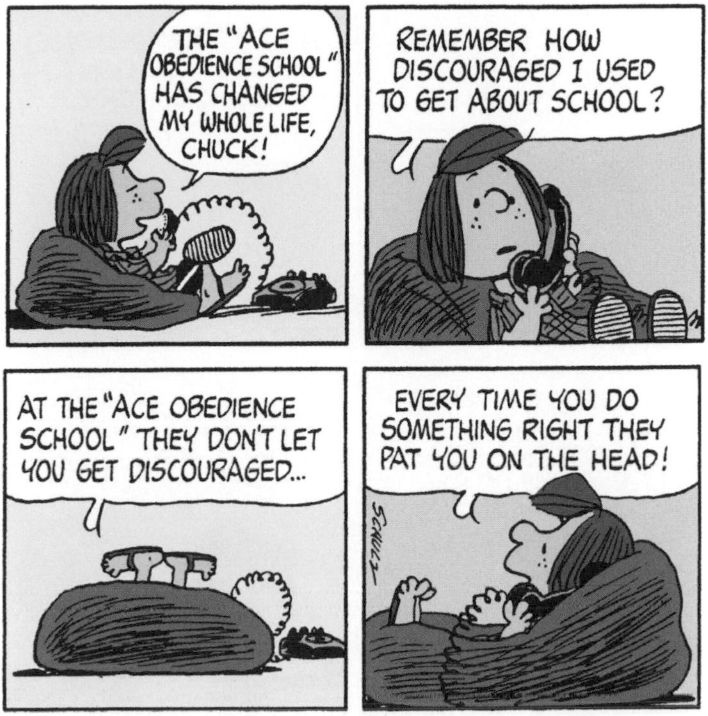
THE "ACE OBEDIENCE SCHOOL" HAS CHANGED MY WHOLE LIFE, CHUCK!
REMEMBER HOW DISCOURAGED I USED TO GET ABOUT SCHOOL?
AT THE "ACE OBEDIENCE SCHOOL" THEY DON'T LET YOU GET DISCOURAGED...
EVERY TIME YOU DO SOMETHING RIGHT THEY PAT YOU ON THE HEAD!
SCHULZ

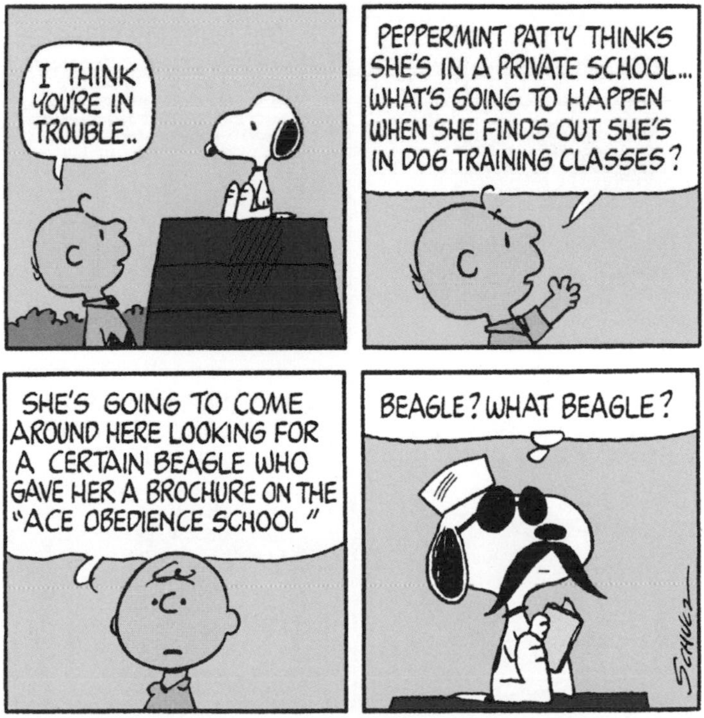
I THINK YOU'RE IN TROUBLE..
PEPPERMINT PATTY THINKS SHE'S IN A PRIVATE SCHOOL... WHAT'S GOING TO HAPPEN WHEN SHE FINDS OUT SHE'S IN DOG TRAINING CLASSES?
SHE'S GOING TO COME AROUND HERE LOOKING FOR A CERTAIN BEAGLE WHO GAVE HER A BROCHURE ON THE "ACE OBEDIENCE SCHOOL"
BEAGLE? WHAT BEAGLE?
SCHULZ

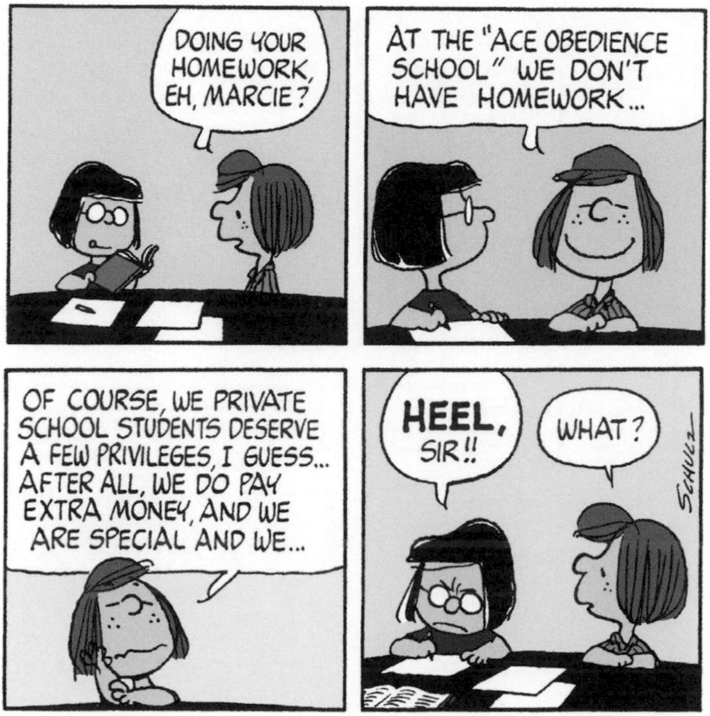
DOING YOUR HOMEWORK, EH, MARCIE?
AT THE "ACE OBEDIENCE SCHOOL" WE DON'T HAVE HOMEWORK...
OF COURSE, WE PRIVATE SCHOOL STUDENTS DESERVE A FEW PRIVILEGES, I GUESS... AFTER ALL, WE DO PAY EXTRA MONEY, AND WE ARE SPECIAL AND WE...
HEEL, SIR!!
WHAT?
SCHULZ

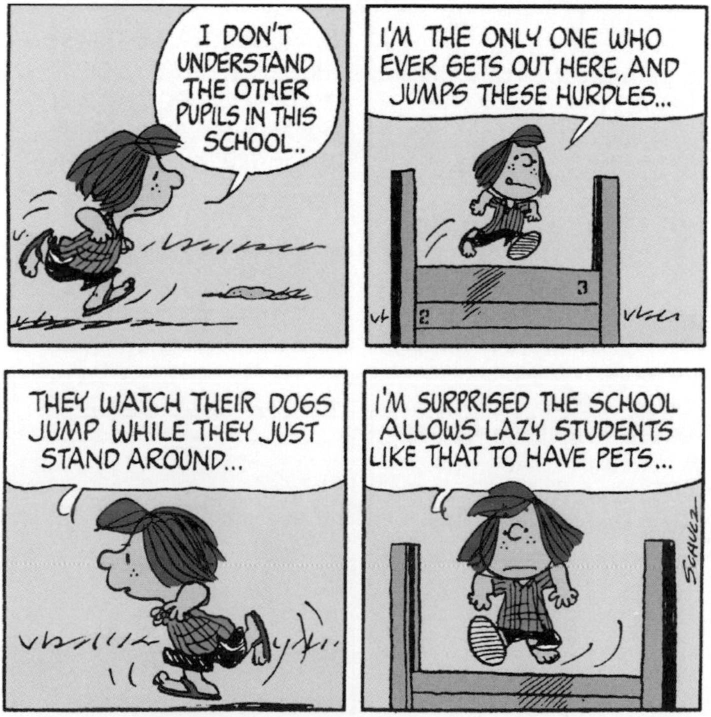
I DON'T UNDERSTAND THE OTHER PUPILS IN THIS SCHOOL..
I'M THE ONLY ONE WHO EVER GETS OUT HERE, AND JUMPS THESE HURDLES...
3
2
THEY WATCH THEIR DOGS JUMP WHILE THEY JUST STAND AROUND...
I'M SURPRISED THE SCHOOL ALLOWS LAZY STUDENTS LIKE THAT TO HAVE PETS...
SCHULZ

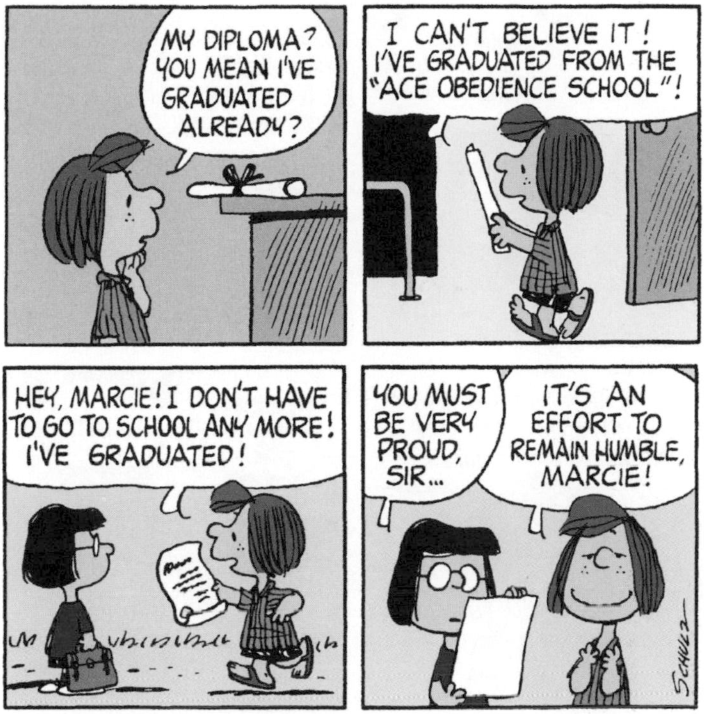
MY DIPLOMA? YOU MEAN I'VE GRADUATED ALREADY?
I CAN'T BELIEVE IT! I'VE GRADUATED FROM THE "ACE OBEDIENCE SCHOOL"!
HEY, MARCIE! I DON'T HAVE TO GO TO SCHOOL ANY MORE! I'VE GRADUATED!
YOU MUST BE VERY PROUD, SIR...
IT'S AN EFFORT TO REMAIN HUMBLE, MARCIE!
SCHULZ

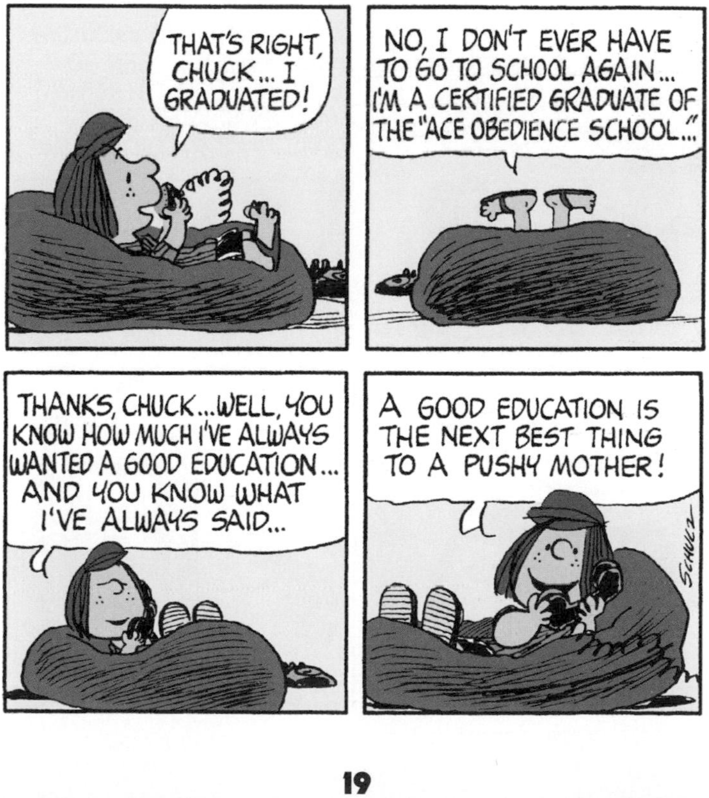
THAT'S RIGHT, CHUCK... I GRADUATED!
NO, I DON'T EVER HAVE TO GO TO SCHOOL AGAIN... I'M A CERTIFIED GRADUATE OF THE "ACE OBEDIENCE SCHOOL..."
THANKS, CHUCK...WELL, YOU KNOW HOW MUCH I'VE ALWAYS WANTED A GOOD EDUCATION... AND YOU KNOW WHAT I'VE ALWAYS SAID...
A GOOD EDUCATION IS THE NEXT BEST THING TO A PUSHY MOTHER!
SCHULZ

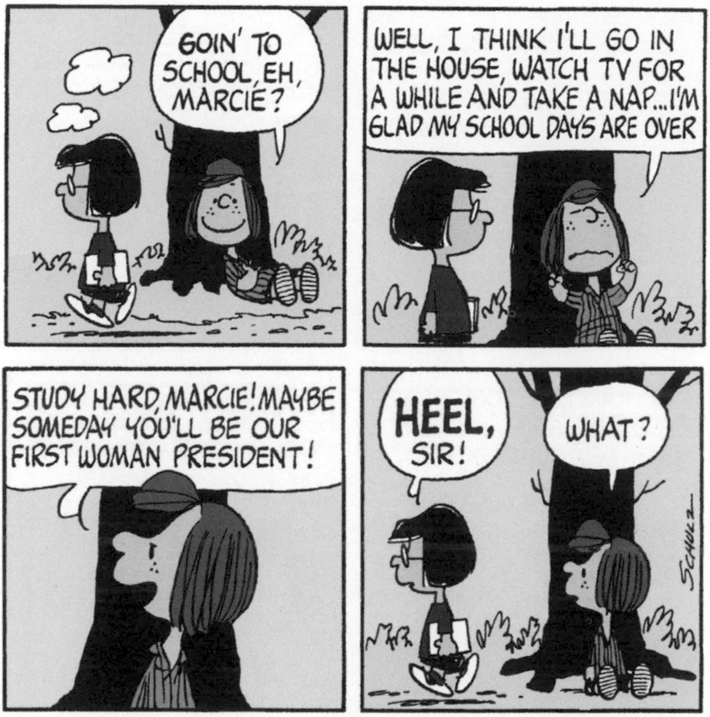
GOIN' TO SCHOOL, EH, MARCIE?
WELL, I THINK I'LL GO IN THE HOUSE, WATCH TV FOR A WHILE AND TAKE A NAP...I'M GLAD MY SCHOOL DAYS ARE OVER
STUDY HARD, MARCIE! MAYBE SOMEDAY YOU'LL BE OUR FIRST WOMAN PRESIDENT!
HEEL, SIR!
WHAT?
SCHULZ

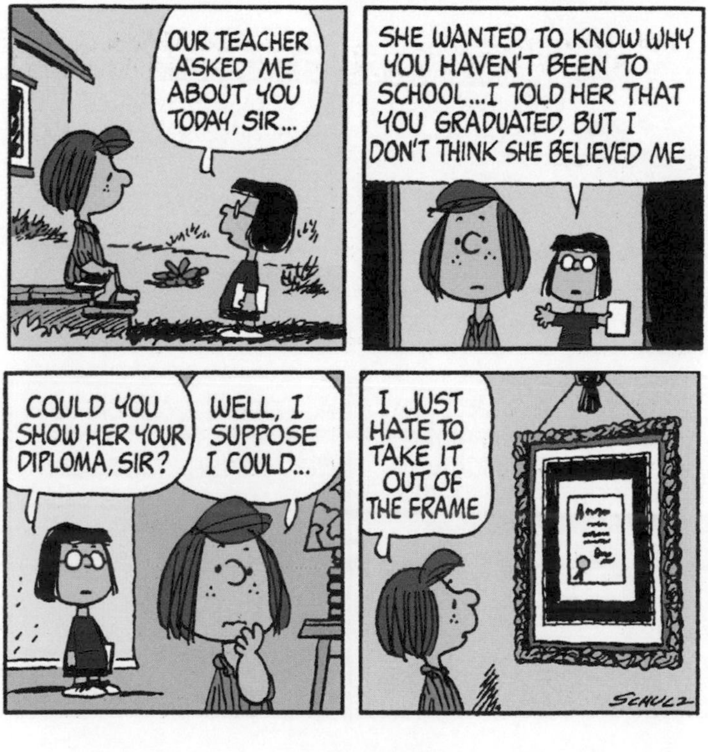
OUR TEACHER ASKED ME ABOUT YOU TODAY, SIR...
SHE WANTED TO KNOW WHY YOU HAVEN'T BEEN TO SCHOOL...I TOLD HER THAT YOU GRADUATED, BUT I DON'T THINK SHE BELIEVED ME
COULD YOU SHOW HER YOUR DIPLOMA, SIR?
WELL, I SUPPOSE I COULD...
I JUST HATE TO TAKE IT OUT OF THE FRAME
SCHULZ

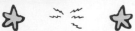

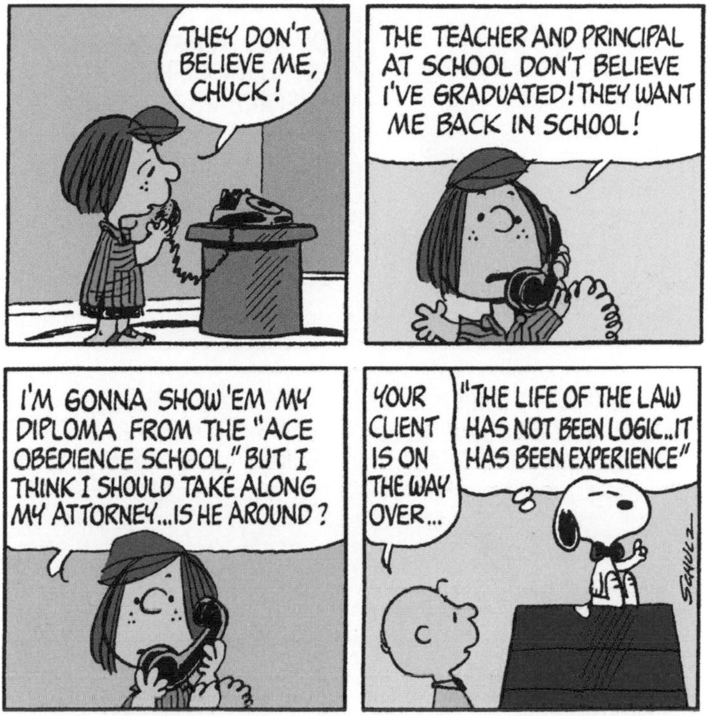
THEY DON'T BELIEVE ME, CHUCK!
THE TEACHER AND PRINCIPAL AT SCHOOL DON'T BELIEVE I'VE GRADUATED! THEY WANT ME BACK IN SCHOOL!
I'M GONNA SHOW 'EM MY DIPLOMA FROM THE "ACE OBEDIENCE SCHOOL," BUT I THINK I SHOULD TAKE ALONG MY ATTORNEY...IS HE AROUND?
YOUR CLIENT IS ON THE WAY OVER...
"THE LIFE OF THE LAW HAS NOT BEEN LOGIC..IT HAS BEEN EXPERIENCE"
SCHULZ

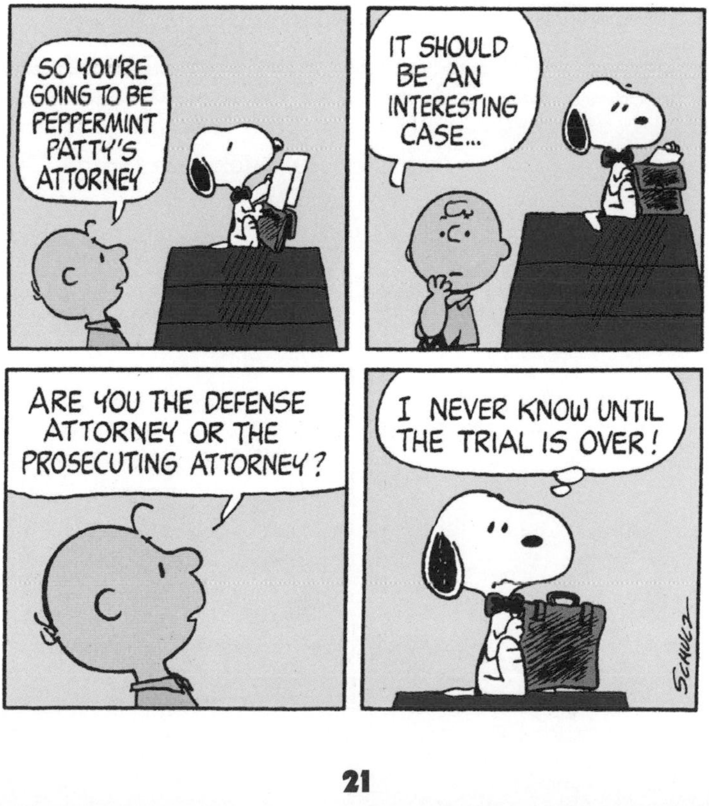
SO YOU'RE GOING TO BE PEPPERMINT PATTY'S ATTORNEY
IT SHOULD BE AN INTERESTING CASE...
ARE YOU THE DEFENSE ATTORNEY OR THE PROSECUTING ATTORNEY?
I NEVER KNOW UNTIL THE TRIAL IS OVER!
SCHULZ

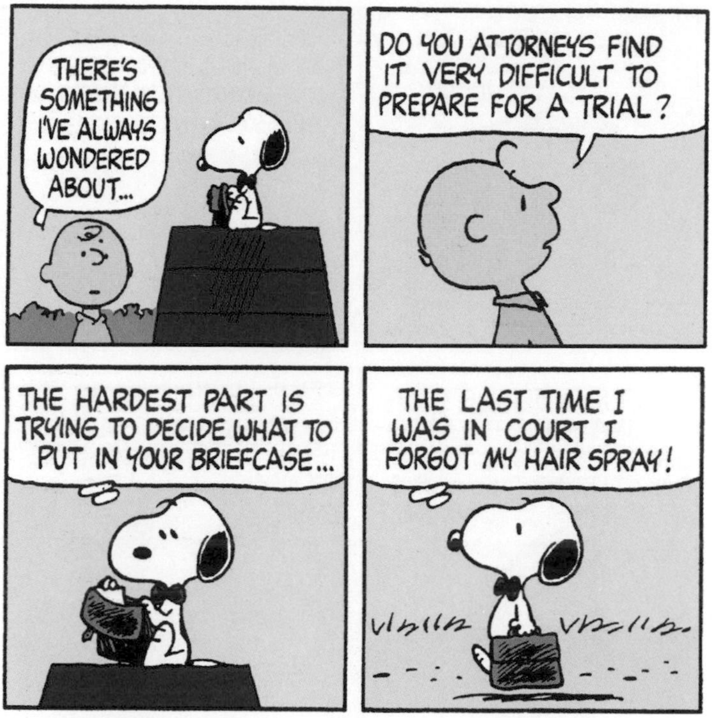
THERE'S SOMETHING I'VE ALWAYS WONDERED ABOUT...
DO YOU ATTORNEYS FIND IT VERY DIFFICULT TO PREPARE FOR A TRIAL?
THE HARDEST PART IS TRYING TO DECIDE WHAT TO PUT IN YOUR BRIEFCASE...
THE LAST TIME I WAS IN COURT I FORGOT MY HAIR SPRAY!

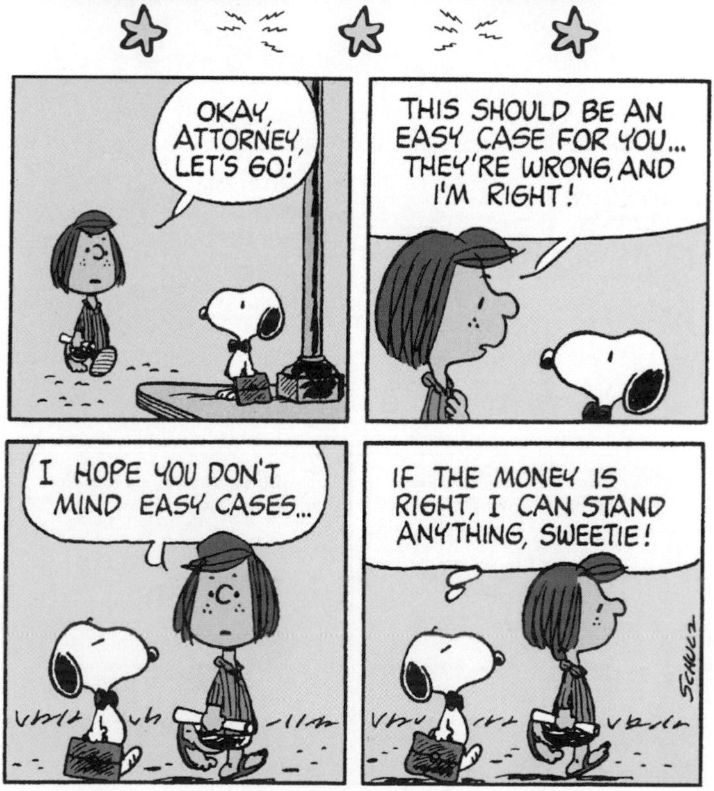
OKAY, ATTORNEY, LET'S GO!
THIS SHOULD BE AN EASY CASE FOR YOU... THEY'RE WRONG, AND I'M RIGHT!
I HOPE YOU DON'T MIND EASY CASES...
IF THE MONEY IS RIGHT, I CAN STAND ANYTHING, SWEETIE!
SCHULZ

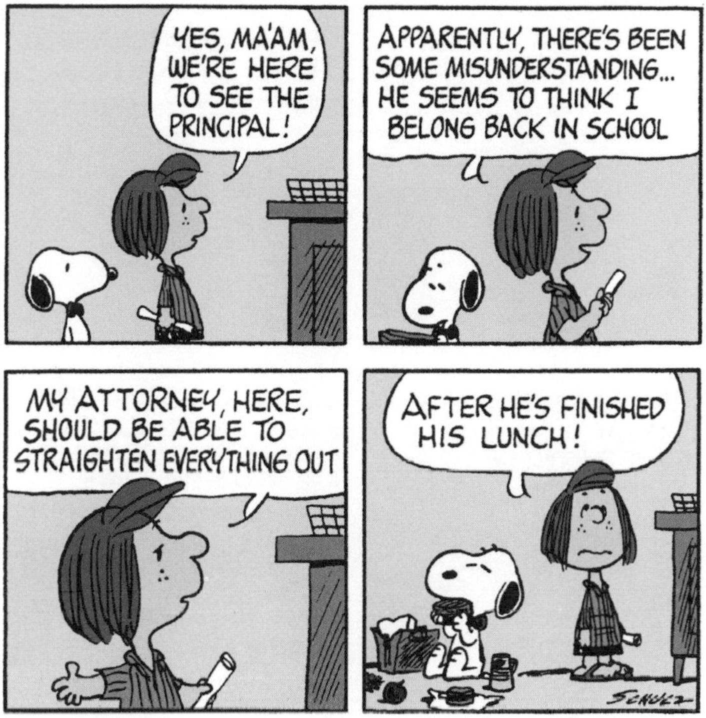
YES, MA'AM, WE'RE HERE TO SEE THE PRINCIPAL!
APPARENTLY, THERE'S BEEN SOME MISUNDERSTANDING... HE SEEMS TO THINK I BELONG BACK IN SCHOOL
MY ATTORNEY, HERE, SHOULD BE ABLE TO STRAIGHTEN EVERYTHING OUT
AFTER HE'S FINISHED HIS LUNCH!
SCHULZ

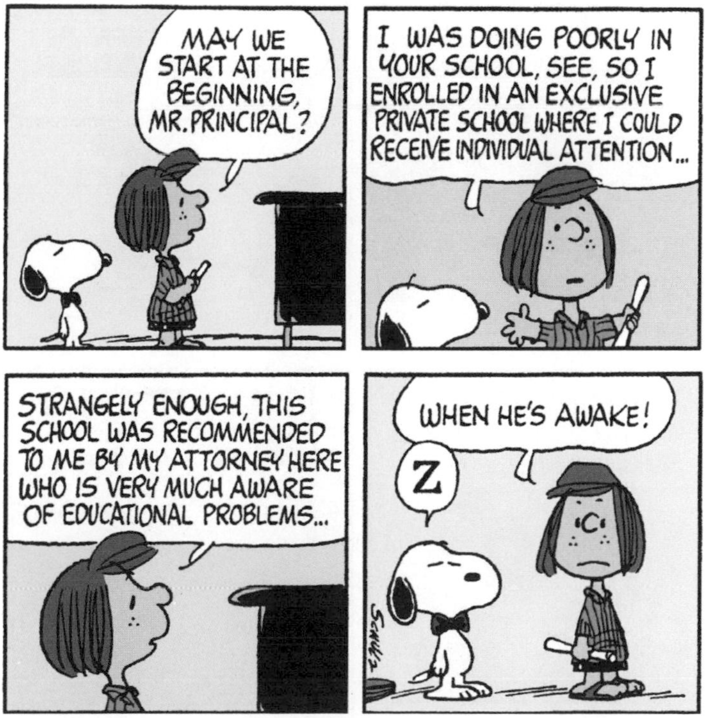
MAY WE START AT THE BEGINNING, MR. PRINCIPAL?
I WAS DOING POORLY IN YOUR SCHOOL, SEE, SO I ENROLLED IN AN EXCLUSIVE PRIVATE SCHOOL WHERE I COULD RECEIVE INDIVIDUAL ATTENTION...
STRANGELY ENOUGH, THIS SCHOOL WAS RECOMMENDED TO ME BY MY ATTORNEY HERE WHO IS VERY MUCH AWARE OF EDUCATIONAL PROBLEMS...
WHEN HE'S AWAKE!
Z
SCHULZ

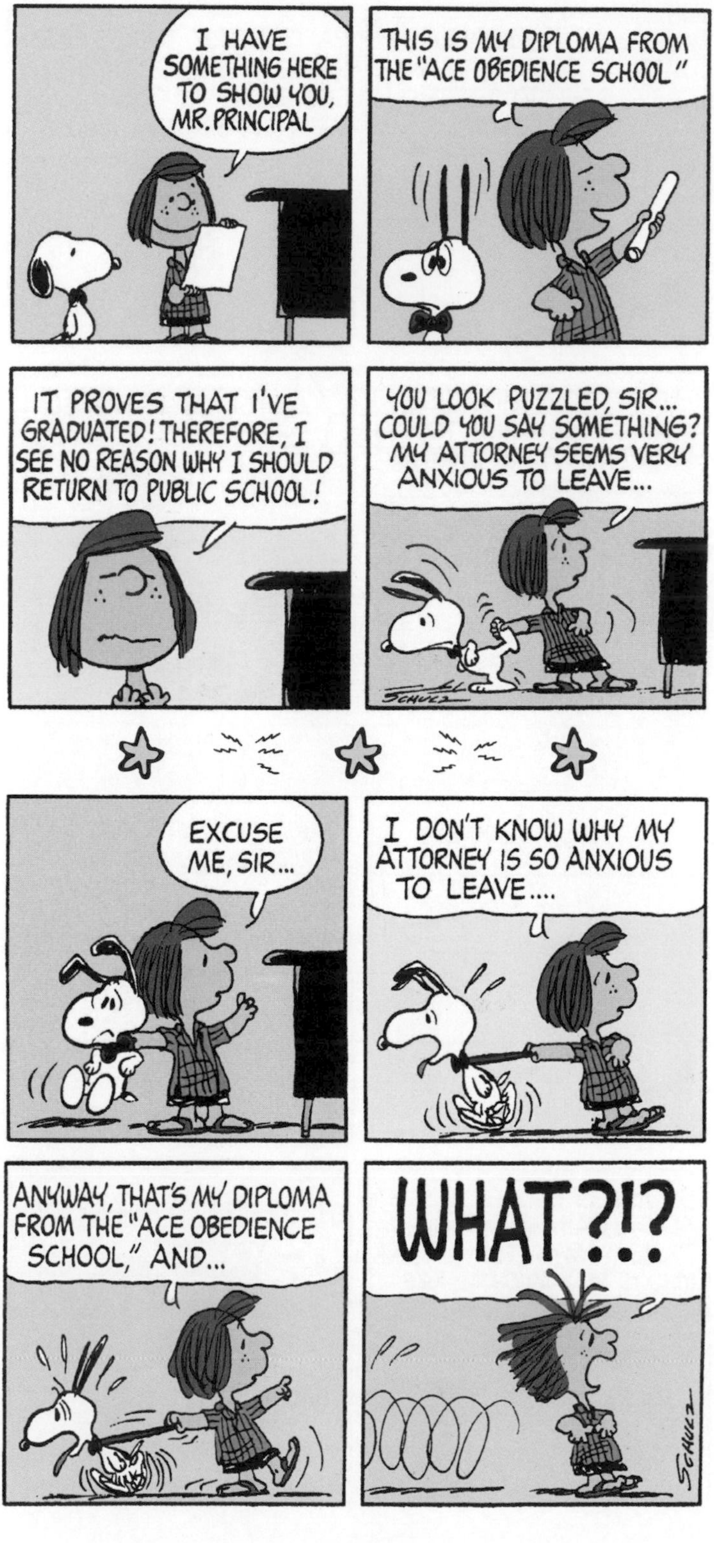
I HAVE SOMETHING HERE TO SHOW YOU, MR. PRINCIPAL
THIS IS MY DIPLOMA FROM THE "ACE OBEDIENCE SCHOOL"
IT PROVES THAT I'VE GRADUATED! THEREFORE, I SEE NO REASON WHY I SHOULD RETURN TO PUBLIC SCHOOL!
YOU LOOK PUZZLED, SIR... COULD YOU SAY SOMETHING? MY ATTORNEY SEEMS VERY ANXIOUS TO LEAVE...
SCHULZ
EXCUSE ME, SIR...
I DON'T KNOW WHY MY ATTORNEY IS SO ANXIOUS TO LEAVE....
ANYWAY, THAT'S MY DIPLOMA FROM THE "ACE OBEDIENCE SCHOOL," AND...
WHAT?!?
SCHULZ

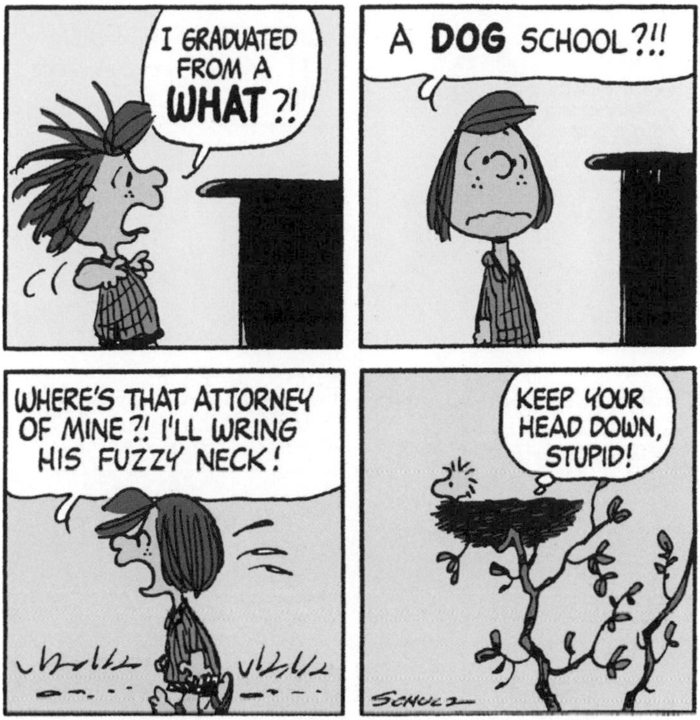
I GRADUATED FROM A WHAT?!
A DOG SCHOOL?!!
WHERE'S THAT ATTORNEY OF MINE?! I'LL WRING HIS FUZZY NECK!
KEEP YOUR HEAD DOWN, STUPID!
SCHULZ

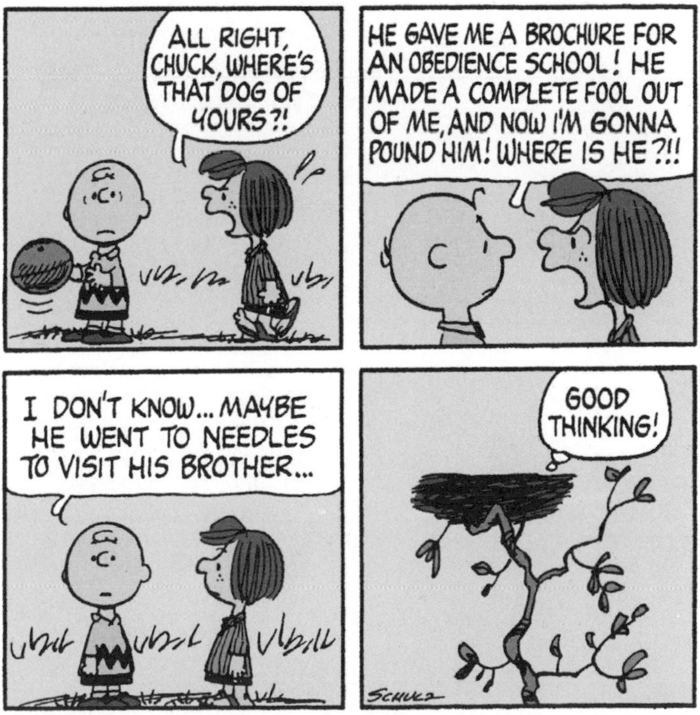
ALL RIGHT, CHUCK, WHERE'S THAT DOG OF YOURS?!
HE GAVE ME A BROCHURE FOR AN OBEDIENCE SCHOOL! HE MADE A COMPLETE FOOL OUT OF ME, AND NOW I'M GONNA POUND HIM! WHERE IS HE?!!
I DON'T KNOW... MAYBE HE WENT TO NEEDLES TO VISIT HIS BROTHER...
GOOD THINKING!
SCHULZ

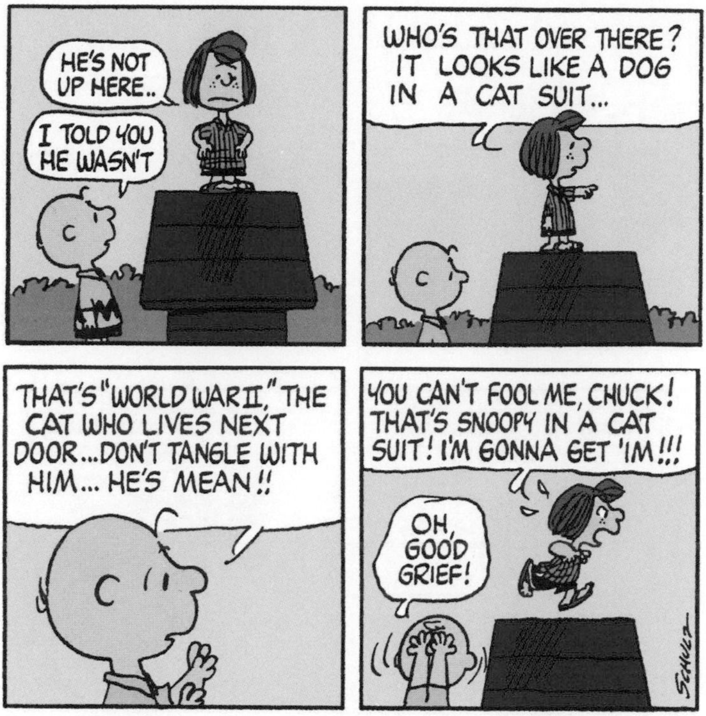
HE'S NOT UP HERE..
I TOLD YOU HE WASN'T
WHO'S THAT OVER THERE? IT LOOKS LIKE A DOG IN A CAT SUIT...
THAT'S "WORLD WAR II," THE CAT WHO LIVES NEXT DOOR...DON'T TANGLE WITH HIM... HE'S MEAN!!
YOU CAN'T FOOL ME, CHUCK! THAT'S SNOOPY IN A CAT SUIT! I'M GONNA GET 'IM!!!
OH, GOOD GRIEF!
SCHULZ

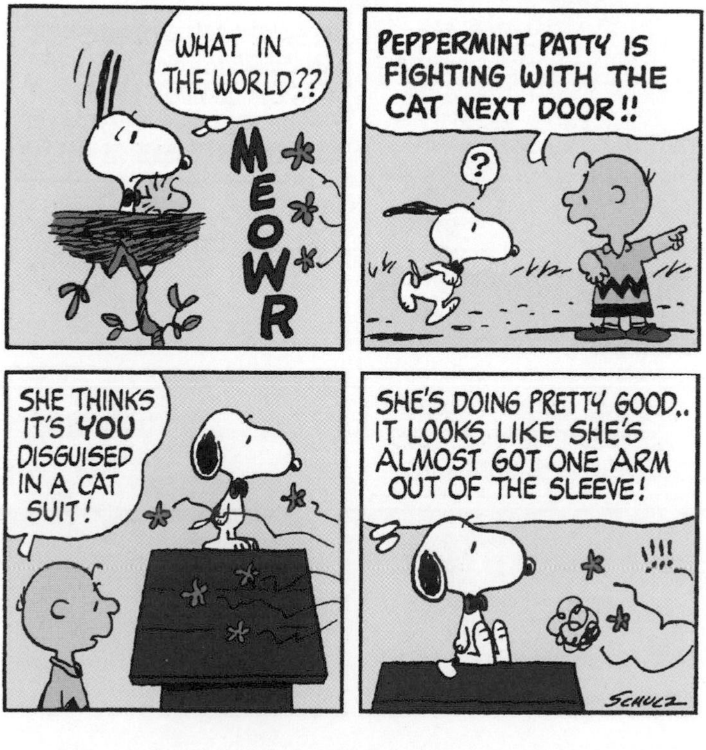
WHAT IN THE WORLD??
MEOWR
PEPPERMINT PATTY IS FIGHTING WITH THE CAT NEXT DOOR!!
?
SHE THINKS IT'S YOU DISGUISED IN A CAT SUIT!
SHE'S DOING PRETTY GOOD.. IT LOOKS LIKE SHE'S ALMOST GOT ONE ARM OUT OF THE SLEEVE!
!!!!
SCHULZ

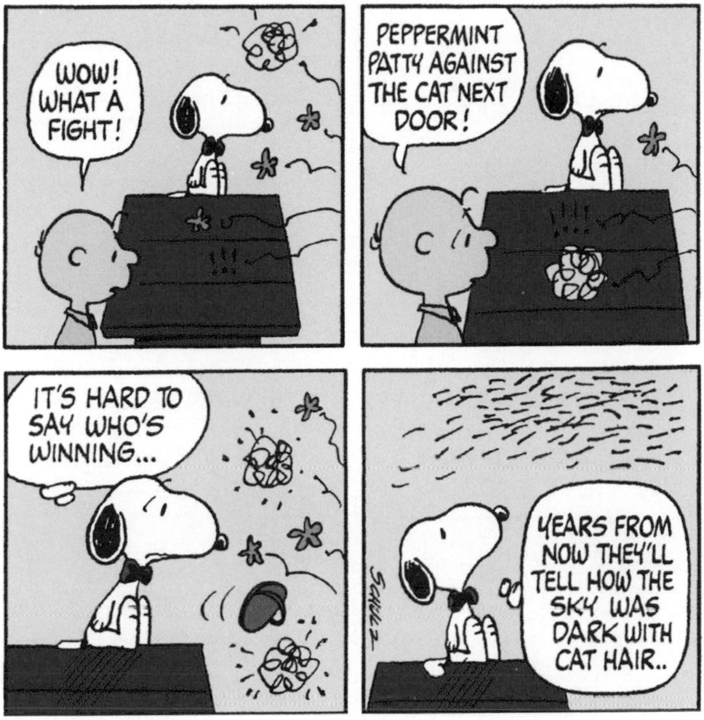
WOW! WHAT A FIGHT!
PEPPERMINT PATTY AGAINST THE CAT NEXT DOOR!
IT'S HARD TO SAY WHO'S WINNING...
YEARS FROM NOW THEY'LL TELL HOW THE SKY WAS DARK WITH CAT HAIR..
SCHULZ

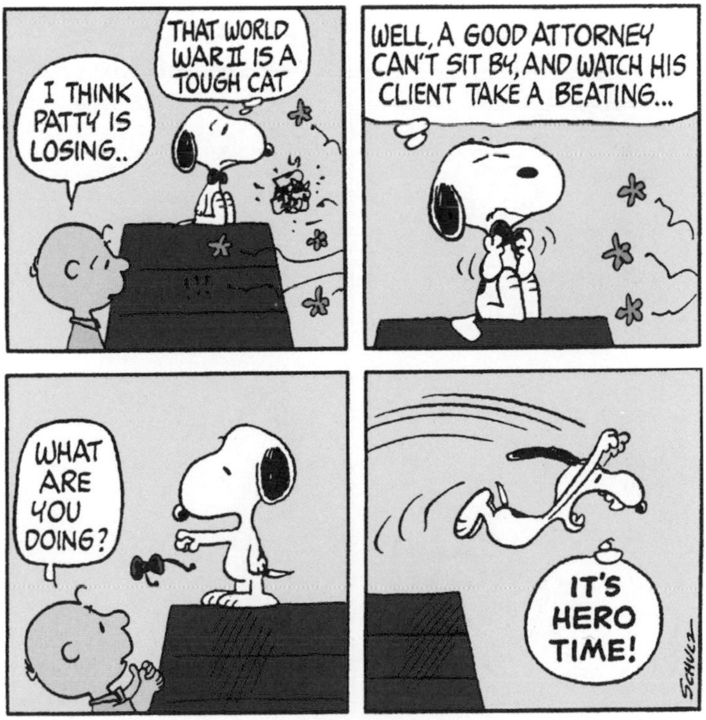
I THINK PATTY IS LOSING..
THAT WORLD WAR II IS A TOUGH CAT
WELL, A GOOD ATTORNEY CAN'T SIT BY, AND WATCH HIS CLIENT TAKE A BEATING...
WHAT ARE YOU DOING?
IT'S HERO TIME!
SCHULZ

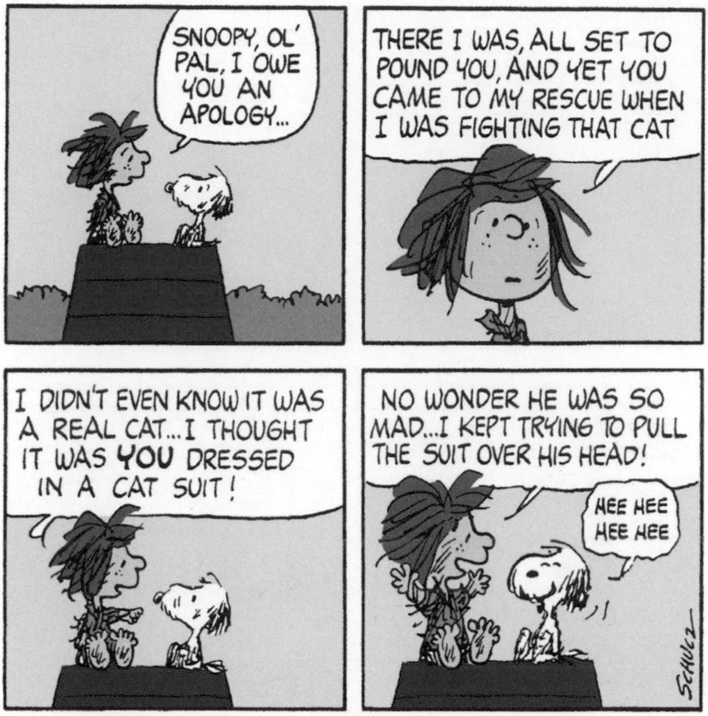
SNOOPY, OL' PAL, I OWE YOU AN APOLOGY...
THERE I WAS, ALL SET TO POUND YOU, AND YET YOU CAME TO MY RESCUE WHEN I WAS FIGHTING THAT CAT
I DIDN'T EVEN KNOW IT WAS A REAL CAT...I THOUGHT IT WAS **YOU** DRESSED IN A CAT SUIT!
NO WONDER HE WAS SO MAD...I KEPT TRYING TO PULL THE SUIT OVER HIS HEAD!
HEE HEE HEE HEE
SCHULZ

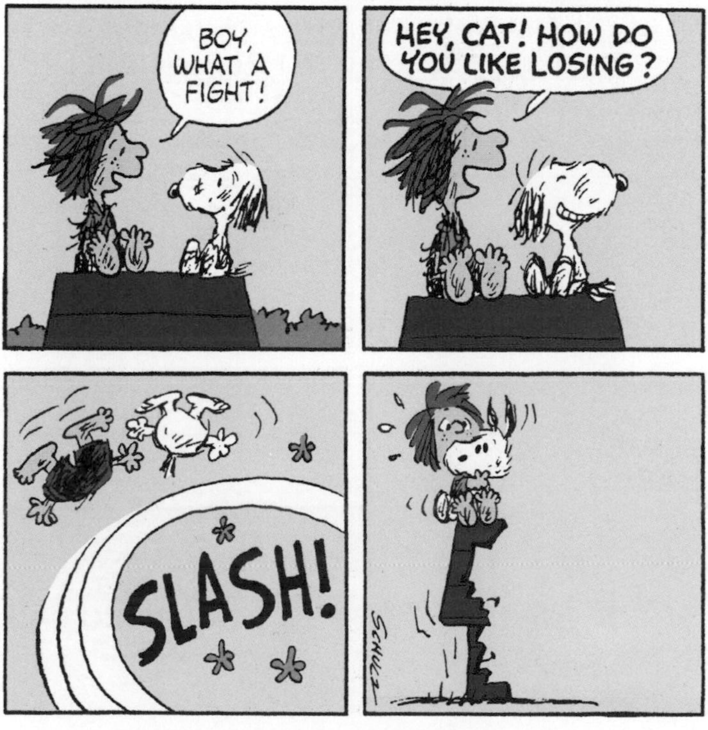
BOY, WHAT A FIGHT!
HEY, CAT! HOW DO YOU LIKE LOSING?
SLASH!
SCHULZ

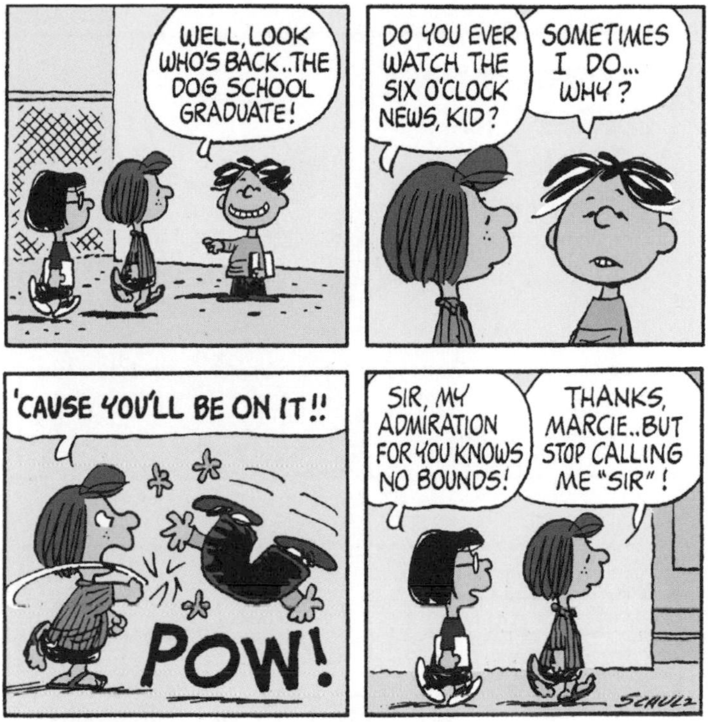
WELL, LOOK WHO'S BACK..THE DOG SCHOOL GRADUATE!
DO YOU EVER WATCH THE SIX O'CLOCK NEWS, KID?
SOMETIMES I DO... WHY?
'CAUSE YOU'LL BE ON IT!!
POW!
SIR, MY ADMIRATION FOR YOU KNOWS NO BOUNDS!
THANKS, MARCIE..BUT STOP CALLING ME "SIR"!
SCHULZ

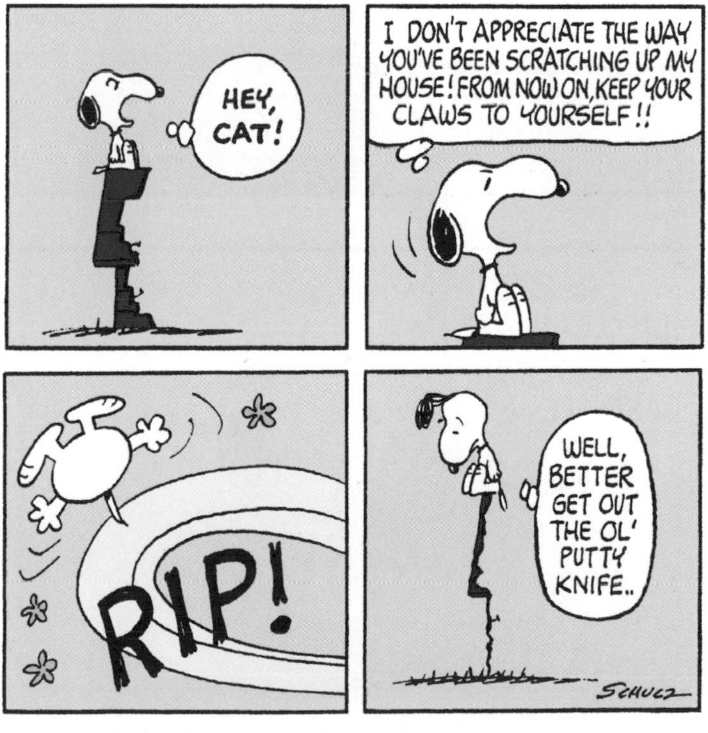
HEY, CAT!
I DON'T APPRECIATE THE WAY YOU'VE BEEN SCRATCHING UP MY HOUSE! FROM NOW ON, KEEP YOUR CLAWS TO YOURSELF!!
RIP!
WELL, BETTER GET OUT THE OL' PUTTY KNIFE..
SCHULZ

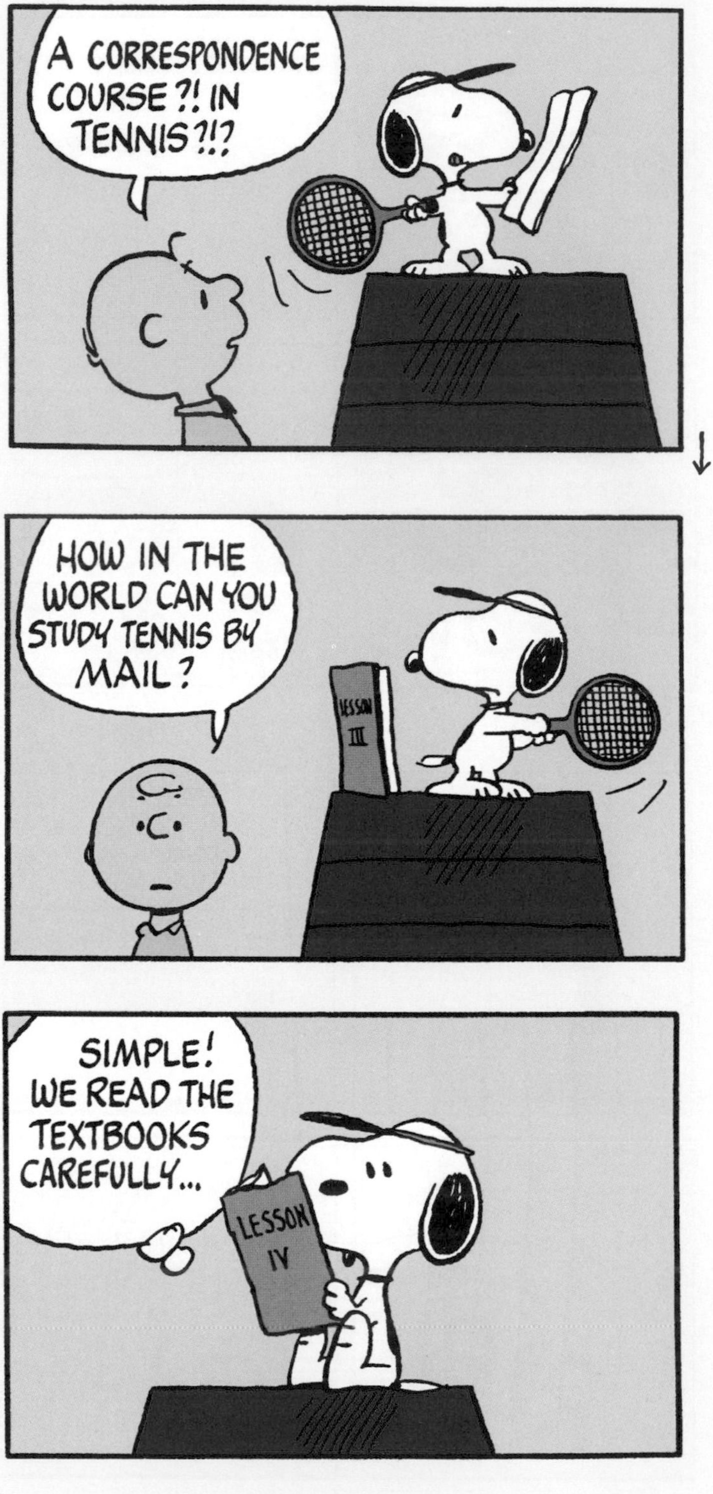
A CORRESPONDENCE COURSE?! IN TENNIS?!?
HOW IN THE WORLD CAN YOU STUDY TENNIS BY MAIL?
LESSON III
SIMPLE! WE READ THE TEXTBOOKS CAREFULLY...
LESSON IV

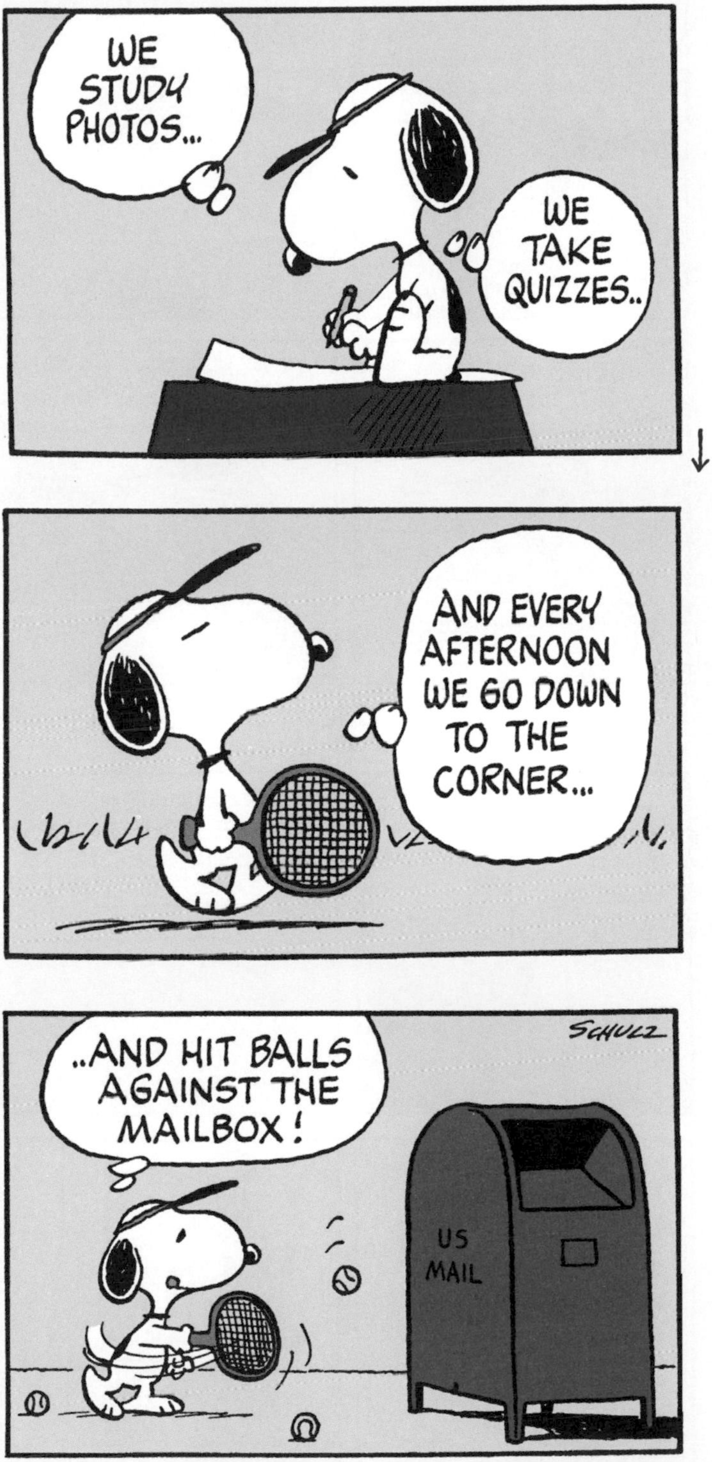
WE STUDY PHOTOS...
WE TAKE QUIZZES..
AND EVERY AFTERNOON WE GO DOWN TO THE CORNER...
SCHULZ
..AND HIT BALLS AGAINST THE MAILBOX!
US MAIL

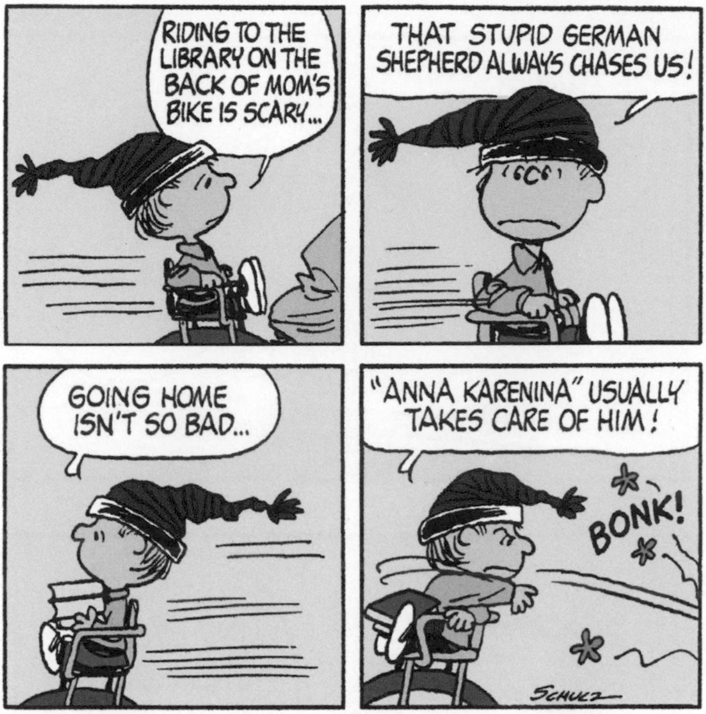
RIDING TO THE LIBRARY ON THE BACK OF MOM'S BIKE IS SCARY...
THAT STUPID GERMAN SHEPHERD ALWAYS CHASES US!
GOING HOME ISN'T SO BAD...
"ANNA KARENINA" USUALLY TAKES CARE OF HIM!
BONK!
SCHULZ

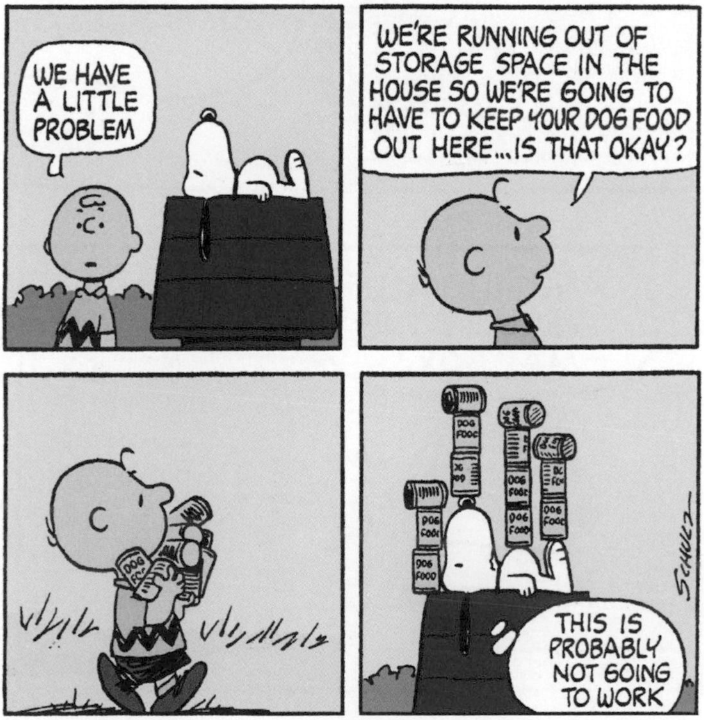
WE HAVE A LITTLE PROBLEM
WE'RE RUNNING OUT OF STORAGE SPACE IN THE HOUSE SO WE'RE GOING TO HAVE TO KEEP YOUR DOG FOOD OUT HERE...IS THAT OKAY?
THIS IS PROBABLY NOT GOING TO WORK
SCHULZ

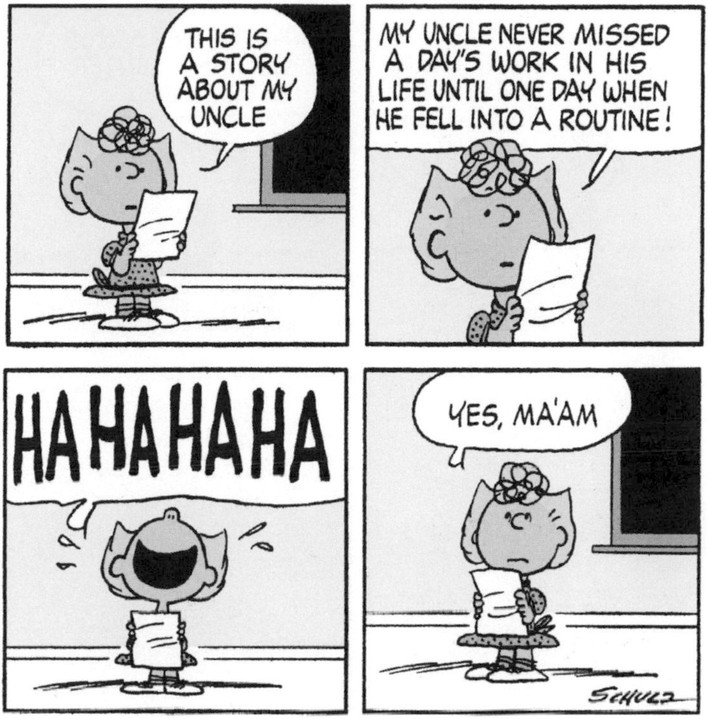
THIS IS A STORY ABOUT MY UNCLE
MY UNCLE NEVER MISSED A DAY'S WORK IN HIS LIFE UNTIL ONE DAY WHEN HE FELL INTO A ROUTINE!
HAHAHAHA
YES, MA'AM
SCHULZ

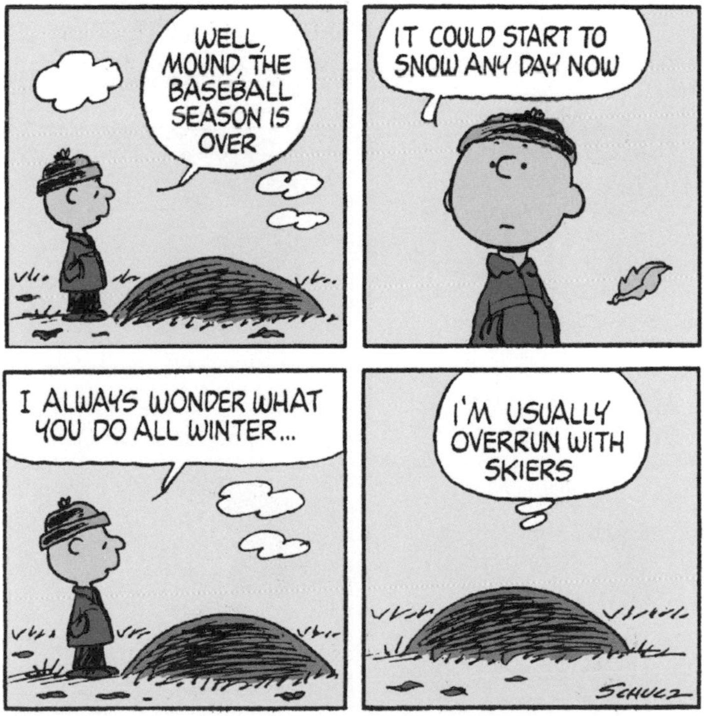
WELL, MOUND, THE BASEBALL SEASON IS OVER
IT COULD START TO SNOW ANY DAY NOW
I ALWAYS WONDER WHAT YOU DO ALL WINTER...
I'M USUALLY OVERRUN WITH SKIERS
SCHULZ

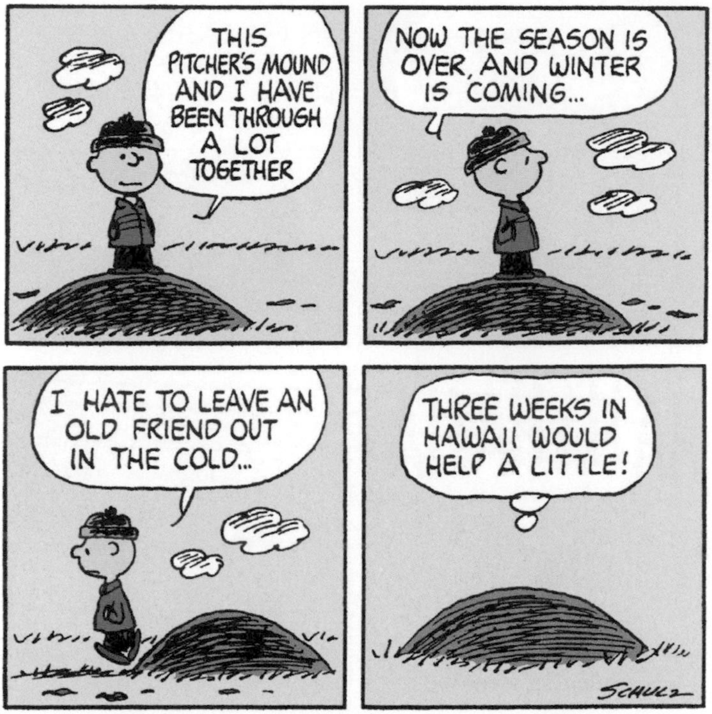
THIS PITCHER'S MOUND AND I HAVE BEEN THROUGH A LOT TOGETHER
NOW THE SEASON IS OVER, AND WINTER IS COMING...
I HATE TO LEAVE AN OLD FRIEND OUT IN THE COLD...
THREE WEEKS IN HAWAII WOULD HELP A LITTLE!

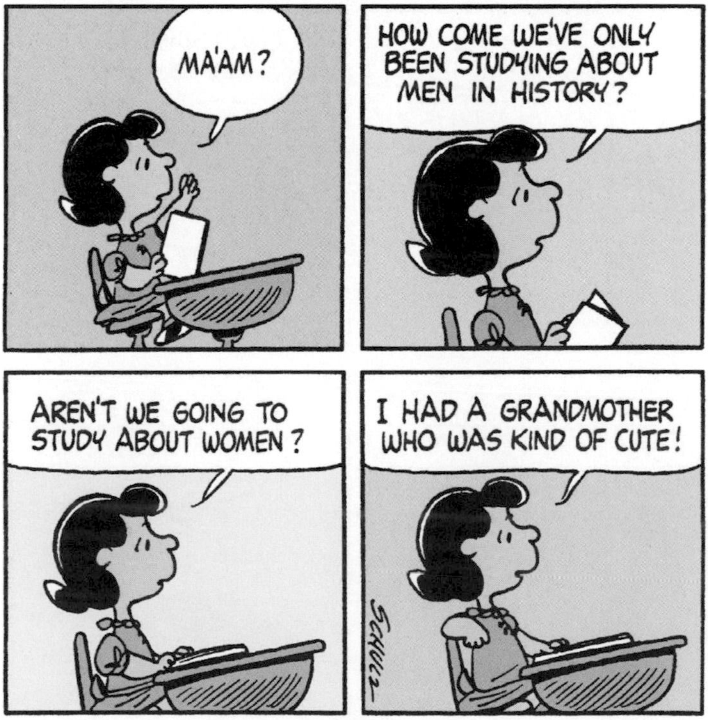
MA'AM?
HOW COME WE'VE ONLY BEEN STUDYING ABOUT MEN IN HISTORY?
AREN'T WE GOING TO STUDY ABOUT WOMEN?
I HAD A GRANDMOTHER WHO WAS KIND OF CUTE!

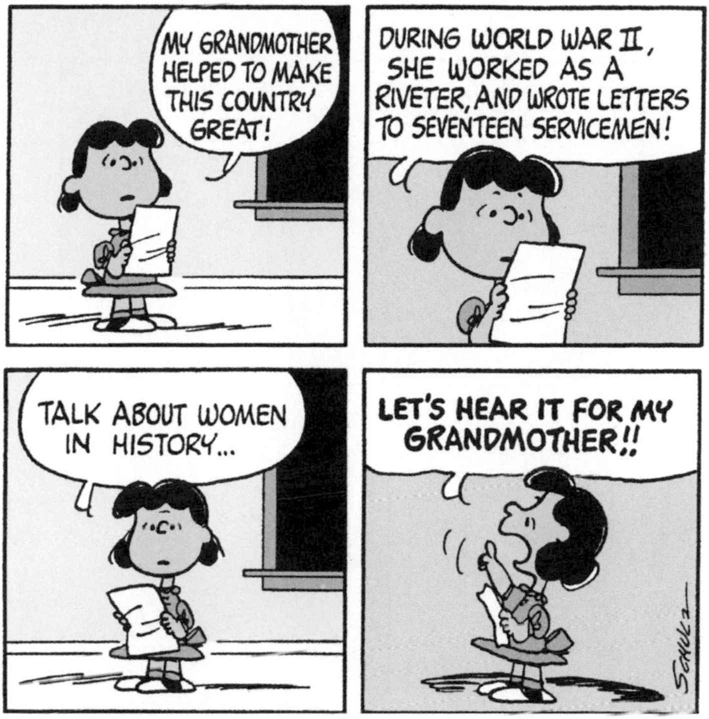
MY GRANDMOTHER HELPED TO MAKE THIS COUNTRY GREAT!
DURING WORLD WAR II, SHE WORKED AS A RIVETER, AND WROTE LETTERS TO SEVENTEEN SERVICEMEN!
TALK ABOUT WOMEN IN HISTORY...
LET'S HEAR IT FOR MY GRANDMOTHER!!
SCHULZ

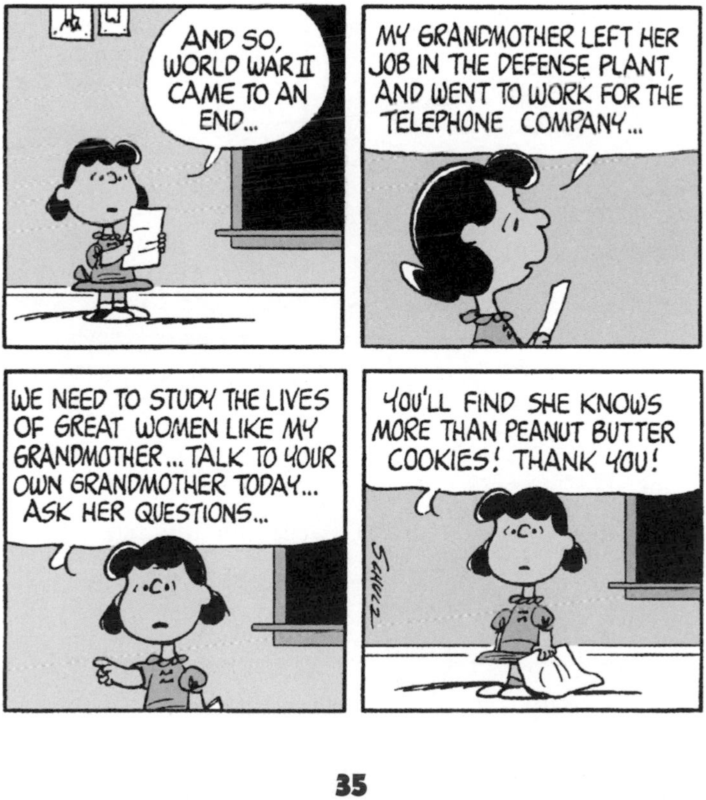
AND SO, WORLD WAR II CAME TO AN END...
MY GRANDMOTHER LEFT HER JOB IN THE DEFENSE PLANT, AND WENT TO WORK FOR THE TELEPHONE COMPANY...
WE NEED TO STUDY THE LIVES OF GREAT WOMEN LIKE MY GRANDMOTHER... TALK TO YOUR OWN GRANDMOTHER TODAY... ASK HER QUESTIONS...
YOU'LL FIND SHE KNOWS MORE THAN PEANUT BUTTER COOKIES! THANK YOU!
SCHULZ

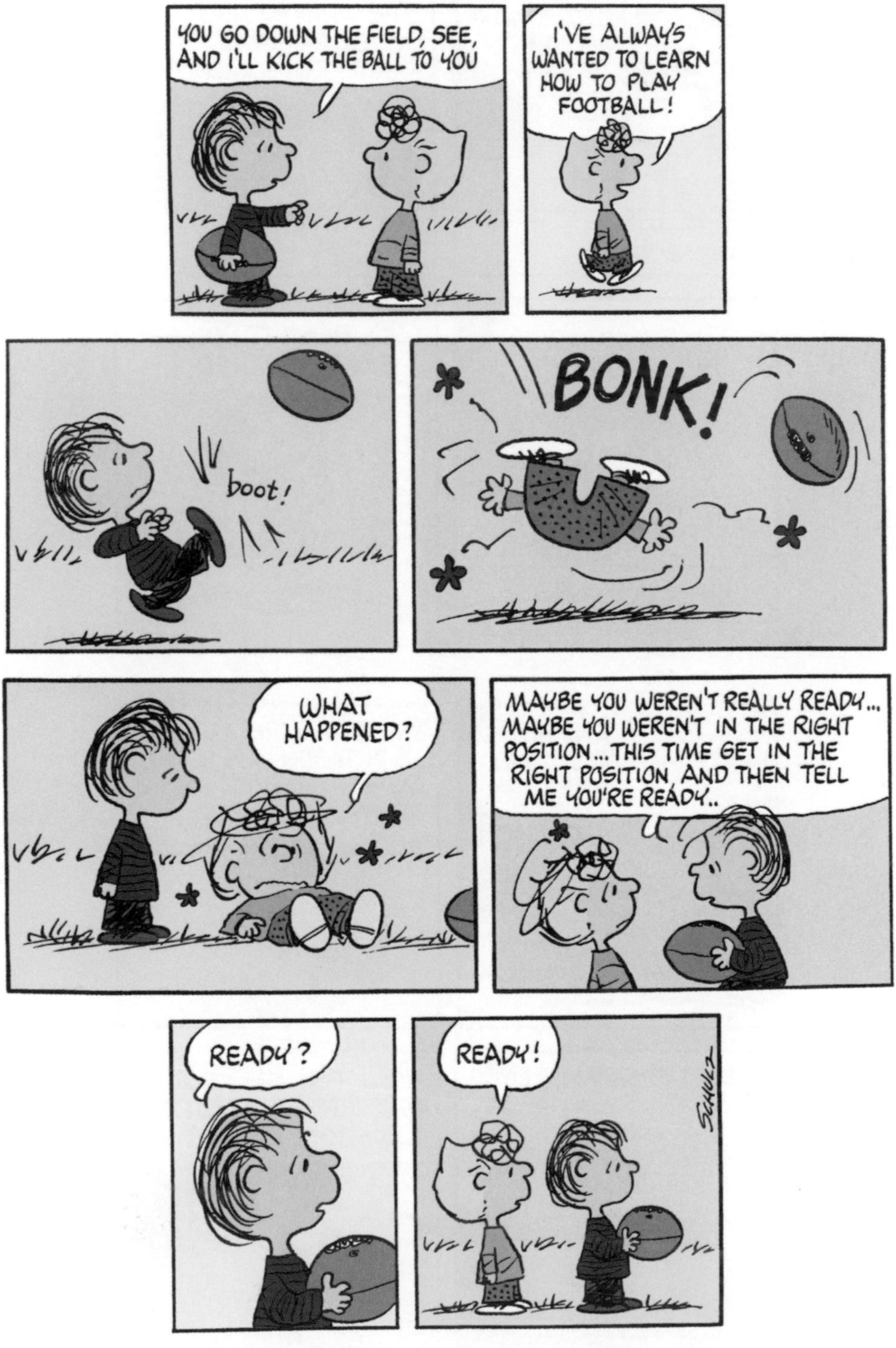
YOU GO DOWN THE FIELD, SEE, AND I'LL KICK THE BALL TO YOU
I'VE ALWAYS WANTED TO LEARN HOW TO PLAY FOOTBALL!
boot!
BONK!
WHAT HAPPENED?
MAYBE YOU WEREN'T REALLY READY... MAYBE YOU WEREN'T IN THE RIGHT POSITION... THIS TIME GET IN THE RIGHT POSITION, AND THEN TELL ME YOU'RE READY..
READY?
READY!
SCHULZ

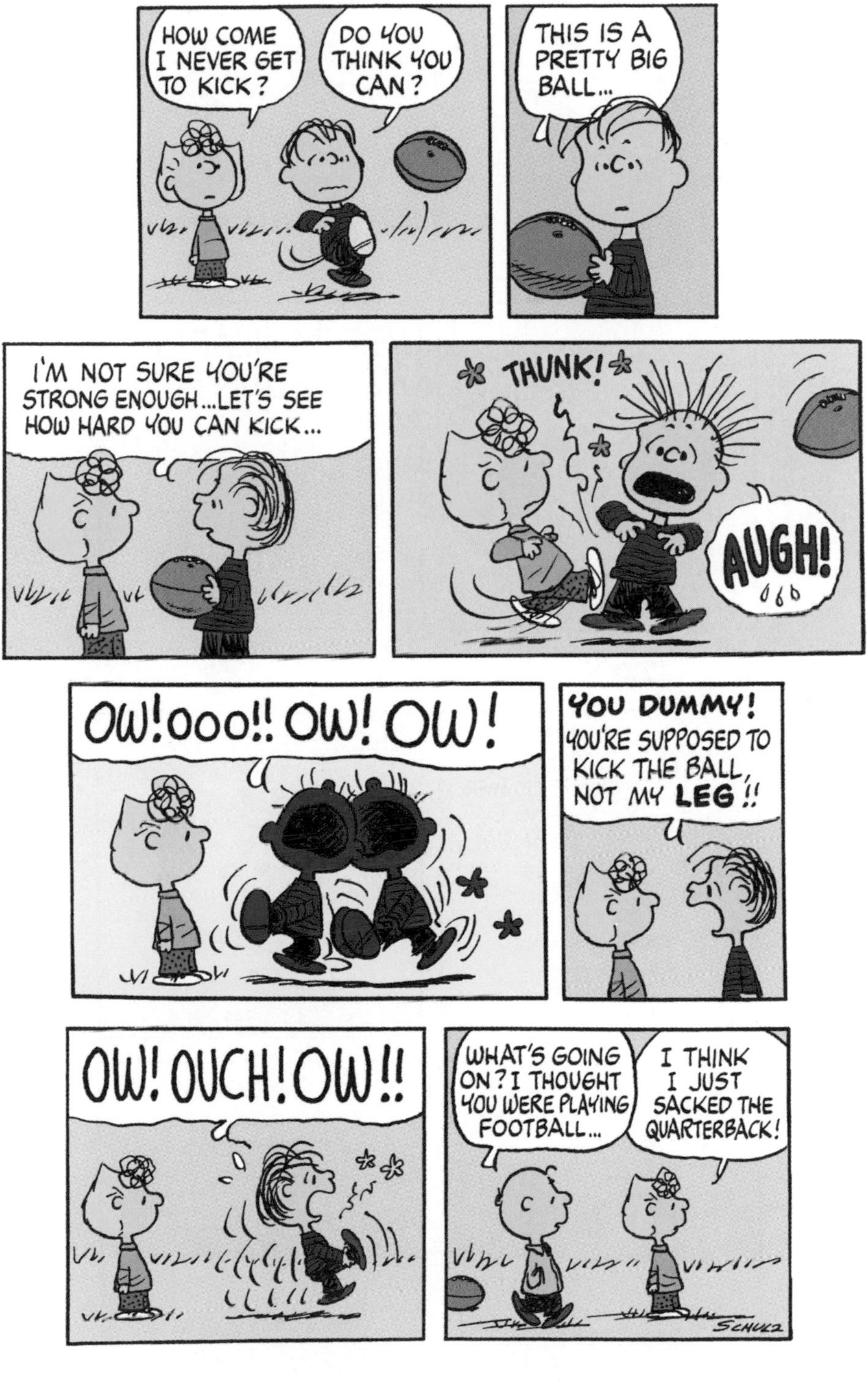
HOW COME I NEVER GET TO KICK?
DO YOU THINK YOU CAN?
THIS IS A PRETTY BIG BALL...
I'M NOT SURE YOU'RE STRONG ENOUGH...LET'S SEE HOW HARD YOU CAN KICK...
THUNK!
AUGH!
OW! OOO!! OW! OW!
YOU DUMMY! YOU'RE SUPPOSED TO KICK THE BALL, NOT MY LEG!!
OW! OUCH! OW!!
WHAT'S GOING ON? I THOUGHT YOU WERE PLAYING FOOTBALL...
I THINK I JUST SACKED THE QUARTERBACK!
SCHULZ

WHO'S THAT MAN RAKING LEAVES?
THE ONE WHO WAVED AT ME? THAT'S MY DENTIST... HE LIVES THERE...
YES, I'M WEARING MY RETAINER!!!
SCHULZ

HERE'S THE WORLD-FAMOUS HOCKEY PLAYER SKATING OUT ONTO THE ICE...
THERE'S A BIG CROWD TONIGHT, AND THEY'RE OUT FOR BLOOD!
HERE'S THE WORLD-FAMOUS HOCKEY PLAYER SKATING OFF THE ICE...
I **NEED** MY BLOOD!
SCHULZ

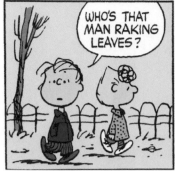

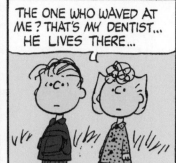

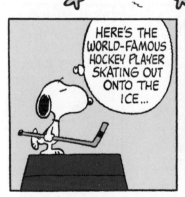

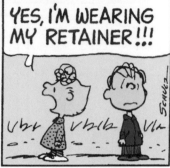

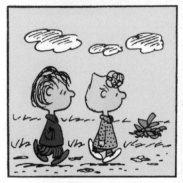

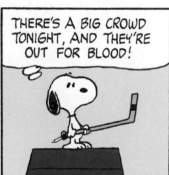

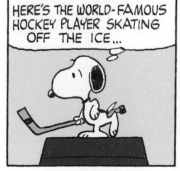

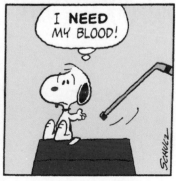

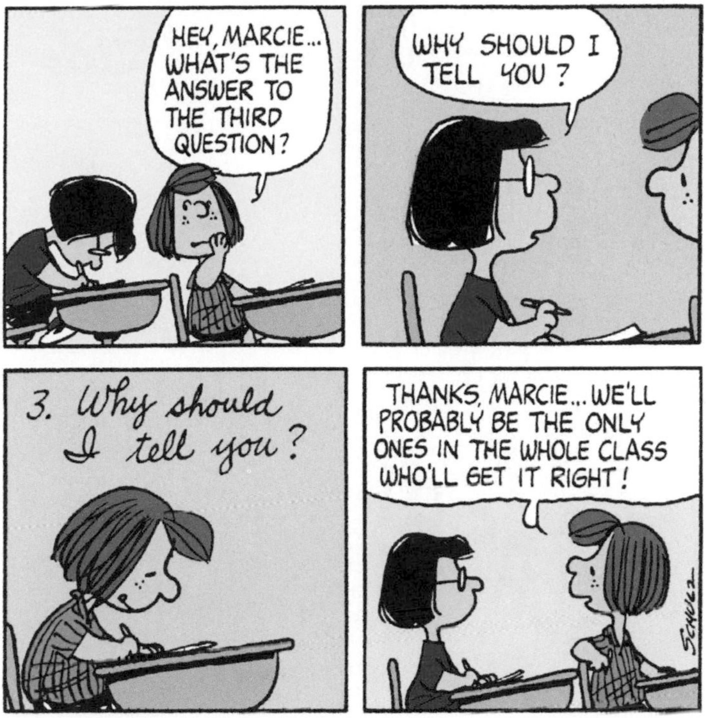
HEY, MARCIE... WHAT'S THE ANSWER TO THE THIRD QUESTION?
WHY SHOULD I TELL YOU?
3. Why should I tell you?
THANKS, MARCIE... WE'LL PROBABLY BE THE ONLY ONES IN THE WHOLE CLASS WHO'LL GET IT RIGHT!

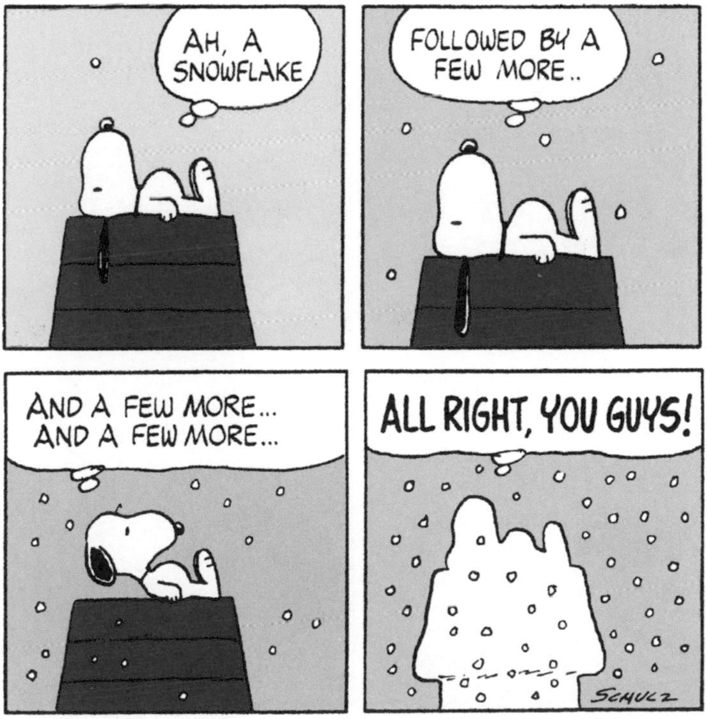
AH, A SNOWFLAKE
FOLLOWED BY A FEW MORE..
AND A FEW MORE... AND A FEW MORE...
ALL RIGHT, YOU GUYS!

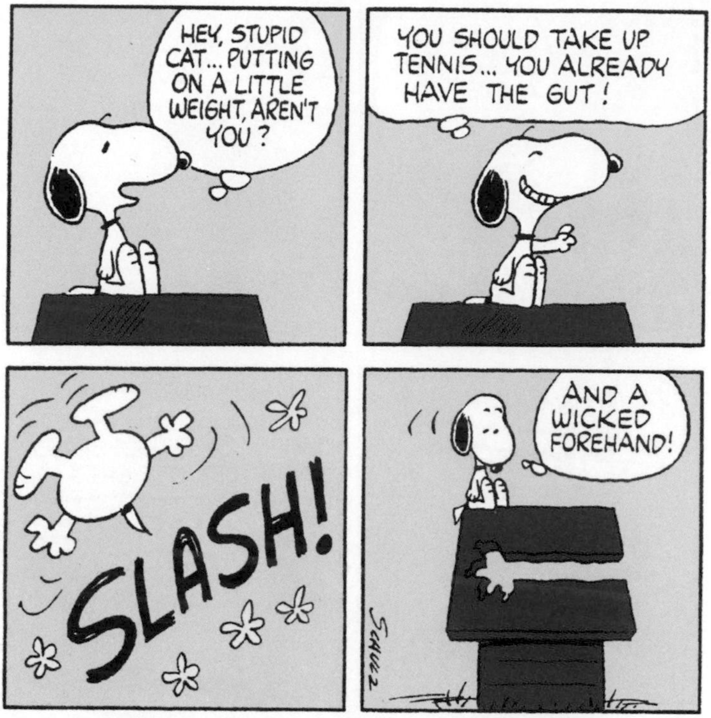
HEY, STUPID CAT... PUTTING ON A LITTLE WEIGHT, AREN'T YOU ?
YOU SHOULD TAKE UP TENNIS... YOU ALREADY HAVE THE GUT !
SLASH!
AND A WICKED FOREHAND!
SCHULZ

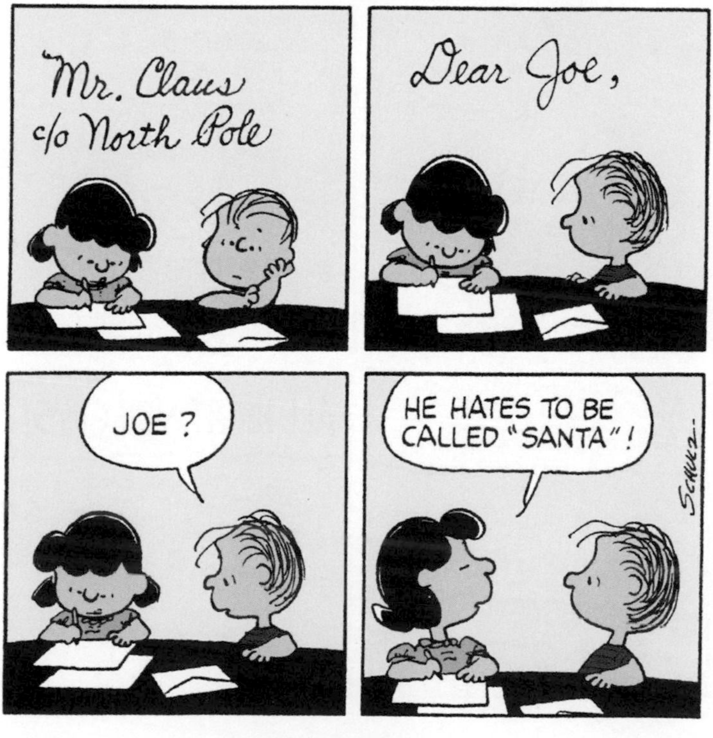
Mr. Claus
c/o North Pole
Dear Joe,
JOE ?
HE HATES TO BE CALLED "SANTA" !
SCHULZ

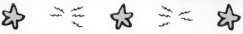

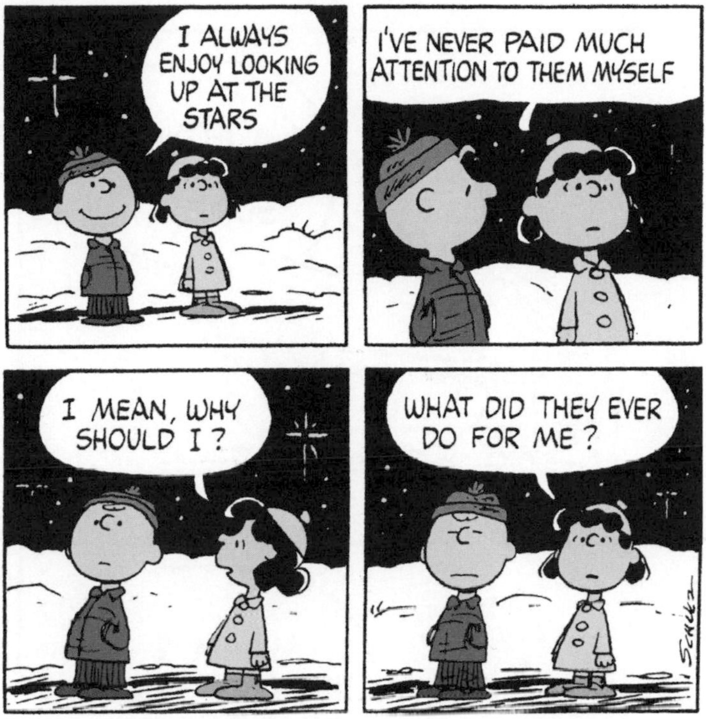
I ALWAYS ENJOY LOOKING UP AT THE STARS
I'VE NEVER PAID MUCH ATTENTION TO THEM MYSELF
I MEAN, WHY SHOULD I ?
WHAT DID THEY EVER DO FOR ME ?
SCHULZ

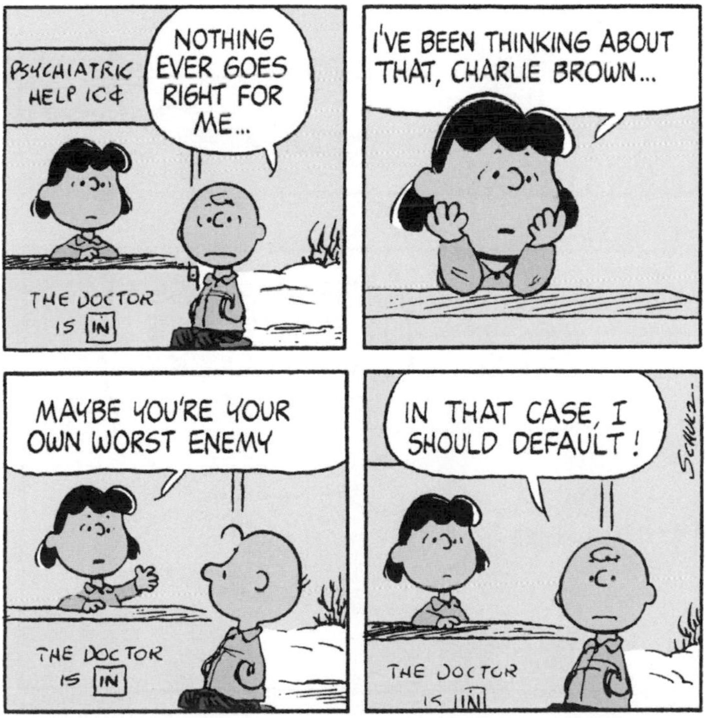
PSYCHIATRIC HELP 10¢
NOTHING EVER GOES RIGHT FOR ME...
THE DOCTOR IS IN
I'VE BEEN THINKING ABOUT THAT, CHARLIE BROWN...
MAYBE YOU'RE YOUR OWN WORST ENEMY
THE DOCTOR IS IN
IN THAT CASE, I SHOULD DEFAULT !
SCHULZ
THE DOCTOR IS IN

I'M GONNA FAIL FOR SURE!
MA'AM, I THINK YOU SHOULD GRADE US ON A CURVE...
THE WAY I SEE IT, THAT'S THE ONLY CHANCE I HAVE TO PASS...

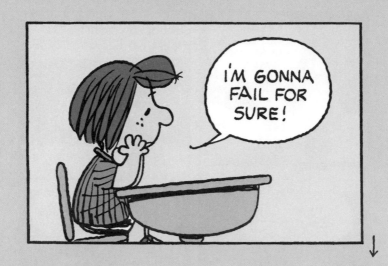

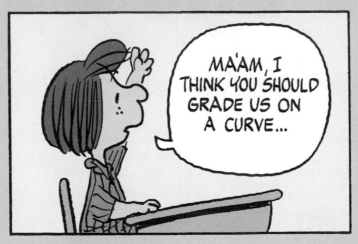

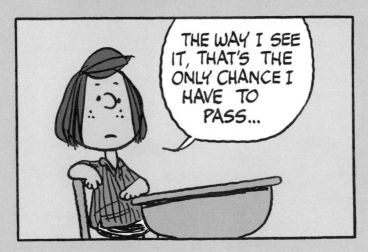

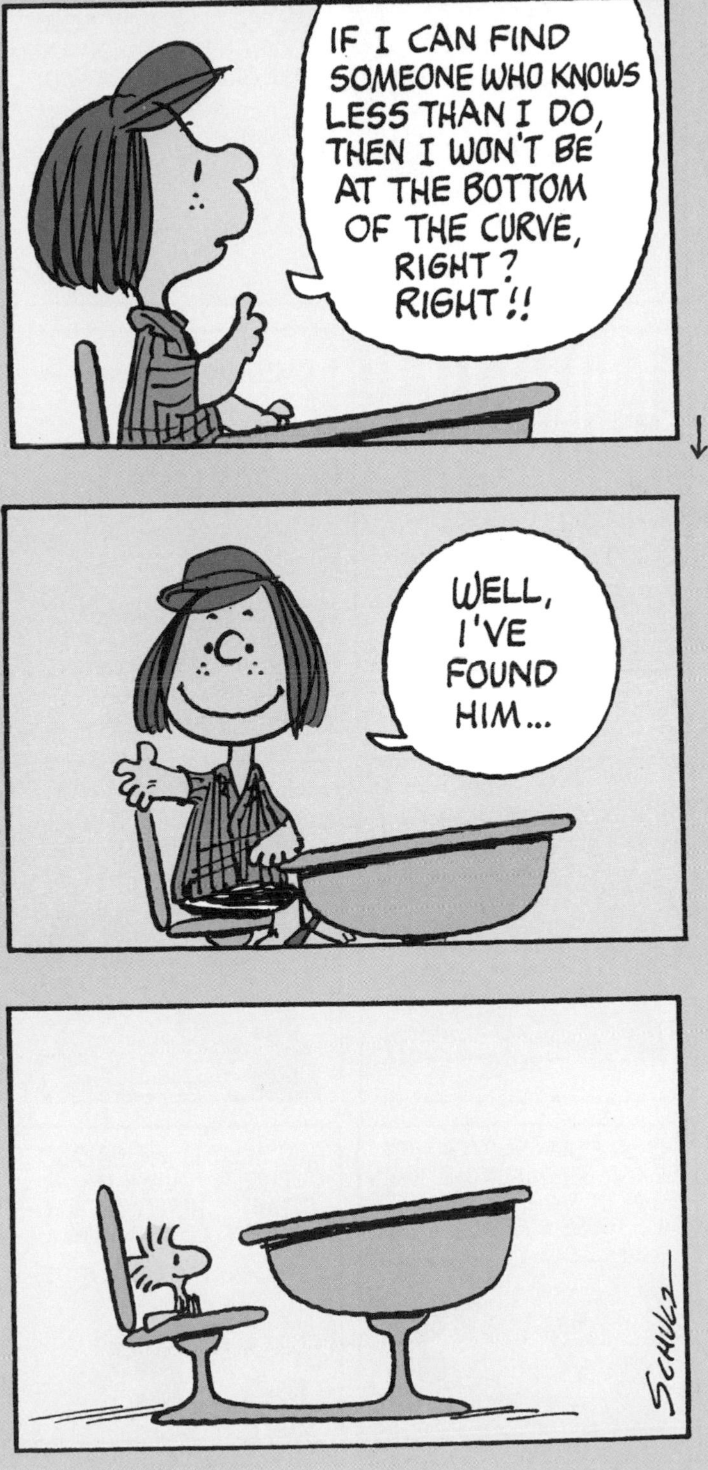
IF I CAN FIND SOMEONE WHO KNOWS LESS THAN I DO, THEN I WON'T BE AT THE BOTTOM OF THE CURVE, RIGHT? RIGHT!!
WELL, I'VE FOUND HIM...
SCHULZ

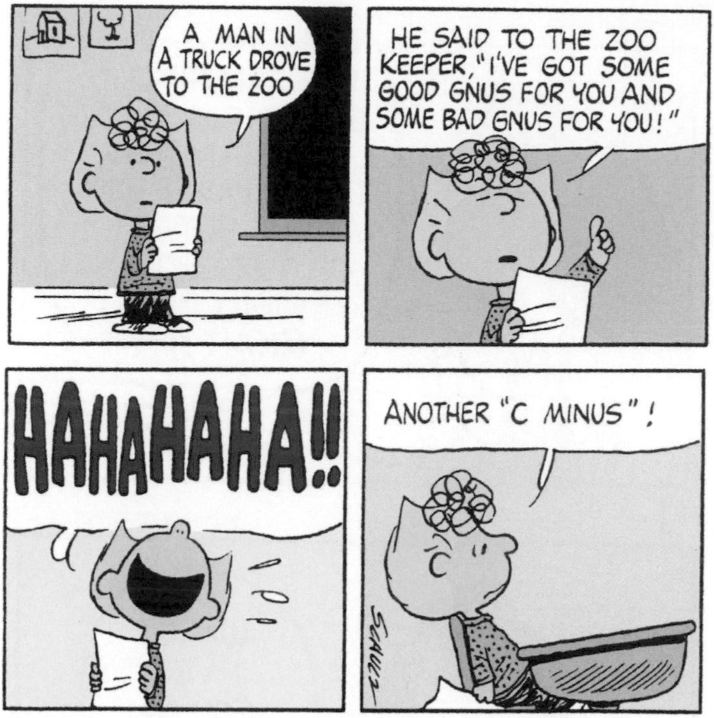
A MAN IN A TRUCK DROVE TO THE ZOO
HE SAID TO THE ZOO KEEPER, "I'VE GOT SOME GOOD GNUS FOR YOU AND SOME BAD GNUS FOR YOU!"
HAHAHAHA!!
ANOTHER "C MINUS"!
SCHULZ

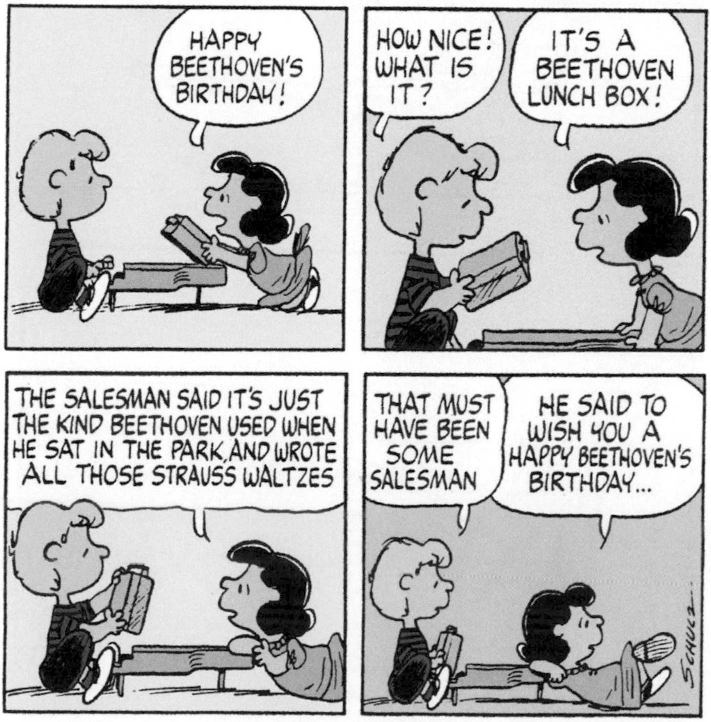
HAPPY BEETHOVEN'S BIRTHDAY!
HOW NICE! WHAT IS IT?
IT'S A BEETHOVEN LUNCH BOX!
THE SALESMAN SAID IT'S JUST THE KIND BEETHOVEN USED WHEN HE SAT IN THE PARK, AND WROTE ALL THOSE STRAUSS WALTZES
THAT MUST HAVE BEEN SOME SALESMAN
HE SAID TO WISH YOU A HAPPY BEETHOVEN'S BIRTHDAY...
SCHULZ

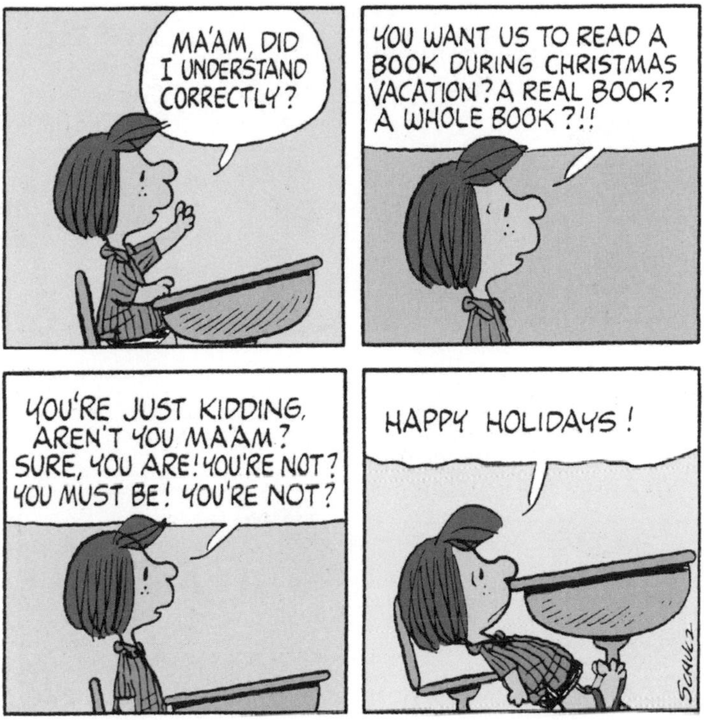
MA'AM, DID I UNDERSTAND CORRECTLY?
YOU WANT US TO READ A BOOK DURING CHRISTMAS VACATION? A REAL BOOK? A WHOLE BOOK?!!
YOU'RE JUST KIDDING, AREN'T YOU MA'AM? SURE, YOU ARE! YOU'RE NOT? YOU MUST BE! YOU'RE NOT?
HAPPY HOLIDAYS!
SCHULZ

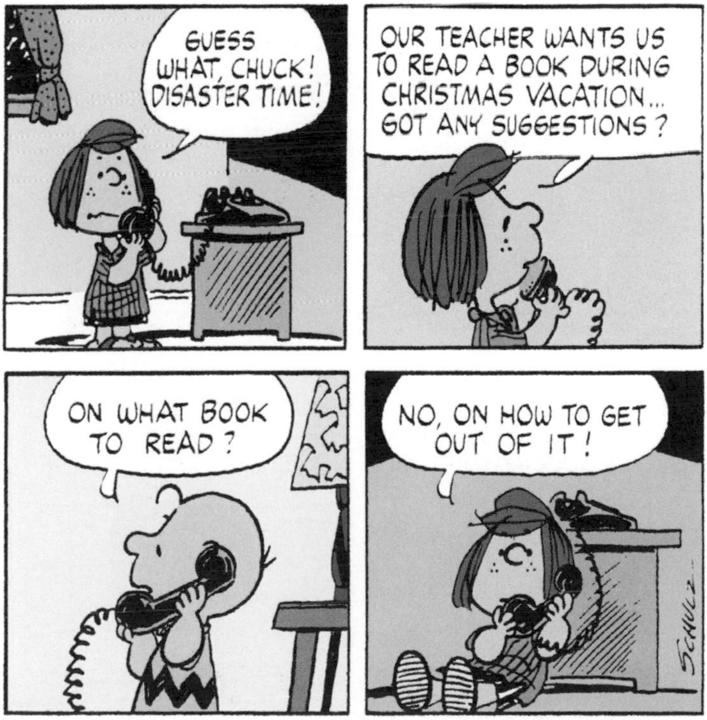
GUESS WHAT, CHUCK! DISASTER TIME!
OUR TEACHER WANTS US TO READ A BOOK DURING CHRISTMAS VACATION... GOT ANY SUGGESTIONS?
ON WHAT BOOK TO READ?
NO, ON HOW TO GET OUT OF IT!
SCHULZ

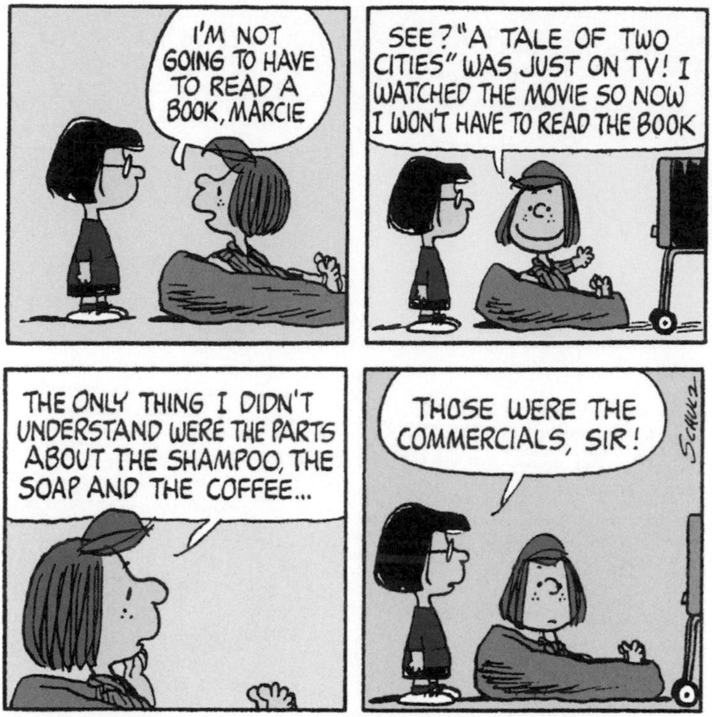
I'M NOT GOING TO HAVE TO READ A BOOK, MARCIE
SEE? "A TALE OF TWO CITIES" WAS JUST ON TV! I WATCHED THE MOVIE SO NOW I WON'T HAVE TO READ THE BOOK
THE ONLY THING I DIDN'T UNDERSTAND WERE THE PARTS ABOUT THE SHAMPOO, THE SOAP AND THE COFFEE...
THOSE WERE THE COMMERCIALS, SIR!
SCHULZ

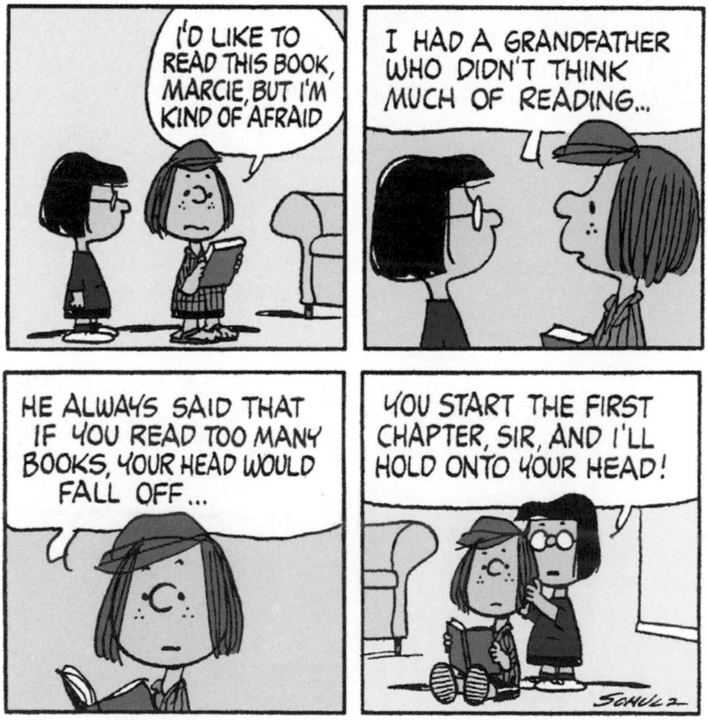
I'D LIKE TO READ THIS BOOK, MARCIE, BUT I'M KIND OF AFRAID
I HAD A GRANDFATHER WHO DIDN'T THINK MUCH OF READING...
HE ALWAYS SAID THAT IF YOU READ TOO MANY BOOKS, YOUR HEAD WOULD FALL OFF...
YOU START THE FIRST CHAPTER, SIR, AND I'LL HOLD ONTO YOUR HEAD!
SCHULZ

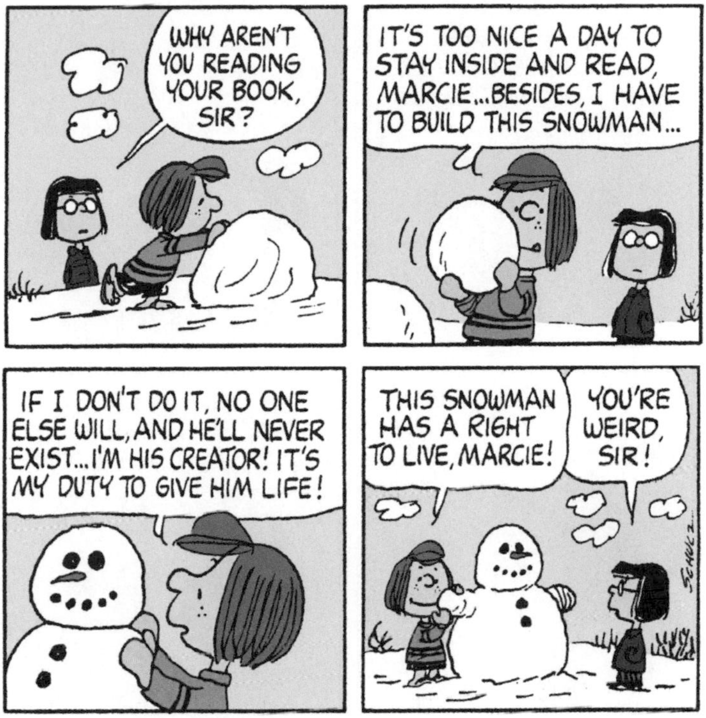
WHY AREN'T YOU READING YOUR BOOK, SIR?
IT'S TOO NICE A DAY TO STAY INSIDE AND READ, MARCIE...BESIDES, I HAVE TO BUILD THIS SNOWMAN...
IF I DON'T DO IT, NO ONE ELSE WILL, AND HE'LL NEVER EXIST...I'M HIS CREATOR! IT'S MY DUTY TO GIVE HIM LIFE!
THIS SNOWMAN HAS A RIGHT TO LIVE, MARCIE!
YOU'RE WEIRD, SIR!
SCHULZ

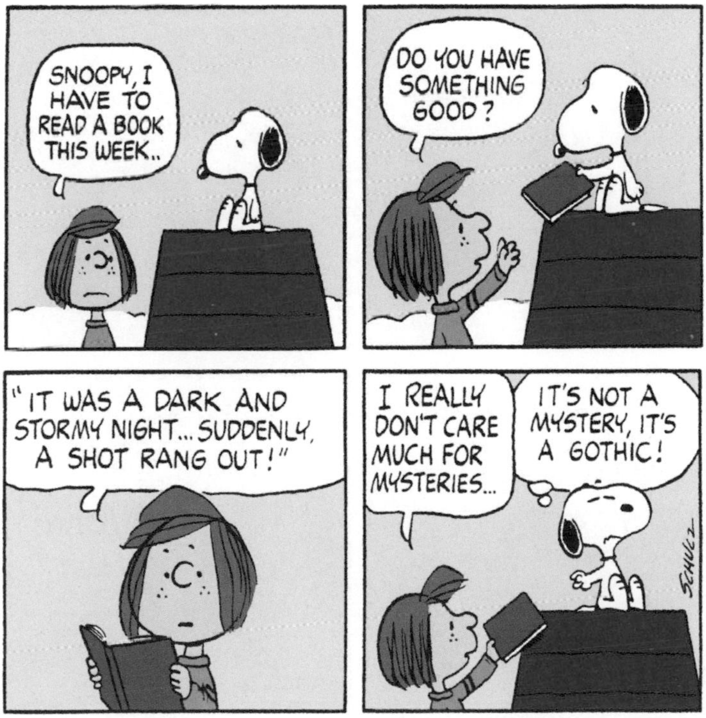
SNOOPY, I HAVE TO READ A BOOK THIS WEEK..
DO YOU HAVE SOMETHING GOOD?
"IT WAS A DARK AND STORMY NIGHT... SUDDENLY, A SHOT RANG OUT!"
I REALLY DON'T CARE MUCH FOR MYSTERIES...
IT'S NOT A MYSTERY, IT'S A GOTHIC!
SCHULZ

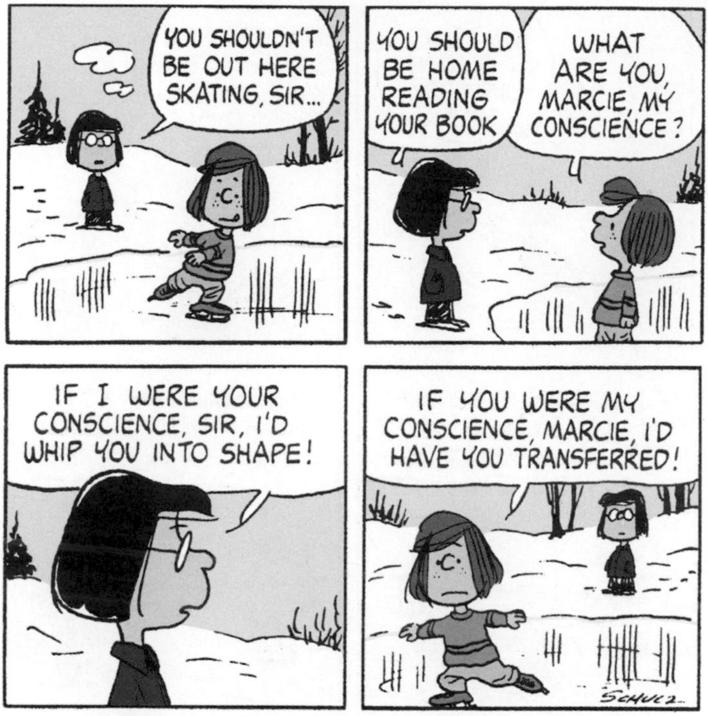
YOU SHOULDN'T BE OUT HERE SKATING, SIR...
YOU SHOULD BE HOME READING YOUR BOOK
WHAT ARE YOU, MARCIE, MY CONSCIENCE?
IF I WERE YOUR CONSCIENCE, SIR, I'D WHIP YOU INTO SHAPE!
IF YOU WERE MY CONSCIENCE, MARCIE, I'D HAVE YOU TRANSFERRED!
SCHULZ

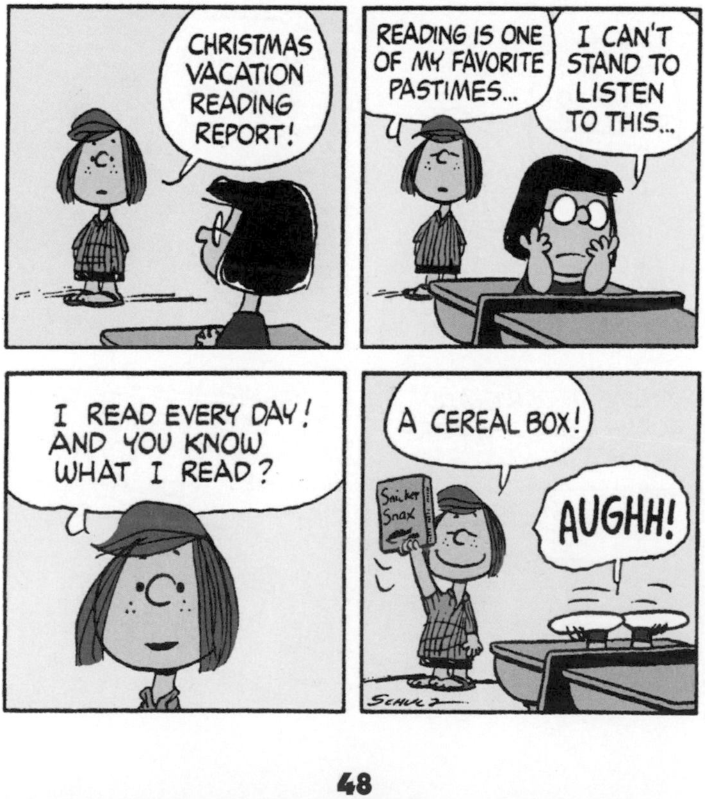
CHRISTMAS VACATION READING REPORT!
READING IS ONE OF MY FAVORITE PASTIMES...
I CAN'T STAND TO LISTEN TO THIS...
I READ EVERY DAY! AND YOU KNOW WHAT I READ?
A CEREAL BOX!
Snicker Snax
AUGHH!
SCHULZ

THERE'S NOTHING WRONG WITH READING CEREAL BOXES...

SOME OF THE BEST STORIES I'VE EVER READ WERE ON CEREAL BOXES...AND YOU DON'T HAVE TO TURN ANY PAGES!

I PREDICT THAT SOME DAY A CEREAL BOX WILL WIN THE PULITZER PRIZE!

SEE, MARCIE? I DID IT!

YOU'RE WEIRD, SIR...

SHE'S TALKING TO YOU, MARCIE...

MA'AM?

MY BOOK REPORT? OH, GOOD GRIEF!

SHE WAS SO BUSY BUGGING ME, MA'AM, THAT SHE FORGOT TO READ ANYTHING HERSELF!

TURN AROUND, MARCIE... I CAN'T AFFORD TO ASSOCIATE WITH SOMEONE WHO DOESN'T DO HER HOMEWORK!

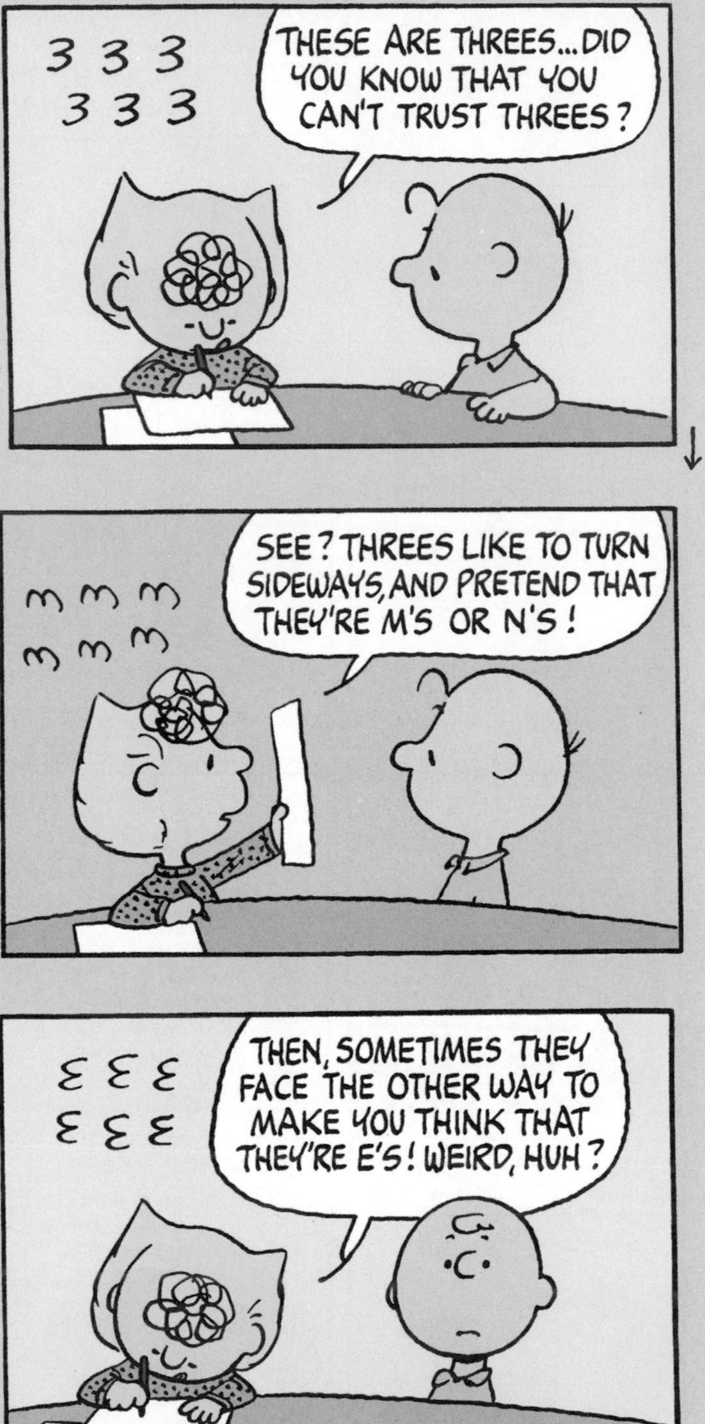
THESE ARE THREES...DID YOU KNOW THAT YOU CAN'T TRUST THREES?
SEE? THREES LIKE TO TURN SIDEWAYS, AND PRETEND THAT THEY'RE M'S OR N'S!
THEN, SOMETIMES THEY FACE THE OTHER WAY TO MAKE YOU THINK THAT THEY'RE E'S! WEIRD, HUH?

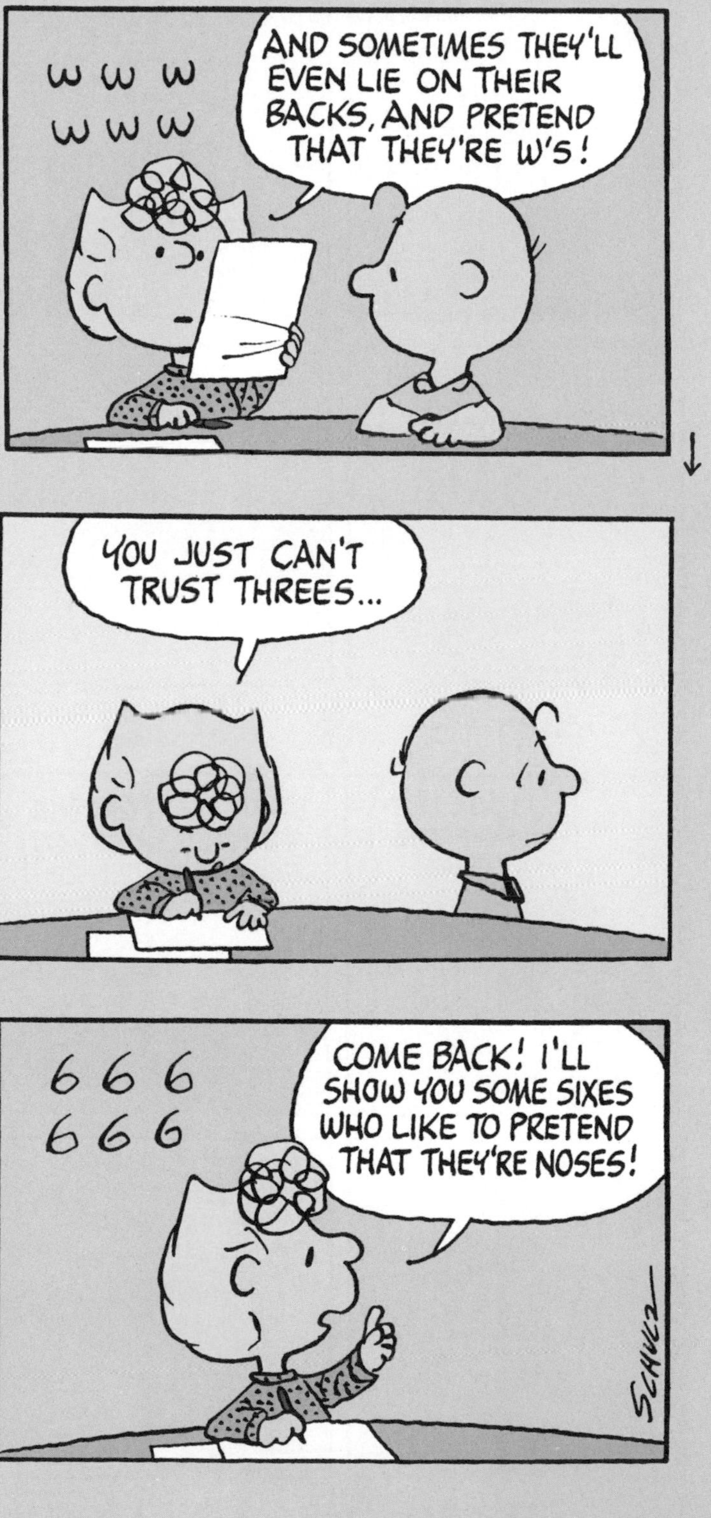
W W W
W W W
AND SOMETIMES THEY'LL EVEN LIE ON THEIR BACKS, AND PRETEND THAT THEY'RE W'S!
YOU JUST CAN'T TRUST THREES...
6 6 6
6 6 6
COME BACK! I'LL SHOW YOU SOME SIXES WHO LIKE TO PRETEND THAT THEY'RE NOSES!
SCHULZ

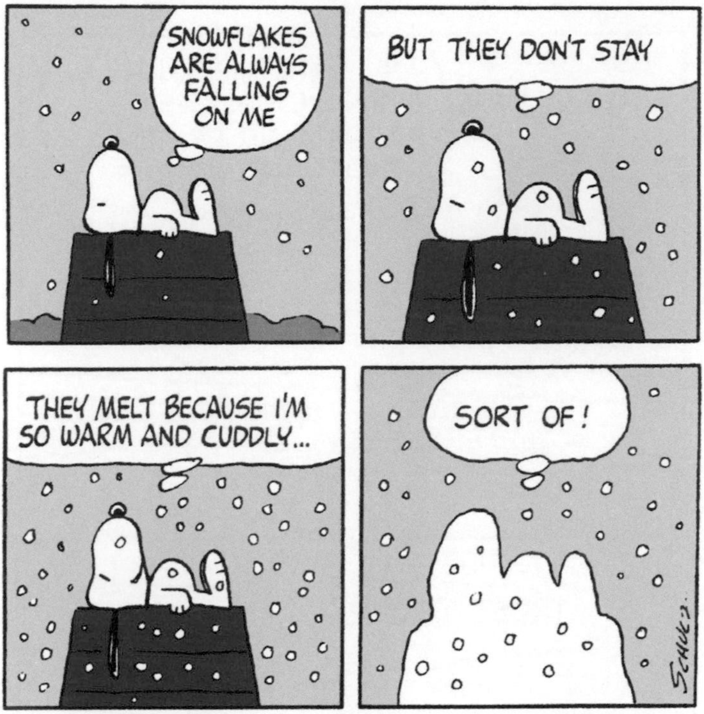

SNOWFLAKES ARE ALWAYS FALLING ON ME
BUT THEY DON'T STAY
THEY MELT BECAUSE I'M SO WARM AND CUDDLY...
SORT OF!

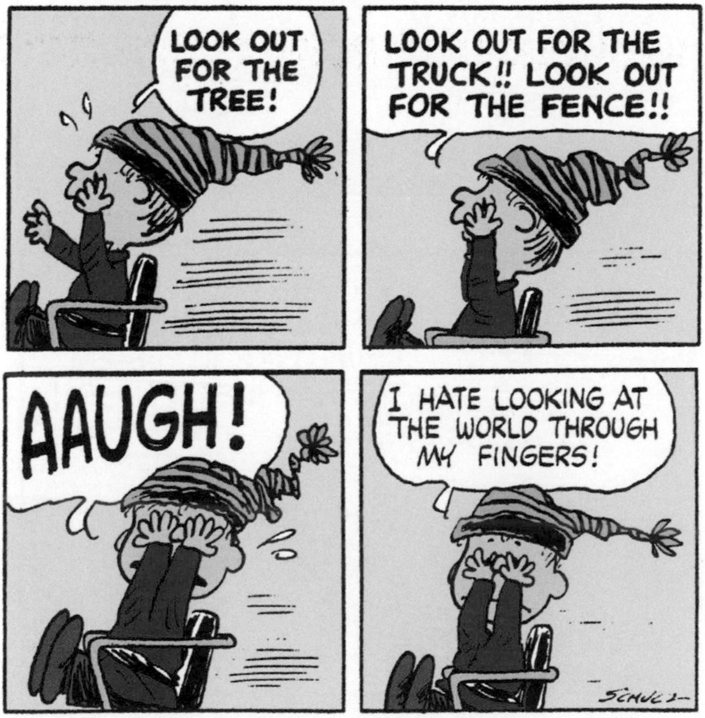

LOOK OUT FOR THE TREE!
LOOK OUT FOR THE TRUCK!! LOOK OUT FOR THE FENCE!!
AAUGH!
I HATE LOOKING AT THE WORLD THROUGH MY FINGERS!

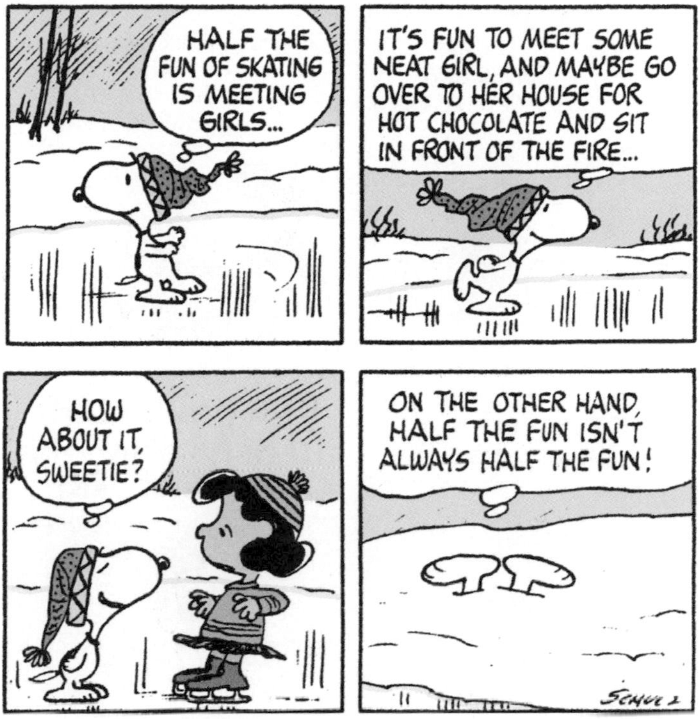
HALF THE FUN OF SKATING IS MEETING GIRLS...
IT'S FUN TO MEET SOME NEAT GIRL, AND MAYBE GO OVER TO HER HOUSE FOR HOT CHOCOLATE AND SIT IN FRONT OF THE FIRE...
HOW ABOUT IT, SWEETIE?
ON THE OTHER HAND, HALF THE FUN ISN'T ALWAYS HALF THE FUN!
SCHULZ

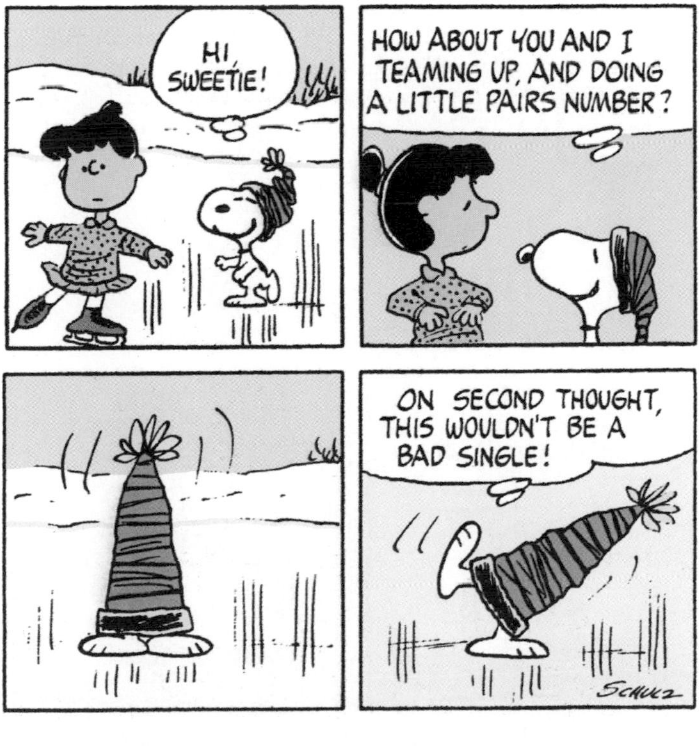
HI, SWEETIE!
HOW ABOUT YOU AND I TEAMING UP, AND DOING A LITTLE PAIRS NUMBER?
ON SECOND THOUGHT, THIS WOULDN'T BE A BAD SINGLE!
SCHULZ

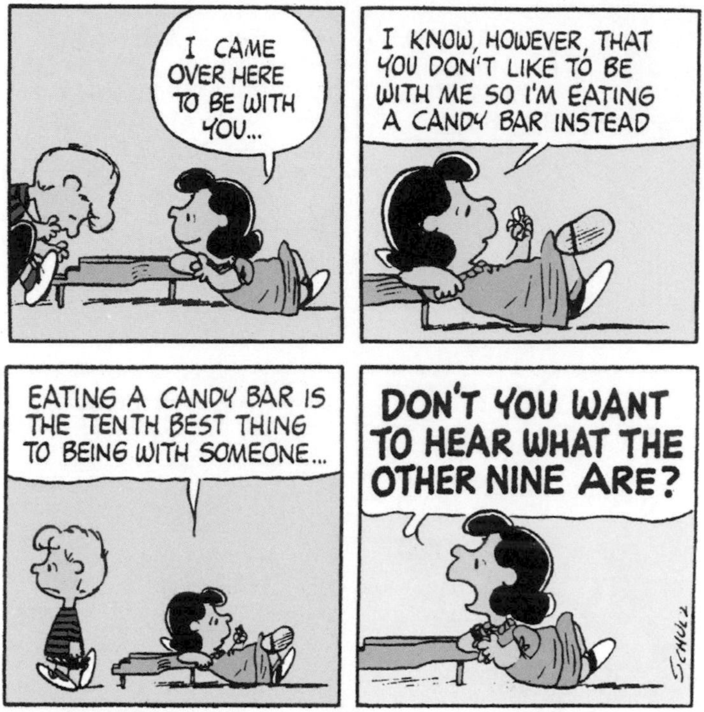
I CAME OVER HERE TO BE WITH YOU...
I KNOW, HOWEVER, THAT YOU DON'T LIKE TO BE WITH ME SO I'M EATING A CANDY BAR INSTEAD
EATING A CANDY BAR IS THE TENTH BEST THING TO BEING WITH SOMEONE...
DON'T YOU WANT TO HEAR WHAT THE OTHER NINE ARE?
SCHULZ

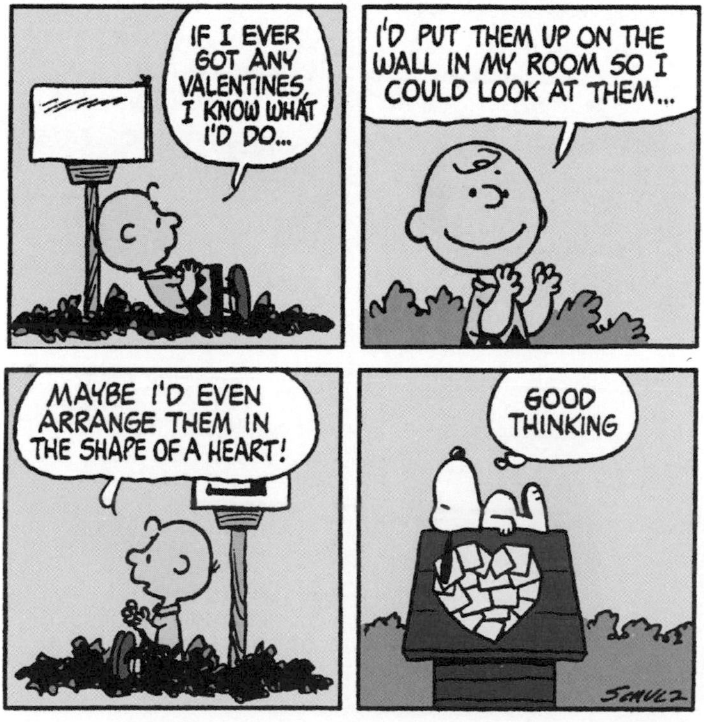
IF I EVER GOT ANY VALENTINES, I KNOW WHAT I'D DO...
I'D PUT THEM UP ON THE WALL IN MY ROOM SO I COULD LOOK AT THEM...
MAYBE I'D EVEN ARRANGE THEM IN THE SHAPE OF A HEART!
GOOD THINKING
SCHULZ

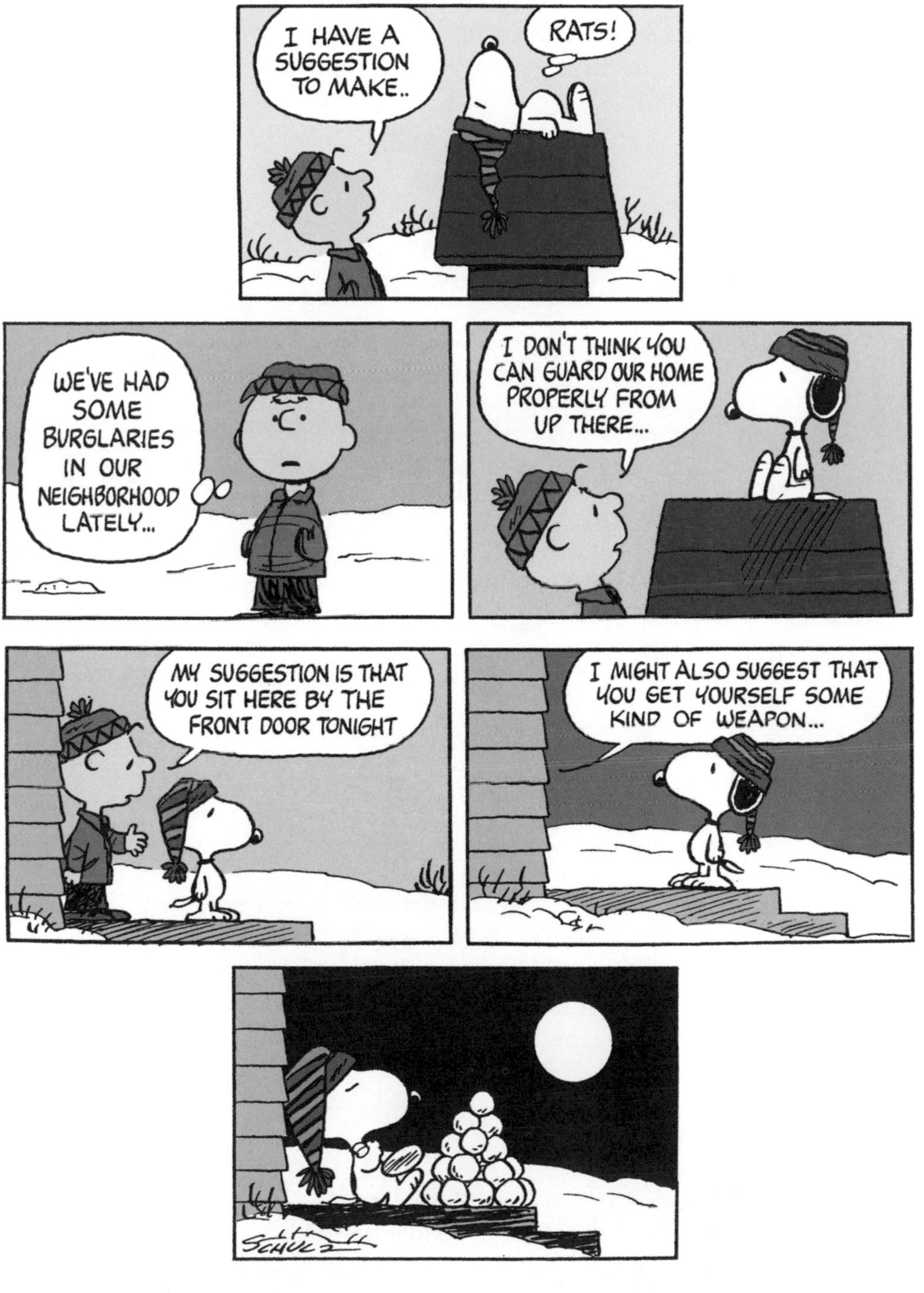
I HAVE A SUGGESTION TO MAKE..
RATS!
WE'VE HAD SOME BURGLARIES IN OUR NEIGHBORHOOD LATELY...
I DON'T THINK YOU CAN GUARD OUR HOME PROPERLY FROM UP THERE...
MY SUGGESTION IS THAT YOU SIT HERE BY THE FRONT DOOR TONIGHT
I MIGHT ALSO SUGGEST THAT YOU GET YOURSELF SOME KIND OF WEAPON...

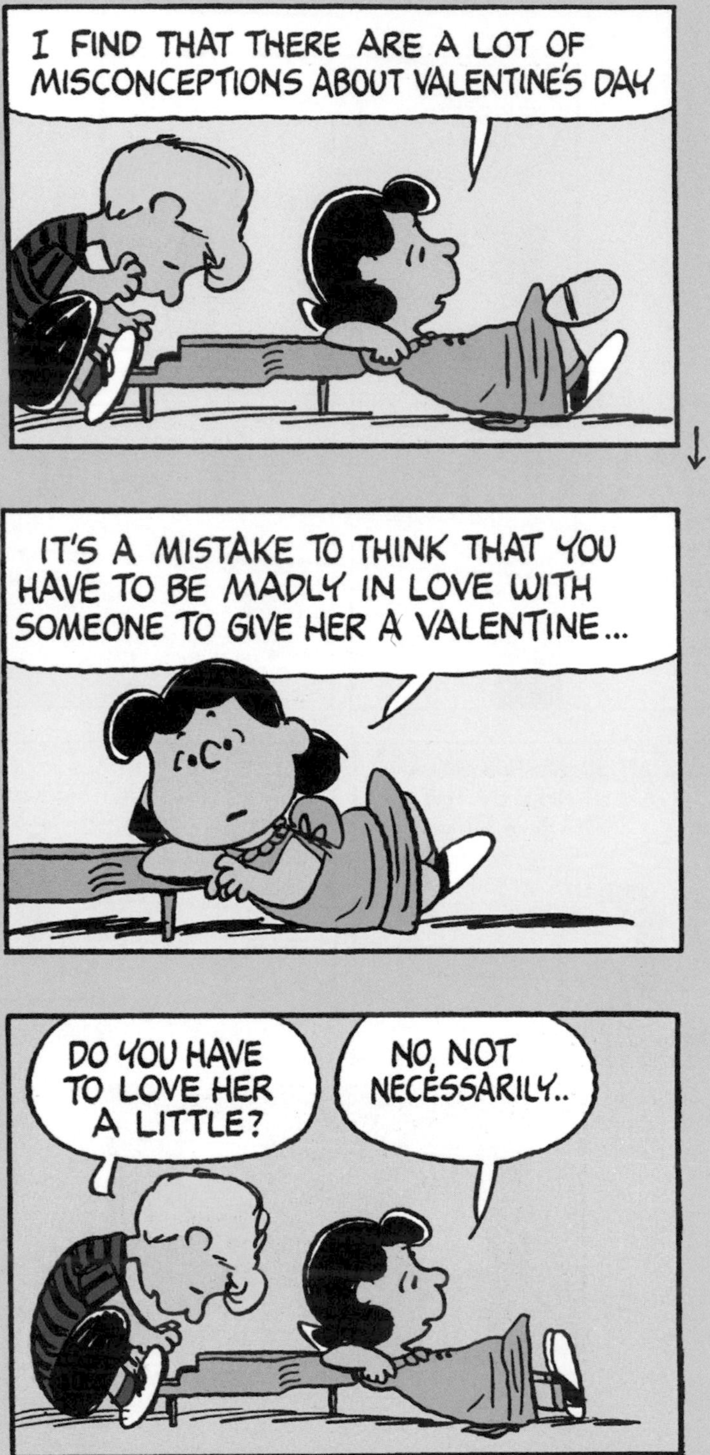
I FIND THAT THERE ARE A LOT OF MISCONCEPTIONS ABOUT VALENTINE'S DAY
IT'S A MISTAKE TO THINK THAT YOU HAVE TO BE MADLY IN LOVE WITH SOMEONE TO GIVE HER A VALENTINE...
DO YOU HAVE TO LOVE HER A LITTLE?
NO, NOT NECESSARILY..

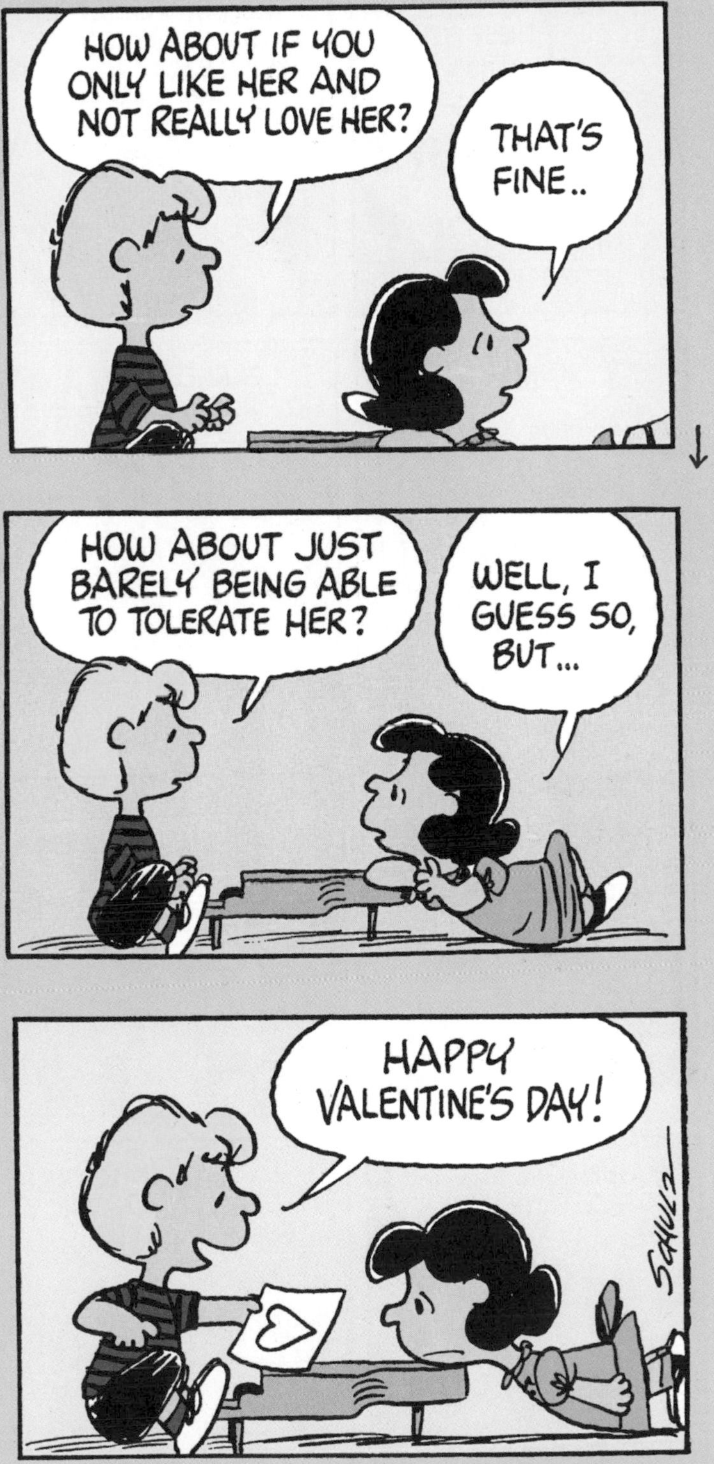
HOW ABOUT IF YOU ONLY LIKE HER AND NOT REALLY LOVE HER?
THAT'S FINE..
HOW ABOUT JUST BARELY BEING ABLE TO TOLERATE HER?
WELL, I GUESS SO, BUT...
HAPPY VALENTINE'S DAY!
SCHULZ

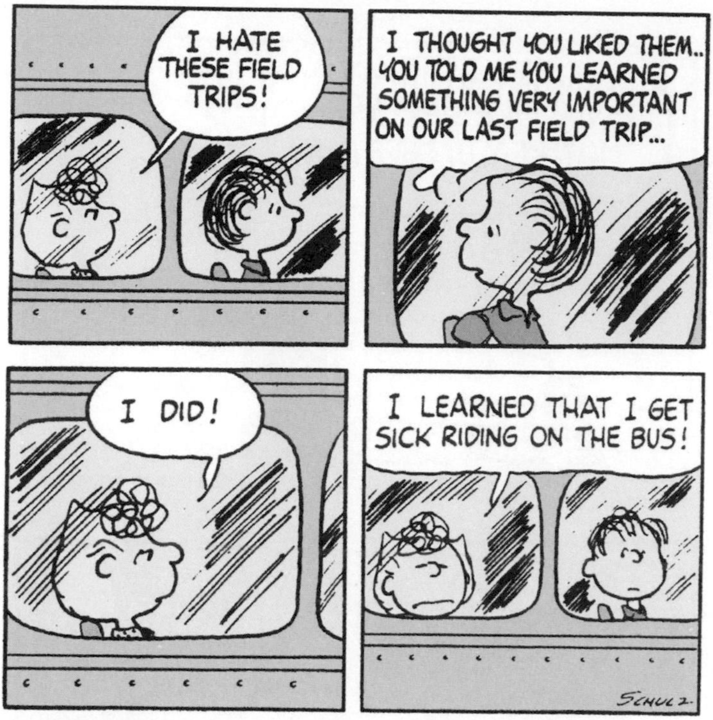
I HATE THESE FIELD TRIPS!
I THOUGHT YOU LIKED THEM.. YOU TOLD ME YOU LEARNED SOMETHING VERY IMPORTANT ON OUR LAST FIELD TRIP...
I DID!
I LEARNED THAT I GET SICK RIDING ON THE BUS!

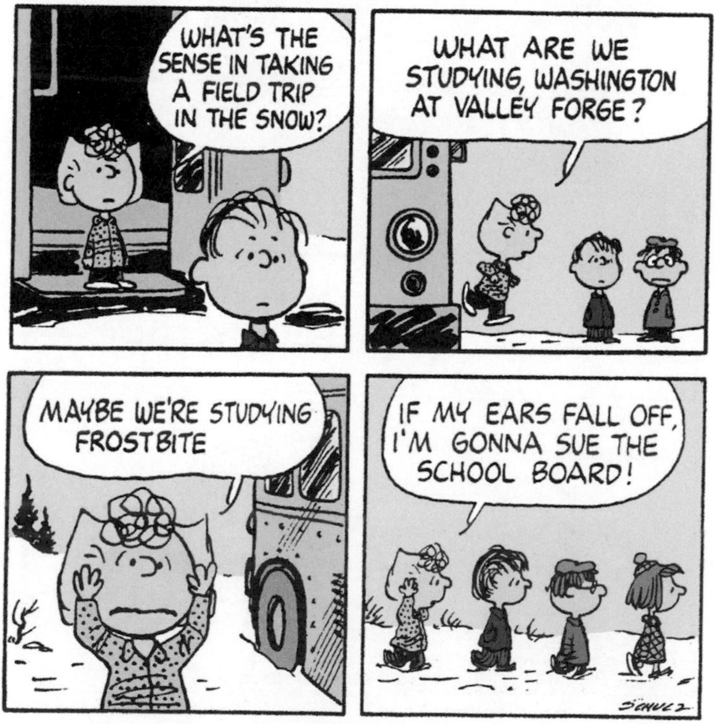
WHAT'S THE SENSE IN TAKING A FIELD TRIP IN THE SNOW?
WHAT ARE WE STUDYING, WASHINGTON AT VALLEY FORGE?
MAYBE WE'RE STUDYING FROSTBITE
IF MY EARS FALL OFF, I'M GONNA SUE THE SCHOOL BOARD!

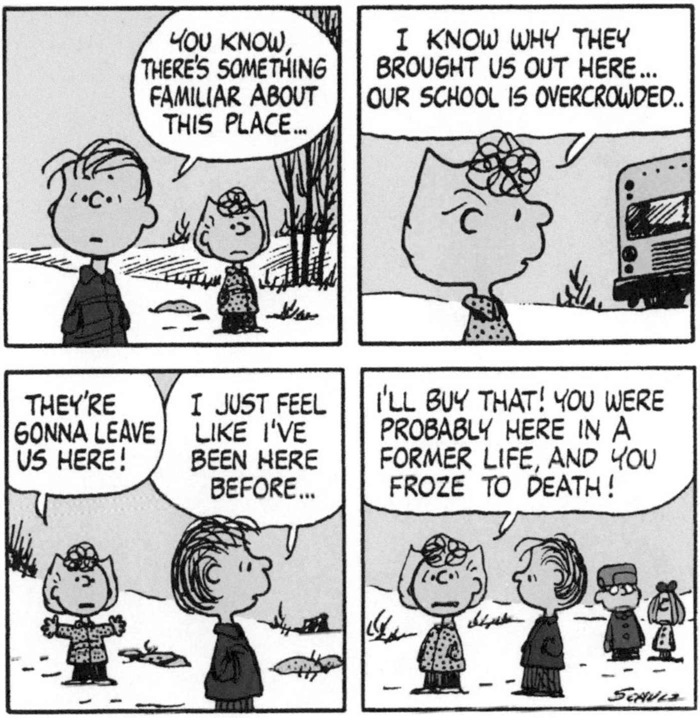
YOU KNOW, THERE'S SOMETHING FAMILIAR ABOUT THIS PLACE...
I KNOW WHY THEY BROUGHT US OUT HERE... OUR SCHOOL IS OVERCROWDED..
THEY'RE GONNA LEAVE US HERE!
I JUST FEEL LIKE I'VE BEEN HERE BEFORE...
I'LL BUY THAT! YOU WERE PROBABLY HERE IN A FORMER LIFE, AND YOU FROZE TO DEATH!

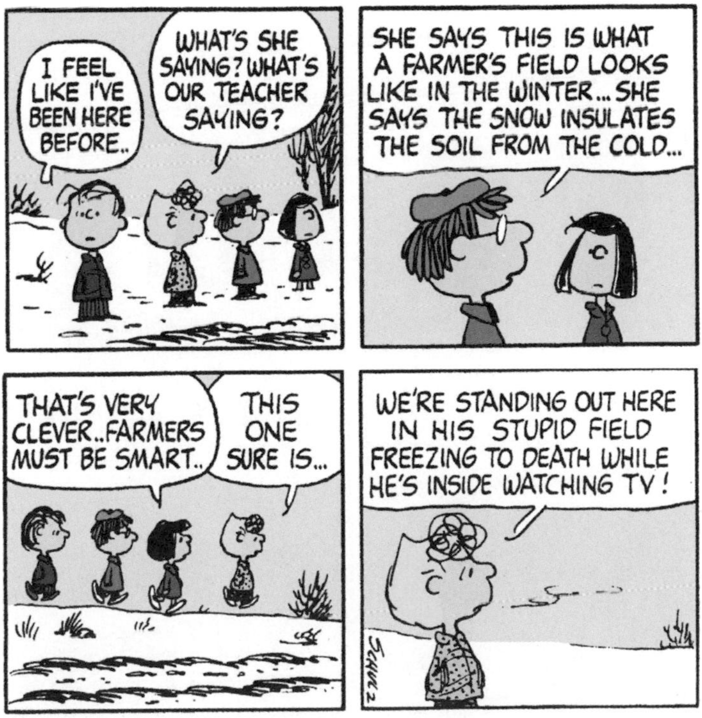
I FEEL LIKE I'VE BEEN HERE BEFORE..
WHAT'S SHE SAYING? WHAT'S OUR TEACHER SAYING?
SHE SAYS THIS IS WHAT A FARMER'S FIELD LOOKS LIKE IN THE WINTER... SHE SAYS THE SNOW INSULATES THE SOIL FROM THE COLD...
THAT'S VERY CLEVER..FARMERS MUST BE SMART..
THIS ONE SURE IS...
WE'RE STANDING OUT HERE IN HIS STUPID FIELD FREEZING TO DEATH WHILE HE'S INSIDE WATCHING TV!

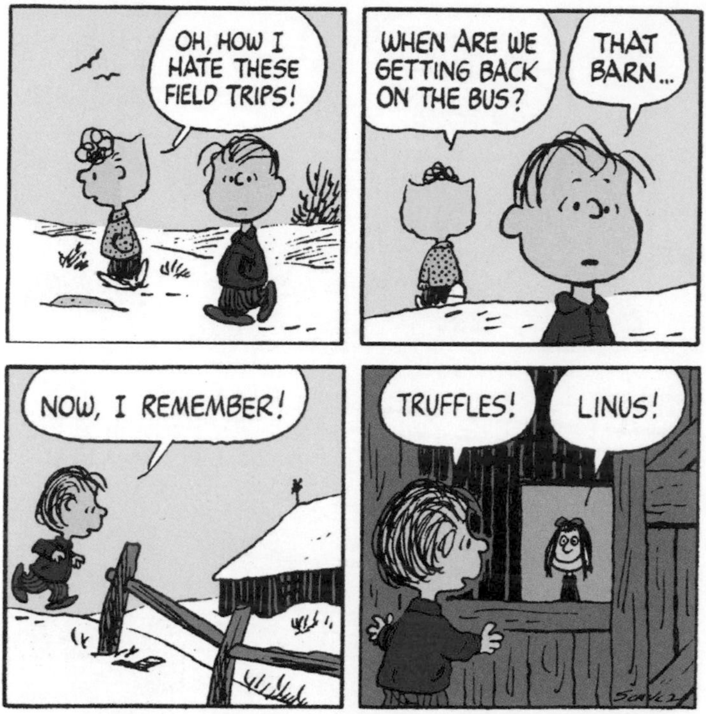
OH, HOW I HATE THESE FIELD TRIPS!
WHEN ARE WE GETTING BACK ON THE BUS?
THAT BARN...
NOW, I REMEMBER!
TRUFFLES!
LINUS!

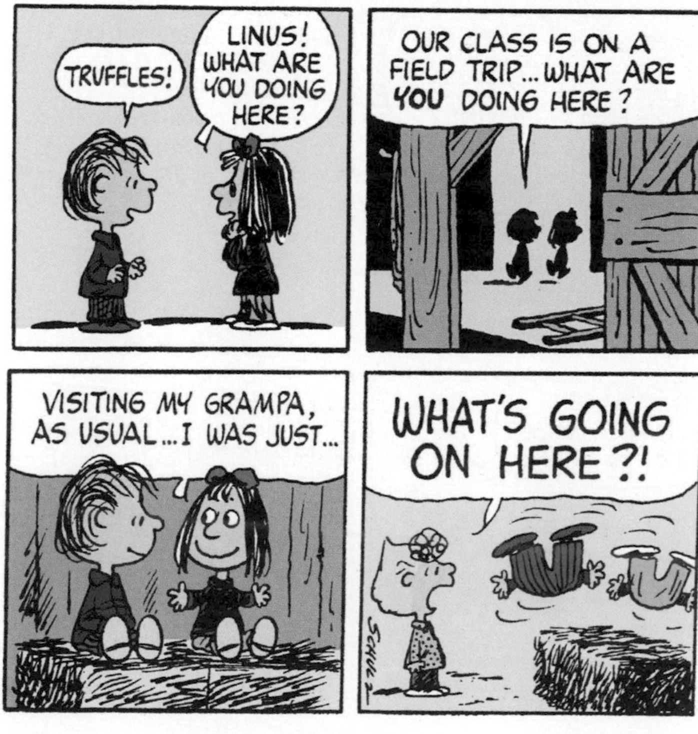
TRUFFLES!
LINUS! WHAT ARE YOU DOING HERE?
OUR CLASS IS ON A FIELD TRIP...WHAT ARE YOU DOING HERE?
VISITING MY GRAMPA, AS USUAL...I WAS JUST...
WHAT'S GOING ON HERE?!

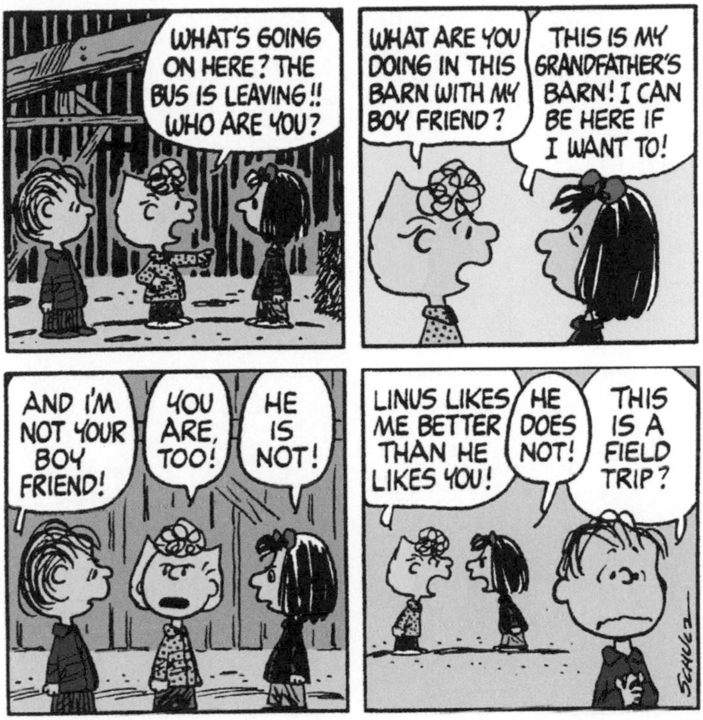
WHAT'S GOING ON HERE? THE BUS IS LEAVING!! WHO ARE YOU?
WHAT ARE YOU DOING IN THIS BARN WITH MY BOY FRIEND?
THIS IS MY GRANDFATHER'S BARN! I CAN BE HERE IF I WANT TO!
AND I'M NOT YOUR BOY FRIEND!
YOU ARE, TOO!
HE IS NOT!
LINUS LIKES ME BETTER THAN HE LIKES YOU!
HE DOES NOT!
THIS IS A FIELD TRIP?

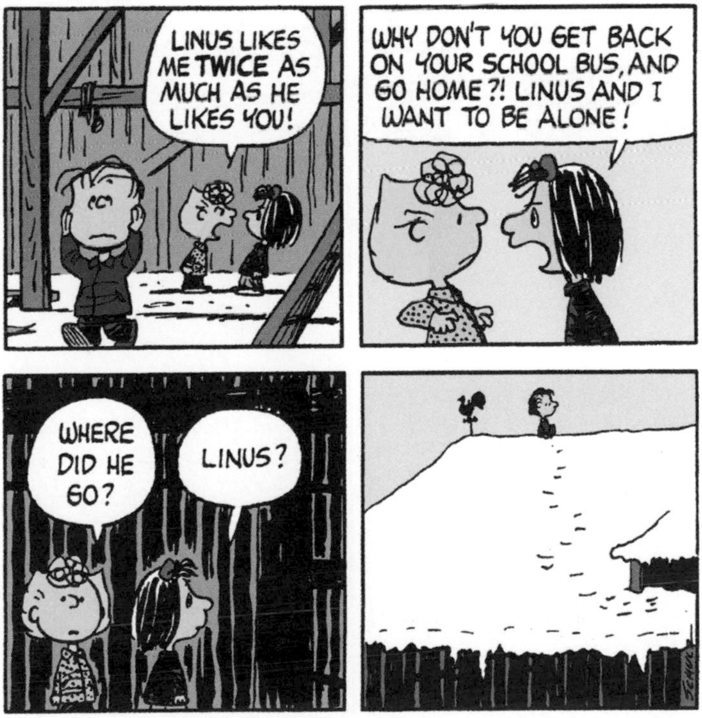
LINUS LIKES ME TWICE AS MUCH AS HE LIKES YOU!
WHY DON'T YOU GET BACK ON YOUR SCHOOL BUS, AND GO HOME?! LINUS AND I WANT TO BE ALONE!
WHERE DID HE GO?
LINUS?

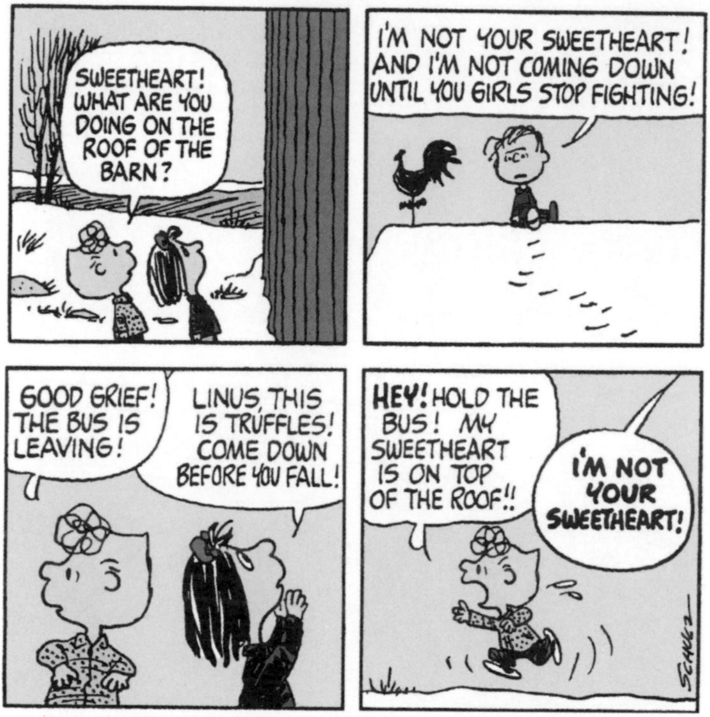
SWEETHEART! WHAT ARE YOU DOING ON THE ROOF OF THE BARN?
I'M NOT YOUR SWEETHEART! AND I'M NOT COMING DOWN UNTIL YOU GIRLS STOP FIGHTING!
GOOD GRIEF! THE BUS IS LEAVING!
LINUS, THIS IS TRUFFLES! COME DOWN BEFORE YOU FALL!
HEY! HOLD THE BUS! MY SWEETHEART IS ON TOP OF THE ROOF!!
I'M NOT YOUR SWEETHEART!
SCHULZ

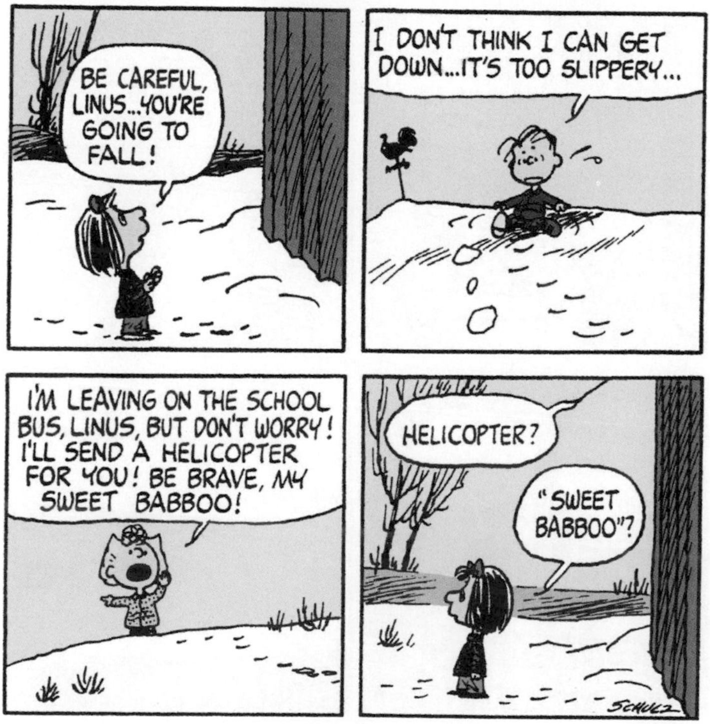
BE CAREFUL, LINUS...YOU'RE GOING TO FALL!
I DON'T THINK I CAN GET DOWN...IT'S TOO SLIPPERY...
I'M LEAVING ON THE SCHOOL BUS, LINUS, BUT DON'T WORRY! I'LL SEND A HELICOPTER FOR YOU! BE BRAVE, MY SWEET BABBOO!
HELICOPTER?
"SWEET BABBOO"?
SCHULZ

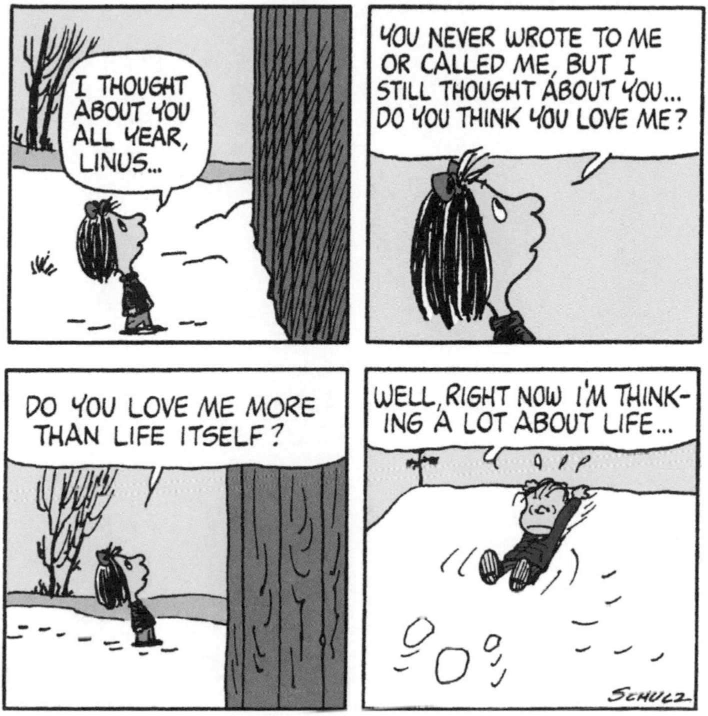
I THOUGHT ABOUT YOU ALL YEAR, LINUS...
YOU NEVER WROTE TO ME OR CALLED ME, BUT I STILL THOUGHT ABOUT YOU... DO YOU THINK YOU LOVE ME?
DO YOU LOVE ME MORE THAN LIFE ITSELF?
WELL, RIGHT NOW I'M THINKING A LOT ABOUT LIFE...
SCHULZ

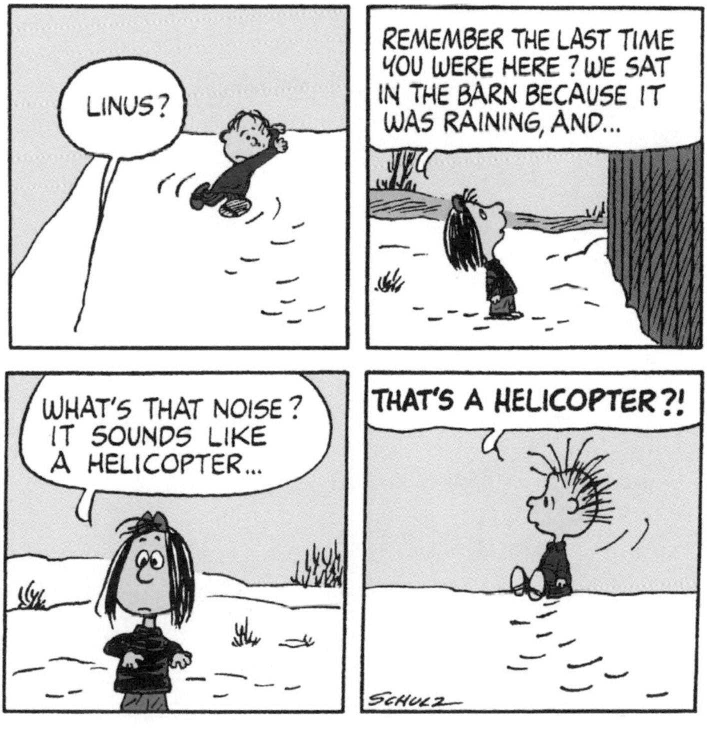
LINUS?
REMEMBER THE LAST TIME YOU WERE HERE? WE SAT IN THE BARN BECAUSE IT WAS RAINING, AND...
WHAT'S THAT NOISE? IT SOUNDS LIKE A HELICOPTER...
THAT'S A HELICOPTER?!
SCHULZ

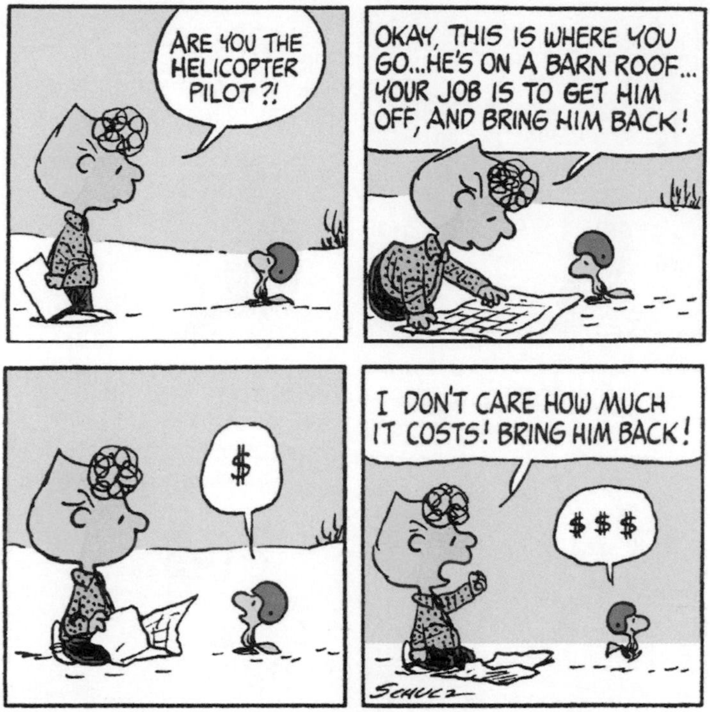
ARE YOU THE HELICOPTER PILOT?!
OKAY, THIS IS WHERE YOU GO...HE'S ON A BARN ROOF... YOUR JOB IS TO GET HIM OFF, AND BRING HIM BACK!
$
I DON'T CARE HOW MUCH IT COSTS! BRING HIM BACK!
$ $ $
SCHULZ

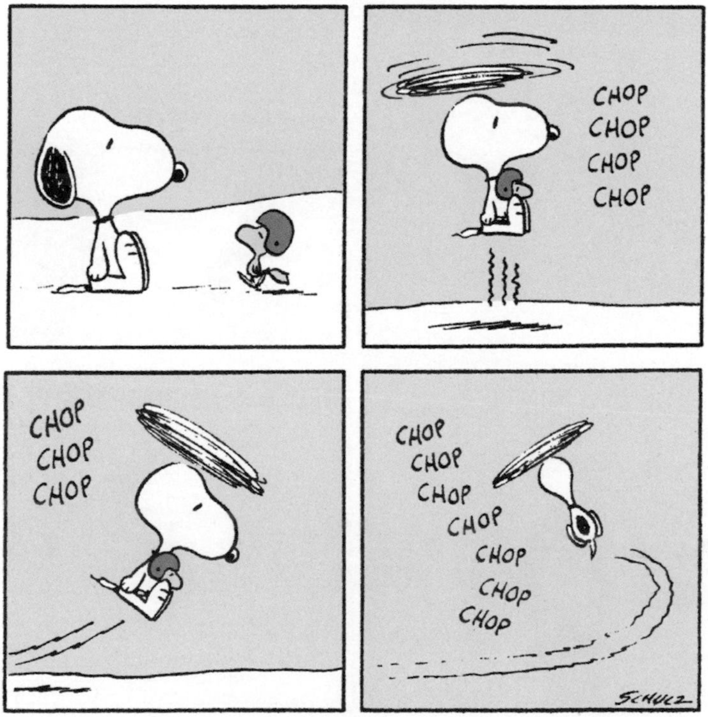
CHOP
CHOP
CHOP
CHOP
CHOP
CHOP
CHOP
CHOP
CHOP
CHOP
CHOP
CHOP
CHOP
CHOP
SCHULZ

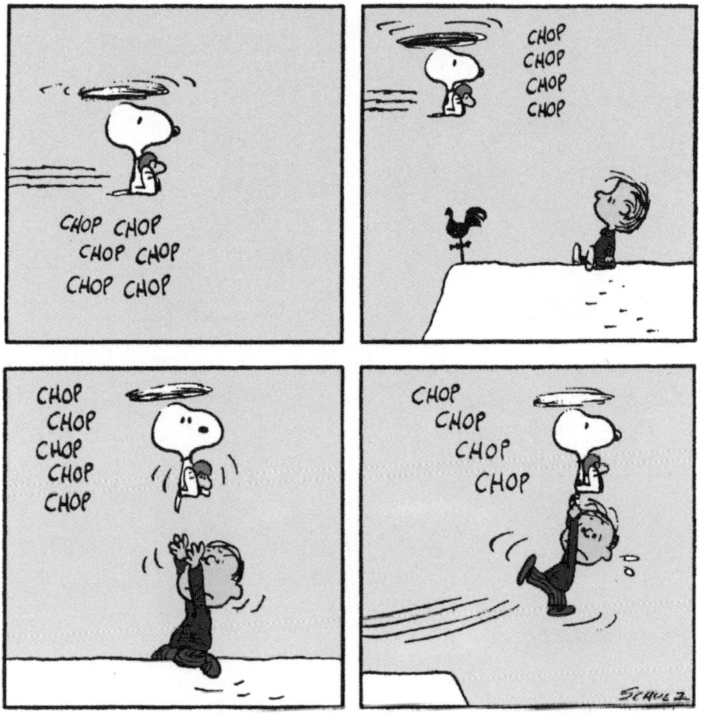
CHOP CHOP
CHOP CHOP
CHOP CHOP
CHOP
CHOP
CHOP
CHOP
CHOP
CHOP
CHOP
CHOP
CHOP
CHOP
CHOP
CHOP
CHOP
CHOP

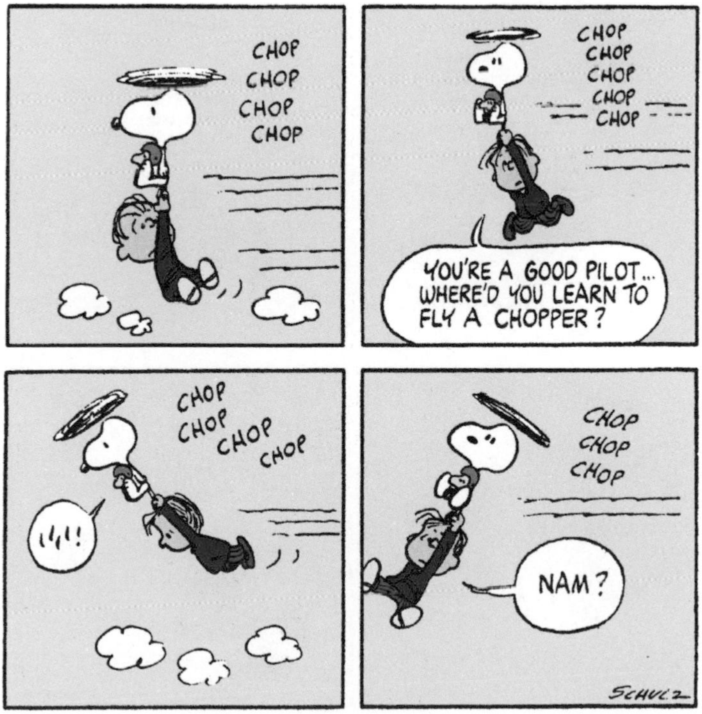
CHOP
CHOP
CHOP
CHOP
CHOP
CHOP
CHOP
CHOP
CHOP
YOU'RE A GOOD PILOT... WHERE'D YOU LEARN TO FLY A CHOPPER?
CHOP
CHOP
CHOP
CHOP
CHOP
CHOP
CHOP
NAM?

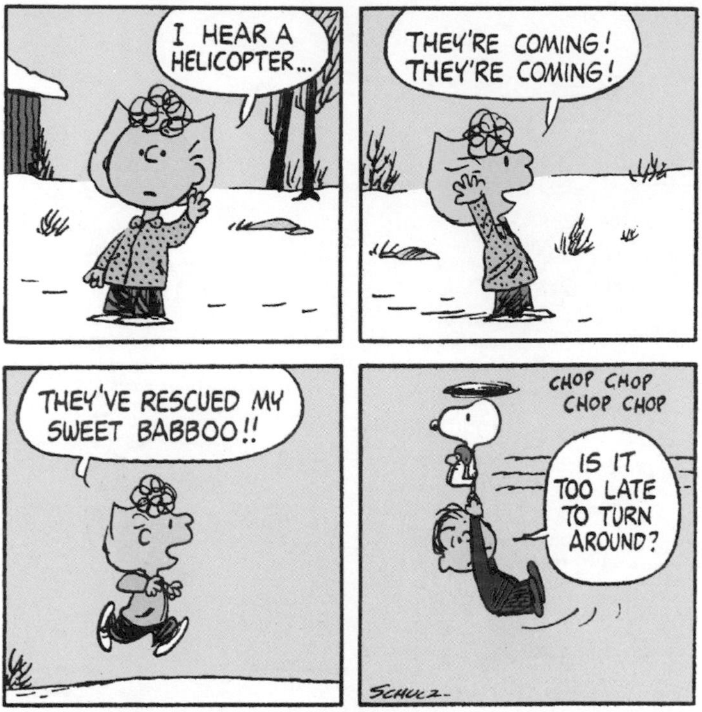
I HEAR A HELICOPTER...
THEY'RE COMING! THEY'RE COMING!
THEY'VE RESCUED MY SWEET BABBOO!!
CHOP CHOP CHOP CHOP
IS IT TOO LATE TO TURN AROUND?
SCHULZ

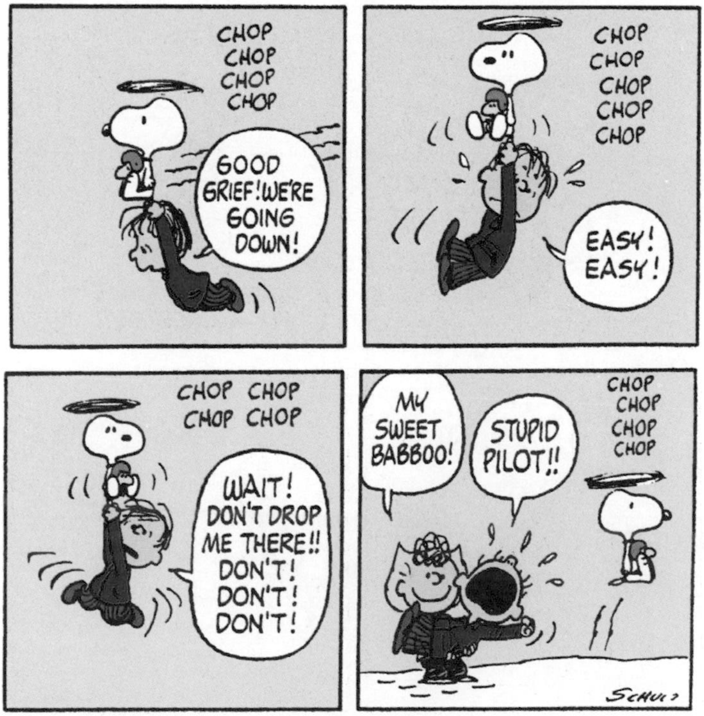
CHOP CHOP CHOP CHOP
GOOD GRIEF! WE'RE GOING DOWN!
CHOP CHOP CHOP CHOP CHOP
EASY! EASY!
CHOP CHOP CHOP CHOP
WAIT! DON'T DROP ME THERE!! DON'T! DON'T! DON'T!
MY SWEET BABBOO!
STUPID PILOT!!
CHOP CHOP CHOP CHOP
SCHULZ

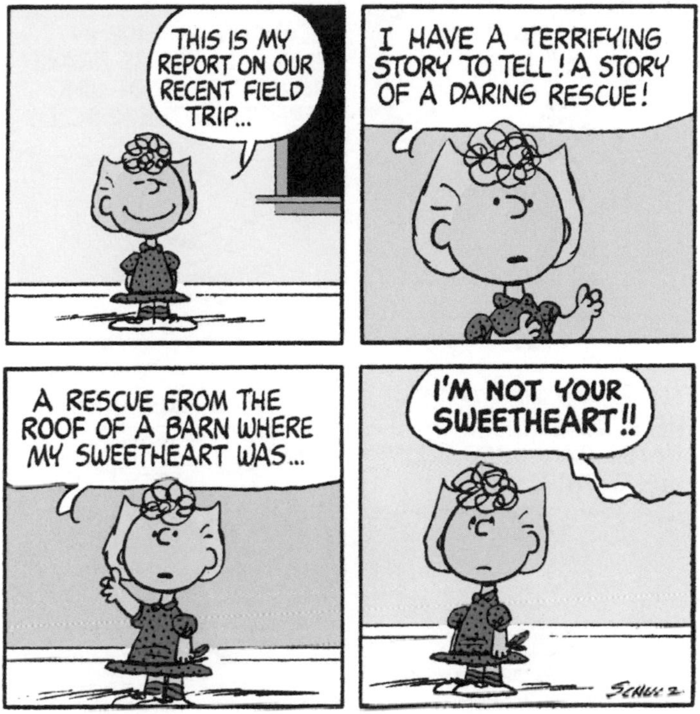
THIS IS MY REPORT ON OUR RECENT FIELD TRIP...
I HAVE A TERRIFYING STORY TO TELL! A STORY OF A DARING RESCUE!
A RESCUE FROM THE ROOF OF A BARN WHERE MY SWEETHEART WAS...
I'M NOT YOUR SWEETHEART!!

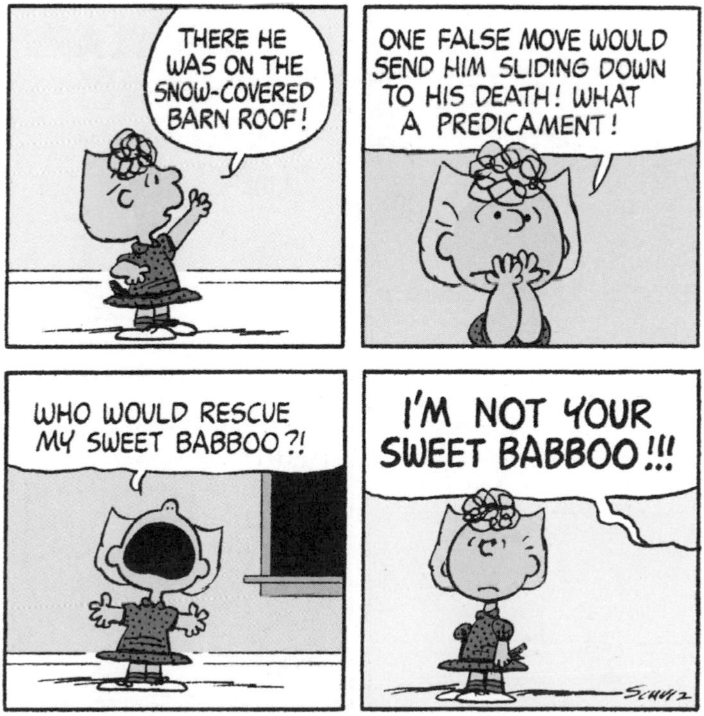
THERE HE WAS ON THE SNOW-COVERED BARN ROOF!
ONE FALSE MOVE WOULD SEND HIM SLIDING DOWN TO HIS DEATH! WHAT A PREDICAMENT!
WHO WOULD RESCUE MY SWEET BABBOO?!
I'M NOT YOUR SWEET BABBOO!!!

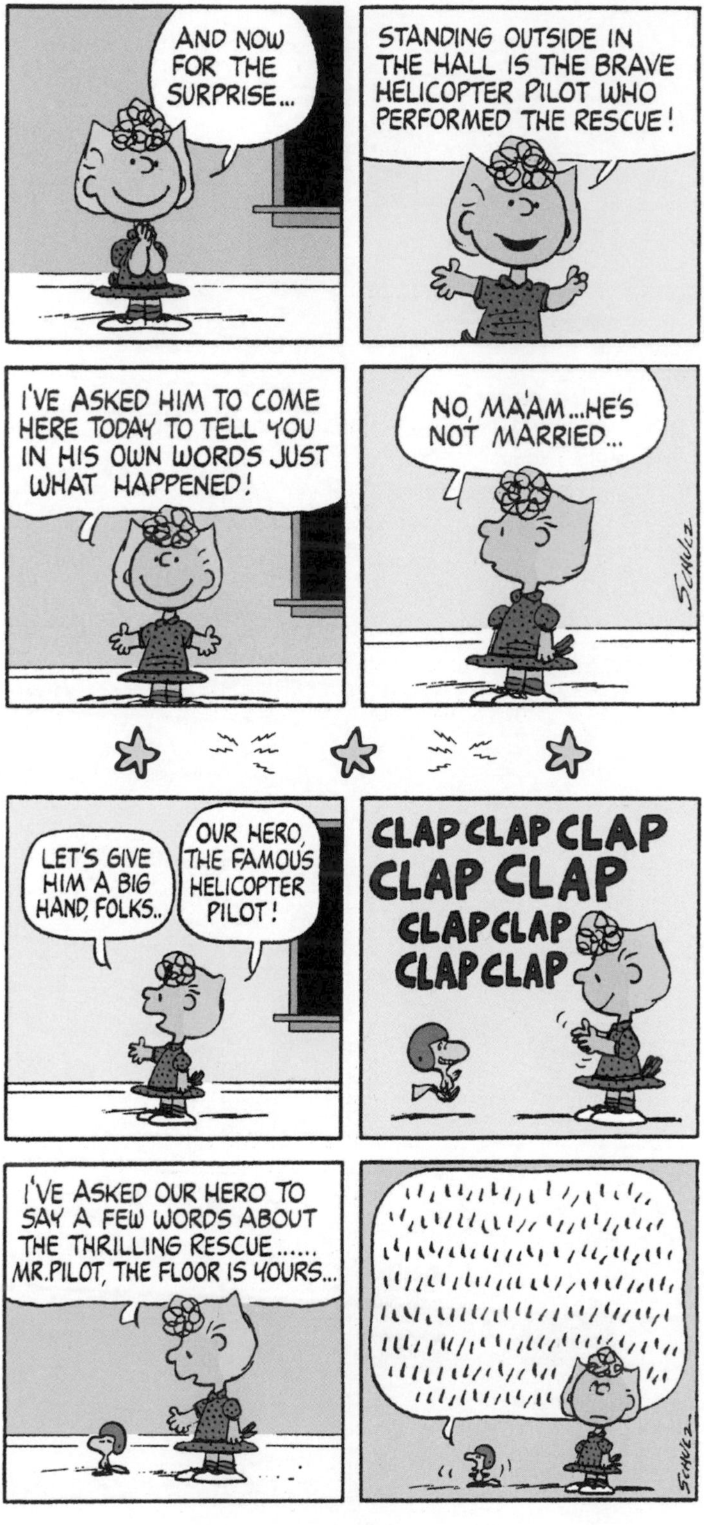
AND NOW FOR THE SURPRISE...
STANDING OUTSIDE IN THE HALL IS THE BRAVE HELICOPTER PILOT WHO PERFORMED THE RESCUE!
I'VE ASKED HIM TO COME HERE TODAY TO TELL YOU IN HIS OWN WORDS JUST WHAT HAPPENED!
NO, MA'AM...HE'S NOT MARRIED...
SCHULZ
OUR HERO, THE FAMOUS HELICOPTER PILOT!
LET'S GIVE HIM A BIG HAND, FOLKS..
CLAP CLAP CLAP
CLAP CLAP
CLAP CLAP
CLAP CLAP
I'VE ASKED OUR HERO TO SAY A FEW WORDS ABOUT THE THRILLING RESCUE...... MR. PILOT, THE FLOOR IS YOURS...
SCHULZ

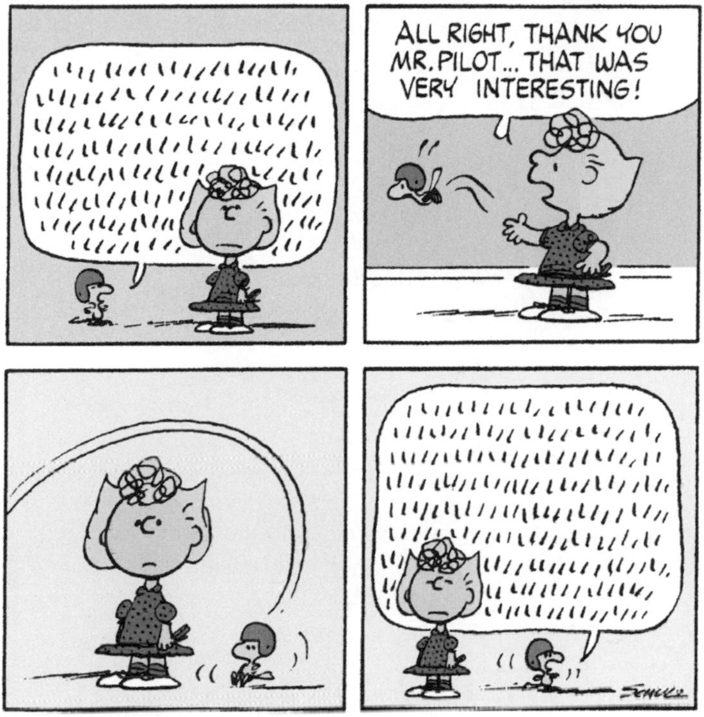
ALL RIGHT, THANK YOU MR. PILOT... THAT WAS VERY INTERESTING!

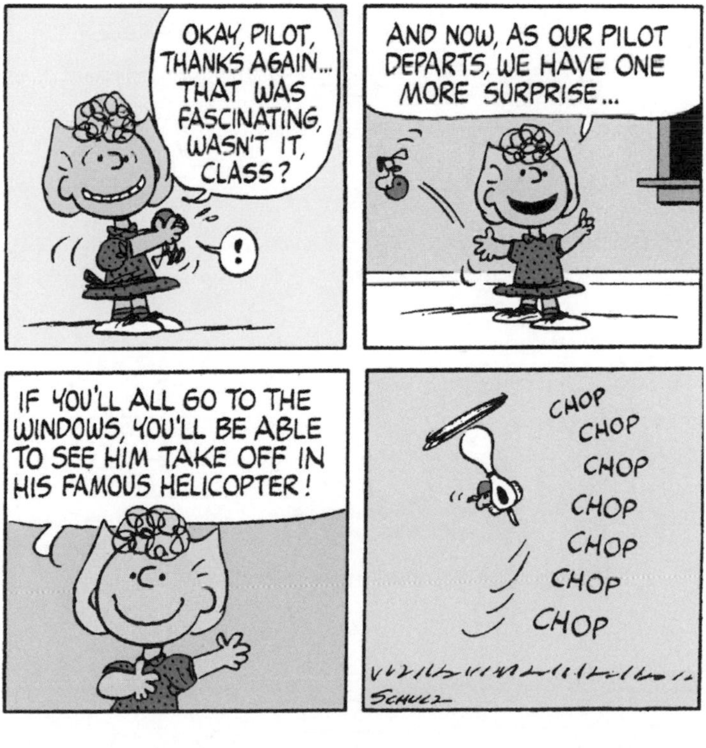
OKAY, PILOT, THANKS AGAIN... THAT WAS FASCINATING, WASN'T IT, CLASS?
!
AND NOW, AS OUR PILOT DEPARTS, WE HAVE ONE MORE SURPRISE...
IF YOU'LL ALL GO TO THE WINDOWS, YOU'LL BE ABLE TO SEE HIM TAKE OFF IN HIS FAMOUS HELICOPTER!
CHOP
CHOP
CHOP
CHOP
CHOP
CHOP
CHOP

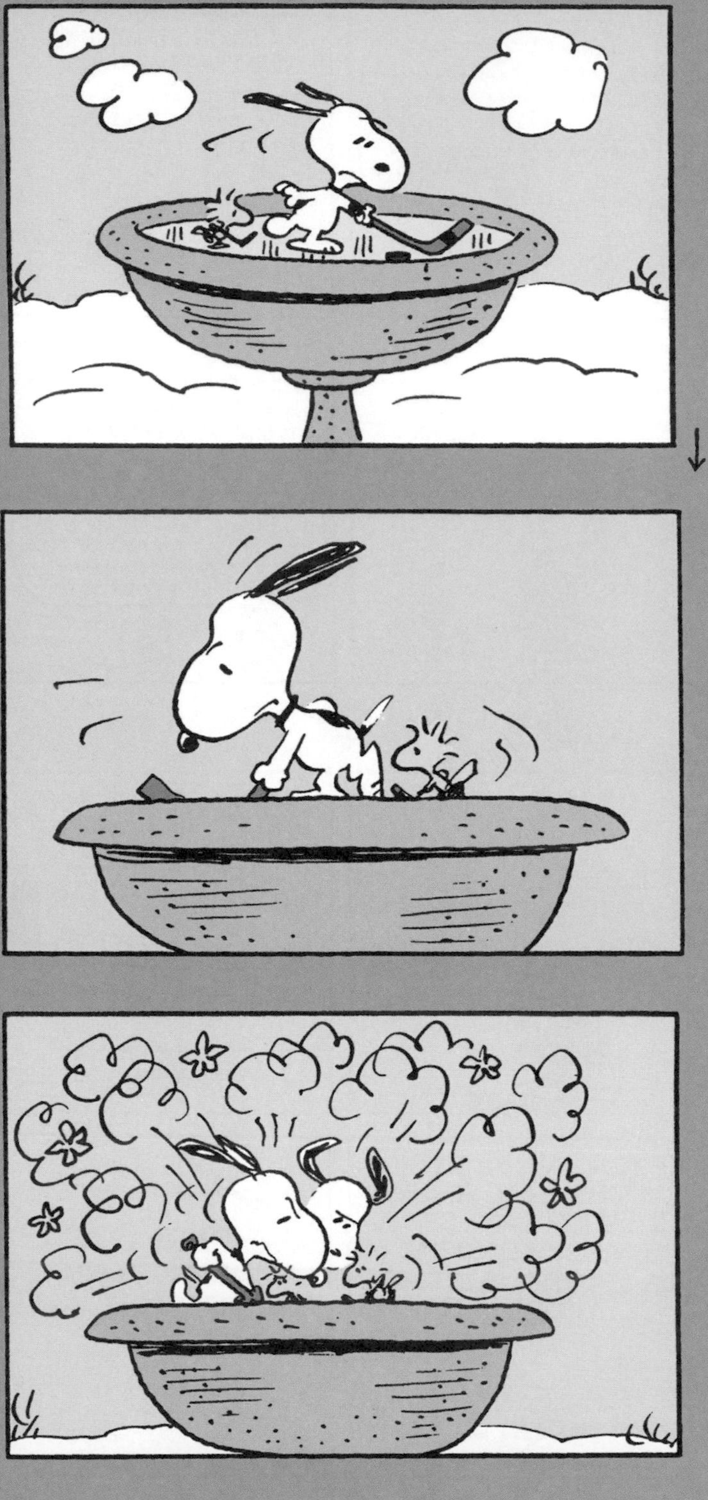

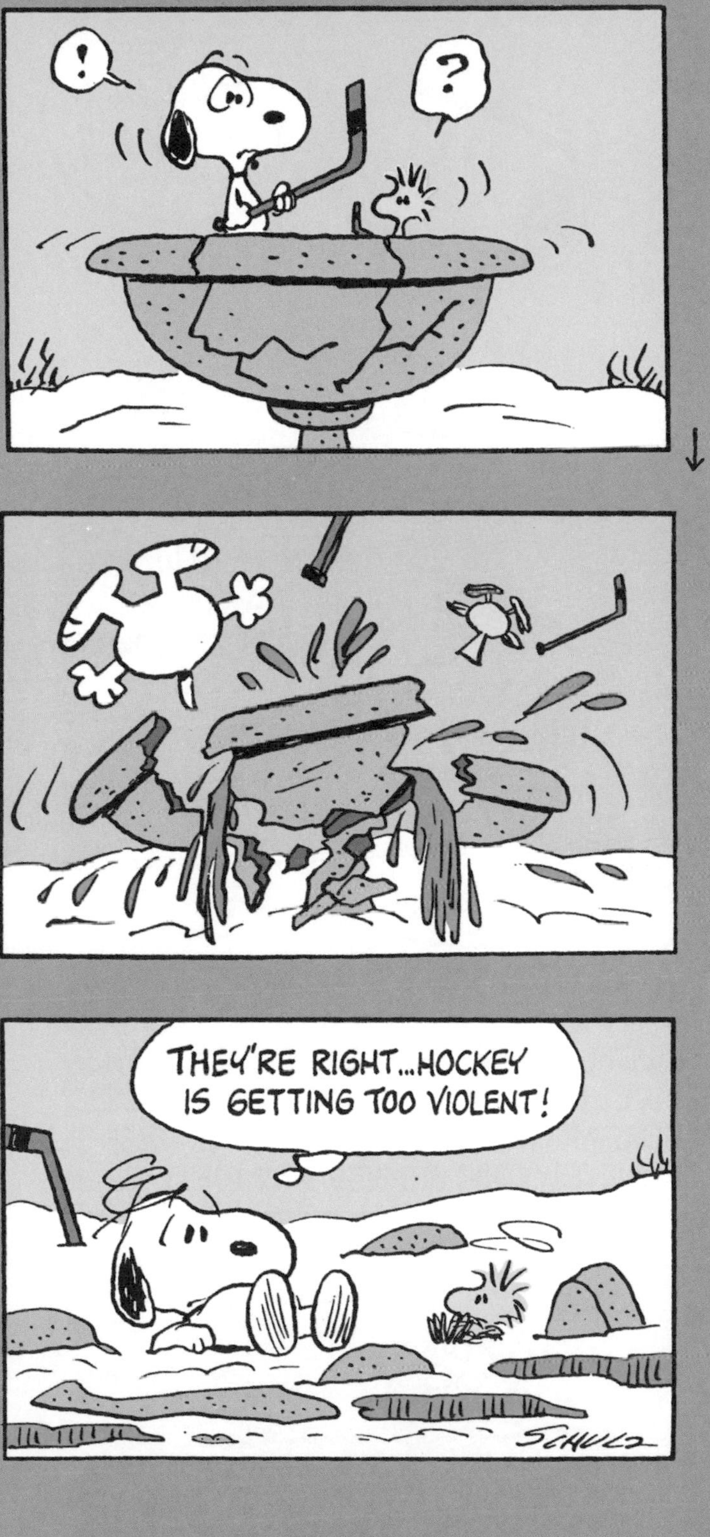
!
?
THEY'RE RIGHT...HOCKEY IS GETTING TOO VIOLENT!
SCHULZ

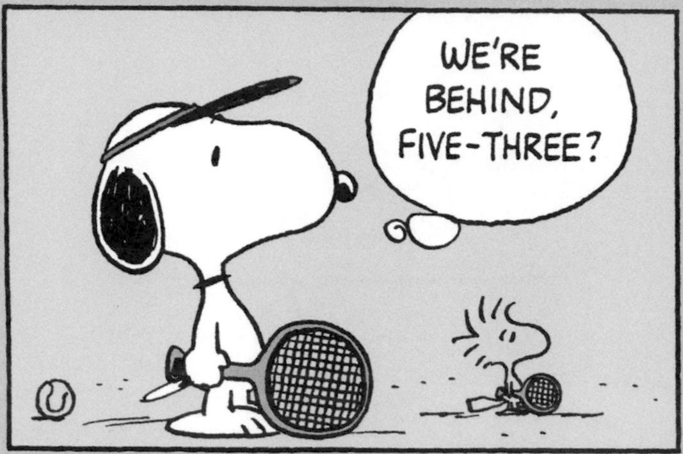
WE'RE BEHIND, FIVE-THREE?

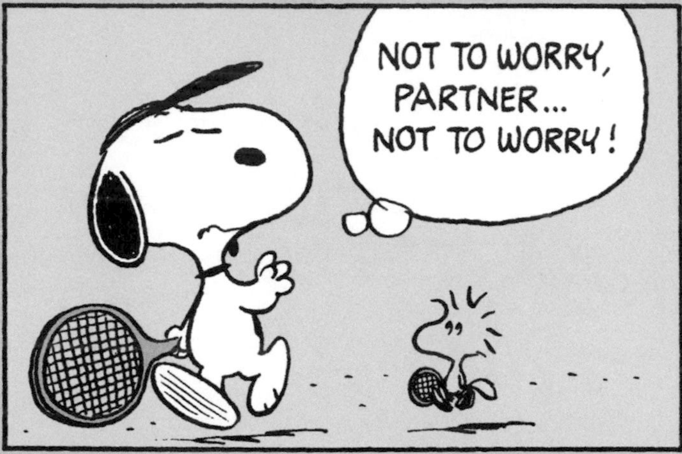
NOT TO WORRY, PARTNER... NOT TO WORRY!

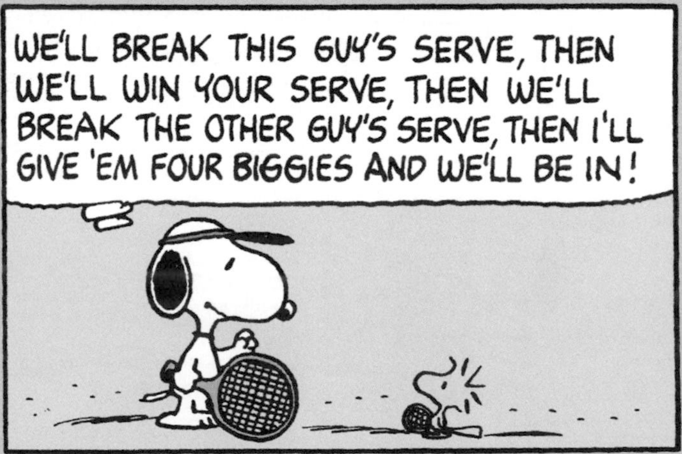
WE'LL BREAK THIS GUY'S SERVE, THEN WE'LL WIN YOUR SERVE, THEN WE'LL BREAK THE OTHER GUY'S SERVE, THEN I'LL GIVE 'EM FOUR BIGGIES AND WE'LL BE IN!

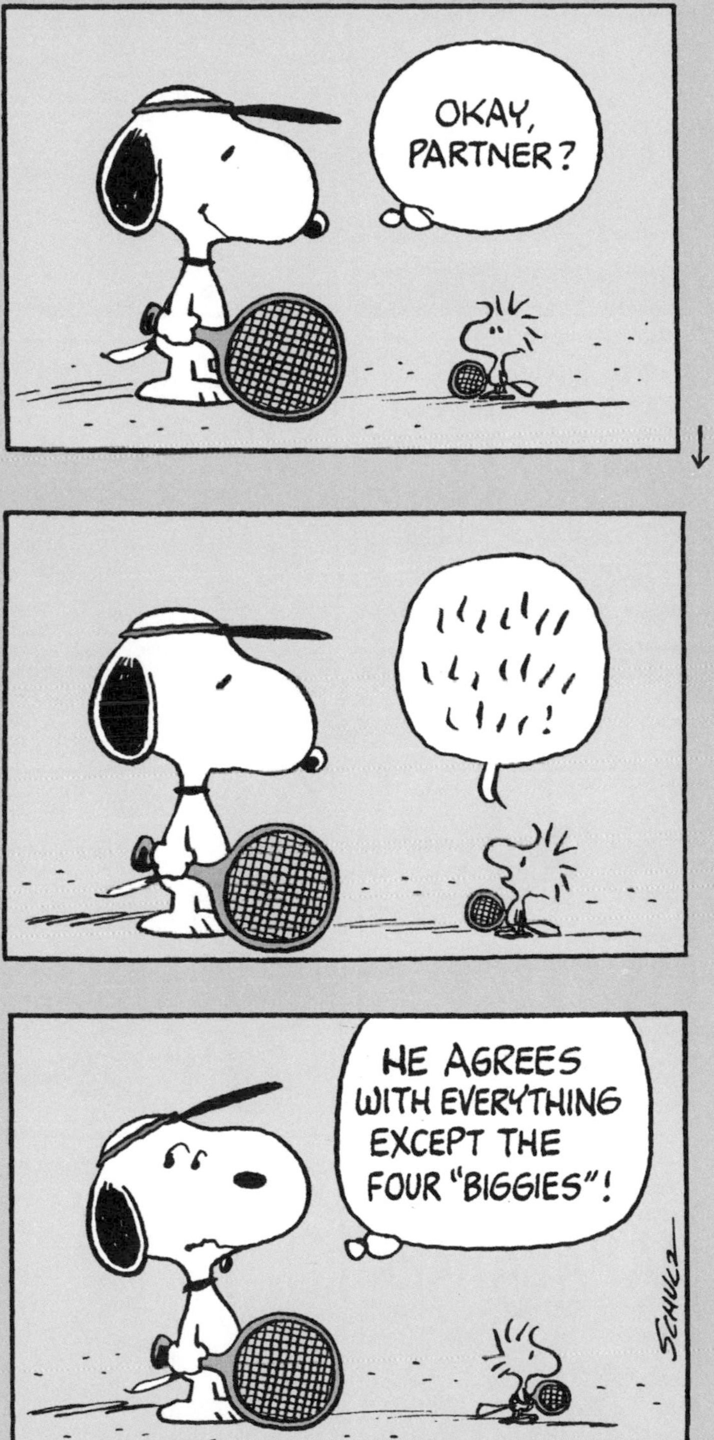
OKAY, PARTNER?
HE AGREES WITH EVERYTHING EXCEPT THE FOUR "BIGGIES"!
SCHULZ

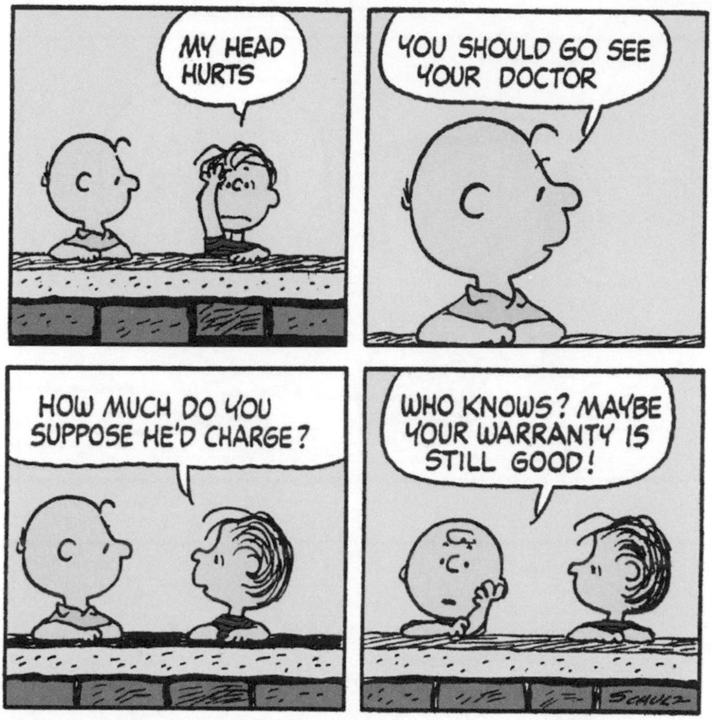
MY HEAD HURTS
YOU SHOULD GO SEE YOUR DOCTOR
HOW MUCH DO YOU SUPPOSE HE'D CHARGE?
WHO KNOWS? MAYBE YOUR WARRANTY IS STILL GOOD!
SCHULZ

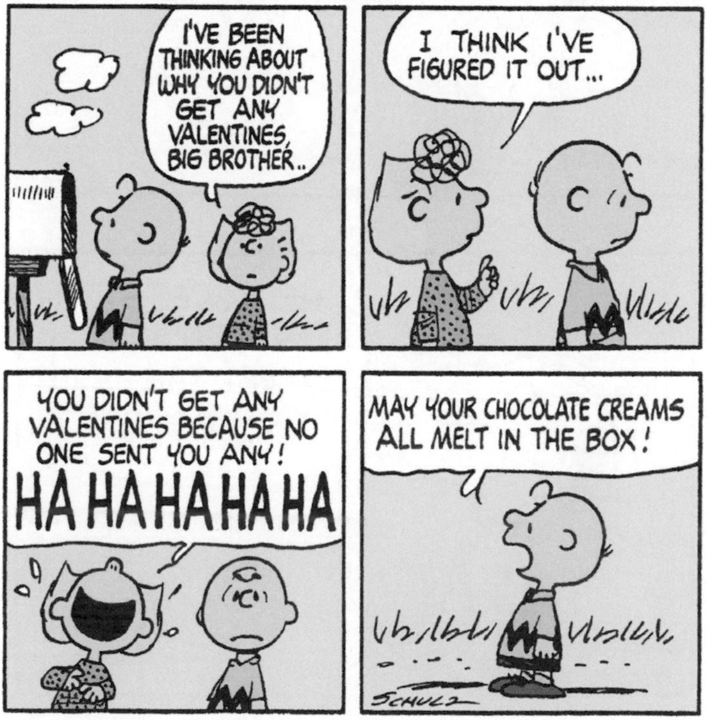
I'VE BEEN THINKING ABOUT WHY YOU DIDN'T GET ANY VALENTINES, BIG BROTHER..
I THINK I'VE FIGURED IT OUT...
YOU DIDN'T GET ANY VALENTINES BECAUSE NO ONE SENT YOU ANY!
HA HA HA HA HA
MAY YOUR CHOCOLATE CREAMS ALL MELT IN THE BOX!
SCHULZ

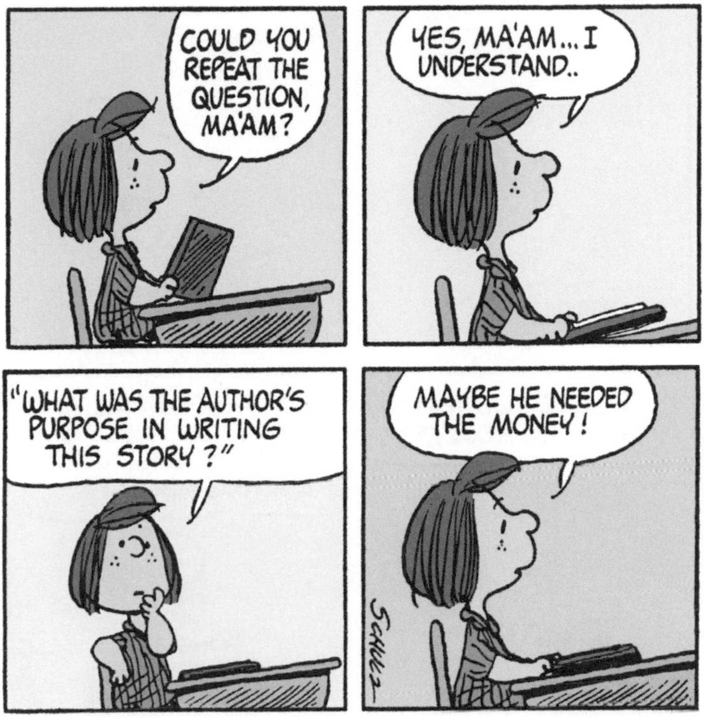
COULD YOU REPEAT THE QUESTION, MA'AM?
YES, MA'AM... I UNDERSTAND..
"WHAT WAS THE AUTHOR'S PURPOSE IN WRITING THIS STORY ?"
MAYBE HE NEEDED THE MONEY !
SCHULZ

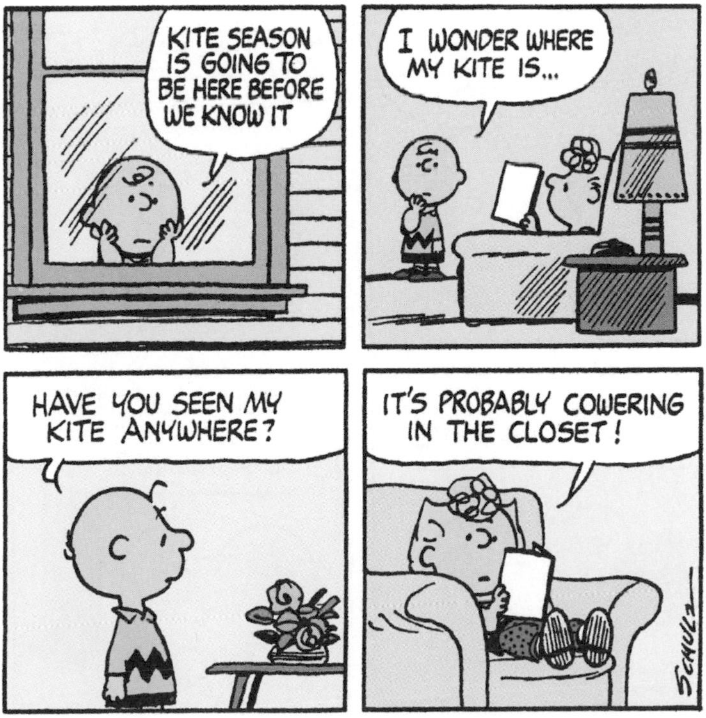
KITE SEASON IS GOING TO BE HERE BEFORE WE KNOW IT
I WONDER WHERE MY KITE IS...
HAVE YOU SEEN MY KITE ANYWHERE?
IT'S PROBABLY COWERING IN THE CLOSET !
SCHULZ

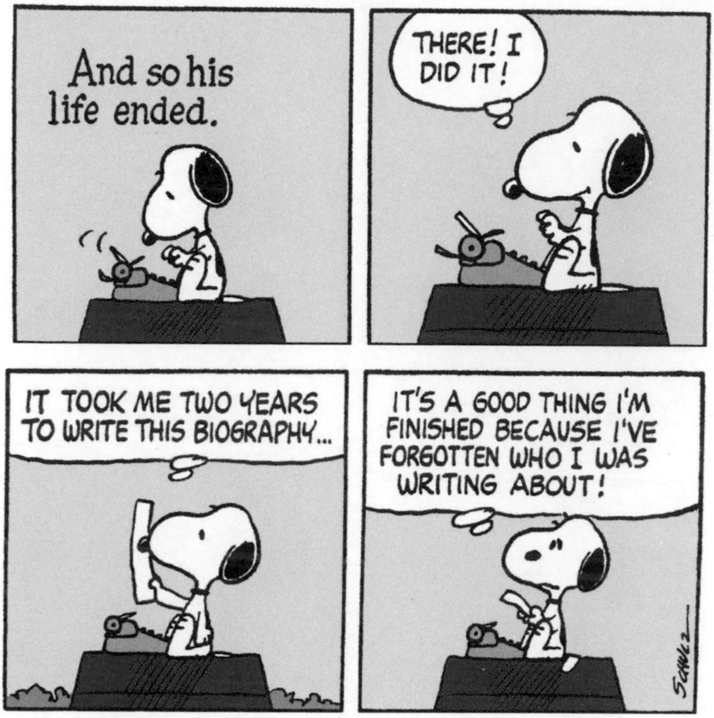
And so his life ended.
THERE! I DID IT!
IT TOOK ME TWO YEARS TO WRITE THIS BIOGRAPHY...
IT'S A GOOD THING I'M FINISHED BECAUSE I'VE FORGOTTEN WHO I WAS WRITING ABOUT!

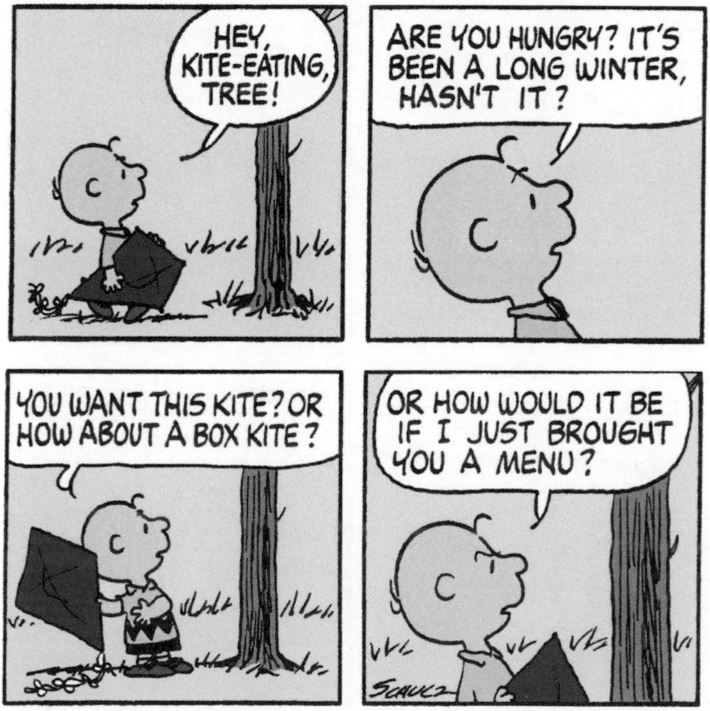
HEY, KITE-EATING, TREE!
ARE YOU HUNGRY? IT'S BEEN A LONG WINTER, HASN'T IT?
YOU WANT THIS KITE? OR HOW ABOUT A BOX KITE?
OR HOW WOULD IT BE IF I JUST BROUGHT YOU A MENU?

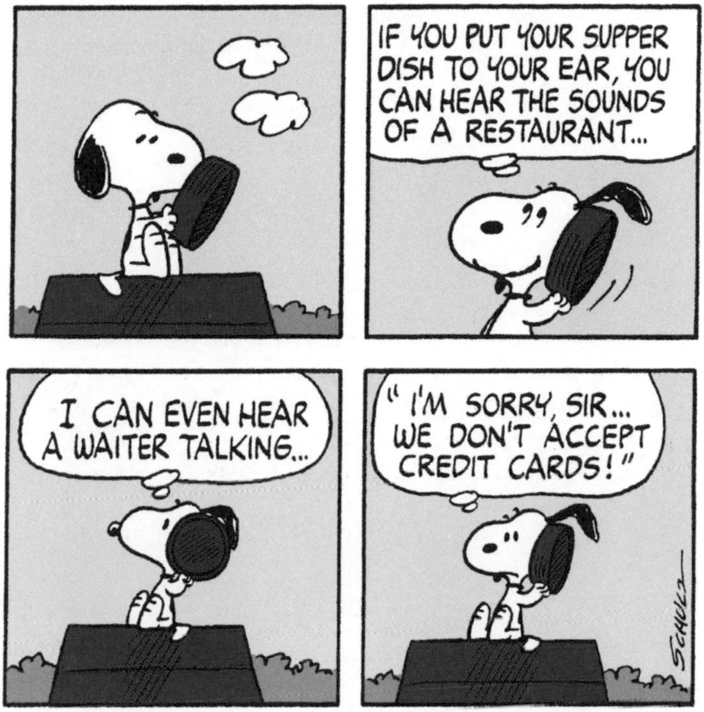
IF YOU PUT YOUR SUPPER DISH TO YOUR EAR, YOU CAN HEAR THE SOUNDS OF A RESTAURANT...
I CAN EVEN HEAR A WAITER TALKING...
"I'M SORRY, SIR... WE DON'T ACCEPT CREDIT CARDS!"
SCHULZ

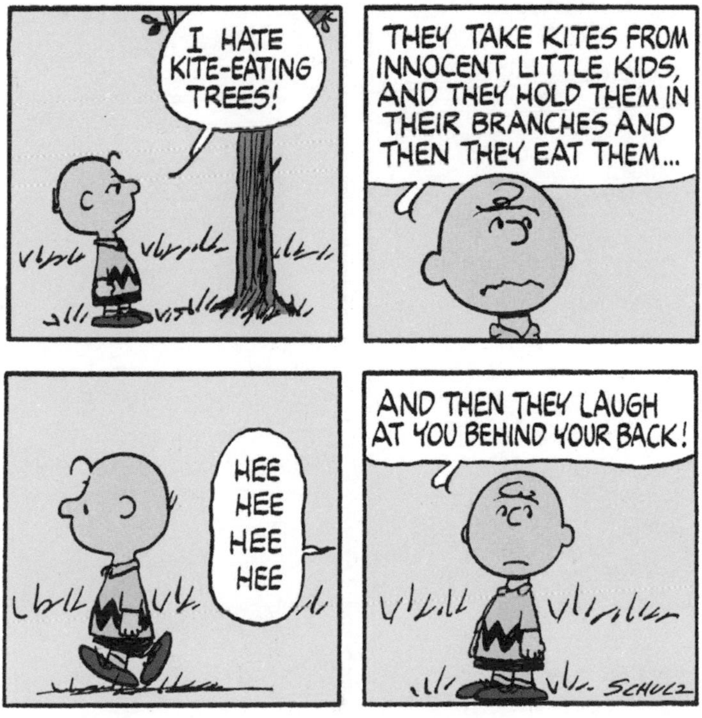
I HATE KITE-EATING TREES!
THEY TAKE KITES FROM INNOCENT LITTLE KIDS, AND THEY HOLD THEM IN THEIR BRANCHES AND THEN THEY EAT THEM...
HEE HEE HEE HEE
AND THEN THEY LAUGH AT YOU BEHIND YOUR BACK!
SCHULZ

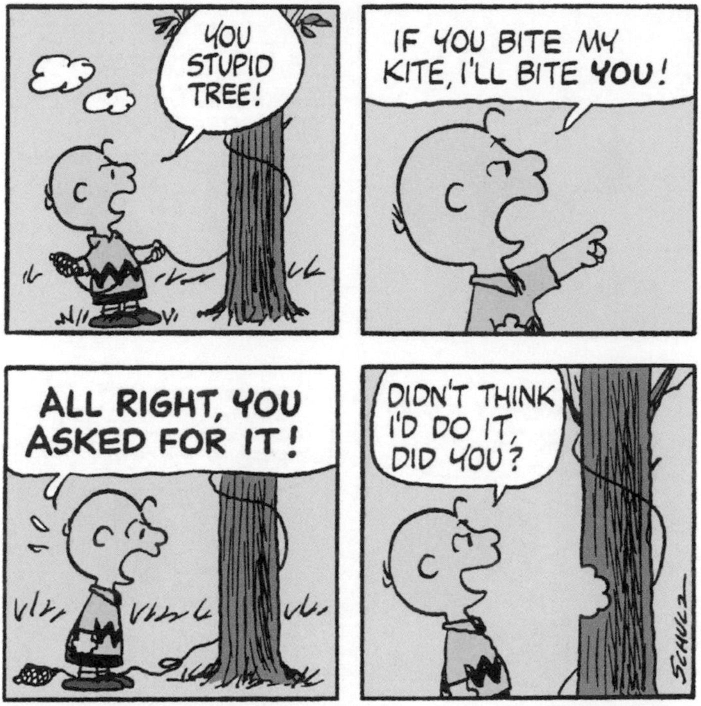
YOU STUPID TREE!
IF YOU BITE MY KITE, I'LL BITE **YOU**!
ALL RIGHT, YOU ASKED FOR IT!
DIDN'T THINK I'D DO IT, DID YOU?
SCHULZ

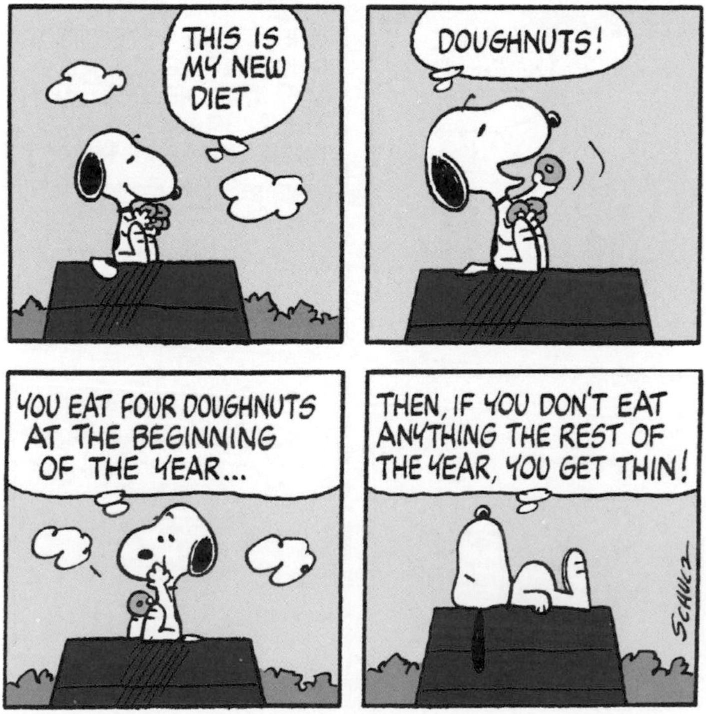
THIS IS MY NEW DIET
DOUGHNUTS!
YOU EAT FOUR DOUGHNUTS AT THE BEGINNING OF THE YEAR...
THEN, IF YOU DON'T EAT ANYTHING THE REST OF THE YEAR, YOU GET THIN!
SCHULZ

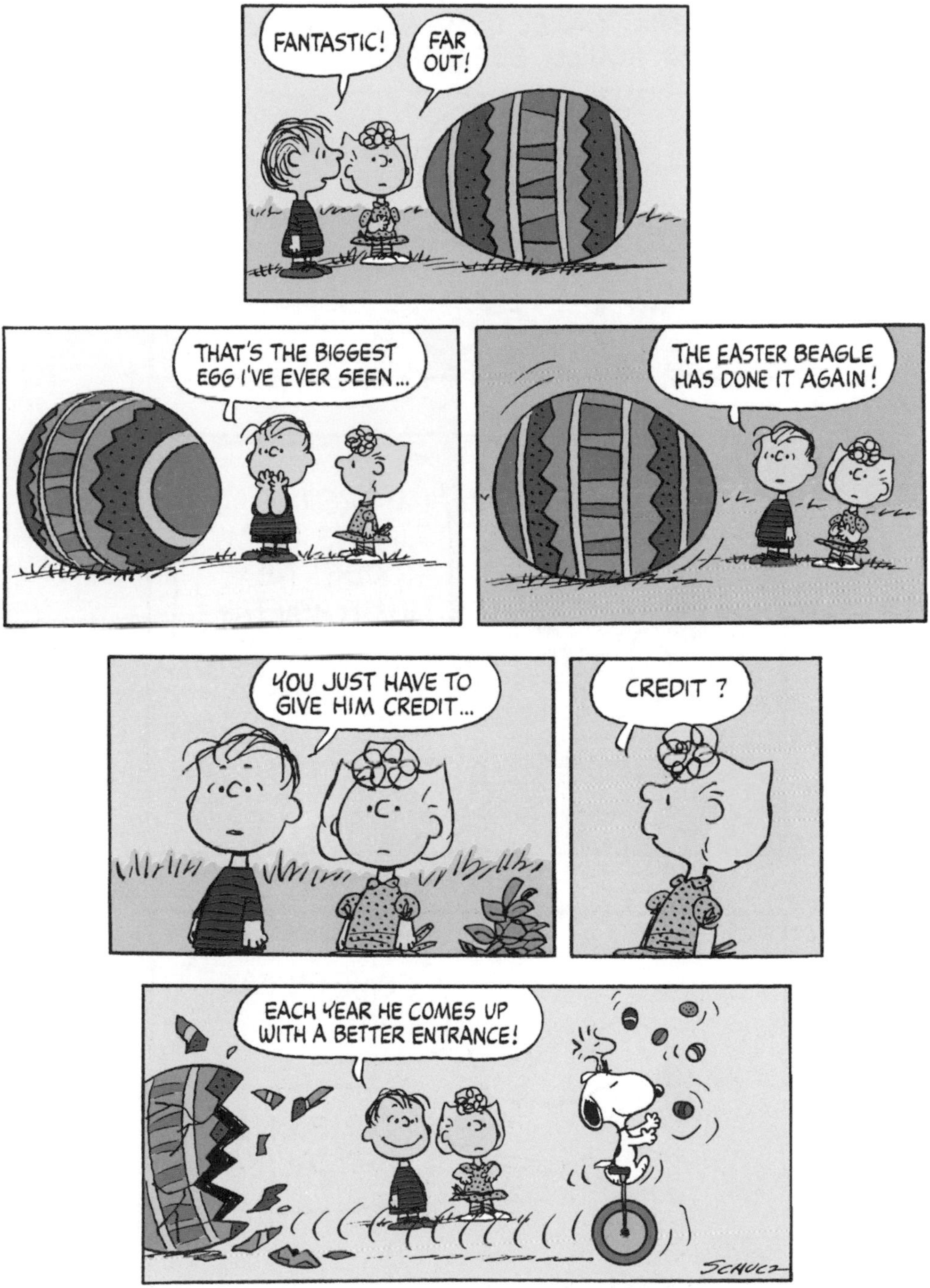
FANTASTIC!
FAR OUT!
THAT'S THE BIGGEST EGG I'VE EVER SEEN...
THE EASTER BEAGLE HAS DONE IT AGAIN!
YOU JUST HAVE TO GIVE HIM CREDIT...
CREDIT ?
EACH YEAR HE COMES UP WITH A BETTER ENTRANCE!
SCHULZ

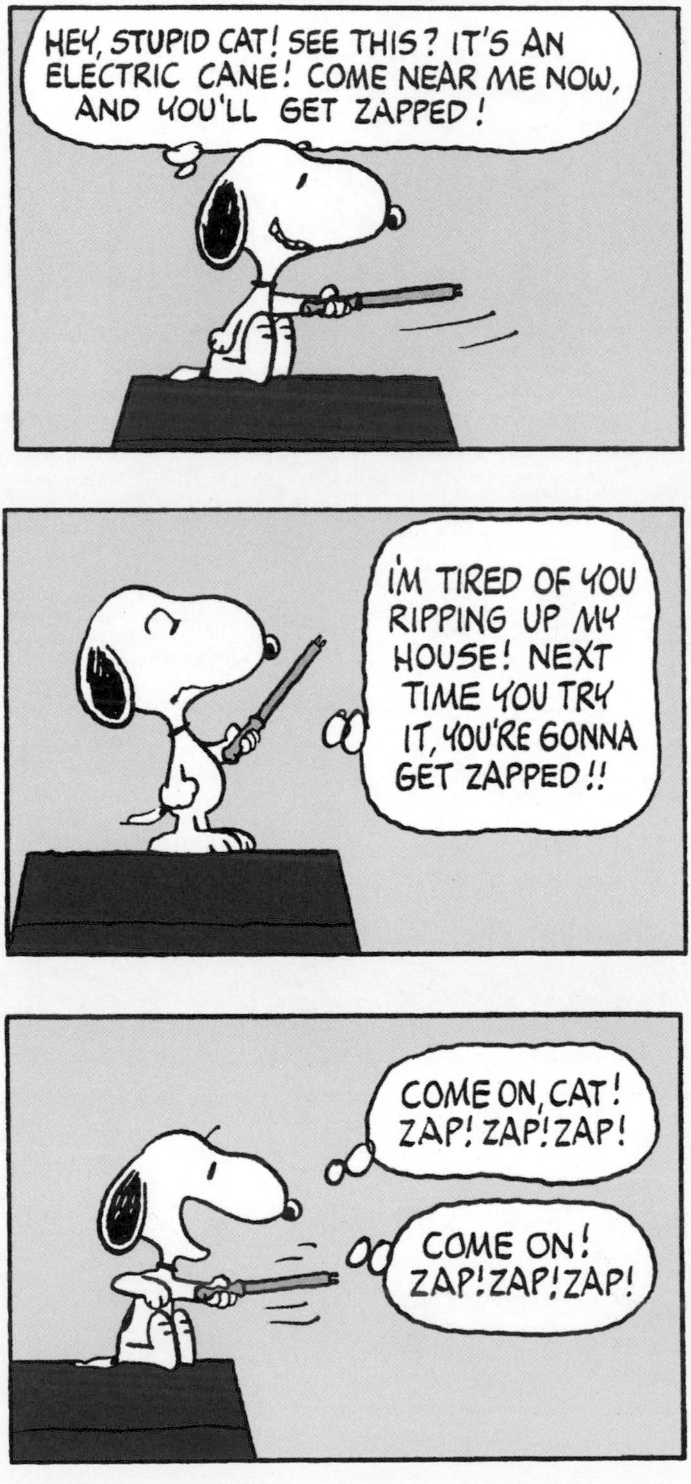
HEY, STUPID CAT! SEE THIS? IT'S AN ELECTRIC CANE! COME NEAR ME NOW, AND YOU'LL GET ZAPPED!
I'M TIRED OF YOU RIPPING UP MY HOUSE! NEXT TIME YOU TRY IT, YOU'RE GONNA GET ZAPPED!!
COME ON, CAT! ZAP! ZAP! ZAP!
COME ON! ZAP! ZAP! ZAP!

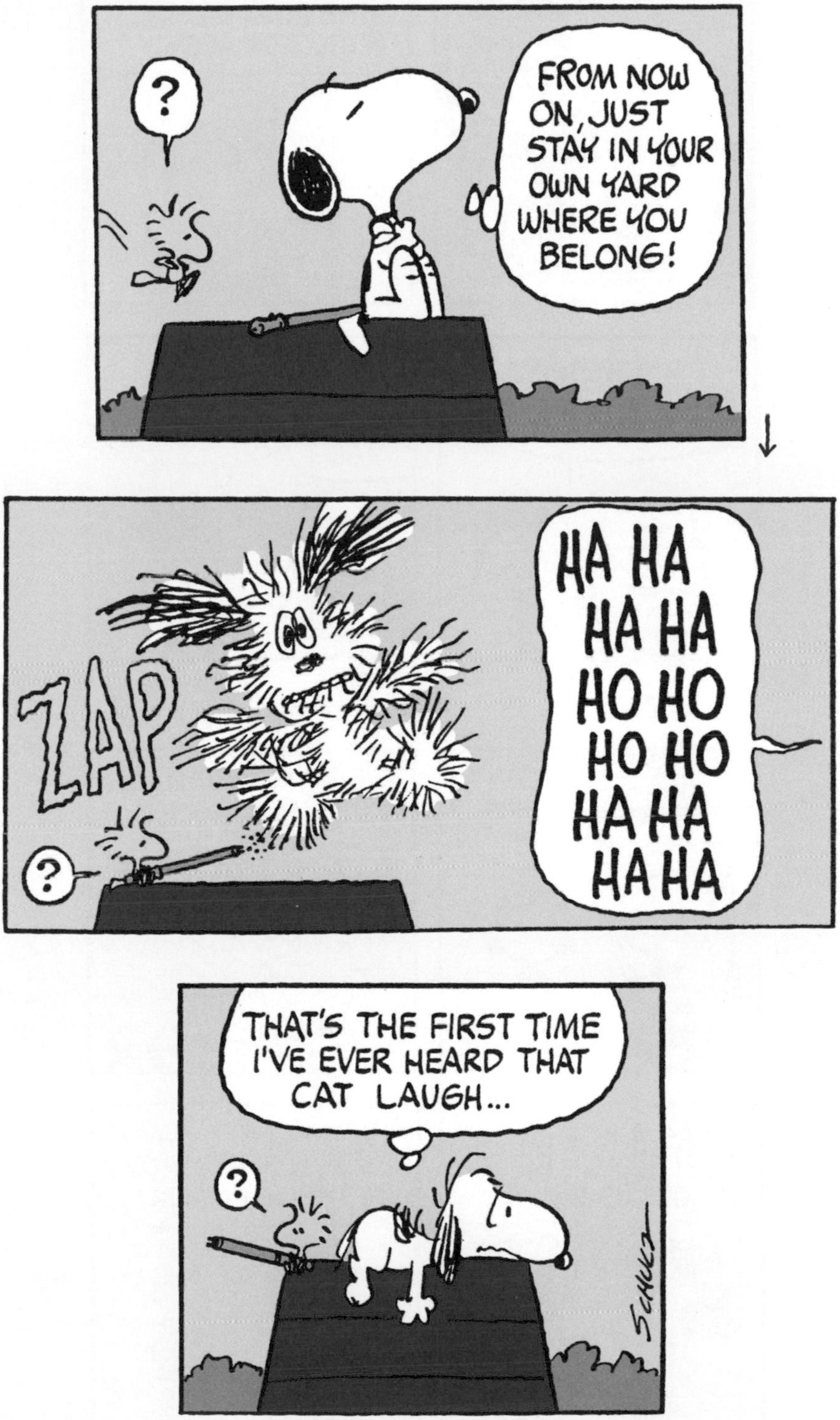
?
FROM NOW ON, JUST STAY IN YOUR OWN YARD WHERE YOU BELONG!
ZAP
?
HA HA HA HA HO HO HO HO HA HA HA HA
THAT'S THE FIRST TIME I'VE EVER HEARD THAT CAT LAUGH...
?
SCHULZ

HERE, BIG BROTHER.. YOU GOT A LETTER
"THE ENVIRONMENTAL PROTECTION AGENCY"
IT'S SOMETHING ABOUT YOU BITING A TREE...
DO YOU ALWAYS READ MY MAIL?
DO YOU ALWAYS BITE TREES?
SCHULZ

I CAN'T BELIEVE IT!
THE ENVIRONMENTAL PROTECTION AGENCY IS AFTER ME JUST BECAUSE I BIT A TREE!
IT WAS A KITE-EATING TREE! I ONLY BIT IT TO GET EVEN...
FIFTY-CENTS SAYS THEY'LL THROW YOU IN THE SLAMMER!
SCHULZ

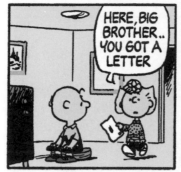

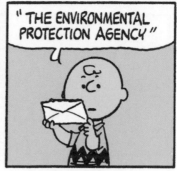

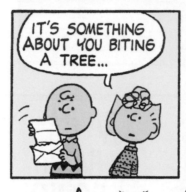

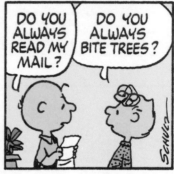

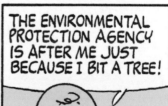

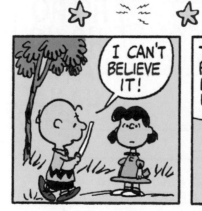

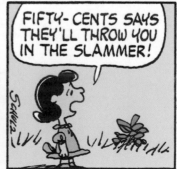

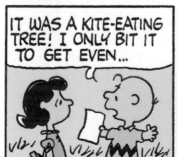

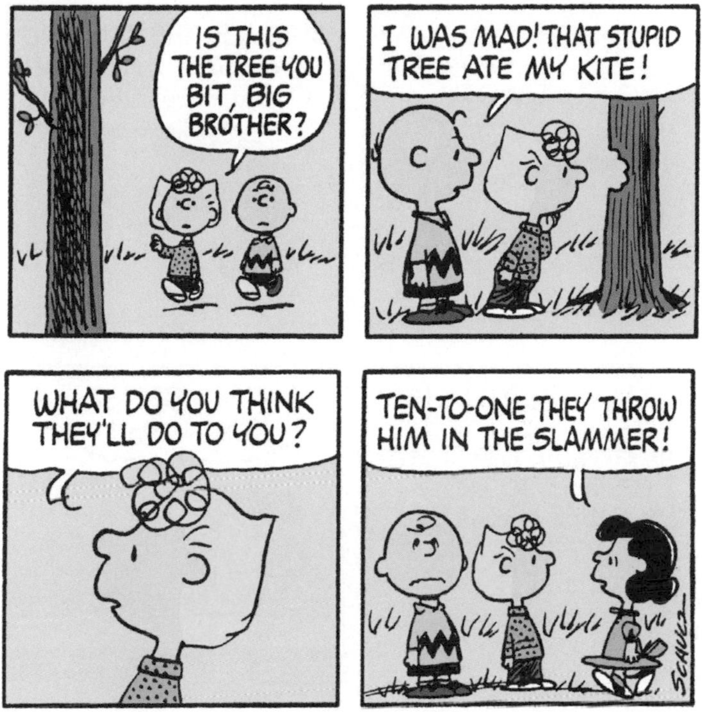
IS THIS THE TREE YOU BIT, BIG BROTHER?
I WAS MAD! THAT STUPID TREE ATE MY KITE!
WHAT DO YOU THINK THEY'LL DO TO YOU?
TEN-TO-ONE THEY THROW HIM IN THE SLAMMER!
SCHULZ

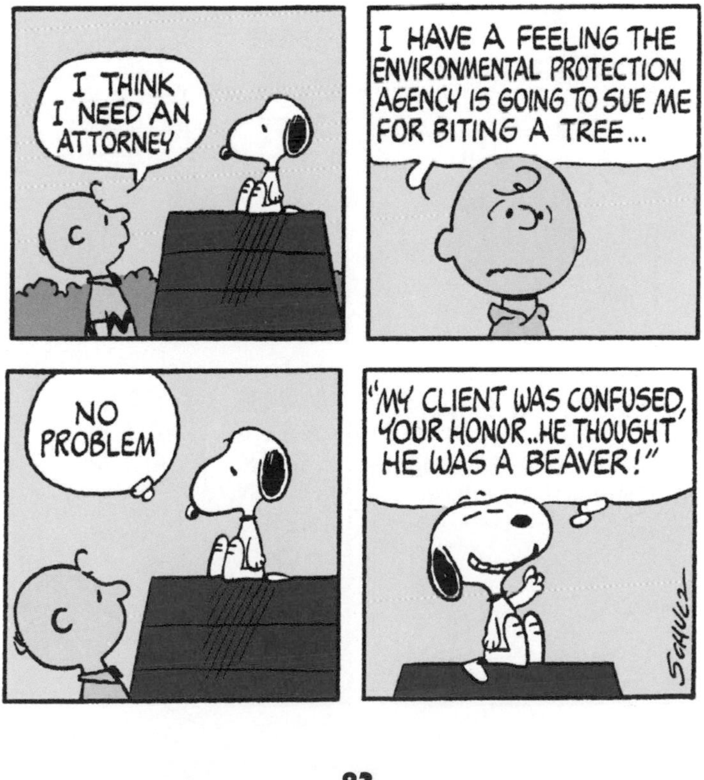
I THINK I NEED AN ATTORNEY
I HAVE A FEELING THE ENVIRONMENTAL PROTECTION AGENCY IS GOING TO SUE ME FOR BITING A TREE...
NO PROBLEM
"MY CLIENT WAS CONFUSED, YOUR HONOR..HE THOUGHT HE WAS A BEAVER!"
SCHULZ

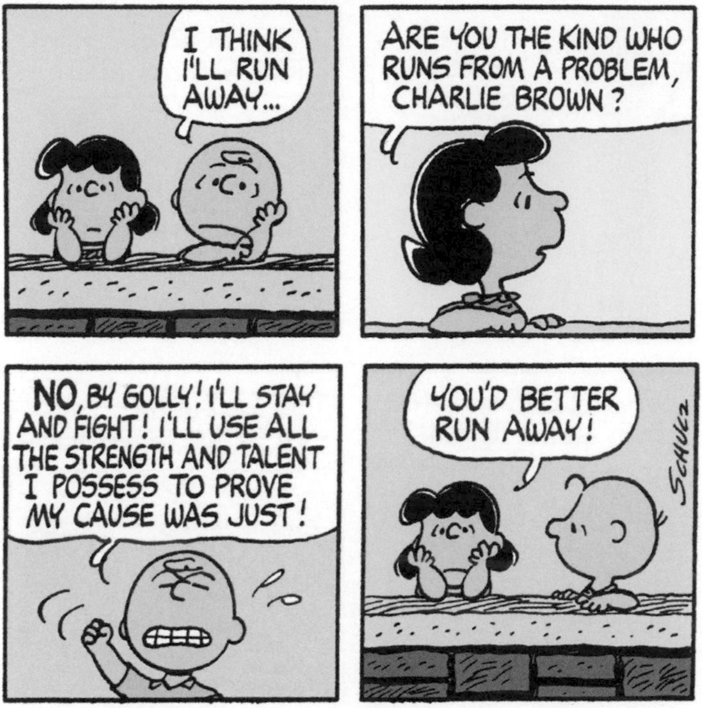
I THINK I'LL RUN AWAY...
ARE YOU THE KIND WHO RUNS FROM A PROBLEM, CHARLIE BROWN ?
NO, BY GOLLY! I'LL STAY AND FIGHT! I'LL USE ALL THE STRENGTH AND TALENT I POSSESS TO PROVE MY CAUSE WAS JUST!
YOU'D BETTER RUN AWAY!
SCHULZ

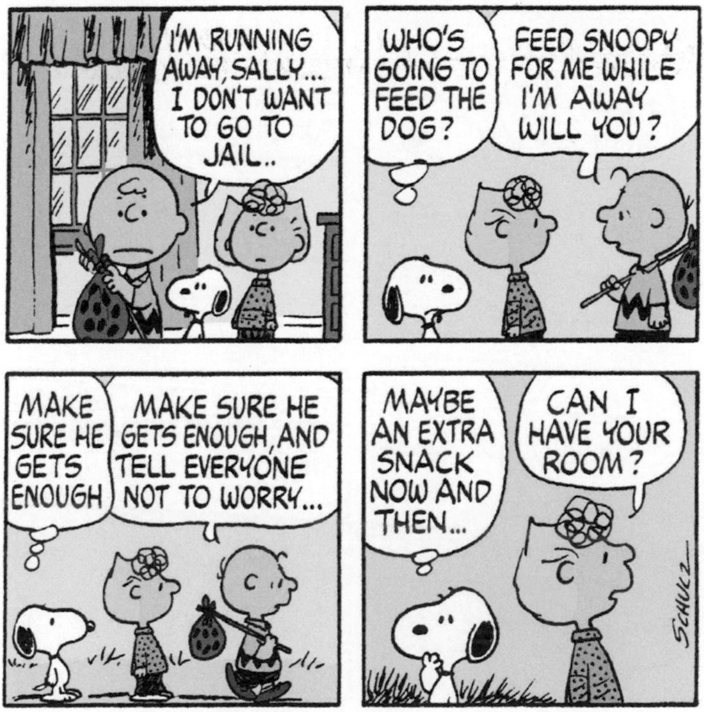
I'M RUNNING AWAY, SALLY... I DON'T WANT TO GO TO JAIL..
WHO'S GOING TO FEED THE DOG?
FEED SNOOPY FOR ME WHILE I'M AWAY WILL YOU ?
MAKE SURE HE GETS ENOUGH
MAKE SURE HE GETS ENOUGH, AND TELL EVERYONE NOT TO WORRY...
MAYBE AN EXTRA SNACK NOW AND THEN...
CAN I HAVE YOUR ROOM ?
SCHULZ

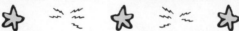

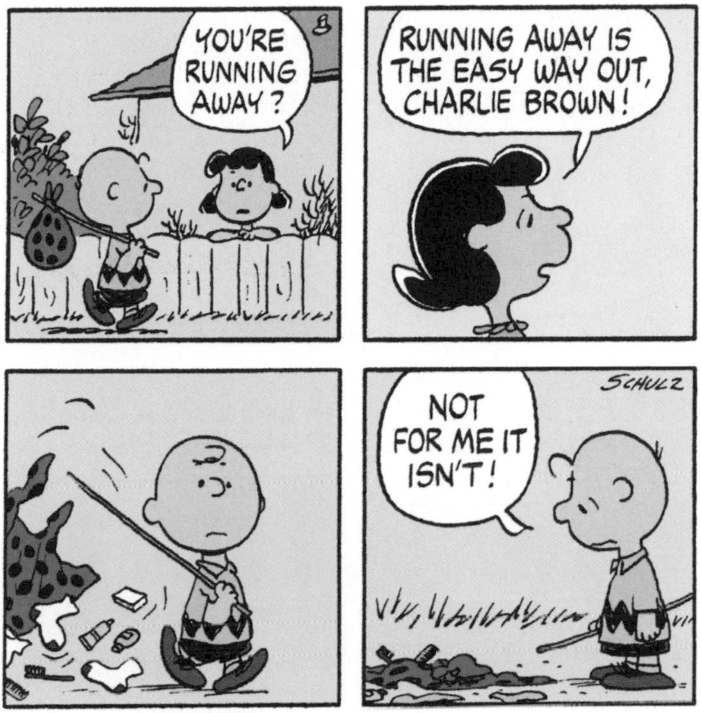
YOU'RE RUNNING AWAY?
RUNNING AWAY IS THE EASY WAY OUT, CHARLIE BROWN!
SCHULZ
NOT FOR ME IT ISN'T!

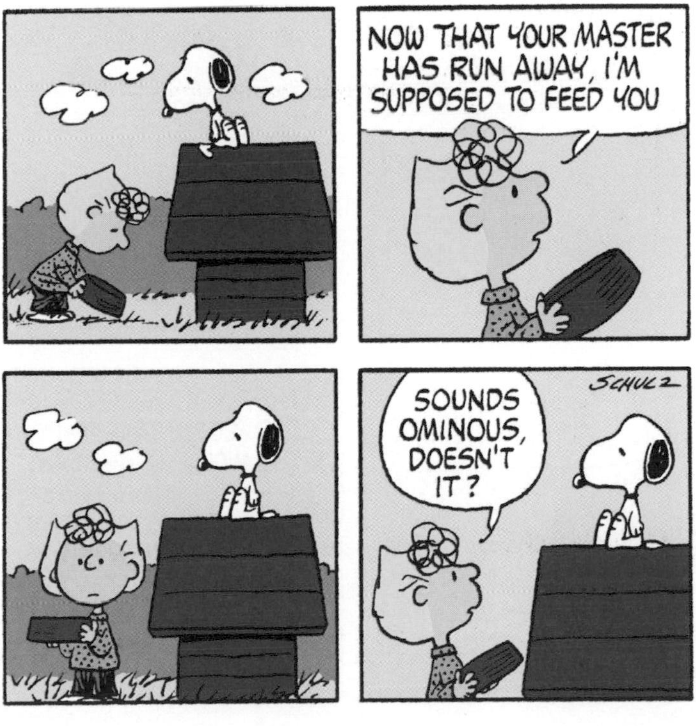
NOW THAT YOUR MASTER HAS RUN AWAY, I'M SUPPOSED TO FEED YOU
SCHULZ
SOUNDS OMINOUS, DOESN'T IT?

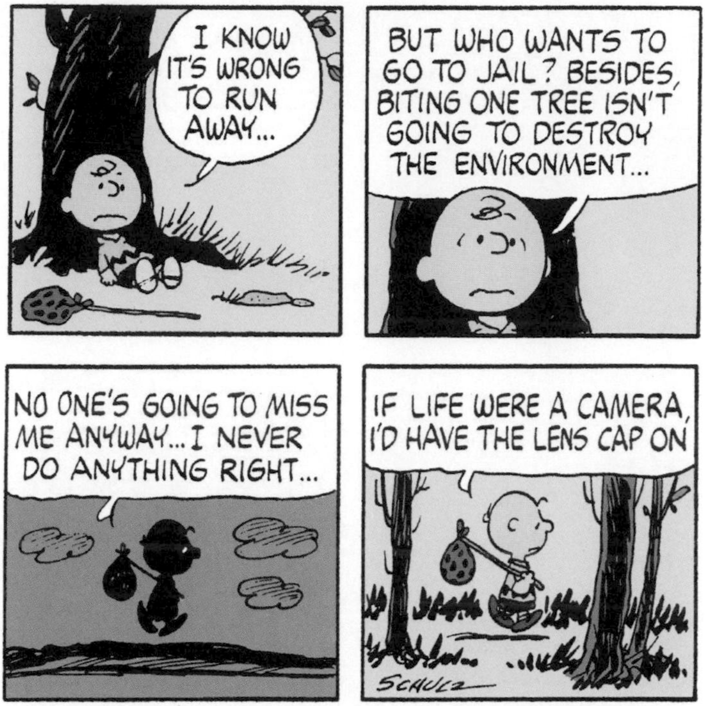
I KNOW IT'S WRONG TO RUN AWAY...
BUT WHO WANTS TO GO TO JAIL? BESIDES, BITING ONE TREE ISN'T GOING TO DESTROY THE ENVIRONMENT...
NO ONE'S GOING TO MISS ME ANYWAY... I NEVER DO ANYTHING RIGHT...
IF LIFE WERE A CAMERA, I'D HAVE THE LENS CAP ON
SCHULZ

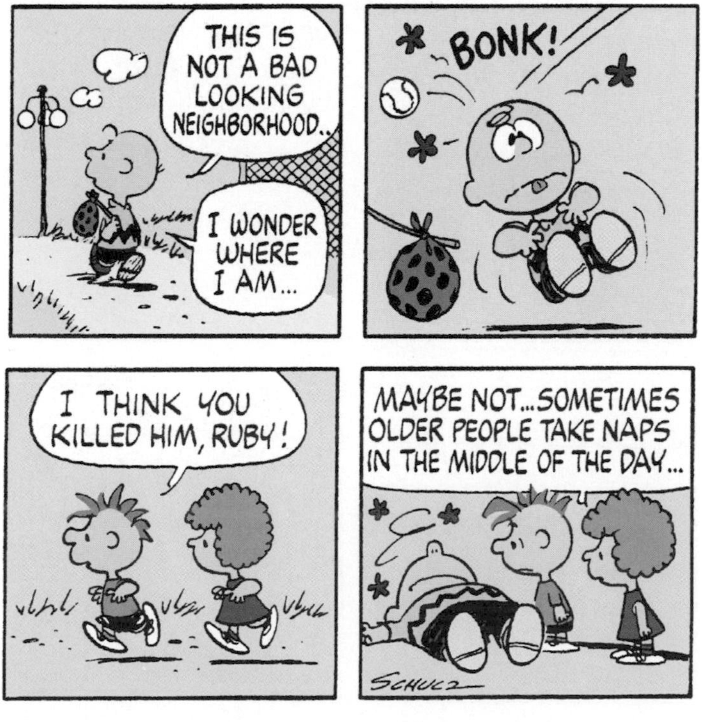
THIS IS NOT A BAD LOOKING NEIGHBORHOOD...
I WONDER WHERE I AM...
BONK!
I THINK YOU KILLED HIM, RUBY!
MAYBE NOT... SOMETIMES OLDER PEOPLE TAKE NAPS IN THE MIDDLE OF THE DAY...
SCHULZ

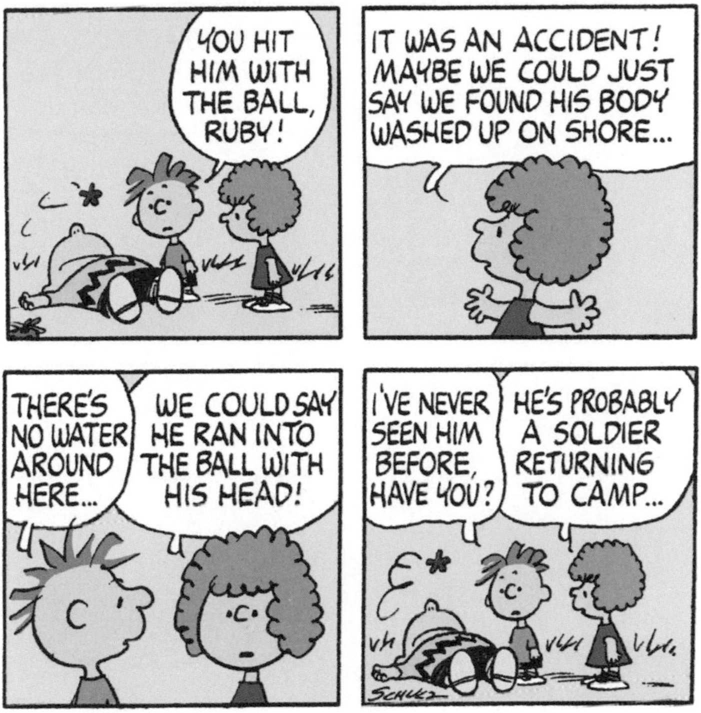
YOU HIT HIM WITH THE BALL, RUBY!
IT WAS AN ACCIDENT! MAYBE WE COULD JUST SAY WE FOUND HIS BODY WASHED UP ON SHORE...
THERE'S NO WATER AROUND HERE...
WE COULD SAY HE RAN INTO THE BALL WITH HIS HEAD!
I'VE NEVER SEEN HIM BEFORE, HAVE YOU?
HE'S PROBABLY A SOLDIER RETURNING TO CAMP...
SCHULZ

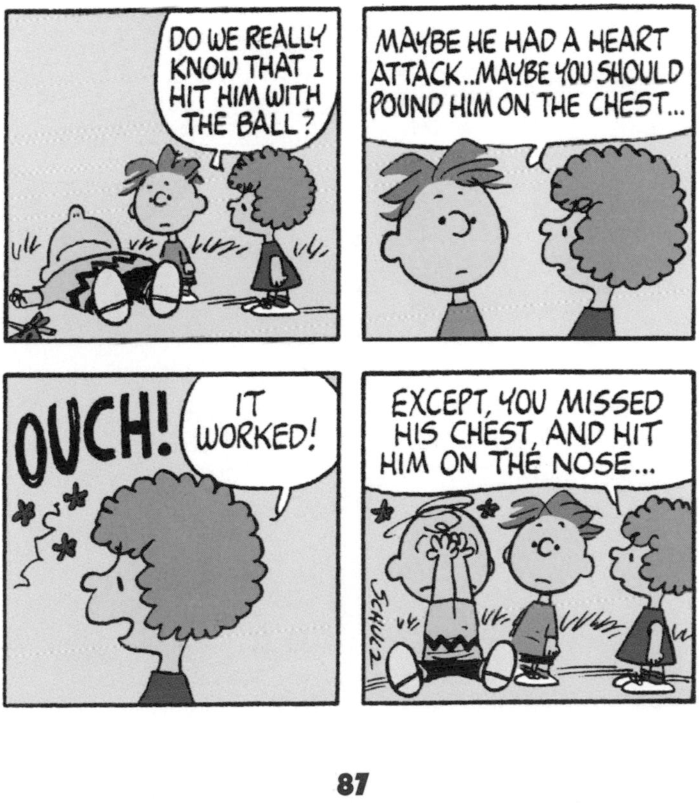
DO WE REALLY KNOW THAT I HIT HIM WITH THE BALL?
MAYBE HE HAD A HEART ATTACK..MAYBE YOU SHOULD POUND HIM ON THE CHEST...
OUCH!
IT WORKED!
EXCEPT, YOU MISSED HIS CHEST, AND HIT HIM ON THE NOSE...
SCHULZ

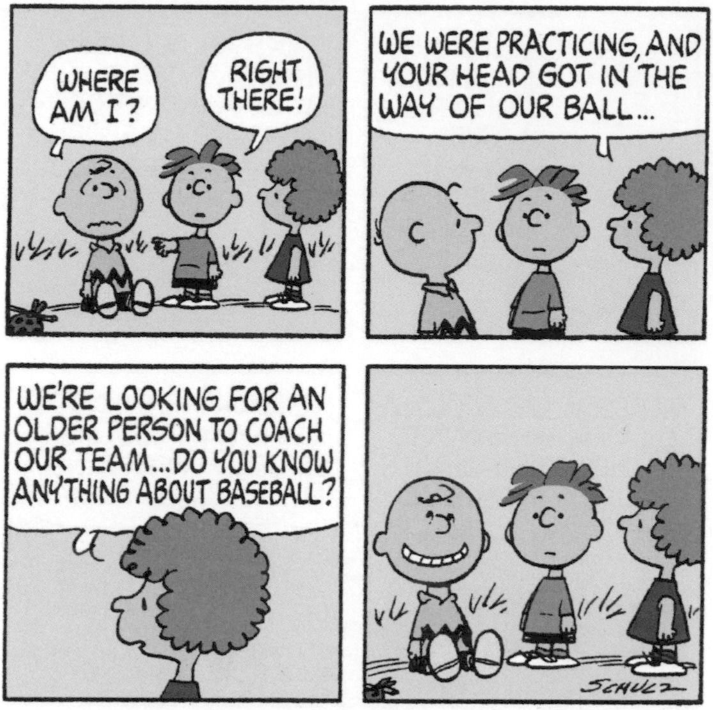
WHERE AM I?
RIGHT THERE!
WE WERE PRACTICING, AND YOUR HEAD GOT IN THE WAY OF OUR BALL...
WE'RE LOOKING FOR AN OLDER PERSON TO COACH OUR TEAM...DO YOU KNOW ANYTHING ABOUT BASEBALL?
SCHULZ

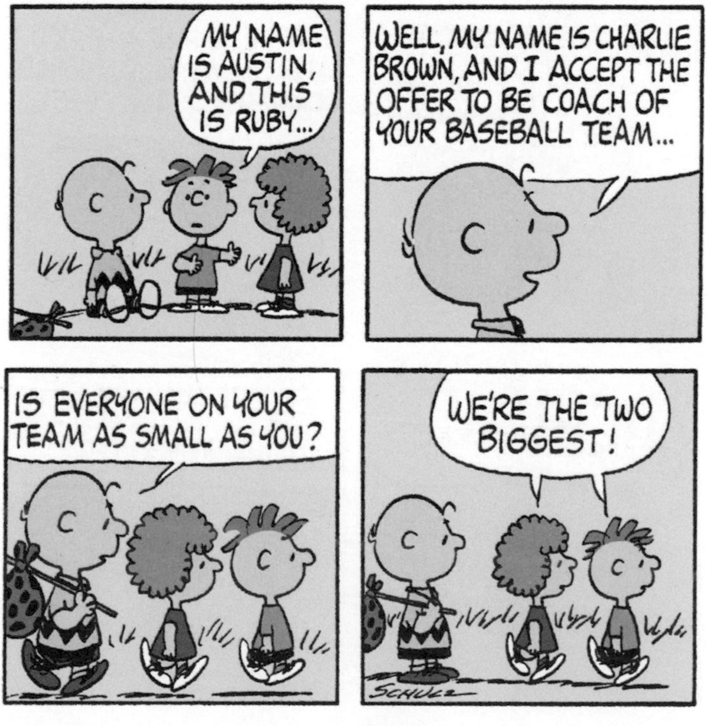
MY NAME IS AUSTIN, AND THIS IS RUBY...
WELL, MY NAME IS CHARLIE BROWN, AND I ACCEPT THE OFFER TO BE COACH OF YOUR BASEBALL TEAM...
IS EVERYONE ON YOUR TEAM AS SMALL AS YOU?
WE'RE THE TWO BIGGEST!
SCHULZ

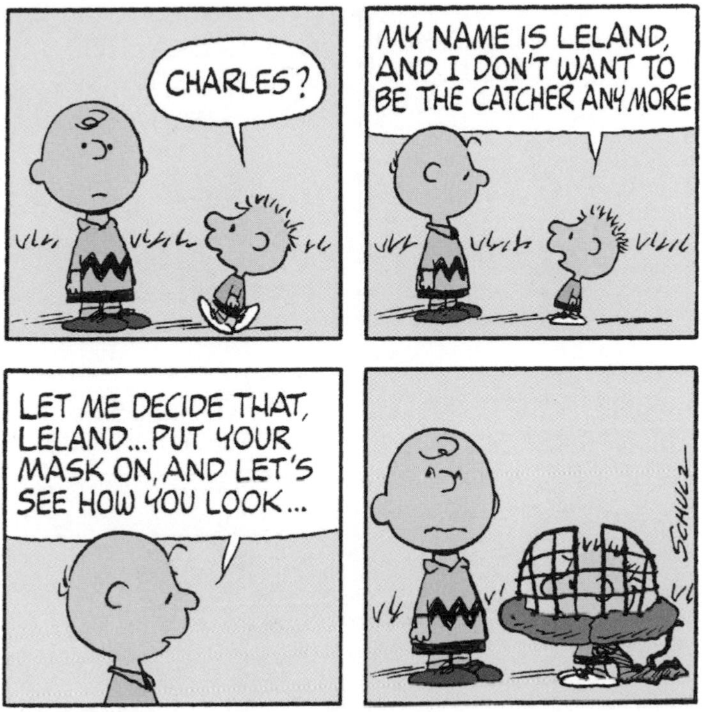
CHARLES ?
MY NAME IS LELAND, AND I DON'T WANT TO BE THE CATCHER ANY MORE
LET ME DECIDE THAT, LELAND... PUT YOUR MASK ON, AND LET'S SEE HOW YOU LOOK...
SCHULZ

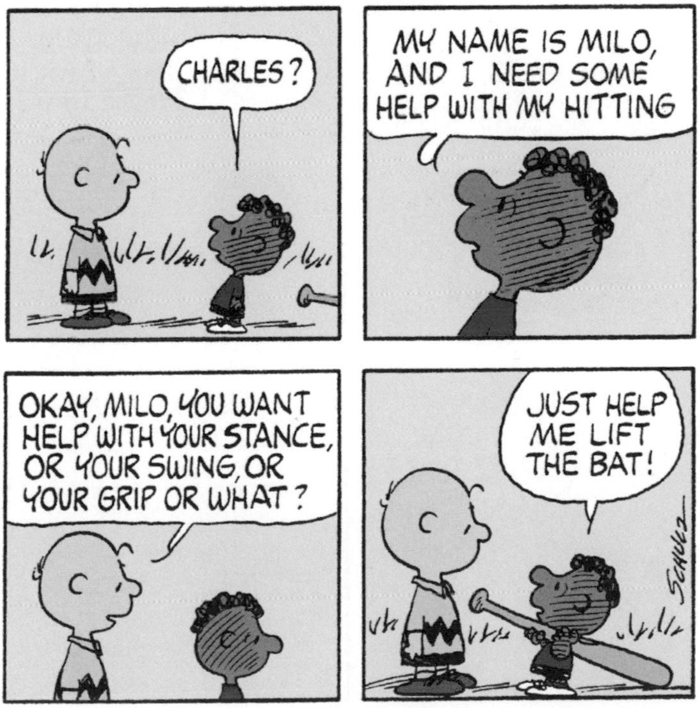
CHARLES ?
MY NAME IS MILO, AND I NEED SOME HELP WITH MY HITTING
OKAY, MILO, YOU WANT HELP WITH YOUR STANCE, OR YOUR SWING, OR YOUR GRIP OR WHAT ?
JUST HELP ME LIFT THE BAT!
SCHULZ

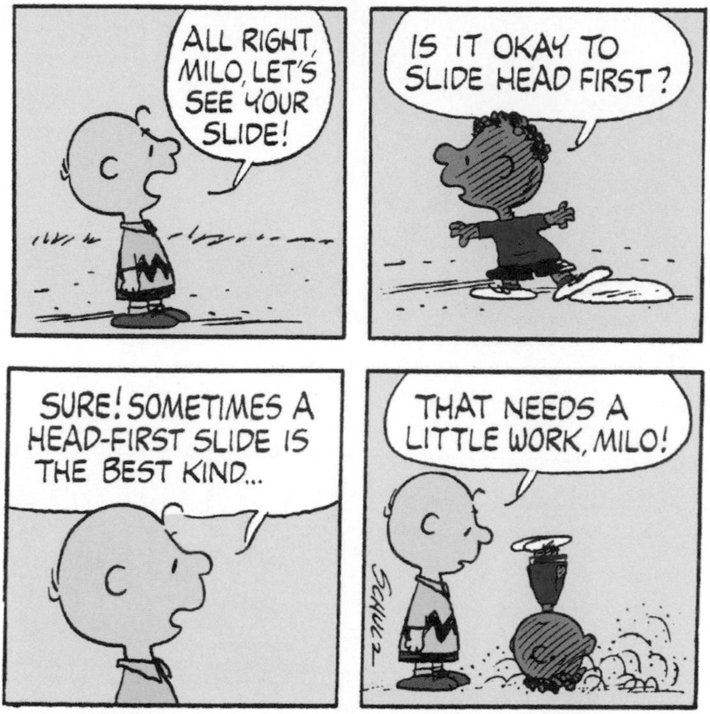
ALL RIGHT, MILO, LET'S SEE YOUR SLIDE!
IS IT OKAY TO SLIDE HEAD FIRST?
SURE! SOMETIMES A HEAD-FIRST SLIDE IS THE BEST KIND...
THAT NEEDS A LITTLE WORK, MILO!
SCHULZ

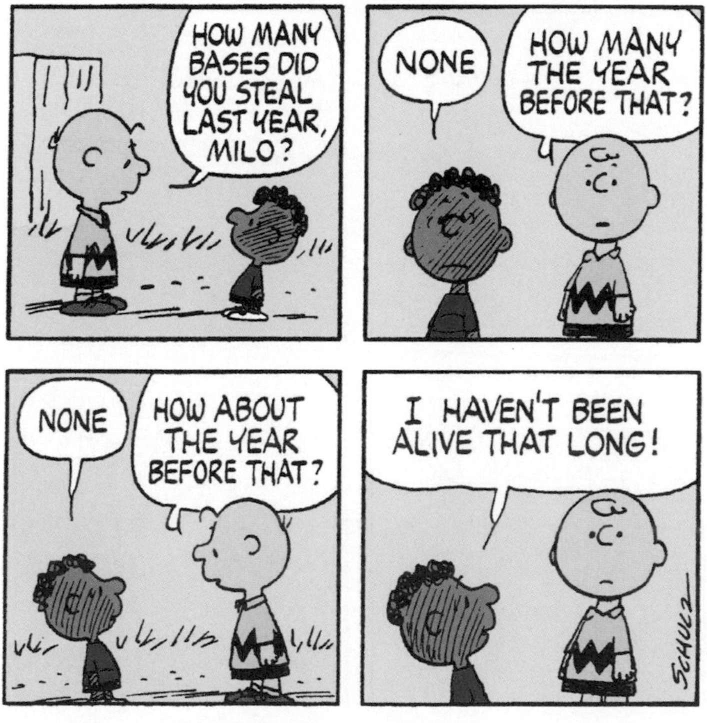
HOW MANY BASES DID YOU STEAL LAST YEAR, MILO?
NONE
HOW MANY THE YEAR BEFORE THAT?
NONE
HOW ABOUT THE YEAR BEFORE THAT?
I HAVEN'T BEEN ALIVE THAT LONG!
SCHULZ

WHERE WILL YOU BE SPENDING THE NIGHT, CHARLES?
OH, I'VE FOUND A LITTLE PLACE...
GOOD... I WAS WORRIED ABOUT YOU
DON'T WORRY, RUBY... IT'S VERY COMFORTABLE
SIGH
SCHULZ

CHARLES?
DO YOU THINK IT WOULD HELP IF I SWUNG THREE BATS BEFORE I GOT UP TO THE PLATE?
IF YOU CAN'T SWING ONE BAT, MILO, HOW ARE YOU GONNA SWING THREE?
GOOD THINKING, CHARLES
THANK YOU, MILO
SCHULZ

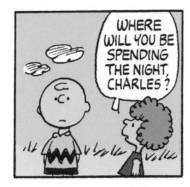

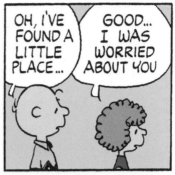

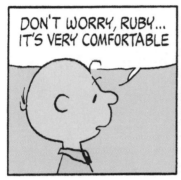

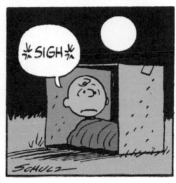

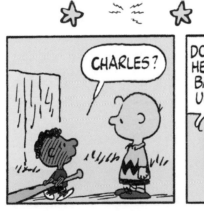

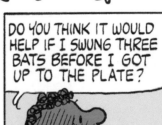

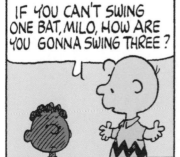

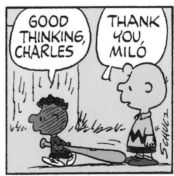

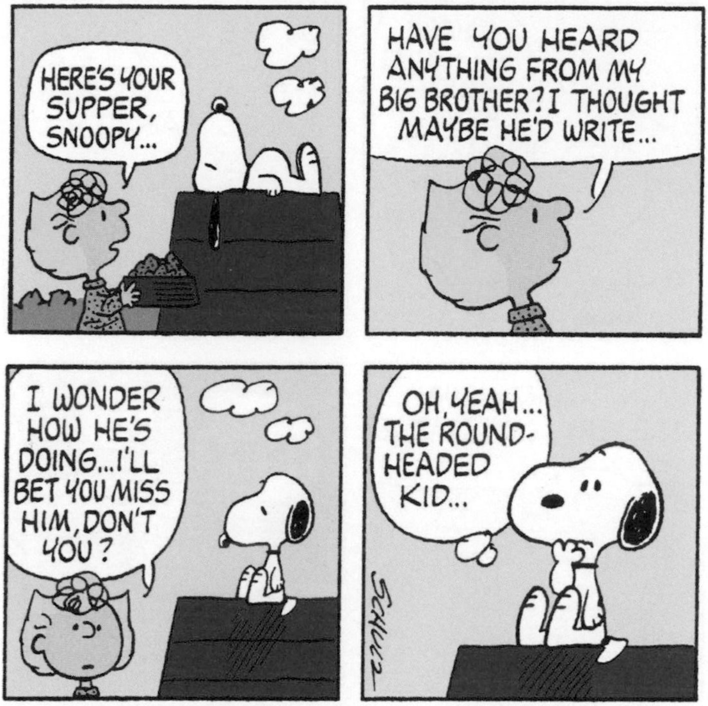
HERE'S YOUR SUPPER, SNOOPY...
HAVE YOU HEARD ANYTHING FROM MY BIG BROTHER? I THOUGHT MAYBE HE'D WRITE...
I WONDER HOW HE'S DOING...I'LL BET YOU MISS HIM, DON'T YOU?
OH, YEAH... THE ROUND-HEADED KID...
SCHULZ

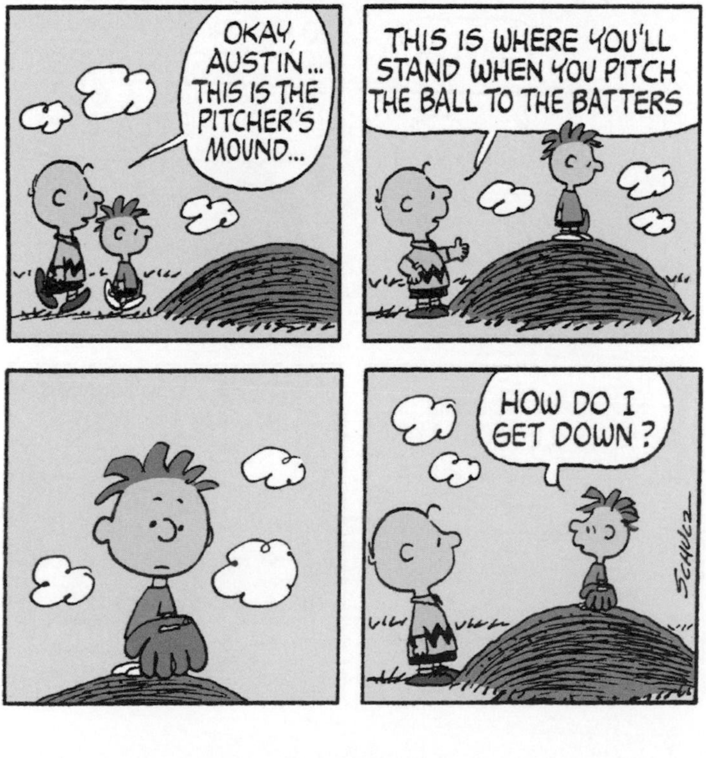
OKAY, AUSTIN... THIS IS THE PITCHER'S MOUND...
THIS IS WHERE YOU'LL STAND WHEN YOU PITCH THE BALL TO THE BATTERS
HOW DO I GET DOWN?
SCHULZ

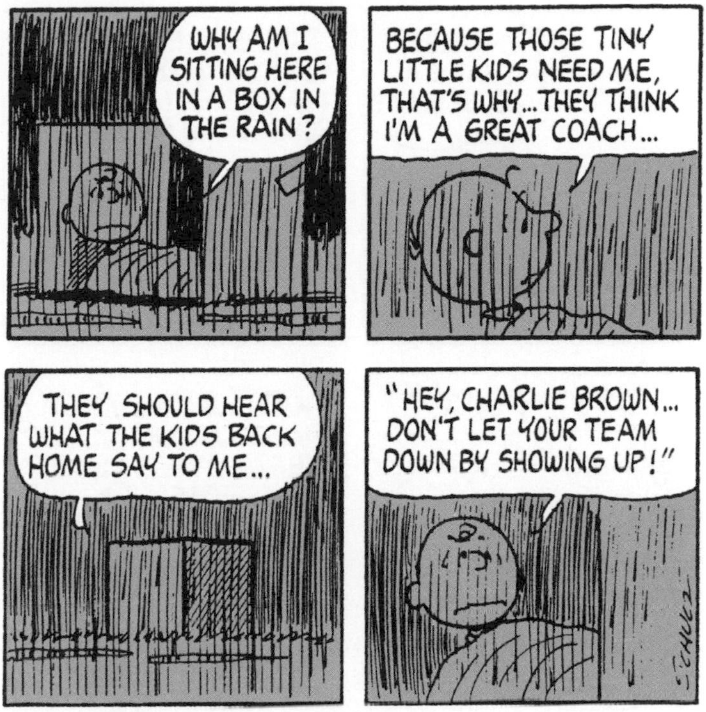
WHY AM I SITTING HERE IN A BOX IN THE RAIN?
BECAUSE THOSE TINY LITTLE KIDS NEED ME, THAT'S WHY...THEY THINK I'M A GREAT COACH...
THEY SHOULD HEAR WHAT THE KIDS BACK HOME SAY TO ME...
"HEY, CHARLIE BROWN... DON'T LET YOUR TEAM DOWN BY SHOWING UP!"
SCHULZ

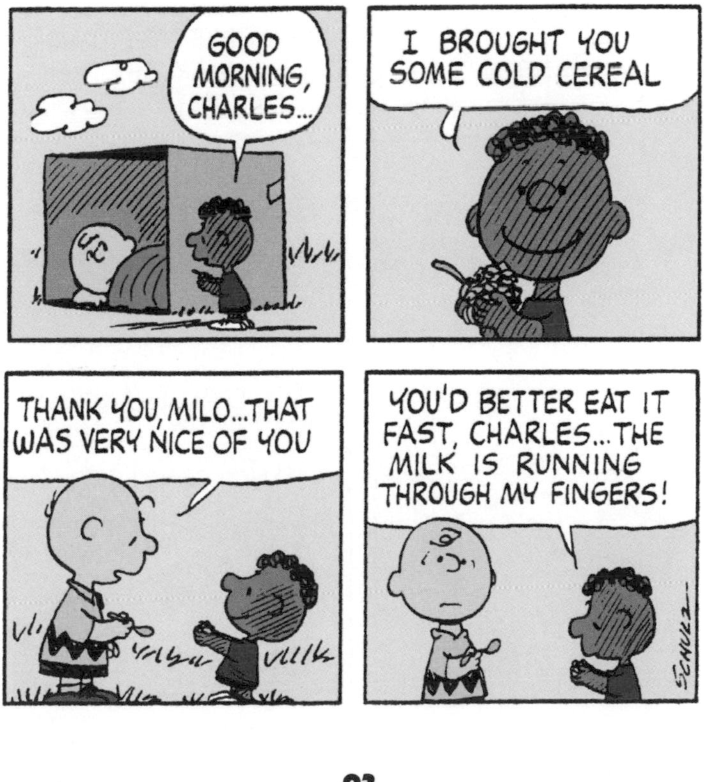
GOOD MORNING, CHARLES...
I BROUGHT YOU SOME COLD CEREAL
THANK YOU, MILO...THAT WAS VERY NICE OF YOU
YOU'D BETTER EAT IT FAST, CHARLES...THE MILK IS RUNNING THROUGH MY FINGERS!
SCHULZ

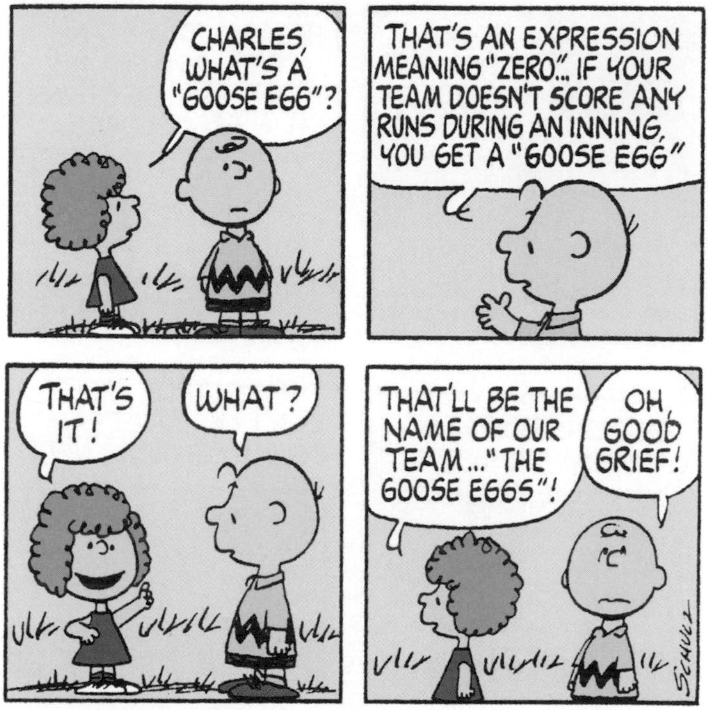
CHARLES, WHAT'S A "GOOSE EGG"?
THAT'S AN EXPRESSION MEANING "ZERO".. IF YOUR TEAM DOESN'T SCORE ANY RUNS DURING AN INNING, YOU GET A "GOOSE EGG"
THAT'S IT!
WHAT?
THAT'LL BE THE NAME OF OUR TEAM..."THE GOOSE EGGS"!
OH, GOOD GRIEF!
SCHULZ

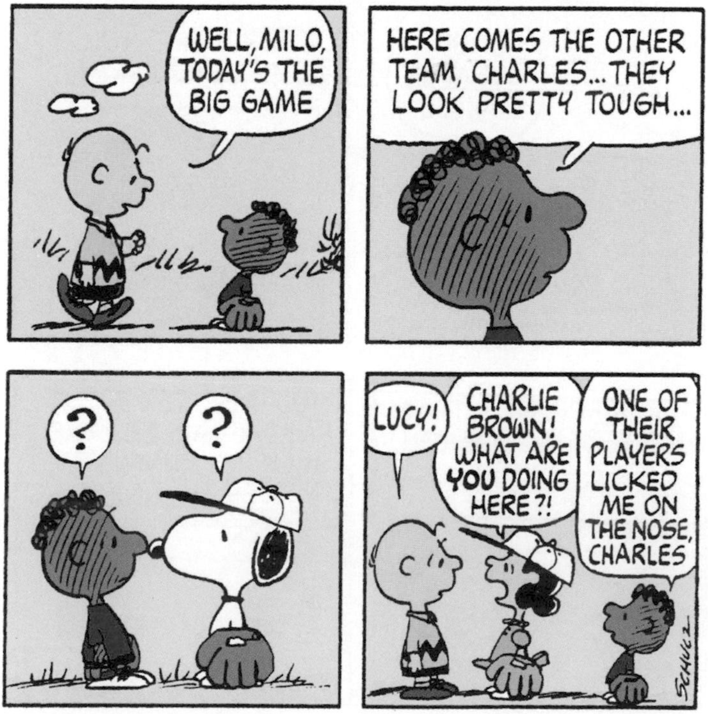
WELL, MILO, TODAY'S THE BIG GAME
HERE COMES THE OTHER TEAM, CHARLES...THEY LOOK PRETTY TOUGH...
?
?
LUCY!
CHARLIE BROWN! WHAT ARE YOU DOING HERE?!
ONE OF THEIR PLAYERS LICKED ME ON THE NOSE, CHARLES
SCHULZ

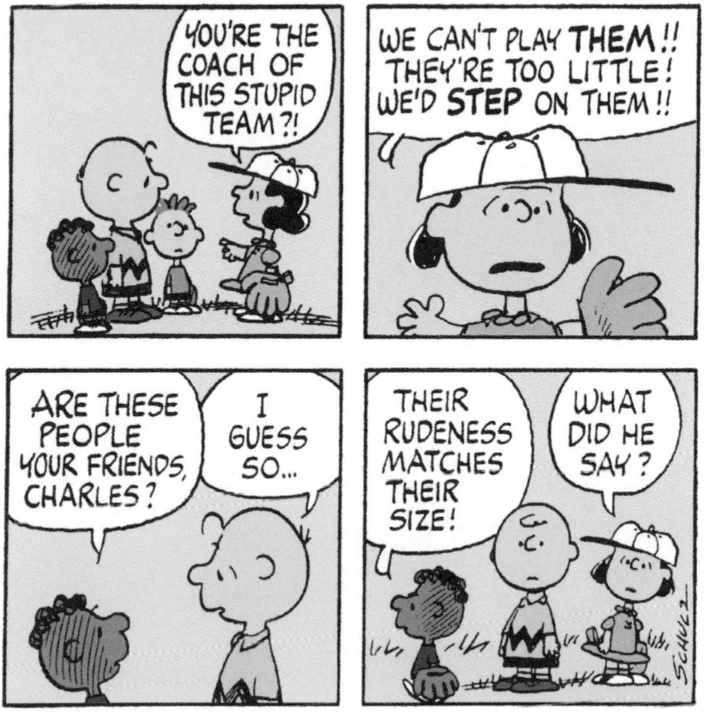
YOU'RE THE COACH OF THIS STUPID TEAM?!
WE CAN'T PLAY **THEM**!! THEY'RE TOO LITTLE! WE'D **STEP** ON THEM!!
ARE THESE PEOPLE YOUR FRIENDS, CHARLES?
I GUESS SO...
THEIR RUDENESS MATCHES THEIR SIZE!
WHAT DID HE SAY?
SCHULZ

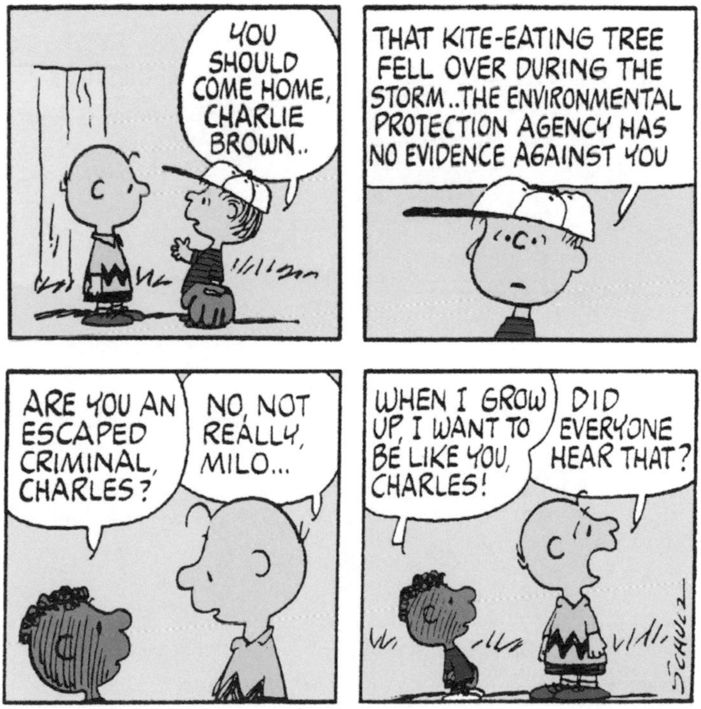
YOU SHOULD COME HOME, CHARLIE BROWN..
THAT KITE-EATING TREE FELL OVER DURING THE STORM..THE ENVIRONMENTAL PROTECTION AGENCY HAS NO EVIDENCE AGAINST YOU
ARE YOU AN ESCAPED CRIMINAL, CHARLES?
NO, NOT REALLY, MILO...
WHEN I GROW UP, I WANT TO BE LIKE YOU, CHARLES!
DID EVERYONE HEAR THAT?
SCHULZ

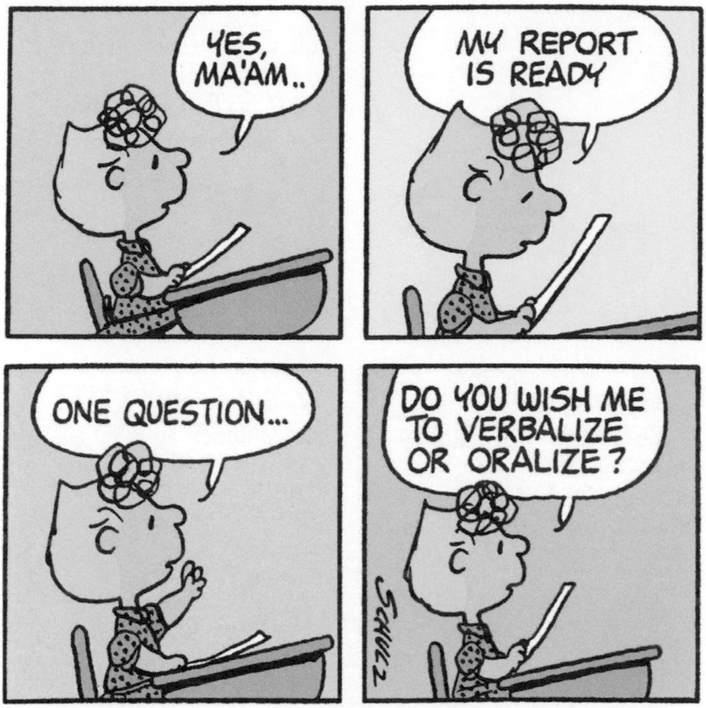
YES, MA'AM..
MY REPORT IS READY
ONE QUESTION...
DO YOU WISH ME TO VERBALIZE OR ORALIZE?
SCHULZ

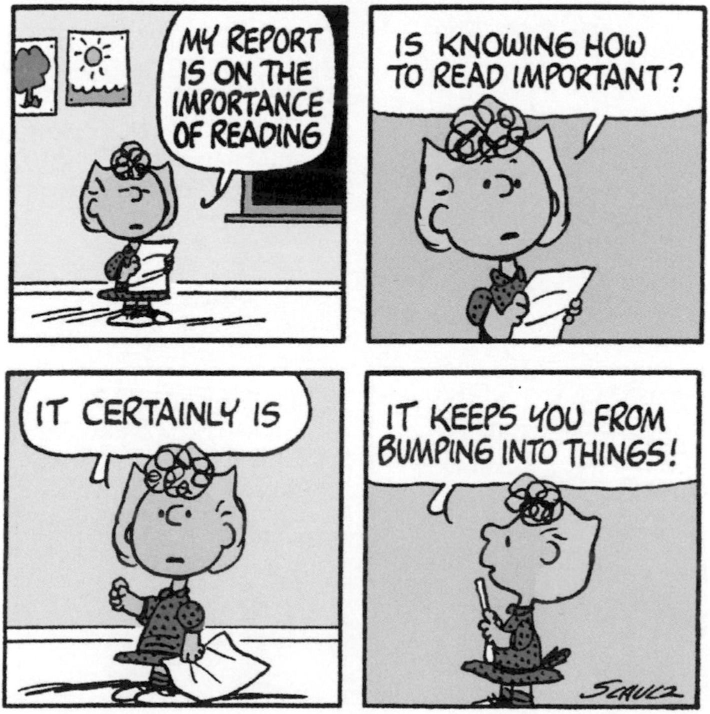
MY REPORT IS ON THE IMPORTANCE OF READING
IS KNOWING HOW TO READ IMPORTANT?
IT CERTAINLY IS
IT KEEPS YOU FROM BUMPING INTO THINGS!
SCHULZ

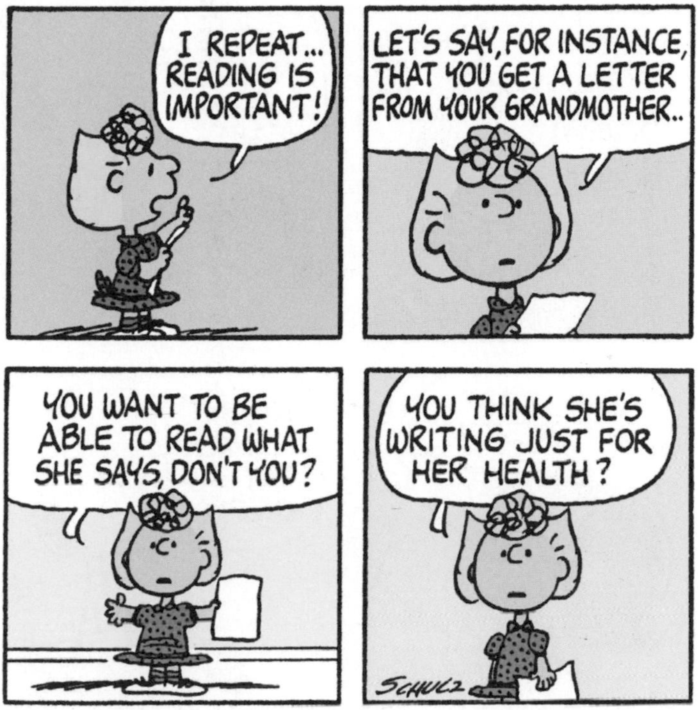
I REPEAT... READING IS IMPORTANT!
LET'S SAY, FOR INSTANCE, THAT YOU GET A LETTER FROM YOUR GRANDMOTHER..
YOU WANT TO BE ABLE TO READ WHAT SHE SAYS, DON'T YOU?
YOU THINK SHE'S WRITING JUST FOR HER HEALTH?
SCHULZ

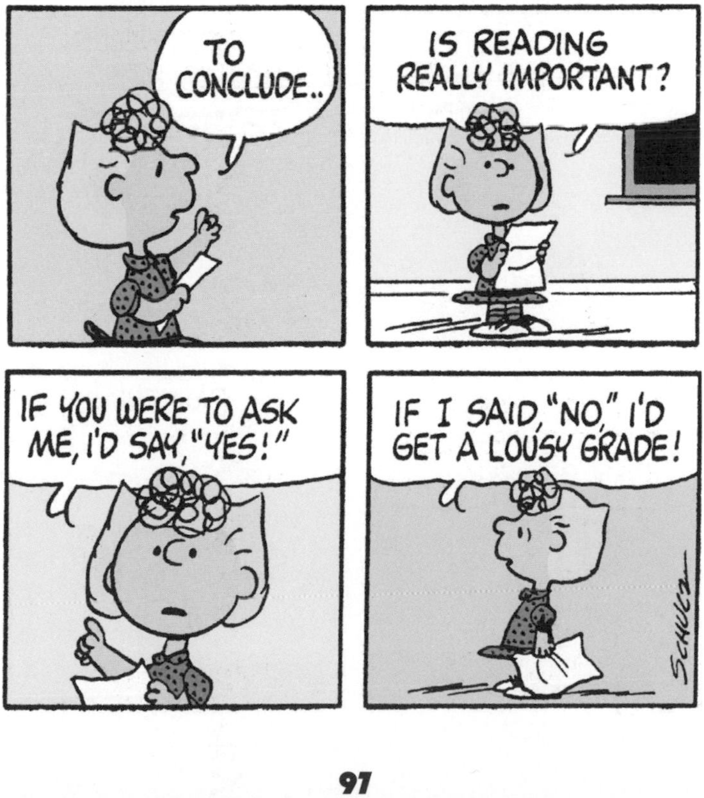
TO CONCLUDE..
IS READING REALLY IMPORTANT?
IF YOU WERE TO ASK ME, I'D SAY, "YES!"
IF I SAID, "NO," I'D GET A LOUSY GRADE!
SCHULZ

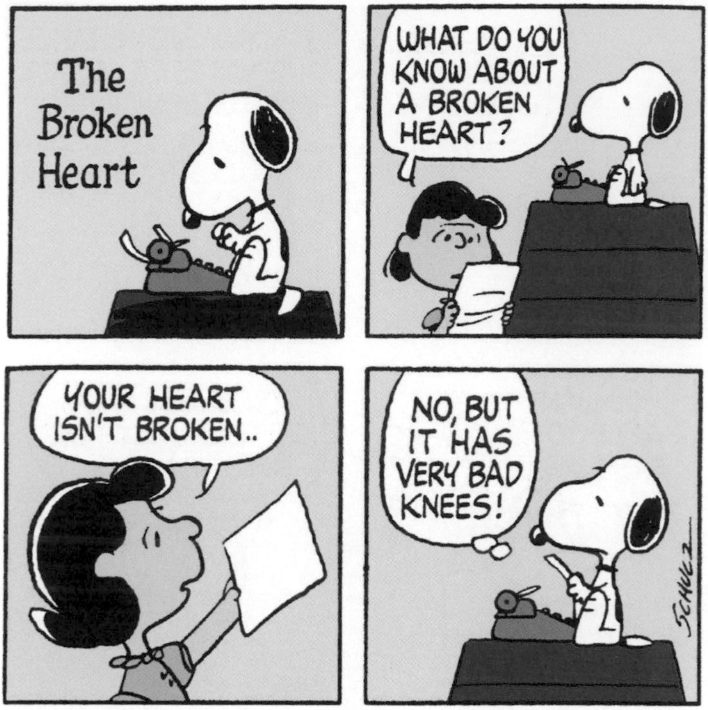
The Broken Heart
WHAT DO YOU KNOW ABOUT A BROKEN HEART?
YOUR HEART ISN'T BROKEN..
NO, BUT IT HAS VERY BAD KNEES!
SCHULZ

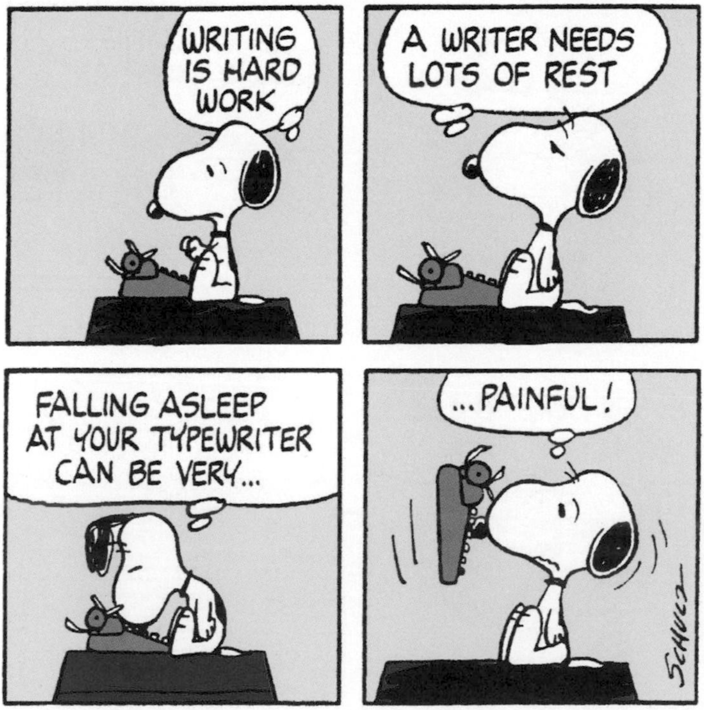
WRITING IS HARD WORK
A WRITER NEEDS LOTS OF REST
FALLING ASLEEP AT YOUR TYPEWRITER CAN BE VERY...
...PAINFUL!
SCHULZ

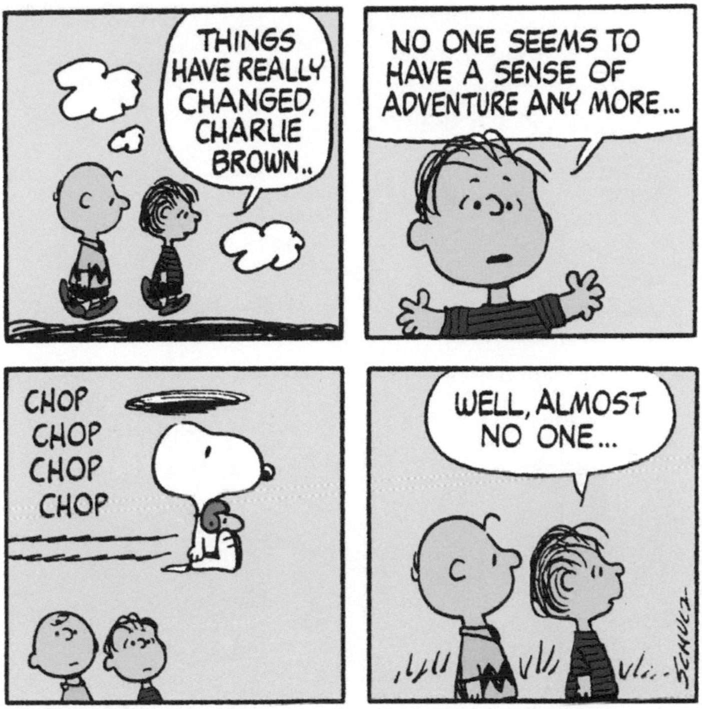
THINGS HAVE REALLY CHANGED, CHARLIE BROWN..
NO ONE SEEMS TO HAVE A SENSE OF ADVENTURE ANY MORE...
CHOP CHOP CHOP CHOP
WELL, ALMOST NO ONE...
SCHULZ

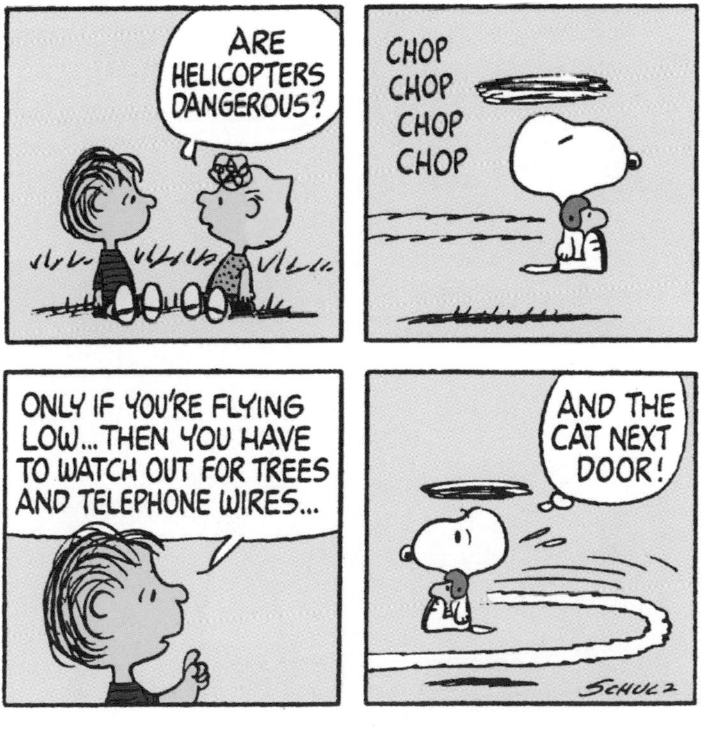
ARE HELICOPTERS DANGEROUS?
CHOP CHOP CHOP CHOP
ONLY IF YOU'RE FLYING LOW...THEN YOU HAVE TO WATCH OUT FOR TREES AND TELEPHONE WIRES...
AND THE CAT NEXT DOOR!
SCHULZ

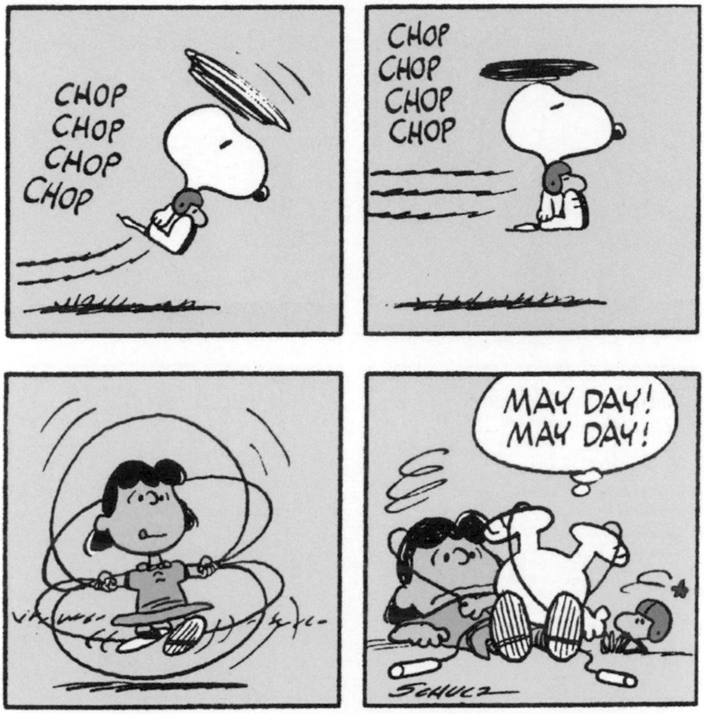
CHOP
CHOP
CHOP
CHOP
CHOP
CHOP
CHOP
CHOP
MAY DAY! MAY DAY!

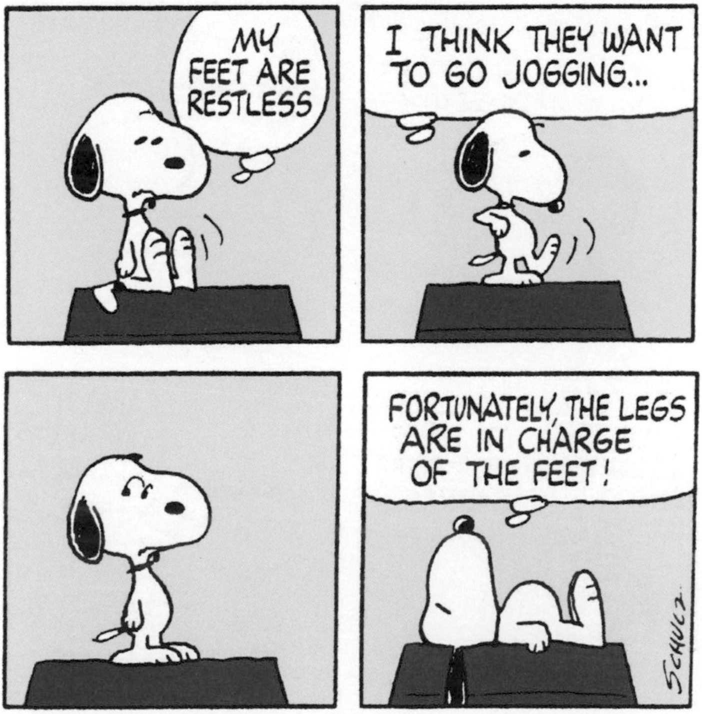
MY FEET ARE RESTLESS
I THINK THEY WANT TO GO JOGGING...
FORTUNATELY, THE LEGS ARE IN CHARGE OF THE FEET!

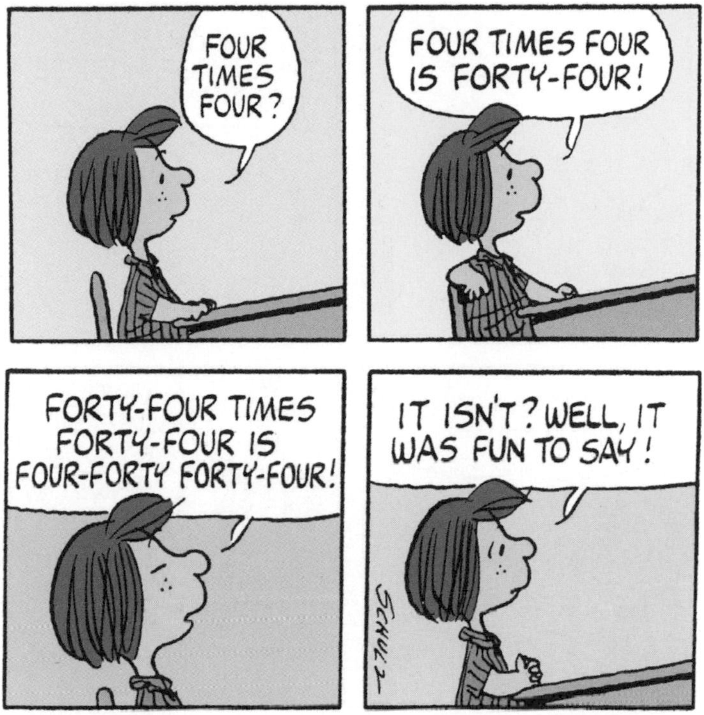
FOUR TIMES FOUR?
FOUR TIMES FOUR IS FORTY-FOUR!
FORTY-FOUR TIMES FORTY-FOUR IS FOUR-FORTY FORTY-FOUR!
IT ISN'T? WELL, IT WAS FUN TO SAY!

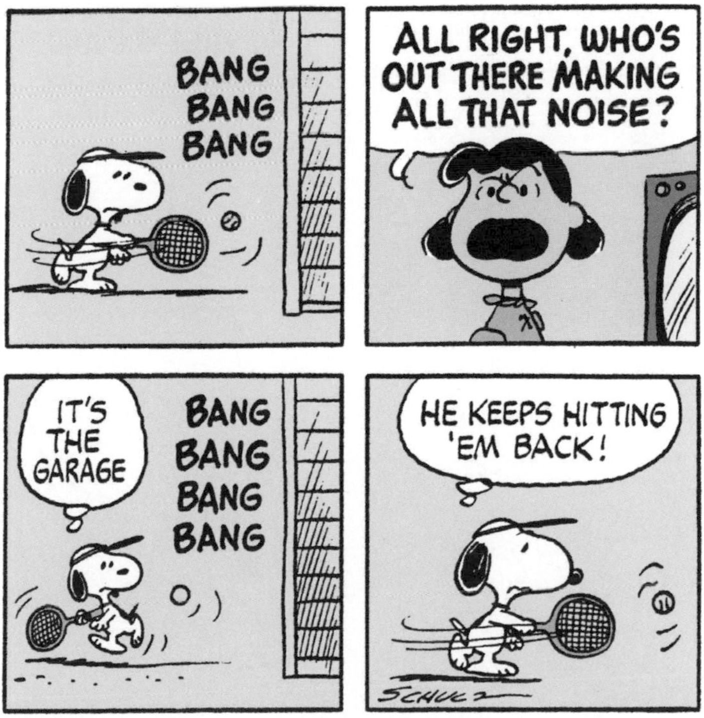
BANG BANG BANG
ALL RIGHT, WHO'S OUT THERE MAKING ALL THAT NOISE?
IT'S THE GARAGE
BANG BANG BANG BANG
HE KEEPS HITTING 'EM BACK!

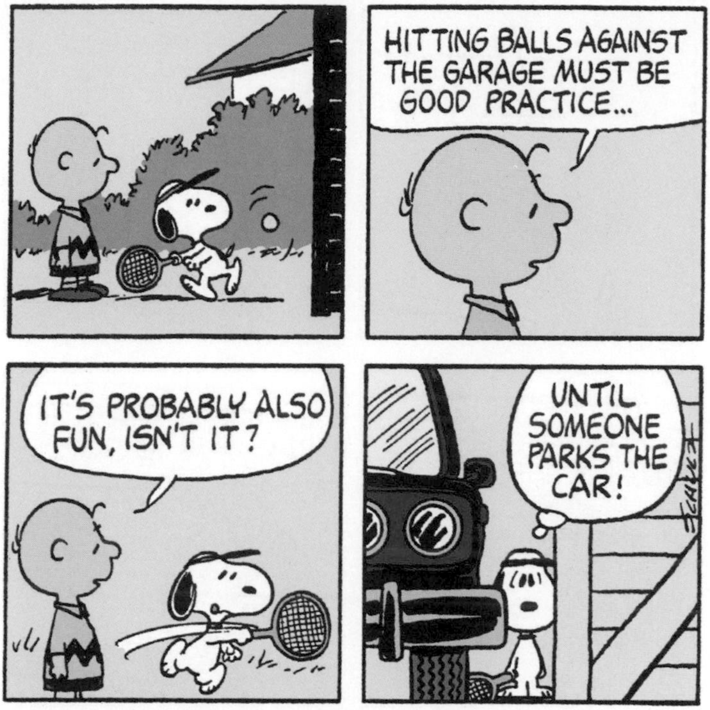
HITTING BALLS AGAINST THE GARAGE MUST BE GOOD PRACTICE...
IT'S PROBABLY ALSO FUN, ISN'T IT?
UNTIL SOMEONE PARKS THE CAR!

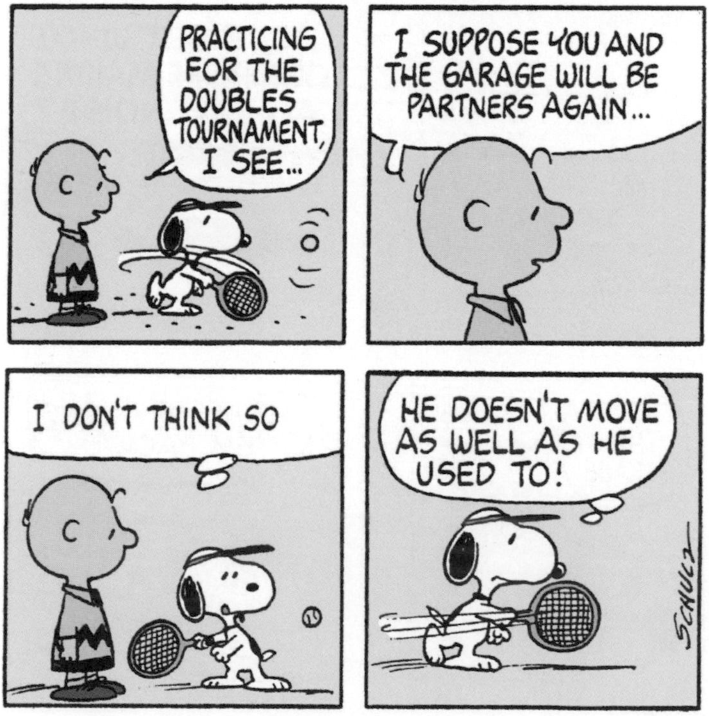
PRACTICING FOR THE DOUBLES TOURNAMENT, I SEE...
I SUPPOSE YOU AND THE GARAGE WILL BE PARTNERS AGAIN...
I DON'T THINK SO
HE DOESN'T MOVE AS WELL AS HE USED TO!
SCHULZ

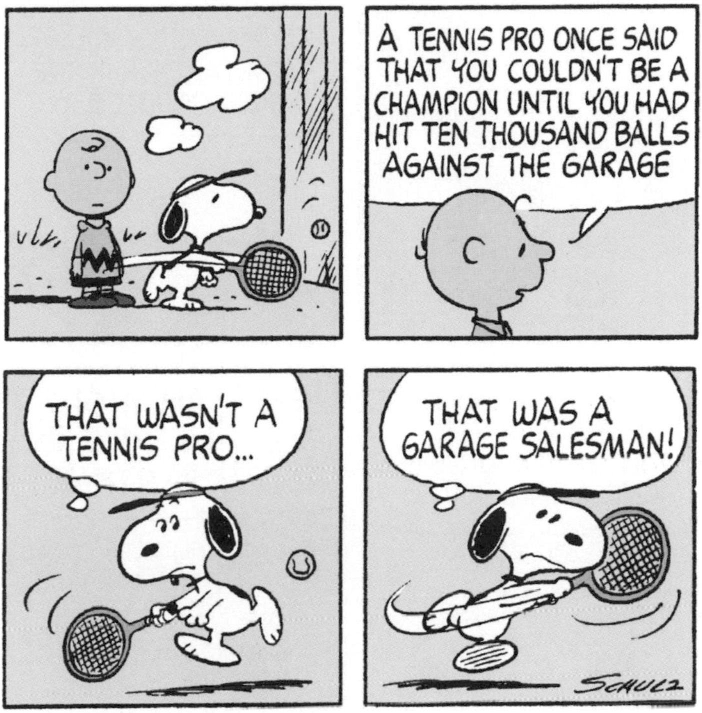
A TENNIS PRO ONCE SAID THAT YOU COULDN'T BE A CHAMPION UNTIL YOU HAD HIT TEN THOUSAND BALLS AGAINST THE GARAGE
THAT WASN'T A TENNIS PRO...
THAT WAS A GARAGE SALESMAN!
SCHULZ

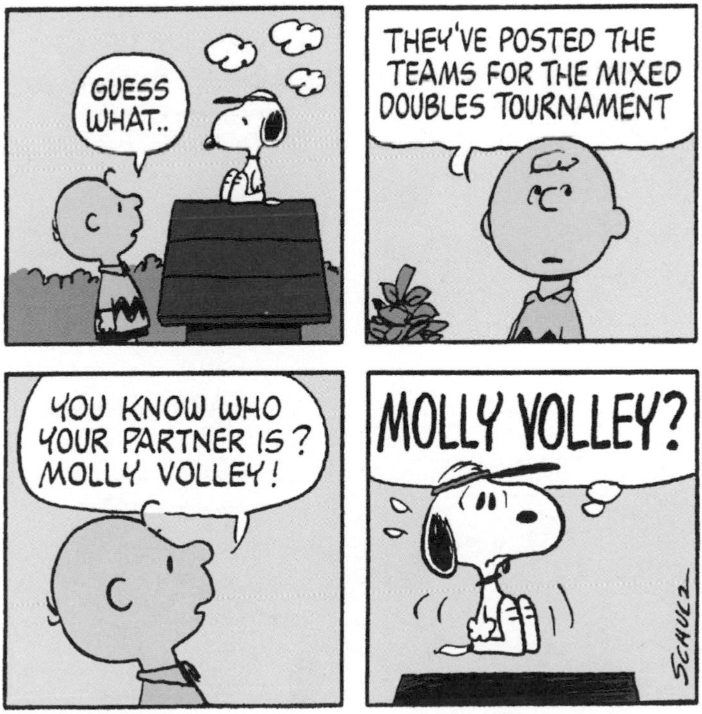
GUESS WHAT..
THEY'VE POSTED THE TEAMS FOR THE MIXED DOUBLES TOURNAMENT
YOU KNOW WHO YOUR PARTNER IS? MOLLY VOLLEY!
MOLLY VOLLEY?
SCHULZ

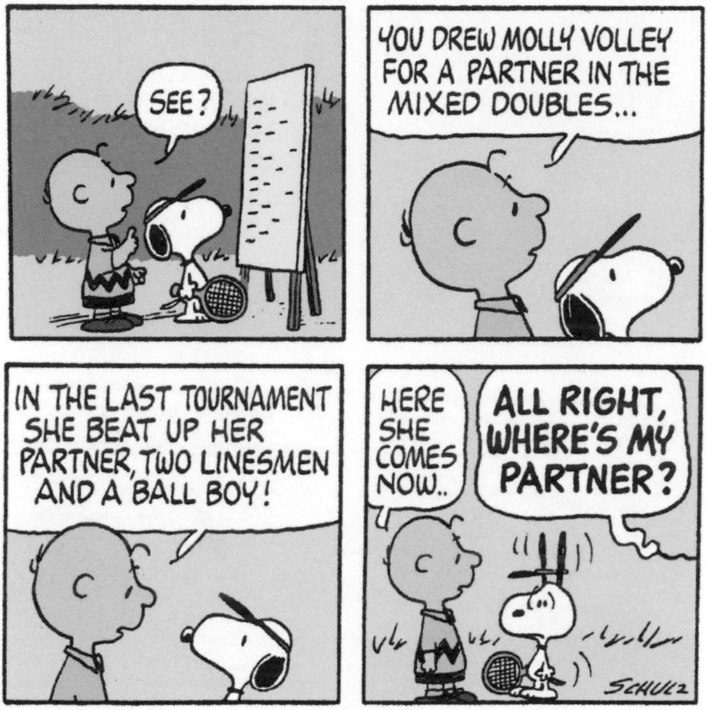
SEE?
YOU DREW MOLLY VOLLEY FOR A PARTNER IN THE MIXED DOUBLES...
IN THE LAST TOURNAMENT SHE BEAT UP HER PARTNER, TWO LINESMEN AND A BALL BOY!
HERE SHE COMES NOW..
ALL RIGHT, WHERE'S MY PARTNER?

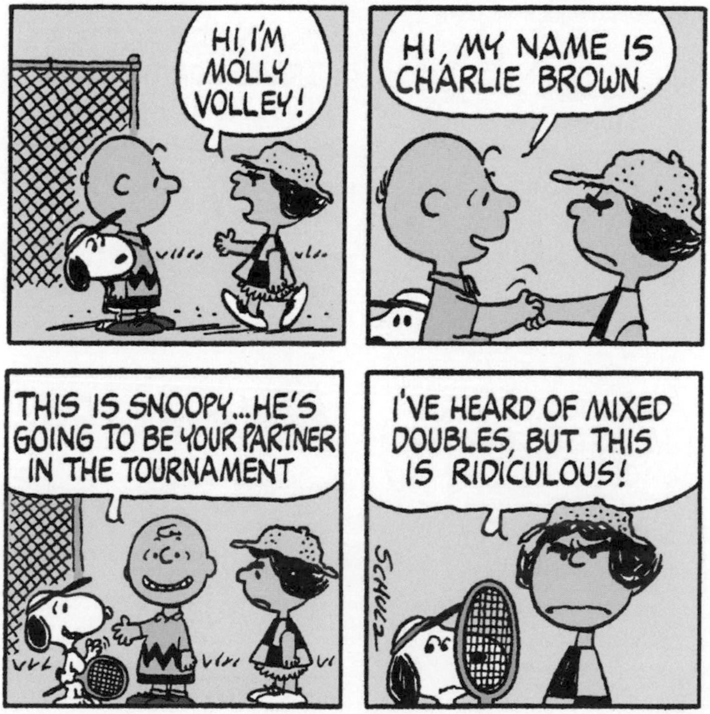
HI, I'M MOLLY VOLLEY!
HI, MY NAME IS CHARLIE BROWN
THIS IS SNOOPY...HE'S GOING TO BE YOUR PARTNER IN THE TOURNAMENT
I'VE HEARD OF MIXED DOUBLES, BUT THIS IS RIDICULOUS!

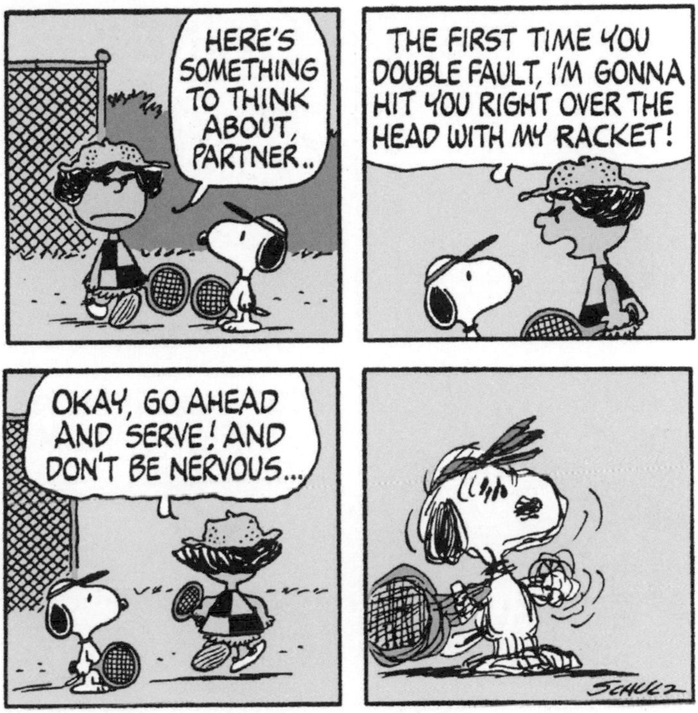
HERE'S SOMETHING TO THINK ABOUT, PARTNER..
THE FIRST TIME YOU DOUBLE FAULT, I'M GONNA HIT YOU RIGHT OVER THE HEAD WITH MY RACKET!
OKAY, GO AHEAD AND SERVE! AND DON'T BE NERVOUS...
SCHULZ

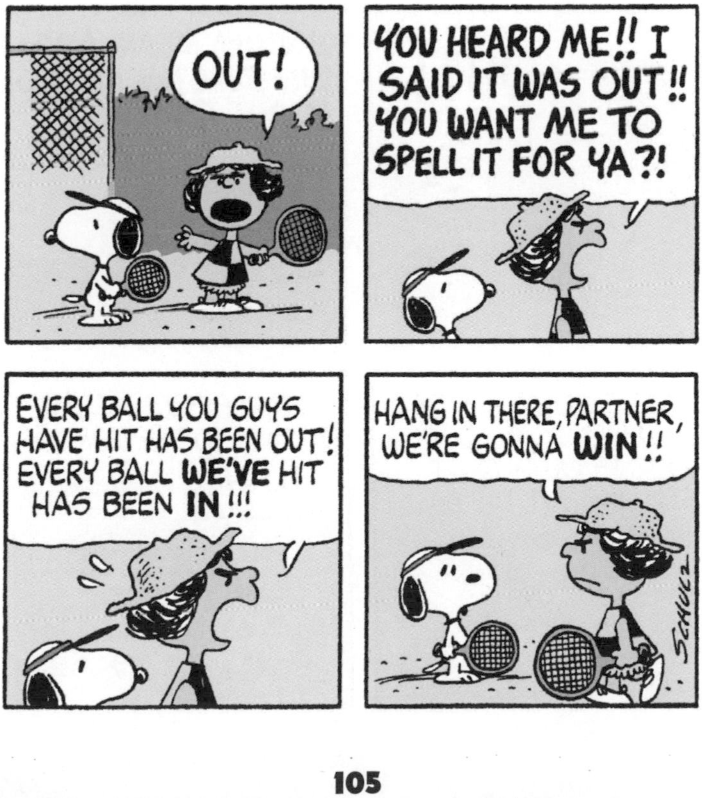
OUT!
YOU HEARD ME!! I SAID IT WAS OUT!! YOU WANT ME TO SPELL IT FOR YA?!
EVERY BALL YOU GUYS HAVE HIT HAS BEEN OUT! EVERY BALL **WE'VE** HIT HAS BEEN **IN**!!!
HANG IN THERE, PARTNER, WE'RE GONNA **WIN**!!
SCHULZ

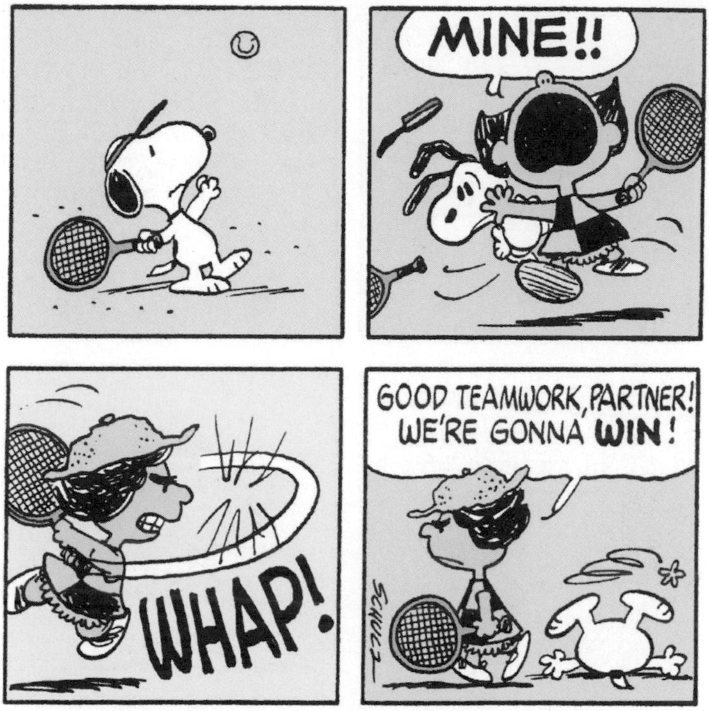
MINE!!
WHAP!
GOOD TEAMWORK, PARTNER! WE'RE GONNA WIN!
SCHULZ

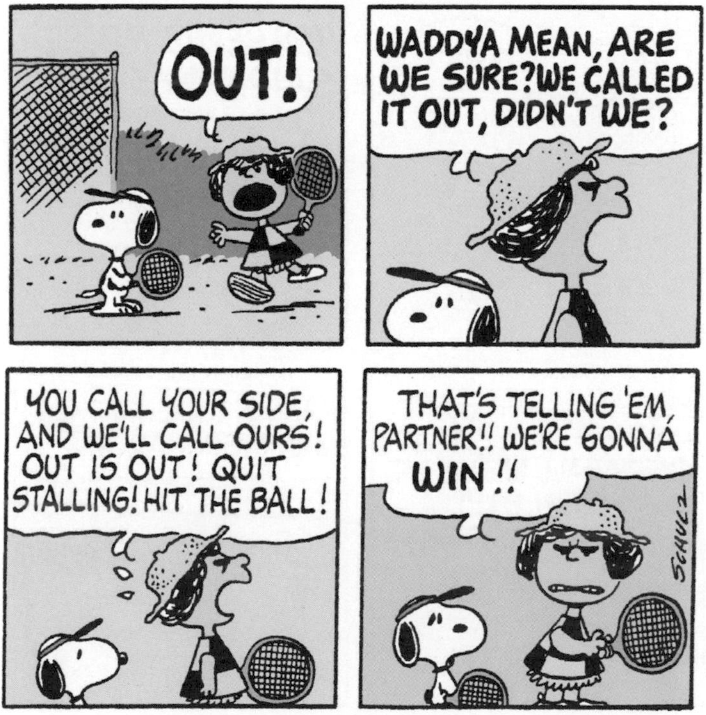
OUT!
WADDYA MEAN, ARE WE SURE? WE CALLED IT OUT, DIDN'T WE?
YOU CALL YOUR SIDE, AND WE'LL CALL OURS! OUT IS OUT! QUIT STALLING! HIT THE BALL!
THAT'S TELLING 'EM, PARTNER!! WE'RE GONNA WIN!!
SCHULZ

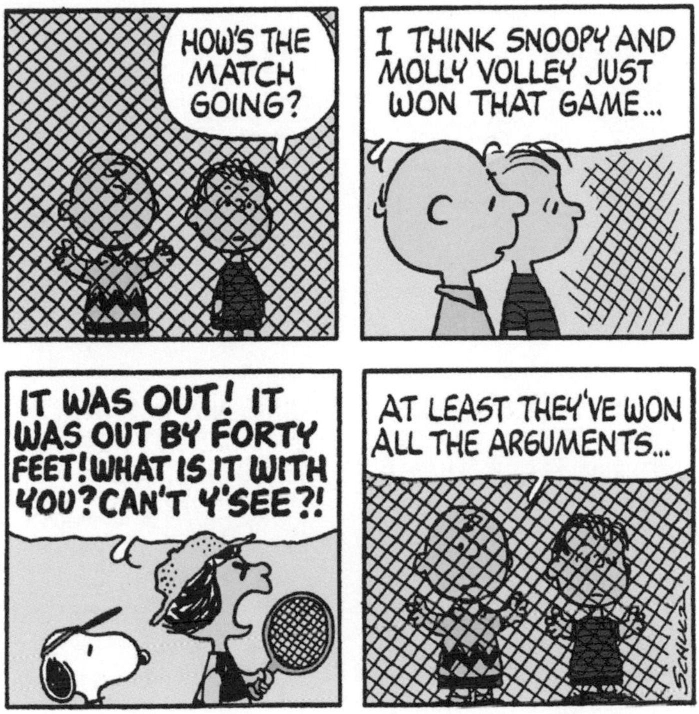
HOW'S THE MATCH GOING?
I THINK SNOOPY AND MOLLY VOLLEY JUST WON THAT GAME...
IT WAS OUT! IT WAS OUT BY FORTY FEET! WHAT IS IT WITH YOU? CAN'T Y'SEE?!
AT LEAST THEY'VE WON ALL THE ARGUMENTS...
SCHULZ

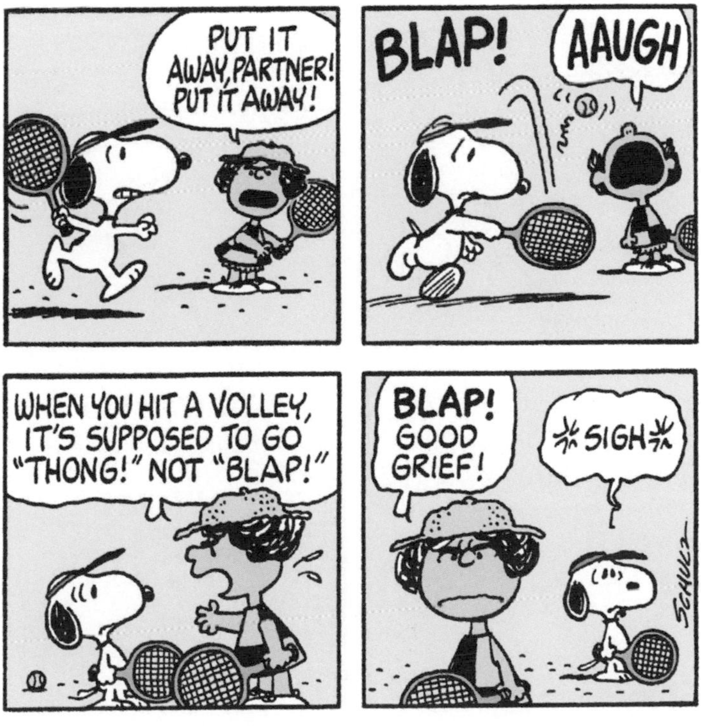
PUT IT AWAY, PARTNER! PUT IT AWAY!
BLAP!
AAUGH
WHEN YOU HIT A VOLLEY, IT'S SUPPOSED TO GO "THONG!" NOT "BLAP!"
BLAP! GOOD GRIEF!
SIGH
SCHULZ

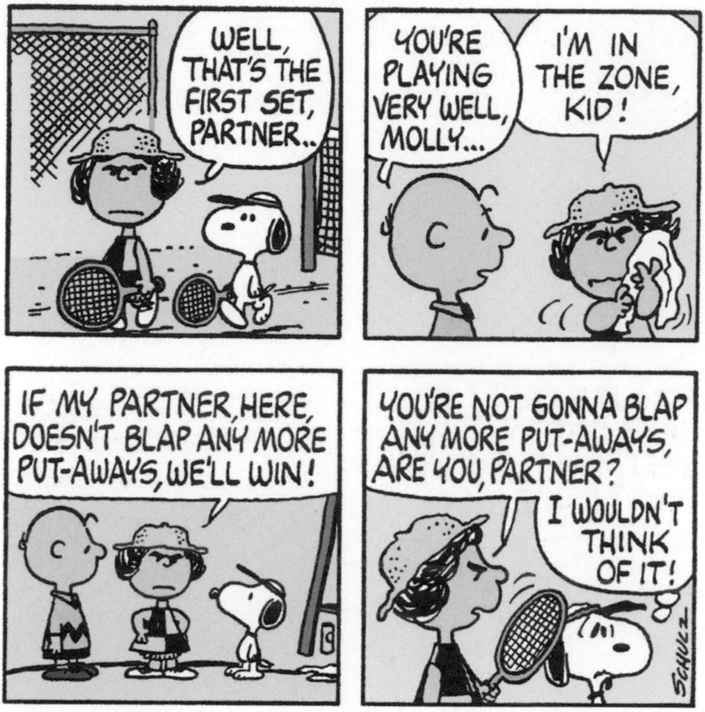
WELL, THAT'S THE FIRST SET, PARTNER..
YOU'RE PLAYING VERY WELL, MOLLY...
I'M IN THE ZONE, KID!
IF MY PARTNER, HERE, DOESN'T BLAP ANY MORE PUT-AWAYS, WE'LL WIN!
YOU'RE NOT GONNA BLAP ANY MORE PUT-AWAYS, ARE YOU, PARTNER?
I WOULDN'T THINK OF IT!
SCHULZ

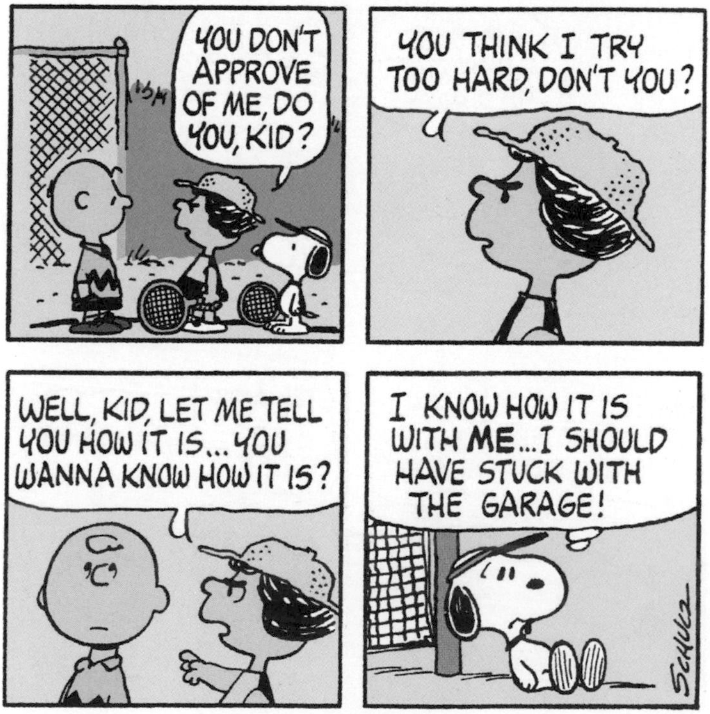
YOU DON'T APPROVE OF ME, DO YOU, KID?
YOU THINK I TRY TOO HARD, DON'T YOU?
WELL, KID, LET ME TELL YOU HOW IT IS... YOU WANNA KNOW HOW IT IS?
I KNOW HOW IT IS WITH **ME**... I SHOULD HAVE STUCK WITH THE GARAGE!
SCHULZ

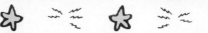

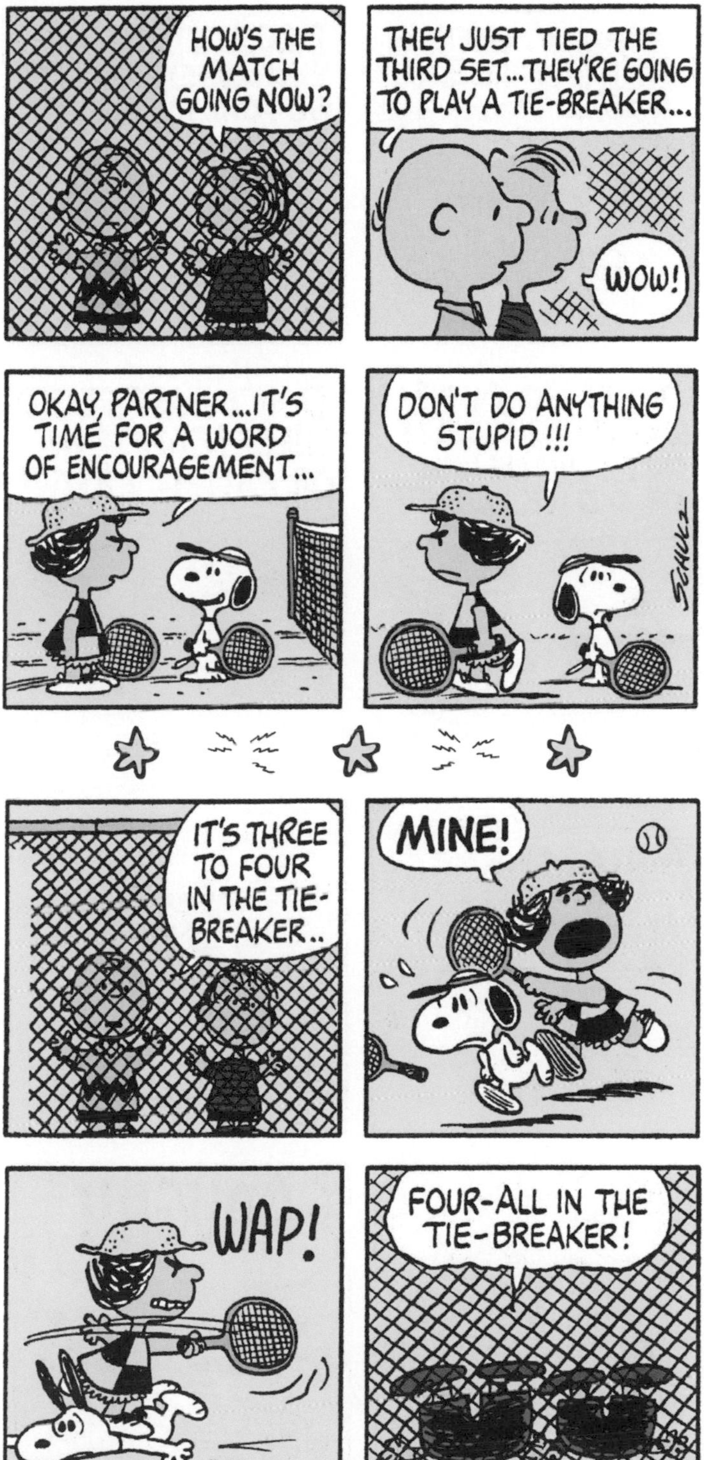
HOW'S THE MATCH GOING NOW?
THEY JUST TIED THE THIRD SET...THEY'RE GOING TO PLAY A TIE-BREAKER...
WOW!
OKAY, PARTNER...IT'S TIME FOR A WORD OF ENCOURAGEMENT...
DON'T DO ANYTHING STUPID!!!
SCHULZ
IT'S THREE TO FOUR IN THE TIE-BREAKER..
MINE!
WAP!
FOUR-ALL IN THE TIE-BREAKER!
SCHULZ

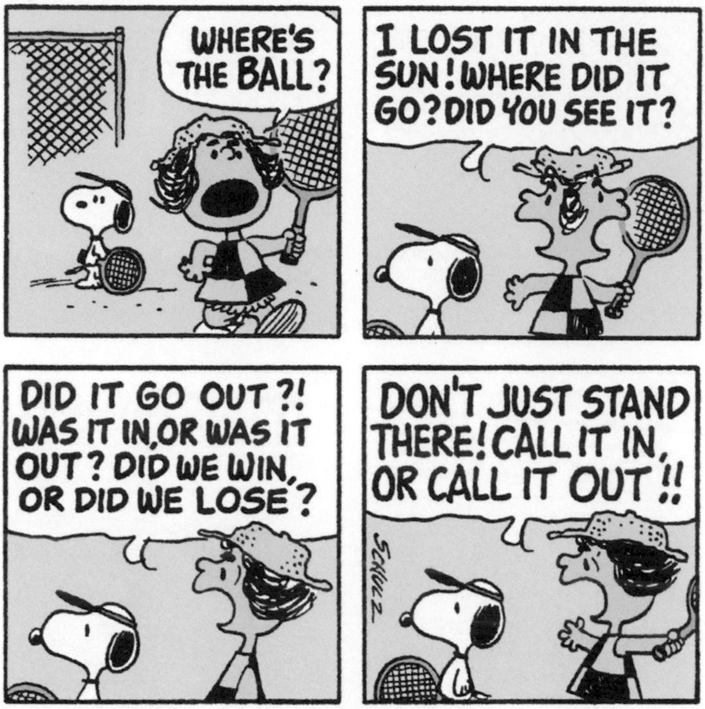
WHERE'S THE BALL?
I LOST IT IN THE SUN! WHERE DID IT GO? DID YOU SEE IT?
DID IT GO OUT?! WAS IT IN, OR WAS IT OUT? DID WE WIN, OR DID WE LOSE?
DON'T JUST STAND THERE! CALL IT IN, OR CALL IT OUT!!
SCHULZ

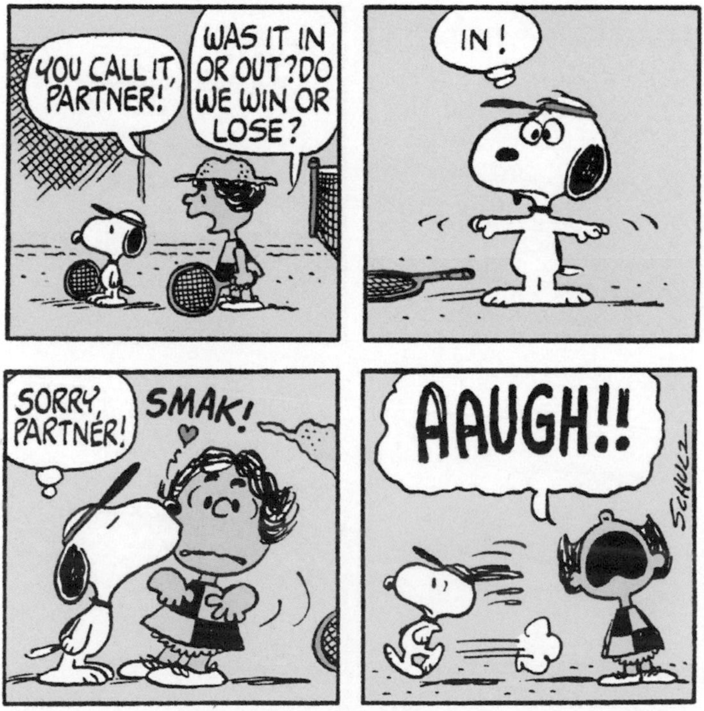
YOU CALL IT, PARTNER!
WAS IT IN OR OUT? DO WE WIN OR LOSE?
IN!
SORRY, PARTNER!
SMAK!
AAUGH!!
SCHULZ

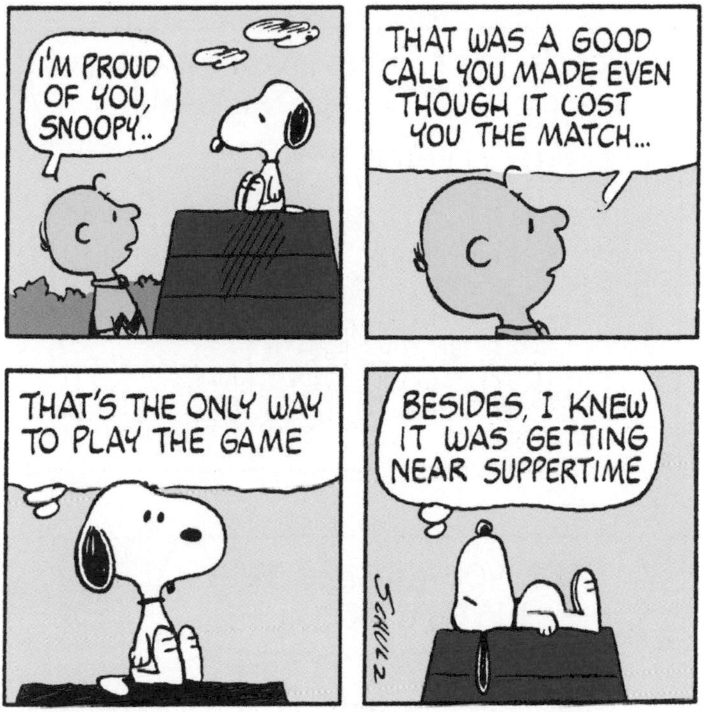
I'M PROUD OF YOU, SNOOPY..
THAT WAS A GOOD CALL YOU MADE EVEN THOUGH IT COST YOU THE MATCH...
THAT'S THE ONLY WAY TO PLAY THE GAME
BESIDES, I KNEW IT WAS GETTING NEAR SUPPERTIME
SCHULZ

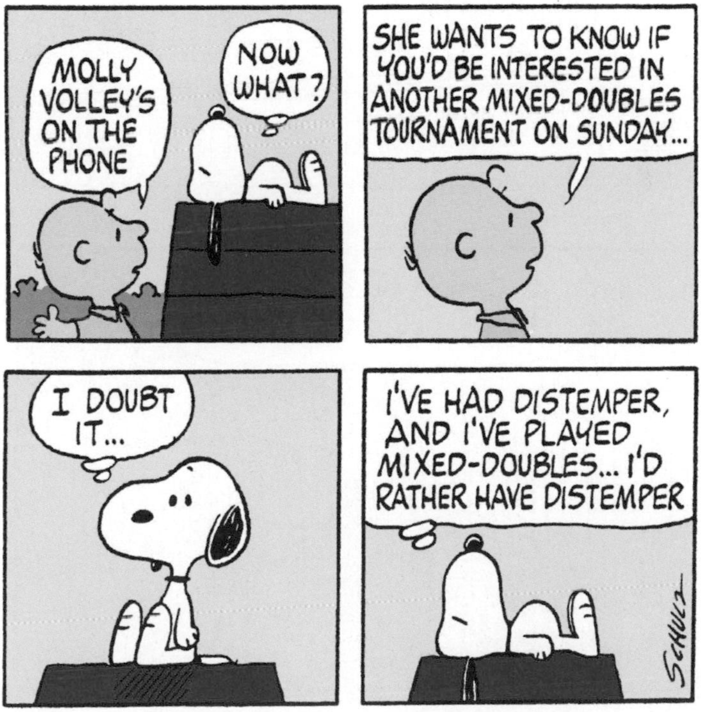
MOLLY VOLLEY'S ON THE PHONE
NOW WHAT?
SHE WANTS TO KNOW IF YOU'D BE INTERESTED IN ANOTHER MIXED-DOUBLES TOURNAMENT ON SUNDAY...
I DOUBT IT...
I'VE HAD DISTEMPER, AND I'VE PLAYED MIXED-DOUBLES... I'D RATHER HAVE DISTEMPER
SCHULZ

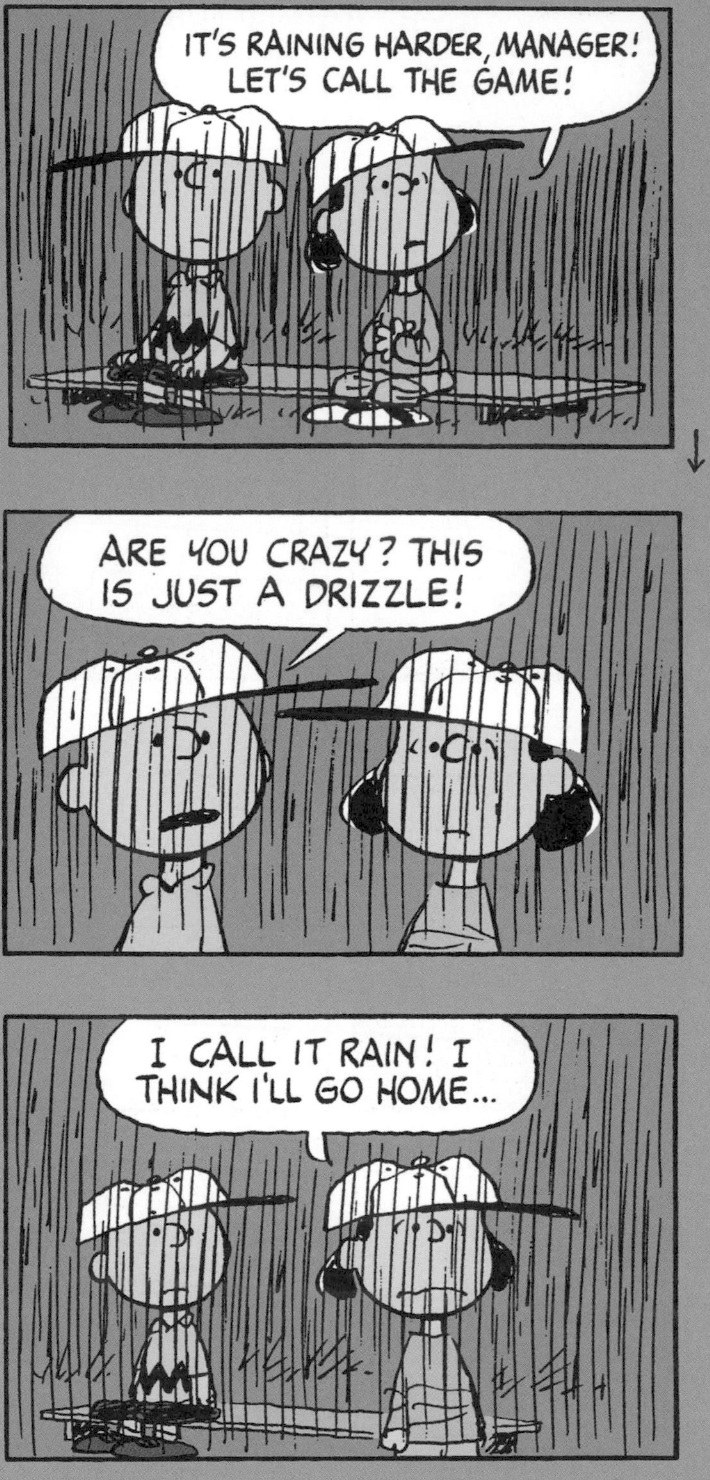
IT'S RAINING HARDER, MANAGER! LET'S CALL THE GAME!
ARE YOU CRAZY? THIS IS JUST A DRIZZLE!
I CALL IT RAIN! I THINK I'LL GO HOME...

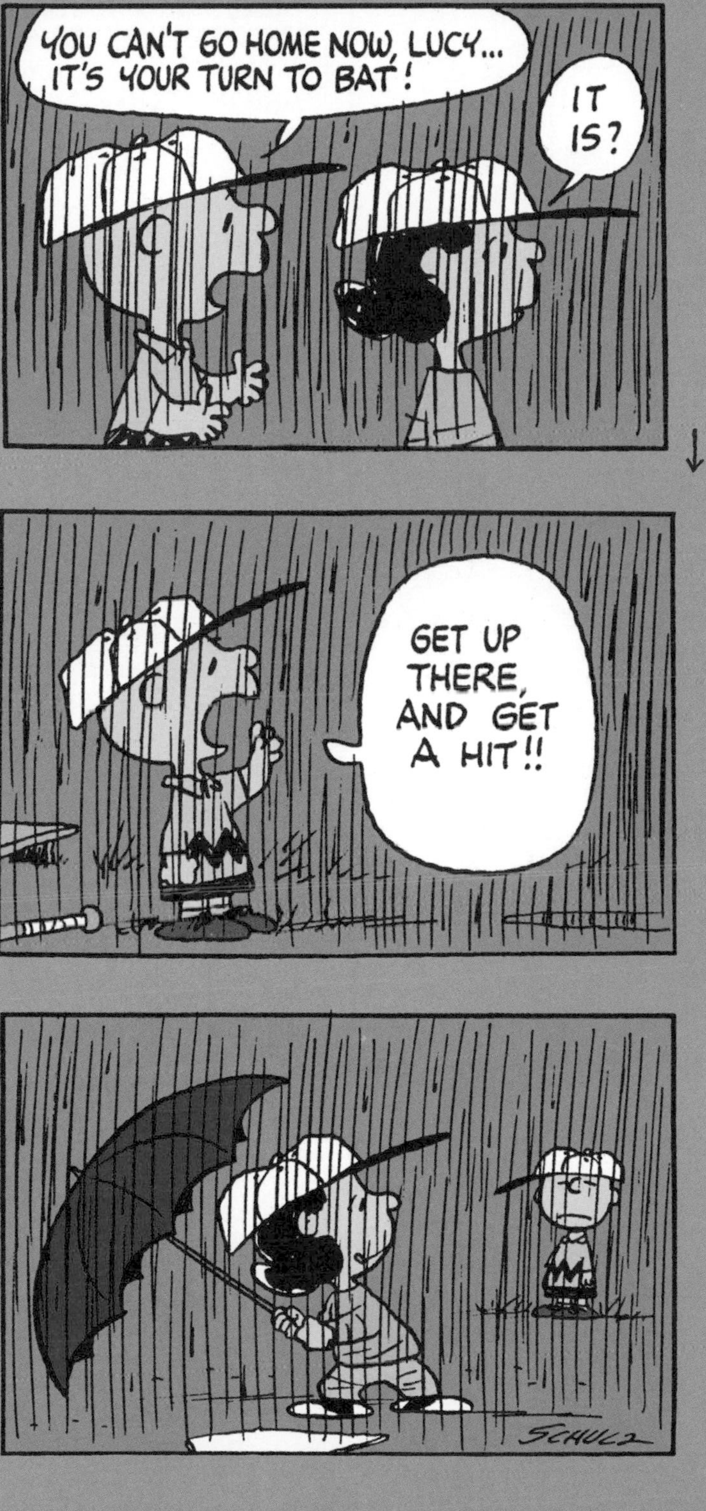
YOU CAN'T GO HOME NOW, LUCY... IT'S YOUR TURN TO BAT!
IT IS?
GET UP THERE, AND GET A HIT!!
SCHULZ

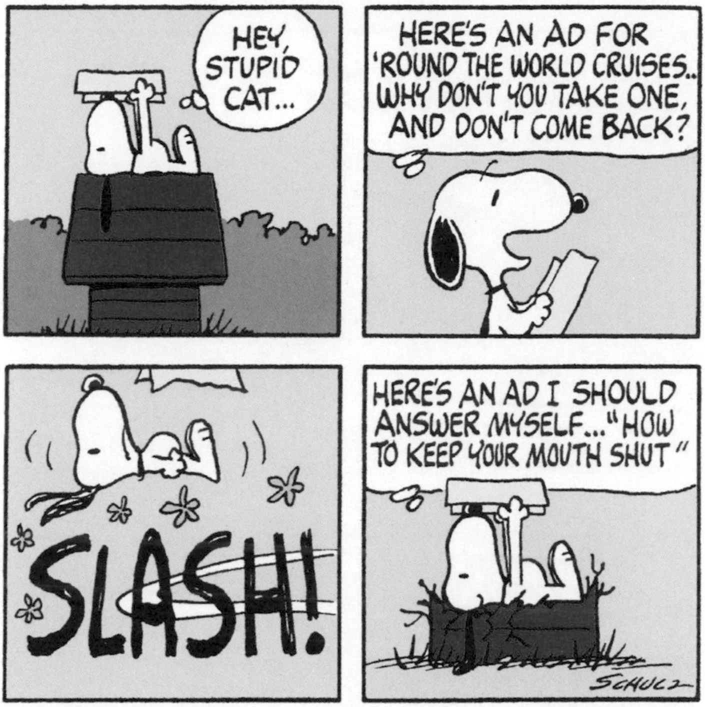
HEY, STUPID CAT...
HERE'S AN AD FOR 'ROUND THE WORLD CRUISES.. WHY DON'T YOU TAKE ONE, AND DON'T COME BACK?
SLASH!
HERE'S AN AD I SHOULD ANSWER MYSELF..."HOW TO KEEP YOUR MOUTH SHUT"
SCHULZ

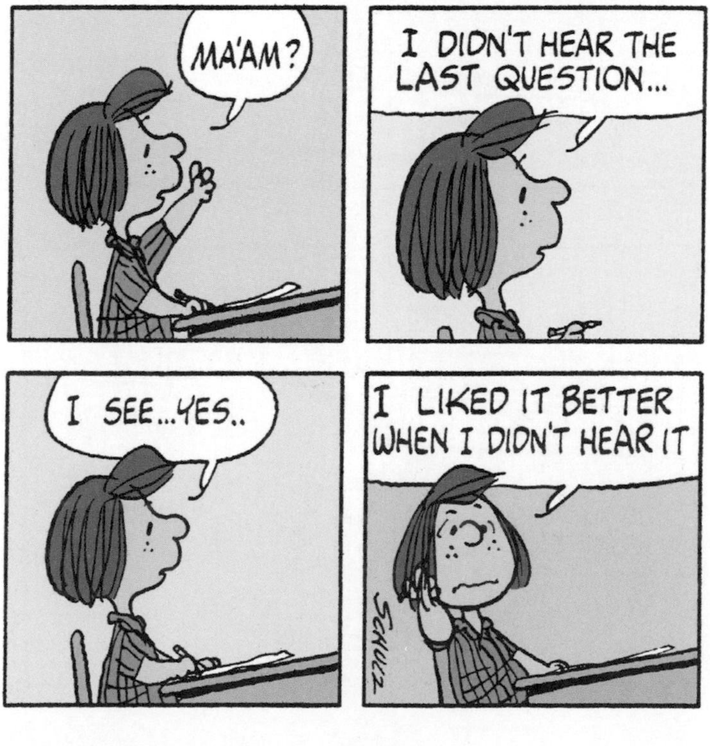
MA'AM?
I DIDN'T HEAR THE LAST QUESTION...
I SEE...YES..
I LIKED IT BETTER WHEN I DIDN'T HEAR IT
SCHULZ

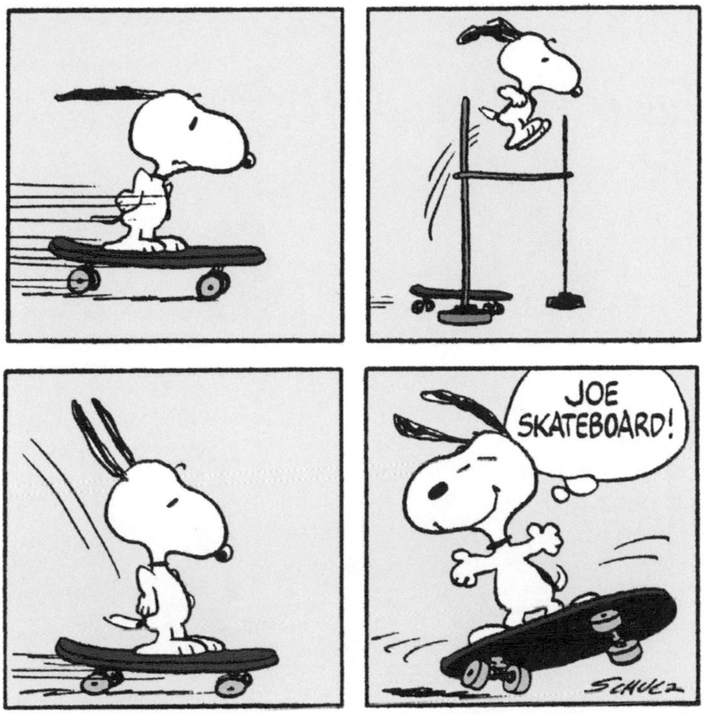
JOE SKATEBOARD!

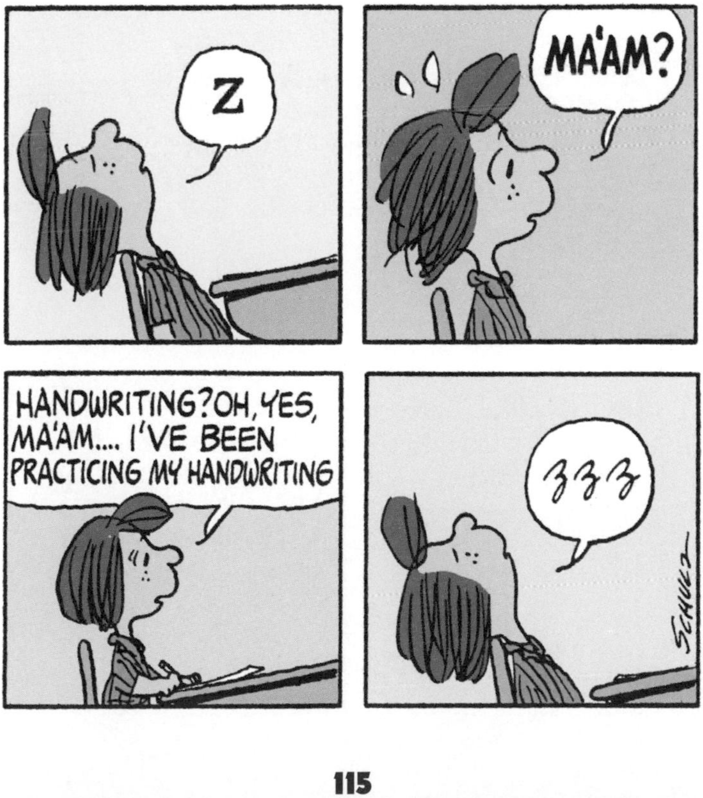
Z
MA'AM?
HANDWRITING? OH, YES, MA'AM.... I'VE BEEN PRACTICING MY HANDWRITING
Z Z Z

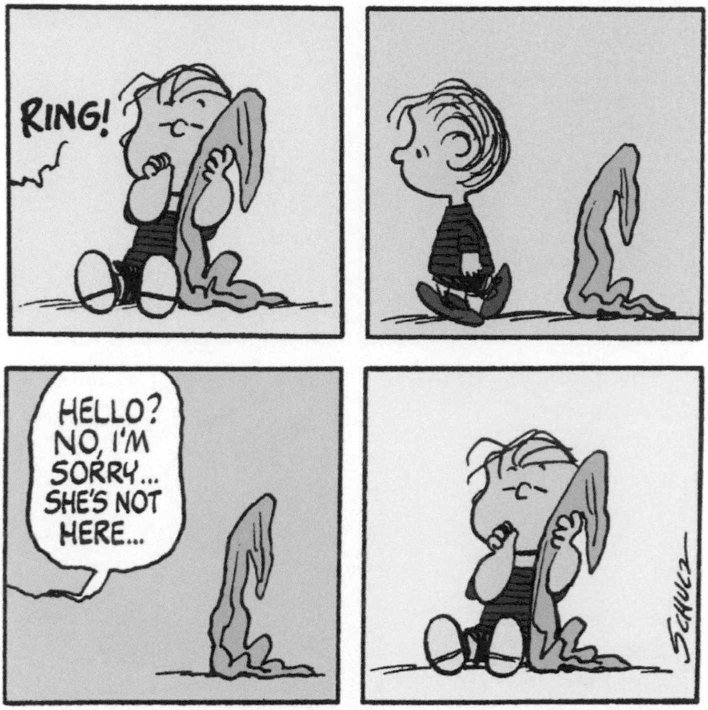
RING!
HELLO? NO, I'M SORRY... SHE'S NOT HERE...
SCHULZ

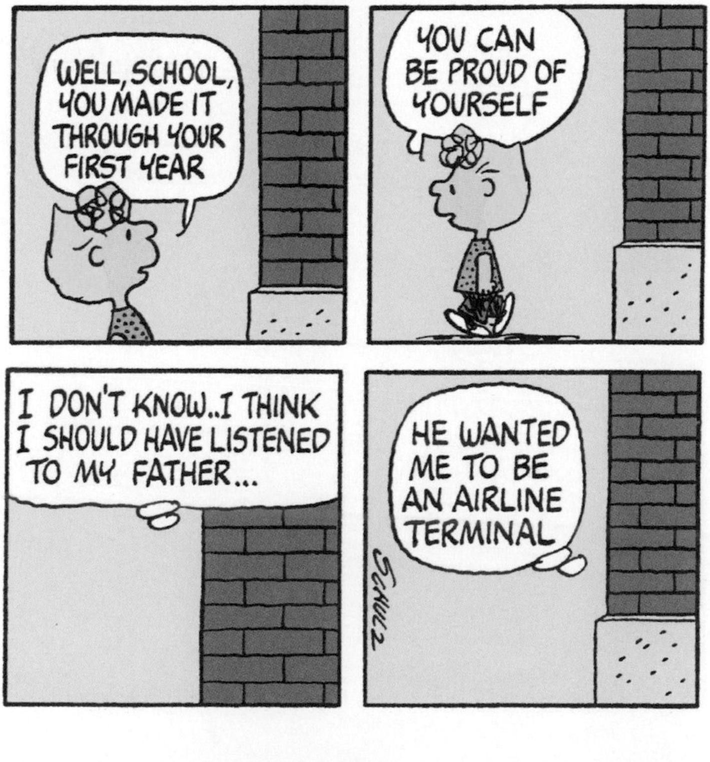
WELL, SCHOOL, YOU MADE IT THROUGH YOUR FIRST YEAR
YOU CAN BE PROUD OF YOURSELF
I DON'T KNOW..I THINK I SHOULD HAVE LISTENED TO MY FATHER...
HE WANTED ME TO BE AN AIRLINE TERMINAL
SCHULZ

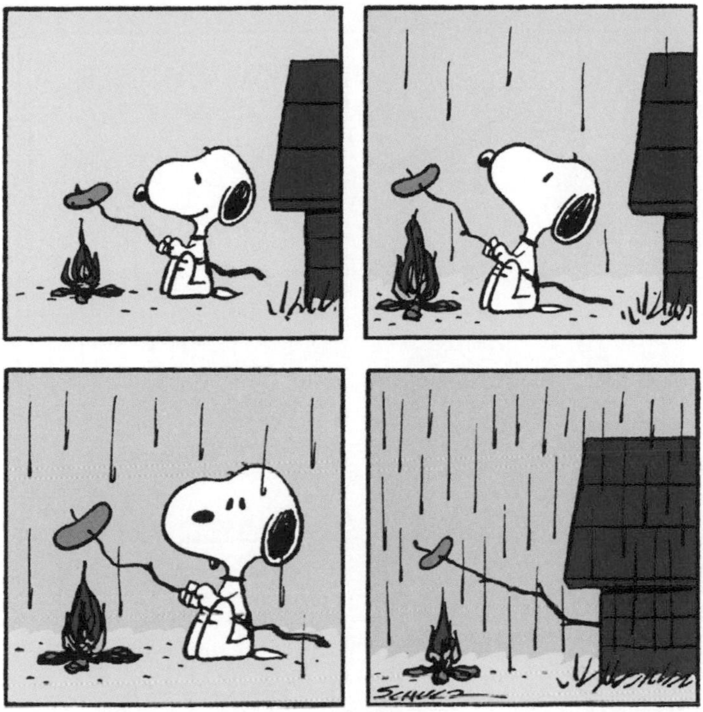

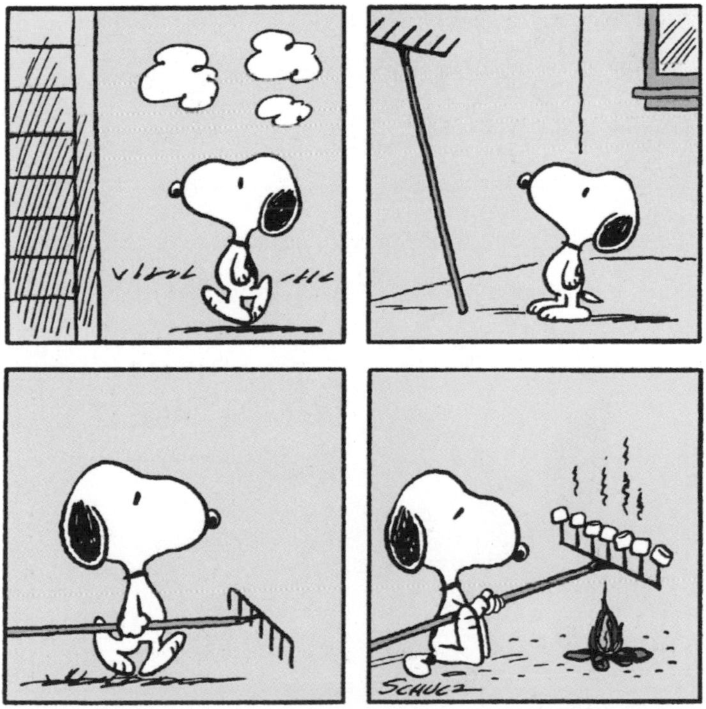

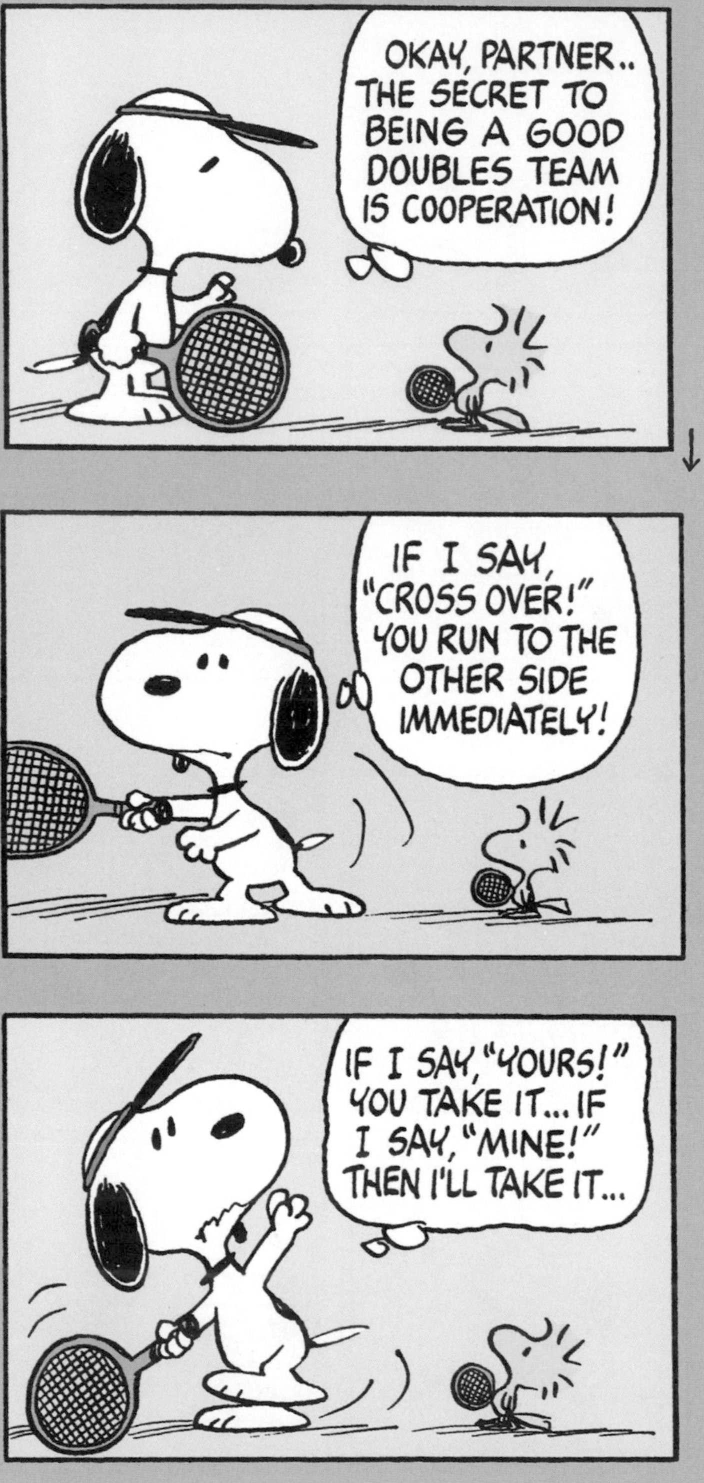
OKAY, PARTNER.. THE SECRET TO BEING A GOOD DOUBLES TEAM IS COOPERATION!
IF I SAY, "CROSS OVER!" YOU RUN TO THE OTHER SIDE IMMEDIATELY!
IF I SAY, "YOURS!" YOU TAKE IT... IF I SAY, "MINE!" THEN I'LL TAKE IT...

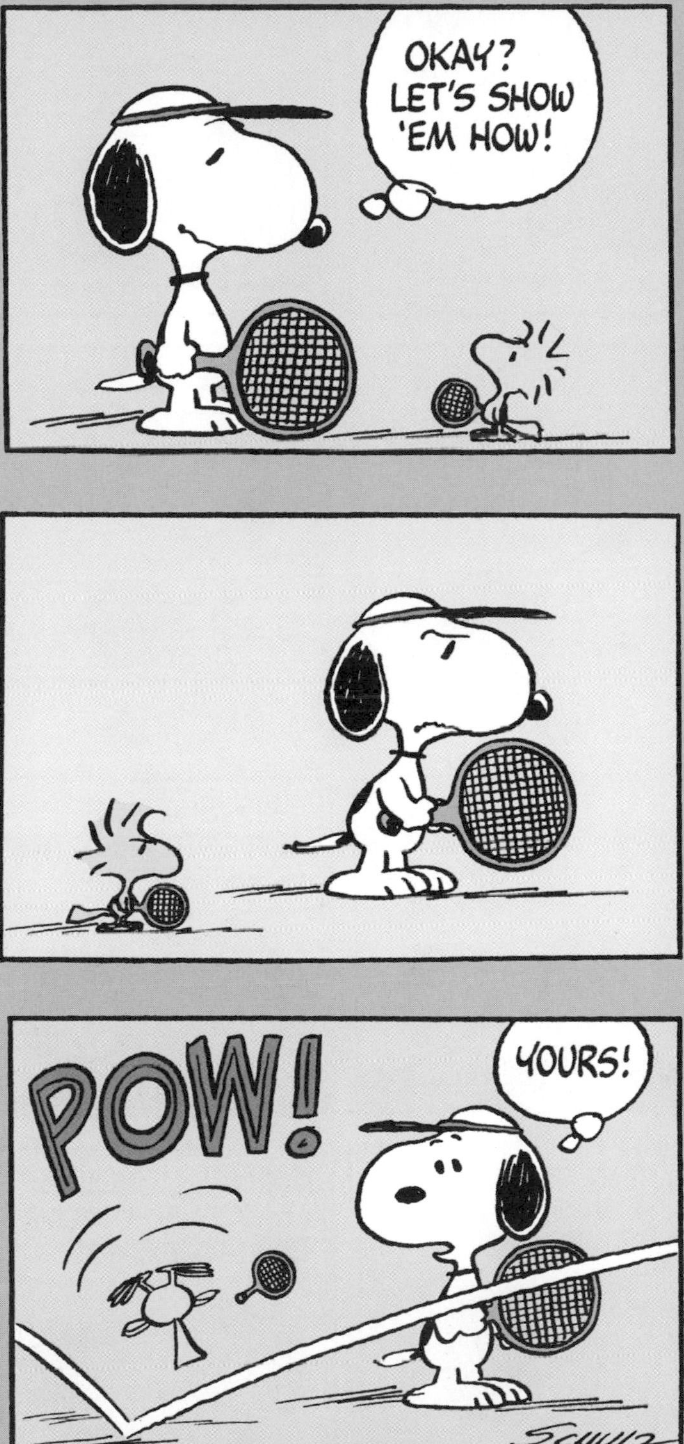
OKAY? LET'S SHOW 'EM HOW!
↓
POW!
YOURS!
SCHULZ

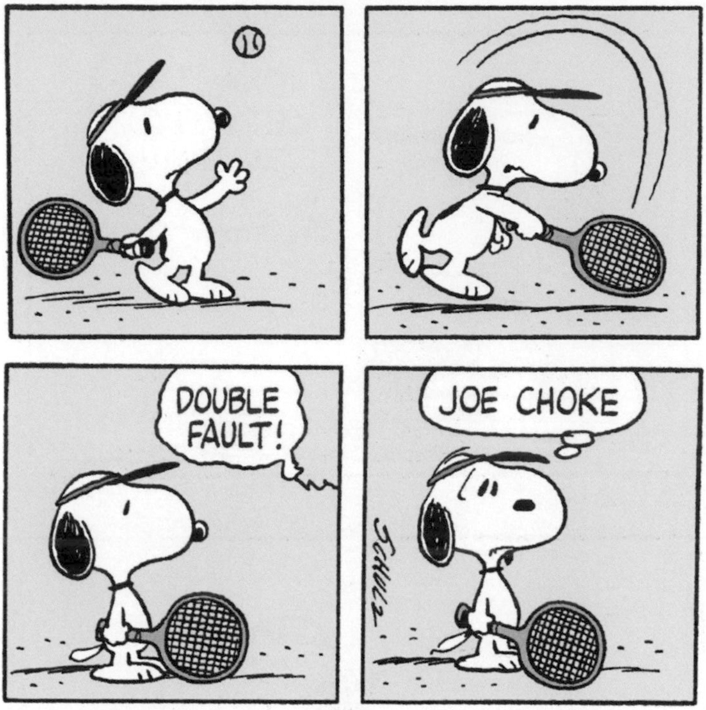
DOUBLE FAULT!
JOE CHOKE
SCHULZ

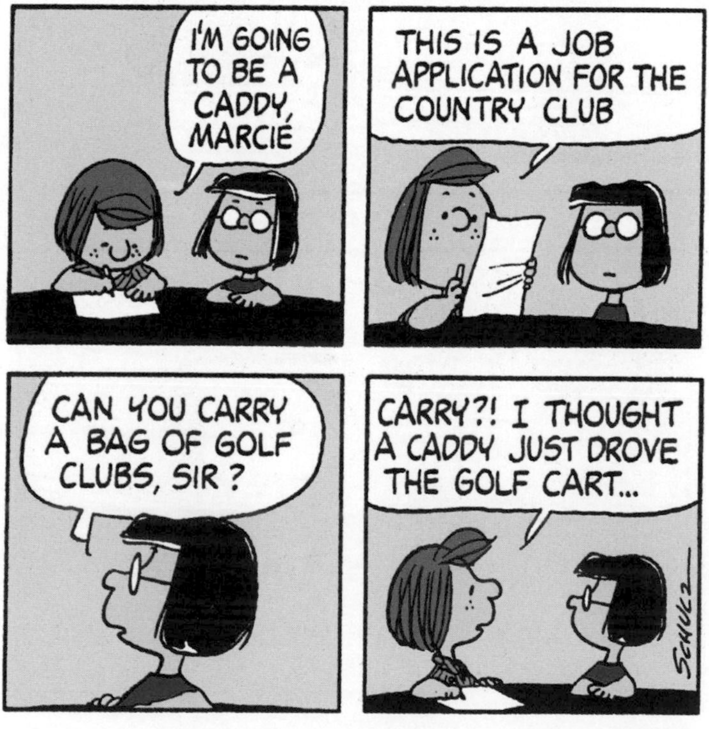
I'M GOING TO BE A CADDY, MARCIE
THIS IS A JOB APPLICATION FOR THE COUNTRY CLUB
CAN YOU CARRY A BAG OF GOLF CLUBS, SIR ?
CARRY?! I THOUGHT A CADDY JUST DROVE THE GOLF CART...
SCHULZ

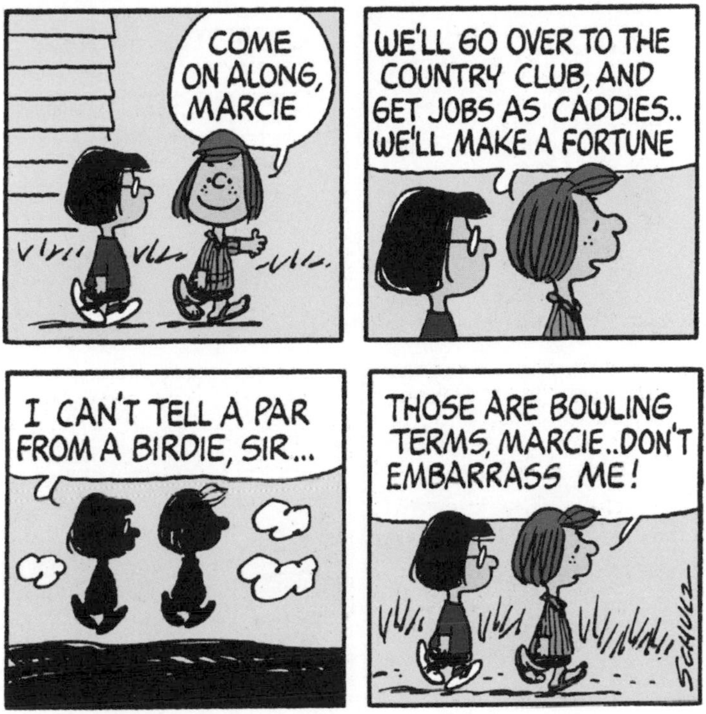
COME ON ALONG, MARCIE
WE'LL GO OVER TO THE COUNTRY CLUB, AND GET JOBS AS CADDIES.. WE'LL MAKE A FORTUNE
I CAN'T TELL A PAR FROM A BIRDIE, SIR...
THOSE ARE BOWLING TERMS, MARCIE..DON'T EMBARRASS ME!
SCHULZ

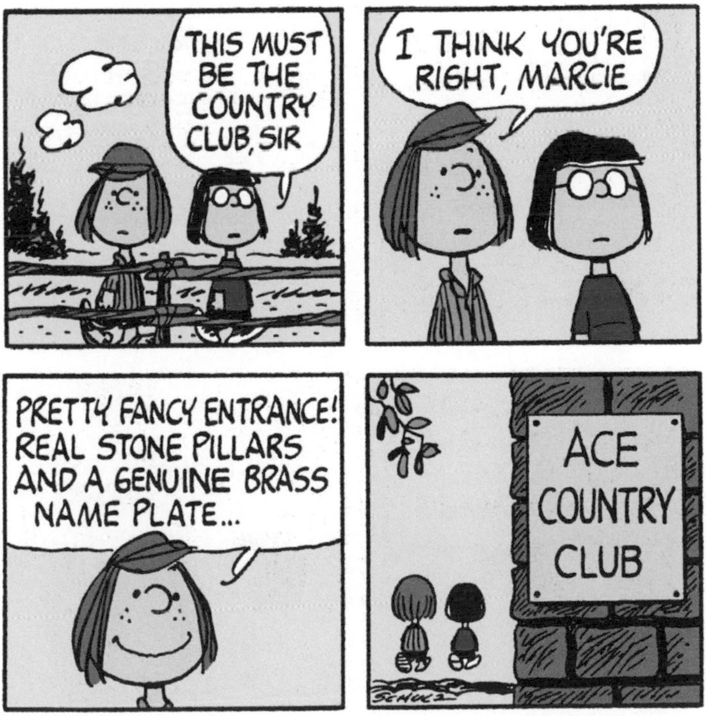
THIS MUST BE THE COUNTRY CLUB, SIR
I THINK YOU'RE RIGHT, MARCIE
PRETTY FANCY ENTRANCE! REAL STONE PILLARS AND A GENUINE BRASS NAME PLATE...
ACE COUNTRY CLUB
SCHULZ

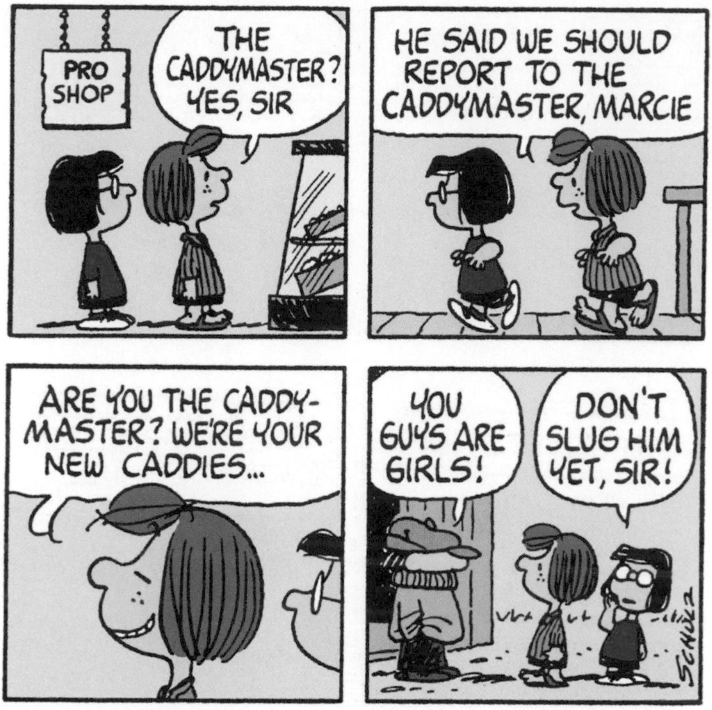
PRO SHOP
THE CADDYMASTER? YES, SIR
HE SAID WE SHOULD REPORT TO THE CADDYMASTER, MARCIE
ARE YOU THE CADDY-MASTER? WE'RE YOUR NEW CADDIES...
YOU GUYS ARE GIRLS!
DON'T SLUG HIM YET, SIR!
SCHULZ

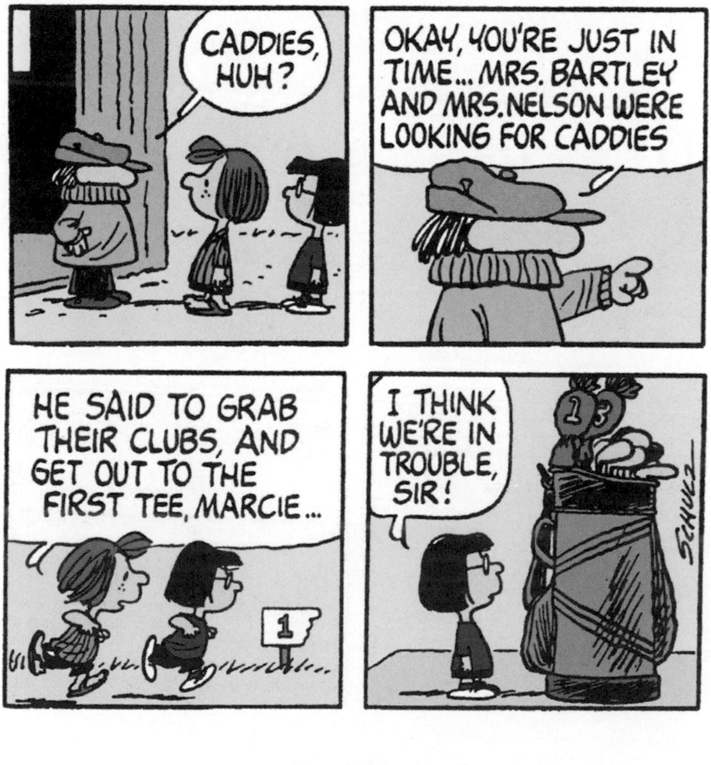
CADDIES, HUH?
OKAY, YOU'RE JUST IN TIME... MRS. BARTLEY AND MRS. NELSON WERE LOOKING FOR CADDIES
HE SAID TO GRAB THEIR CLUBS, AND GET OUT TO THE FIRST TEE, MARCIE...
1
I THINK WE'RE IN TROUBLE, SIR!
SCHULZ

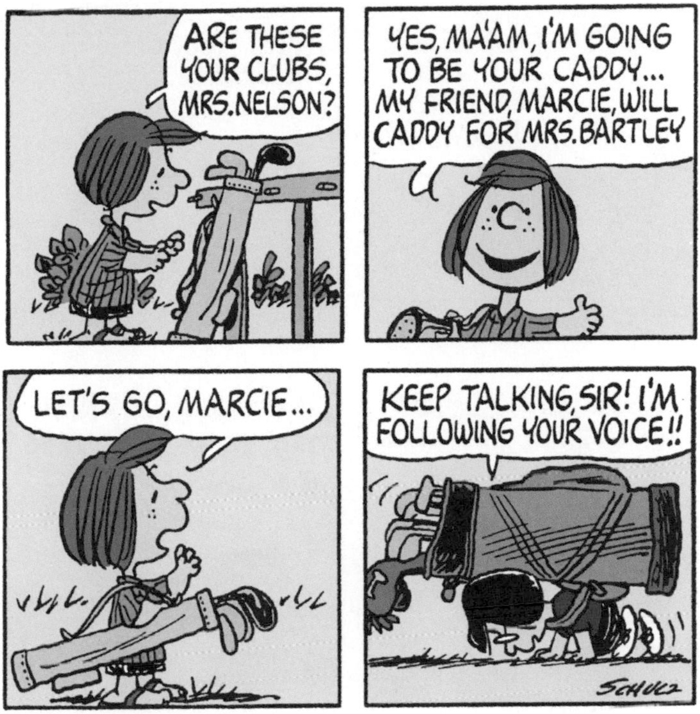
ARE THESE YOUR CLUBS, MRS.NELSON?
YES, MA'AM, I'M GOING TO BE YOUR CADDY... MY FRIEND, MARCIE, WILL CADDY FOR MRS.BARTLEY
LET'S GO, MARCIE...
KEEP TALKING, SIR! I'M FOLLOWING YOUR VOICE!!
SCHULZ

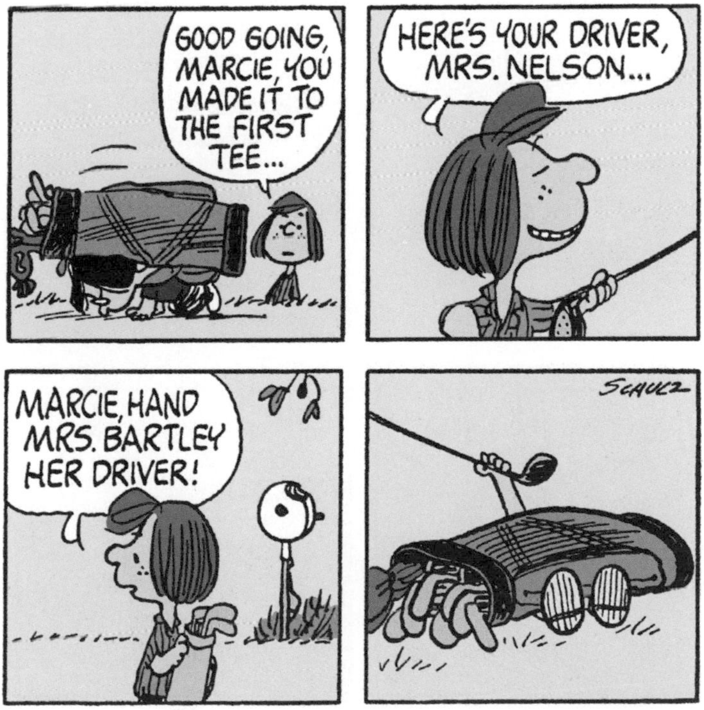
GOOD GOING, MARCIE, YOU MADE IT TO THE FIRST TEE...
HERE'S YOUR DRIVER, MRS. NELSON...
MARCIE, HAND MRS. BARTLEY HER DRIVER!
SCHULZ

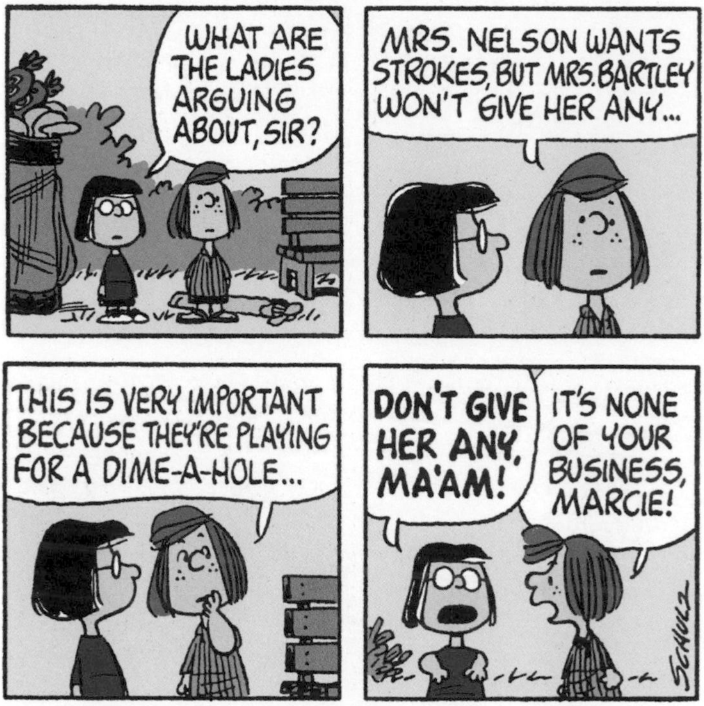
WHAT ARE THE LADIES ARGUING ABOUT, SIR?
MRS. NELSON WANTS STROKES, BUT MRS. BARTLEY WON'T GIVE HER ANY...
THIS IS VERY IMPORTANT BECAUSE THEY'RE PLAYING FOR A DIME-A-HOLE...
DON'T GIVE HER ANY, MA'AM!
IT'S NONE OF YOUR BUSINESS, MARCIE!
SCHULZ

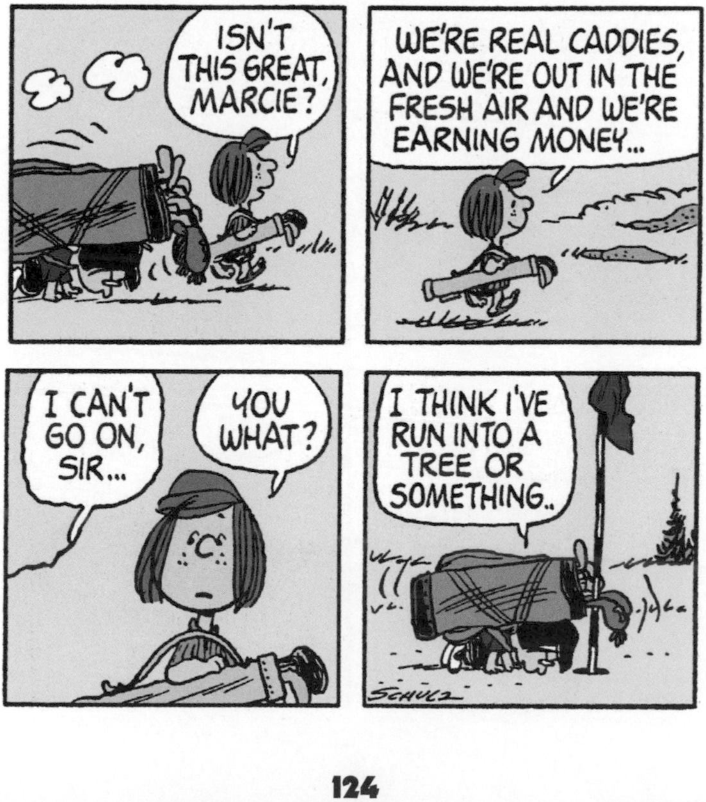
ISN'T THIS GREAT, MARCIE?
WE'RE REAL CADDIES, AND WE'RE OUT IN THE FRESH AIR AND WE'RE EARNING MONEY...
I CAN'T GO ON, SIR...
YOU WHAT?
I THINK I'VE RUN INTO A TREE OR SOMETHING..
SCHULZ

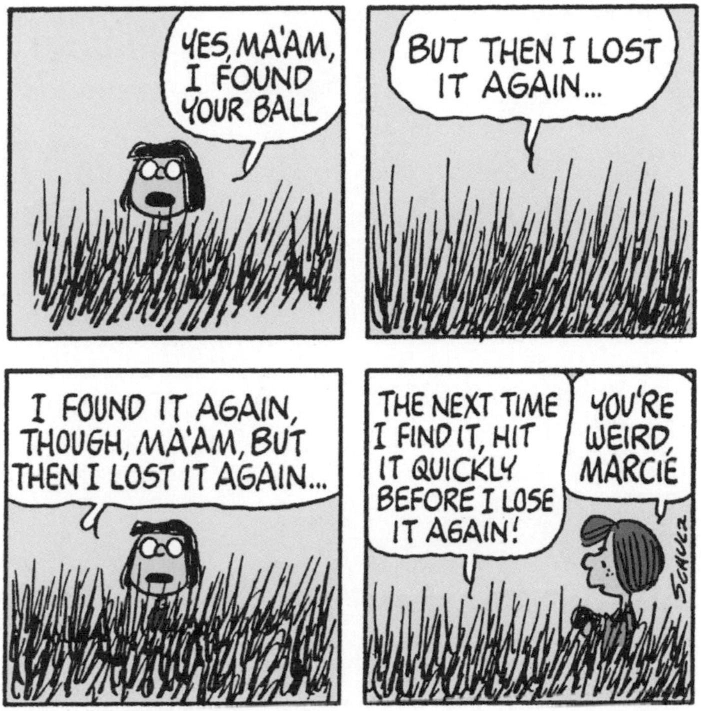
YES, MA'AM, I FOUND YOUR BALL
BUT THEN I LOST IT AGAIN...
I FOUND IT AGAIN, THOUGH, MA'AM, BUT THEN I LOST IT AGAIN...
THE NEXT TIME I FIND IT, HIT IT QUICKLY BEFORE I LOSE IT AGAIN!
YOU'RE WEIRD, MARCIE
SCHULZ

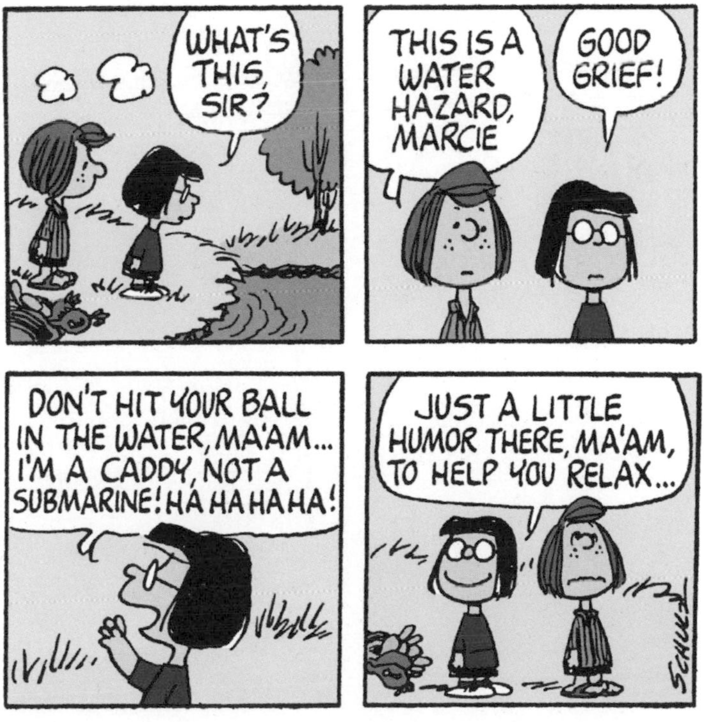
WHAT'S THIS, SIR?
THIS IS A WATER HAZARD, MARCIE
GOOD GRIEF!
DON'T HIT YOUR BALL IN THE WATER, MA'AM... I'M A CADDY, NOT A SUBMARINE! HA HA HA HA!
JUST A LITTLE HUMOR THERE, MA'AM, TO HELP YOU RELAX...
SCHULZ

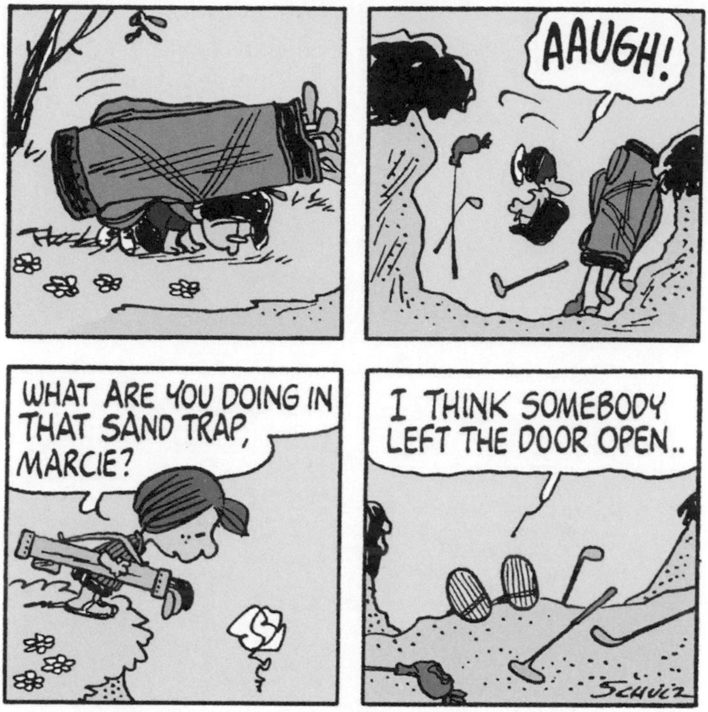
AAUGH!
WHAT ARE YOU DOING IN THAT SAND TRAP, MARCIE?
I THINK SOMEBODY LEFT THE DOOR OPEN..
SCHULZ

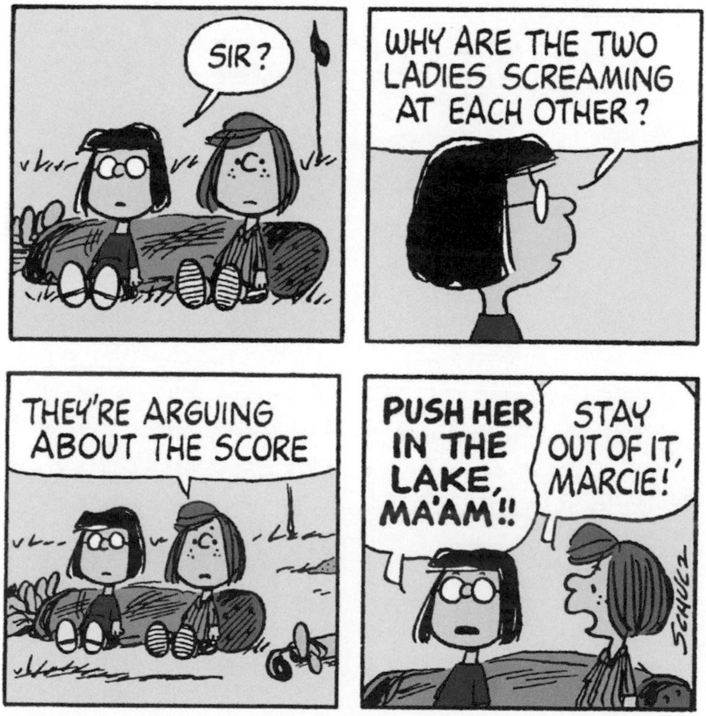
SIR?
WHY ARE THE TWO LADIES SCREAMING AT EACH OTHER?
THEY'RE ARGUING ABOUT THE SCORE
PUSH HER IN THE LAKE, MA'AM!!
STAY OUT OF IT, MARCIE!
SCHULZ

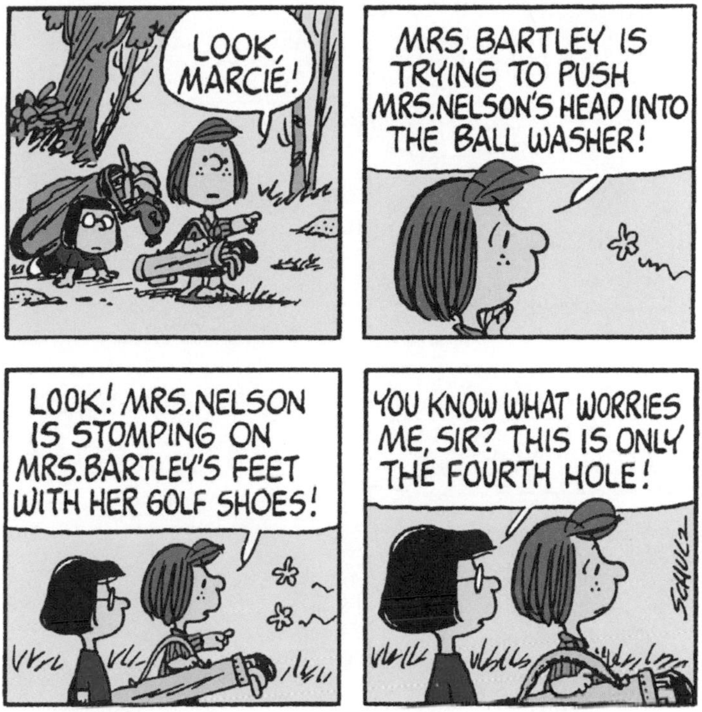
LOOK, MARCIÉ!
MRS. BARTLEY IS TRYING TO PUSH MRS.NELSON'S HEAD INTO THE BALL WASHER!
LOOK! MRS.NELSON IS STOMPING ON MRS.BARTLEY'S FEET WITH HER GOLF SHOES!
YOU KNOW WHAT WORRIES ME, SIR? THIS IS ONLY THE FOURTH HOLE!
SCHULZ

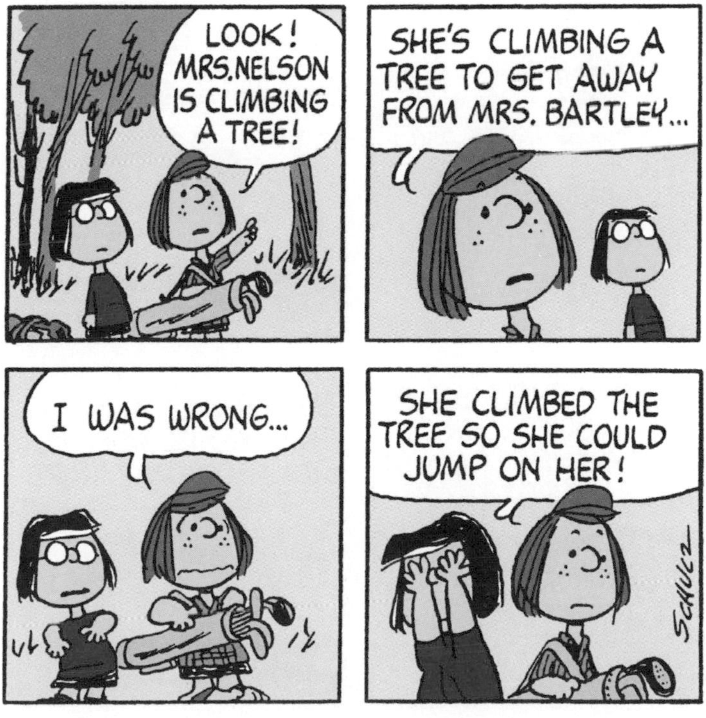
LOOK! MRS.NELSON IS CLIMBING A TREE!
SHE'S CLIMBING A TREE TO GET AWAY FROM MRS. BARTLEY...
I WAS WRONG...
SHE CLIMBED THE TREE SO SHE COULD JUMP ON HER!
SCHULZ

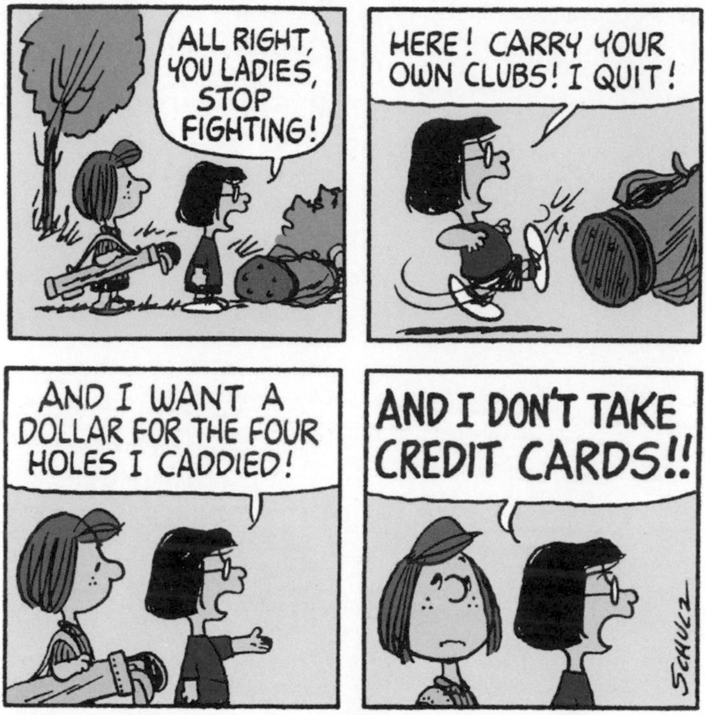
ALL RIGHT, YOU LADIES, STOP FIGHTING!
HERE! CARRY YOUR OWN CLUBS! I QUIT!
AND I WANT A DOLLAR FOR THE FOUR HOLES I CADDIED!
AND I DON'T TAKE CREDIT CARDS!!
SCHULZ

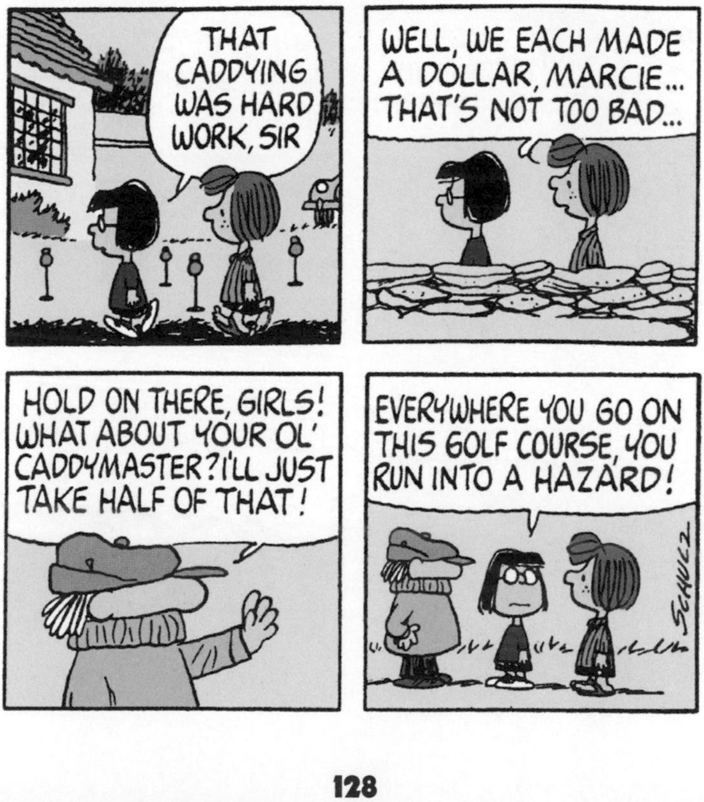
THAT CADDYING WAS HARD WORK, SIR
WELL, WE EACH MADE A DOLLAR, MARCIE... THAT'S NOT TOO BAD...
HOLD ON THERE, GIRLS! WHAT ABOUT YOUR OL' CADDYMASTER? I'LL JUST TAKE HALF OF THAT!
EVERYWHERE YOU GO ON THIS GOLF COURSE, YOU RUN INTO A HAZARD!
SCHULZ

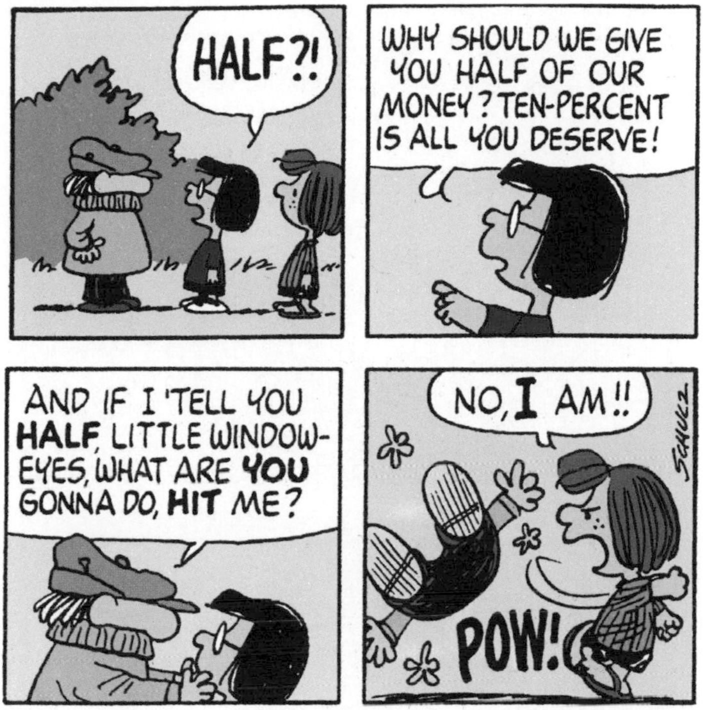
HALF?!
WHY SHOULD WE GIVE YOU HALF OF OUR MONEY? TEN-PERCENT IS ALL YOU DESERVE!
AND IF I 'TELL YOU **HALF**, LITTLE WINDOW-EYES, WHAT ARE **YOU** GONNA DO, **HIT** ME?
NO, **I** AM!!
POW!
SCHULZ

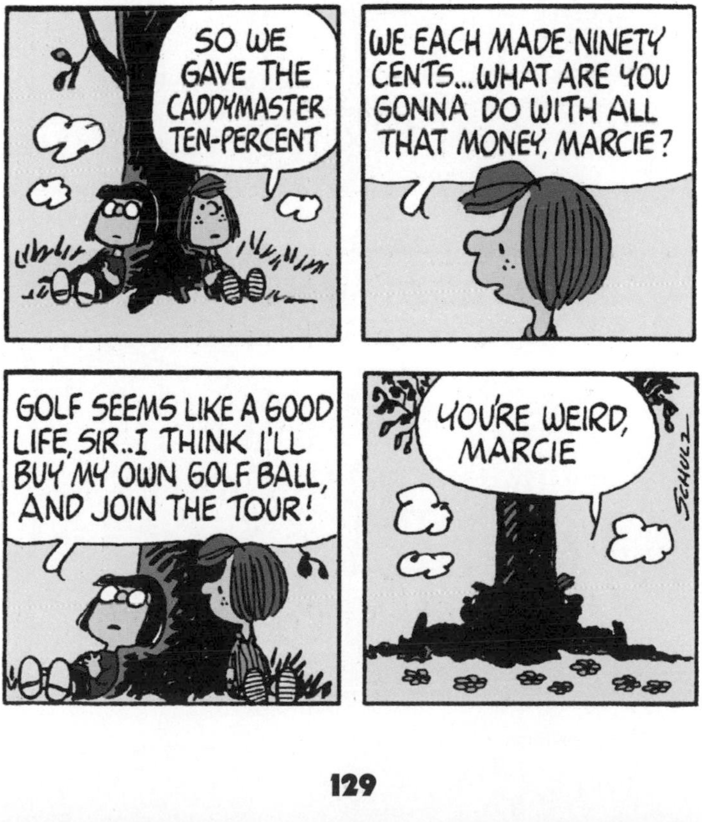
SO WE GAVE THE CADDYMASTER TEN-PERCENT
WE EACH MADE NINETY CENTS...WHAT ARE YOU GONNA DO WITH ALL THAT MONEY, MARCIE?
GOLF SEEMS LIKE A GOOD LIFE, SIR..I THINK I'LL BUY MY OWN GOLF BALL, AND JOIN THE TOUR!
YOU'RE WEIRD, MARCIE
SCHULZ

WHAT ABOUT MY STOMACH? MY STOMACH IS GETTING WET!
HOW ABOUT MY FEET?
MY FEET ARE GETTING SOAKED!
SO HOW ABOUT MY NOSE? NOW, MY NOSE IS GETTING WET!
!

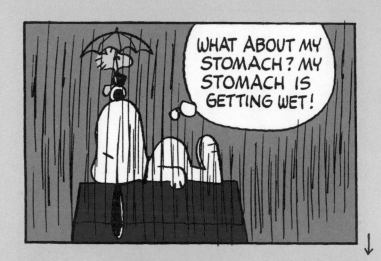

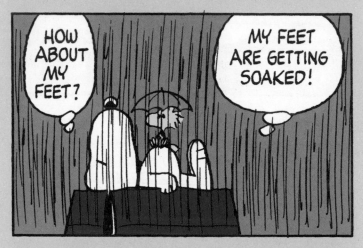

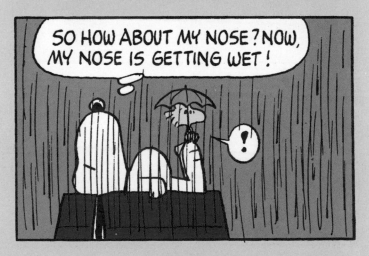

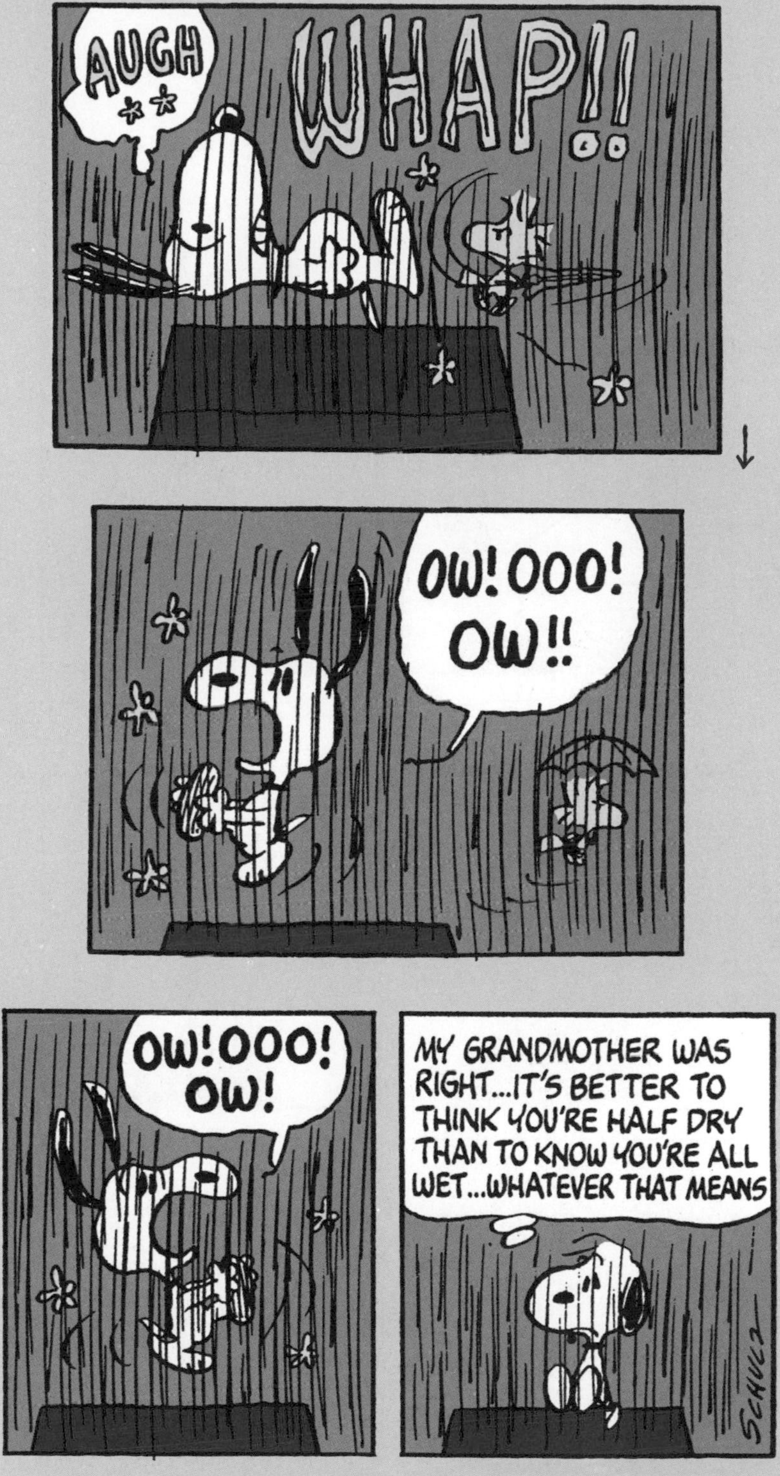
AUGH
WHAP!!
OW! OOO! OW!!
OW! OOO! OW!
MY GRANDMOTHER WAS RIGHT...IT'S BETTER TO THINK YOU'RE HALF DRY THAN TO KNOW YOU'RE ALL WET...WHATEVER THAT MEANS
SCHULZ

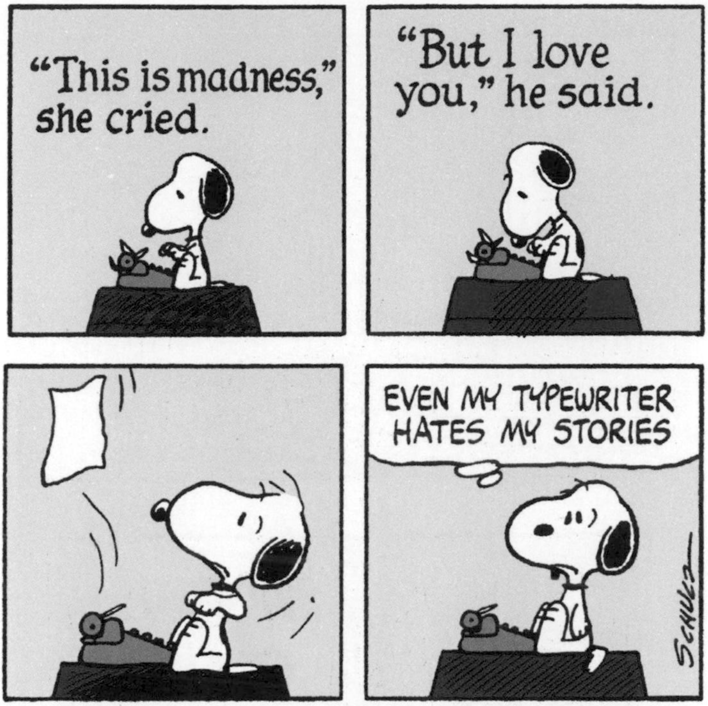
"This is madness," she cried.
"But I love you," he said.
EVEN MY TYPEWRITER HATES MY STORIES
SCHULZ

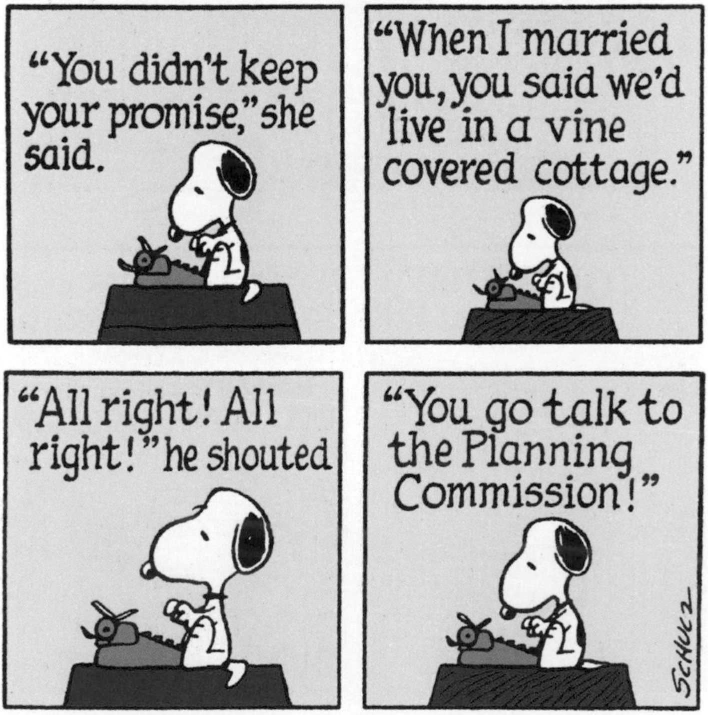
"You didn't keep your promise," she said.
"When I married you, you said we'd live in a vine covered cottage."
"All right! All right!" he shouted
"You go talk to the Planning Commission!"
SCHULZ

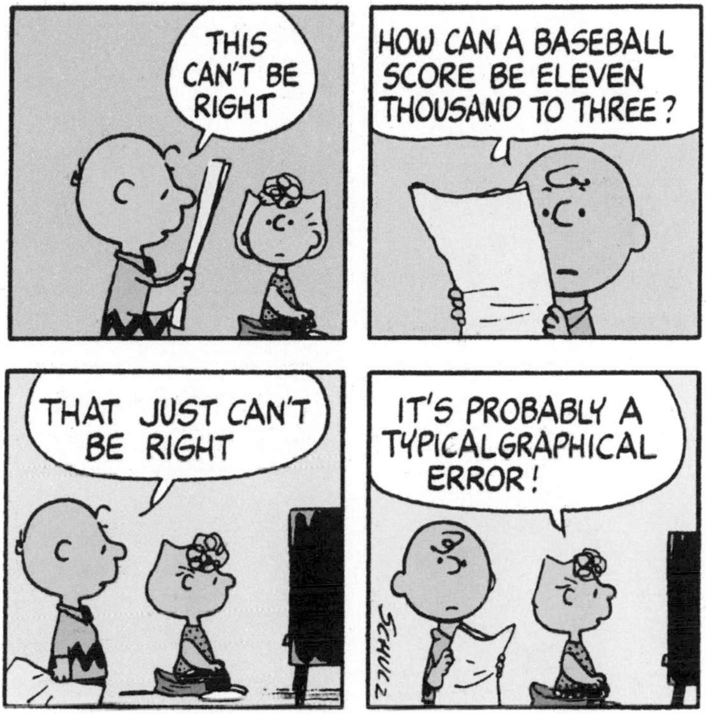
THIS CAN'T BE RIGHT
HOW CAN A BASEBALL SCORE BE ELEVEN THOUSAND TO THREE?
THAT JUST CAN'T BE RIGHT
IT'S PROBABLY A TYPICALGRAPHICAL ERROR!

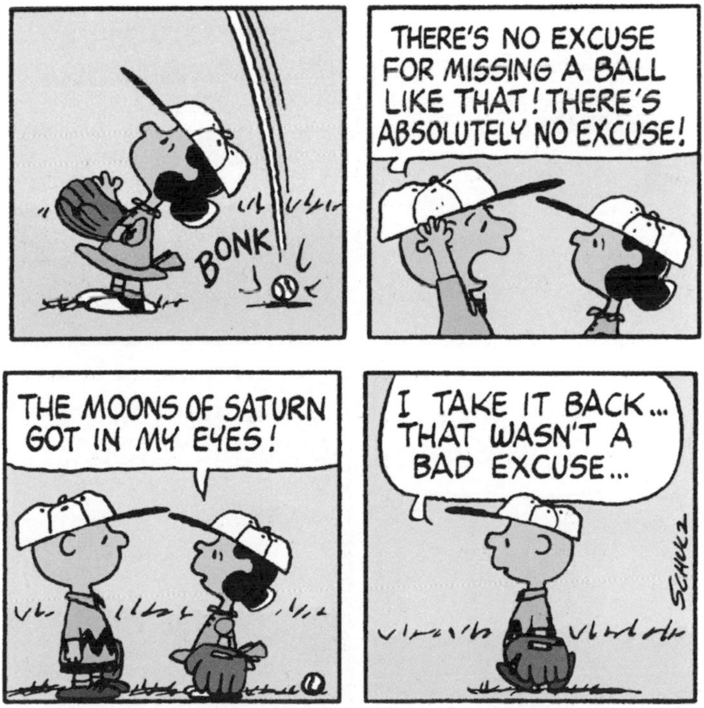
BONK
THERE'S NO EXCUSE FOR MISSING A BALL LIKE THAT! THERE'S ABSOLUTELY NO EXCUSE!
THE MOONS OF SATURN GOT IN MY EYES!
I TAKE IT BACK... THAT WASN'T A BAD EXCUSE...

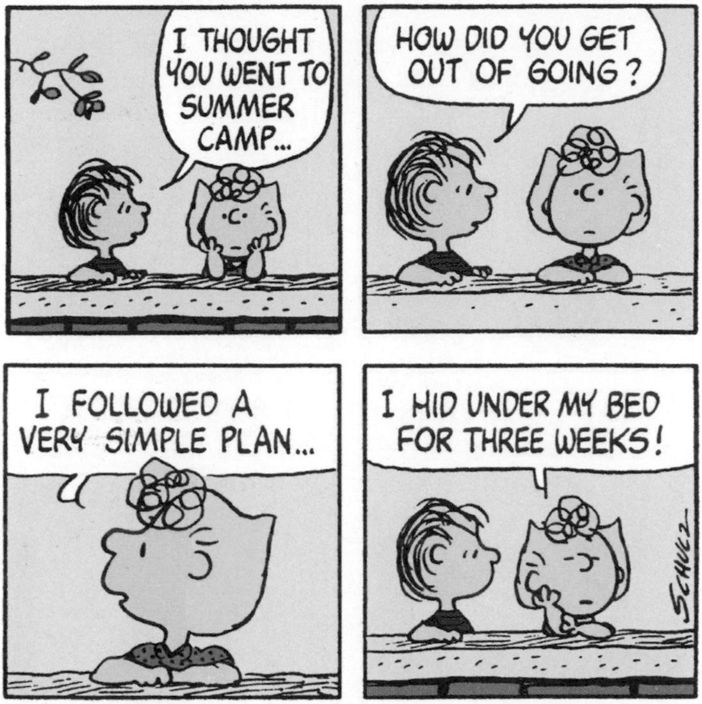
I THOUGHT YOU WENT TO SUMMER CAMP...
HOW DID YOU GET OUT OF GOING?
I FOLLOWED A VERY SIMPLE PLAN...
I HID UNDER MY BED FOR THREE WEEKS!
SCHULZ

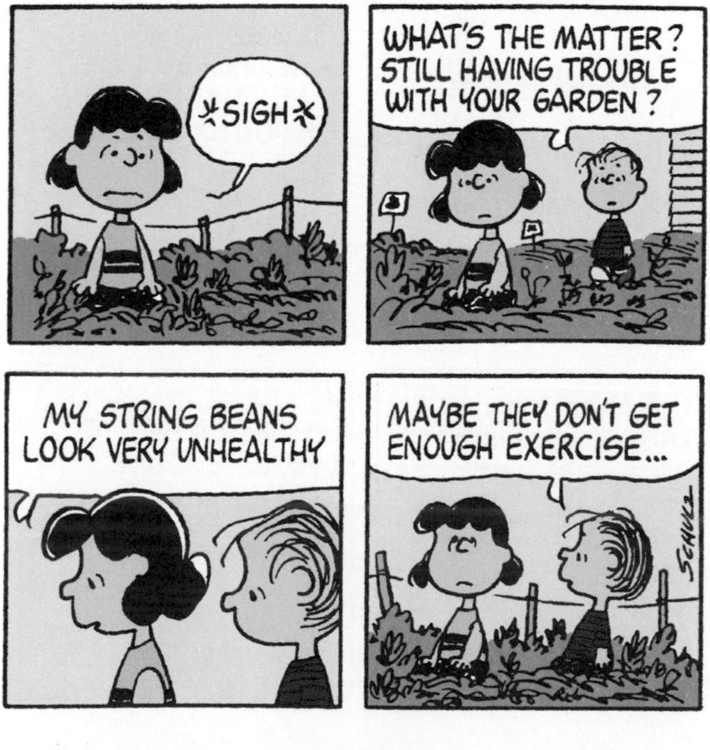
SIGH
WHAT'S THE MATTER? STILL HAVING TROUBLE WITH YOUR GARDEN?
MY STRING BEANS LOOK VERY UNHEALTHY
MAYBE THEY DON'T GET ENOUGH EXERCISE...
SCHULZ

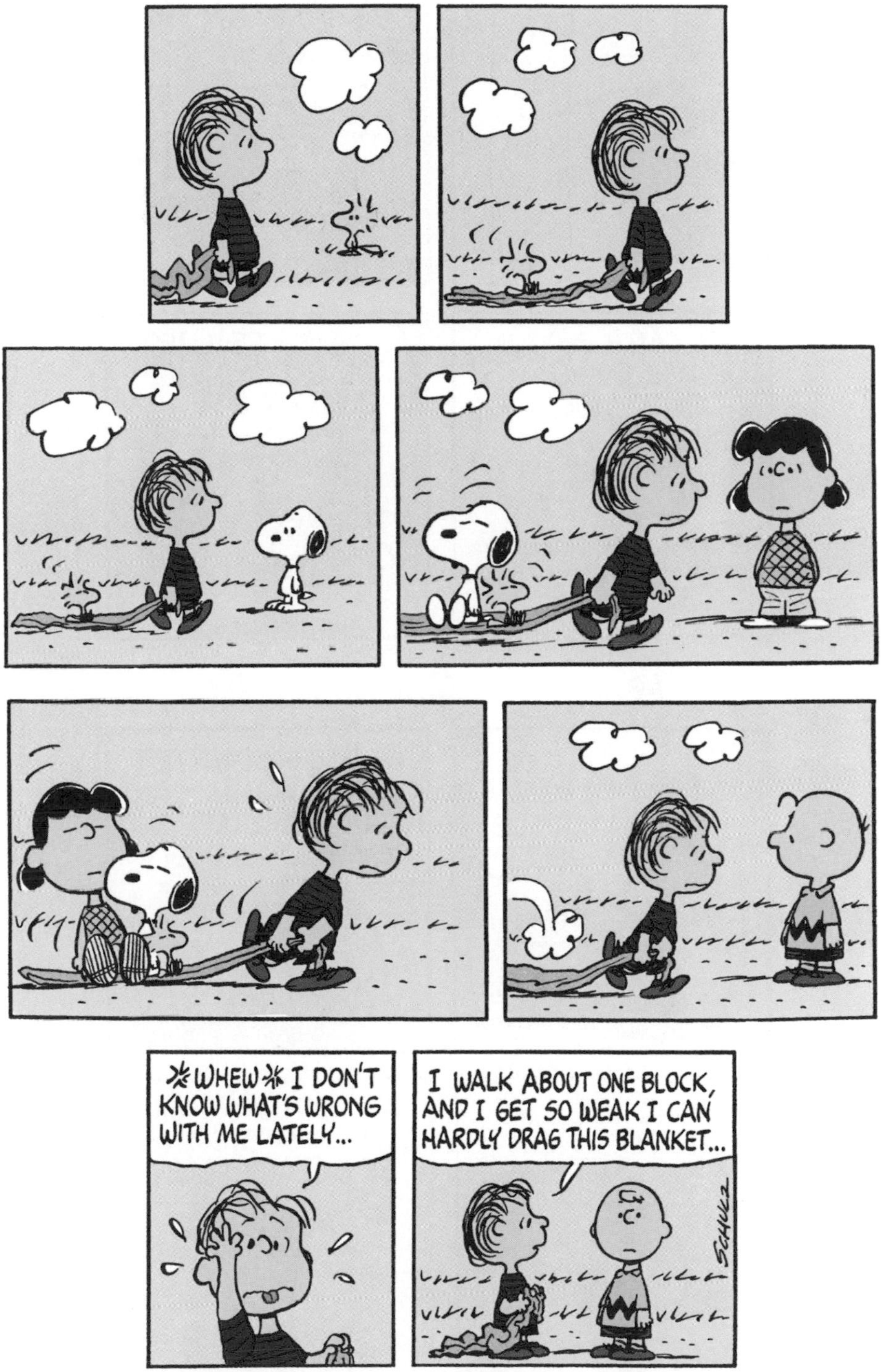
WHEW I DON'T KNOW WHAT'S WRONG WITH ME LATELY...
I WALK ABOUT ONE BLOCK, AND I GET SO WEAK I CAN HARDLY DRAG THIS BLANKET...
SCHULZ

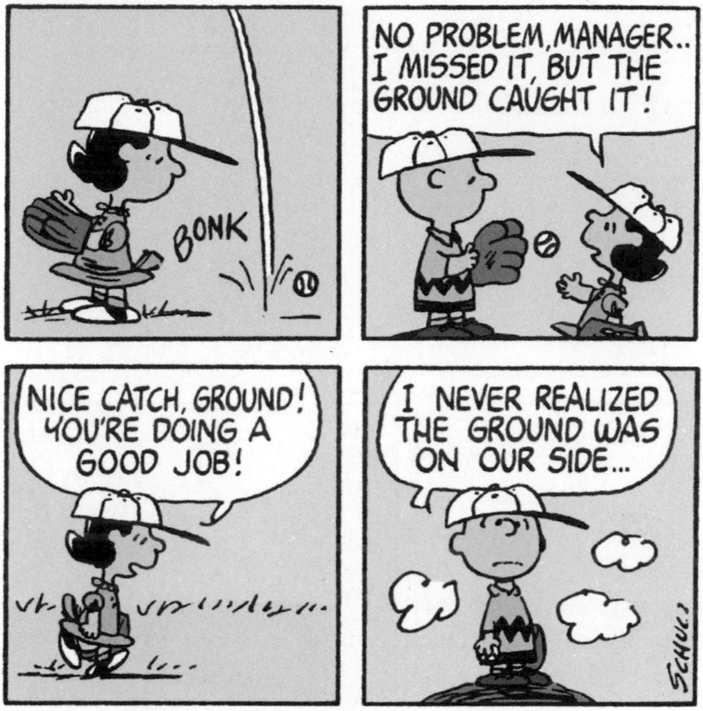
BONK
NO PROBLEM, MANAGER.. I MISSED IT, BUT THE GROUND CAUGHT IT!
NICE CATCH, GROUND! YOU'RE DOING A GOOD JOB!
I NEVER REALIZED THE GROUND WAS ON OUR SIDE...

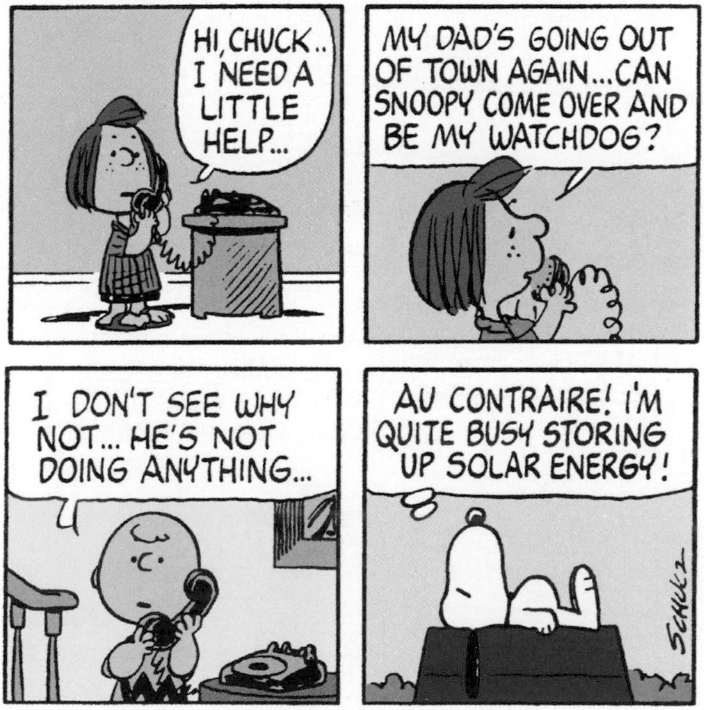
HI, CHUCK.. I NEED A LITTLE HELP...
MY DAD'S GOING OUT OF TOWN AGAIN...CAN SNOOPY COME OVER AND BE MY WATCHDOG?
I DON'T SEE WHY NOT... HE'S NOT DOING ANYTHING...
AU CONTRAIRE! I'M QUITE BUSY STORING UP SOLAR ENERGY!

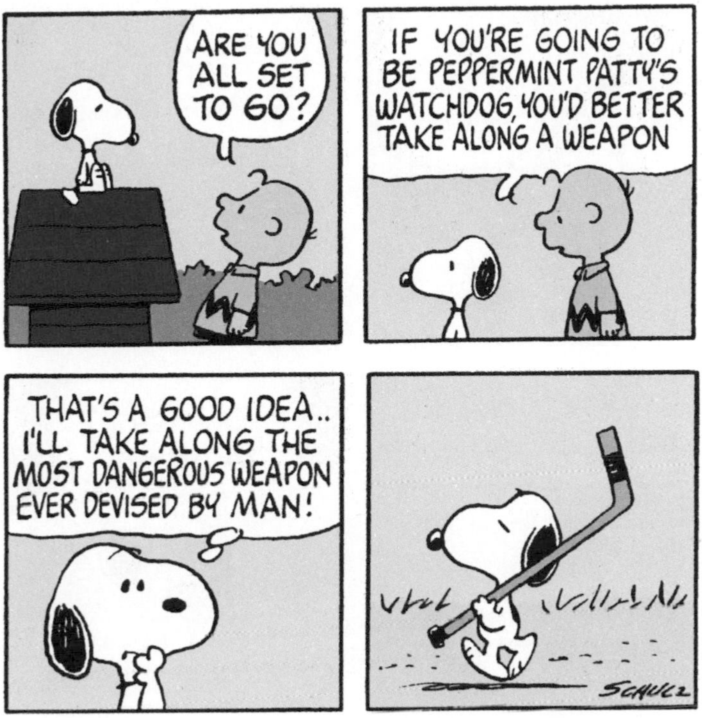
ARE YOU ALL SET TO GO?
IF YOU'RE GOING TO BE PEPPERMINT PATTY'S WATCHDOG, YOU'D BETTER TAKE ALONG A WEAPON
THAT'S A GOOD IDEA.. I'LL TAKE ALONG THE MOST DANGEROUS WEAPON EVER DEVISED BY MAN!
SCHULZ

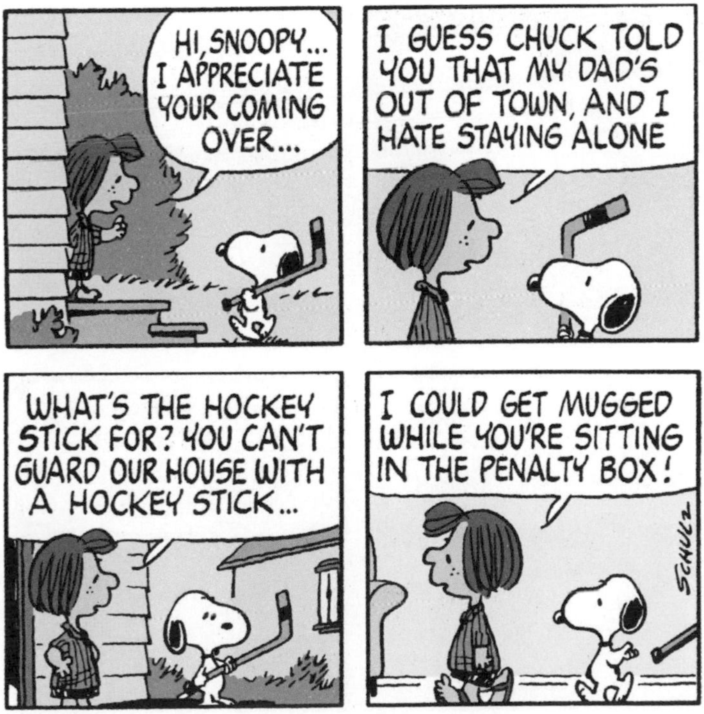
HI, SNOOPY... I APPRECIATE YOUR COMING OVER...
I GUESS CHUCK TOLD YOU THAT MY DAD'S OUT OF TOWN, AND I HATE STAYING ALONE
WHAT'S THE HOCKEY STICK FOR? YOU CAN'T GUARD OUR HOUSE WITH A HOCKEY STICK...
I COULD GET MUGGED WHILE YOU'RE SITTING IN THE PENALTY BOX!
SCHULZ

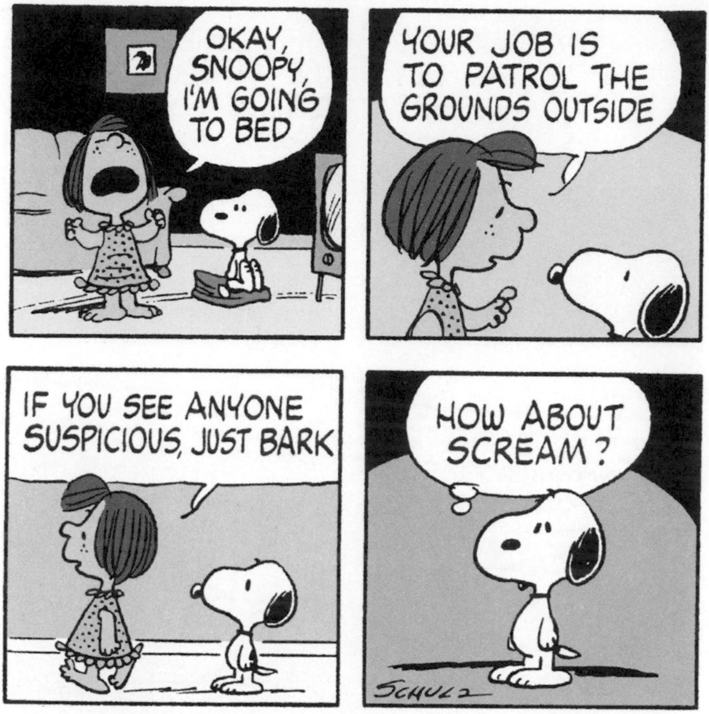
OKAY, SNOOPY, I'M GOING TO BED
YOUR JOB IS TO PATROL THE GROUNDS OUTSIDE
IF YOU SEE ANYONE SUSPICIOUS, JUST BARK
HOW ABOUT SCREAM?
SCHULZ

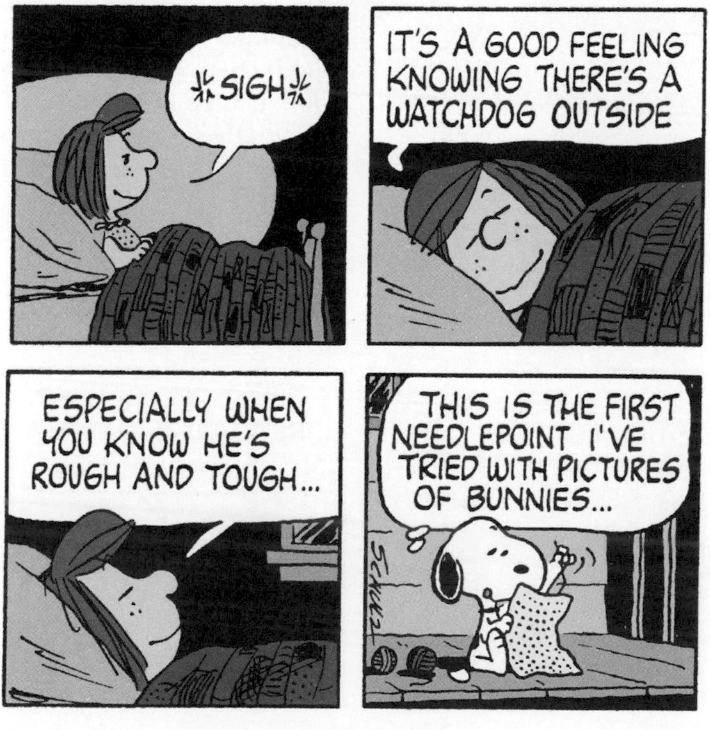
SIGH
IT'S A GOOD FEELING KNOWING THERE'S A WATCHDOG OUTSIDE
ESPECIALLY WHEN YOU KNOW HE'S ROUGH AND TOUGH...
THIS IS THE FIRST NEEDLEPOINT I'VE TRIED WITH PICTURES OF BUNNIES...
SCHULZ

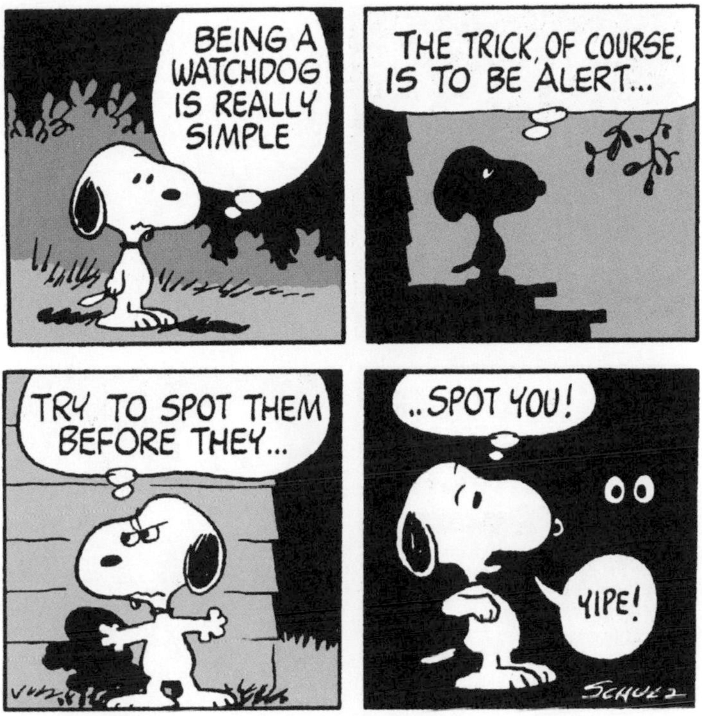
BEING A WATCHDOG IS REALLY SIMPLE
THE TRICK, OF COURSE, IS TO BE ALERT...
TRY TO SPOT THEM BEFORE THEY...
..SPOT YOU!
YIPE!
SCHULZ

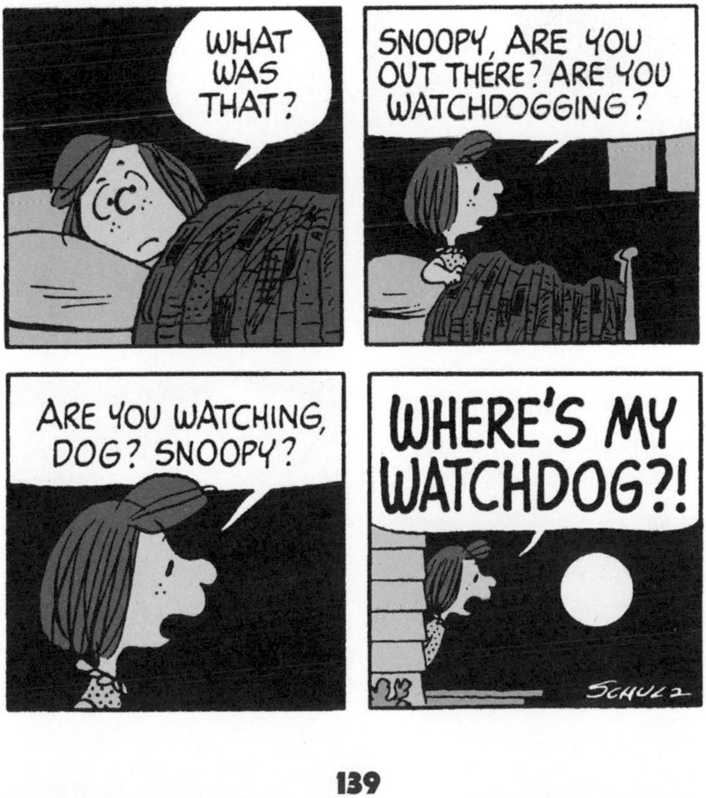
WHAT WAS THAT?
SNOOPY, ARE YOU OUT THERE? ARE YOU WATCHDOGGING?
ARE YOU WATCHING, DOG? SNOOPY?
WHERE'S MY WATCHDOG?!
SCHULZ

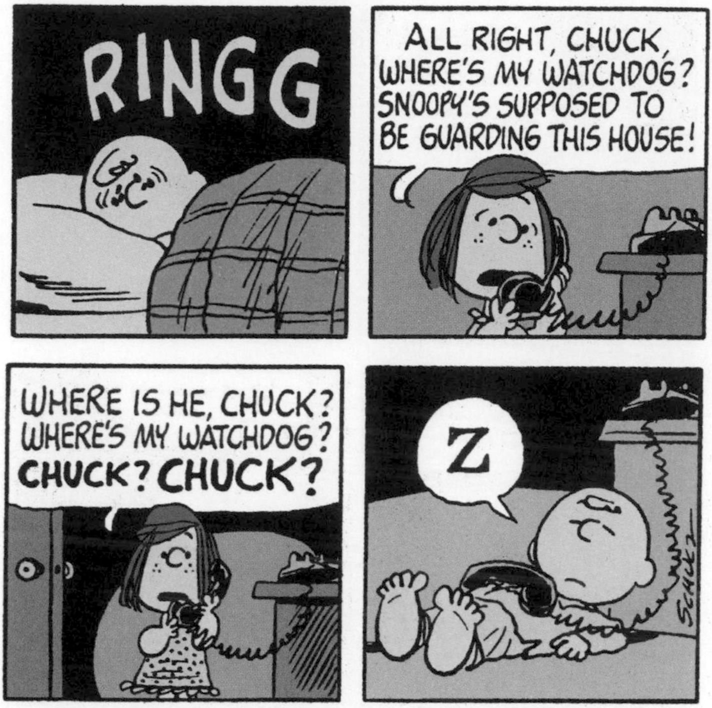
RINGG
ALL RIGHT, CHUCK, WHERE'S MY WATCHDOG? SNOOPY'S SUPPOSED TO BE GUARDING THIS HOUSE!
WHERE IS HE, CHUCK? WHERE'S MY WATCHDOG? CHUCK? CHUCK?
Z

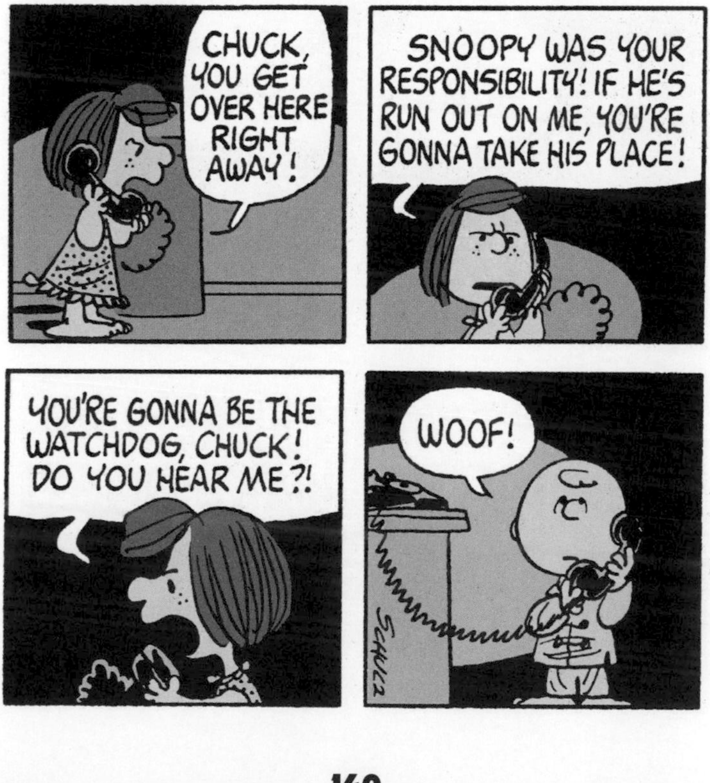
CHUCK, YOU GET OVER HERE RIGHT AWAY!
SNOOPY WAS YOUR RESPONSIBILITY! IF HE'S RUN OUT ON ME, YOU'RE GONNA TAKE HIS PLACE!
YOU'RE GONNA BE THE WATCHDOG, CHUCK! DO YOU HEAR ME?!
WOOF!

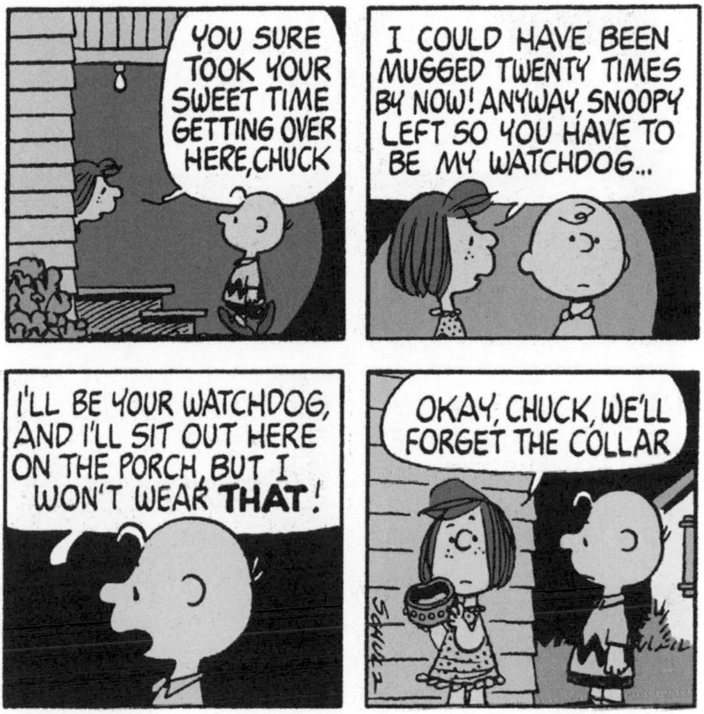
YOU SURE TOOK YOUR SWEET TIME GETTING OVER HERE, CHUCK
I COULD HAVE BEEN MUGGED TWENTY TIMES BY NOW! ANYWAY, SNOOPY LEFT SO YOU HAVE TO BE MY WATCHDOG...
I'LL BE YOUR WATCHDOG, AND I'LL SIT OUT HERE ON THE PORCH, BUT I WON'T WEAR THAT!
OKAY, CHUCK, WE'LL FORGET THE COLLAR
SCHULZ

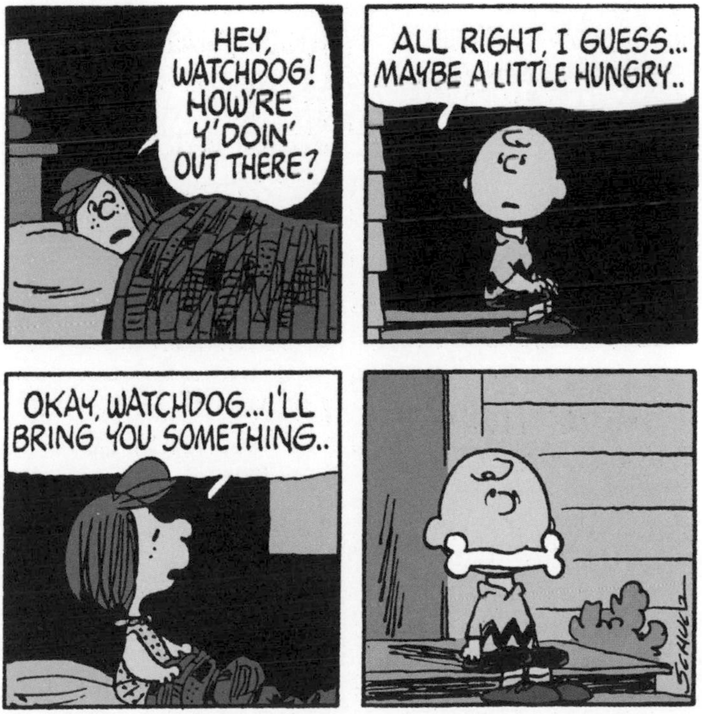
HEY, WATCHDOG! HOW'RE Y'DOIN' OUT THERE?
ALL RIGHT, I GUESS... MAYBE A LITTLE HUNGRY..
OKAY, WATCHDOG...I'LL BRING YOU SOMETHING..
SCHULZ

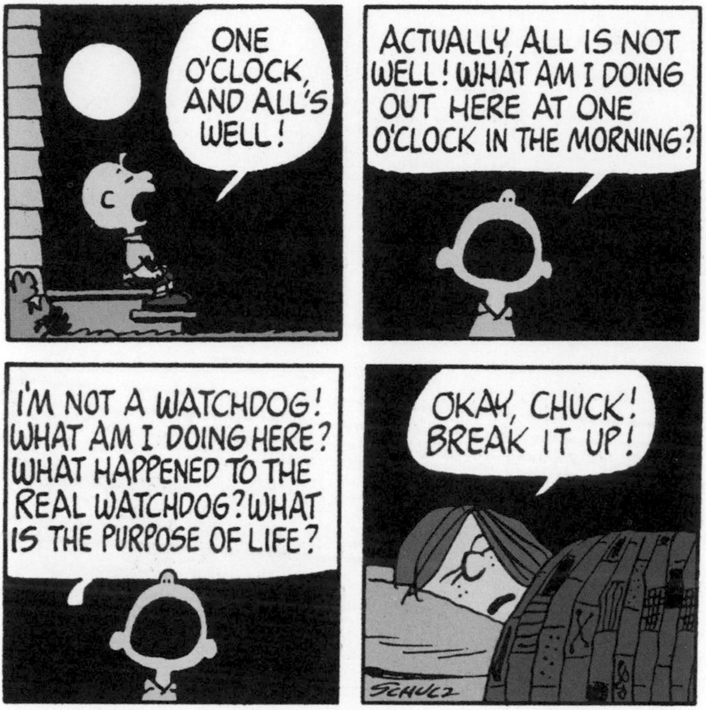
ONE O'CLOCK, AND ALL'S WELL!
ACTUALLY, ALL IS NOT WELL! WHAT AM I DOING OUT HERE AT ONE O'CLOCK IN THE MORNING?
I'M NOT A WATCHDOG! WHAT AM I DOING HERE? WHAT HAPPENED TO THE REAL WATCHDOG? WHAT IS THE PURPOSE OF LIFE?
OKAY, CHUCK! BREAK IT UP!
SCHULZ

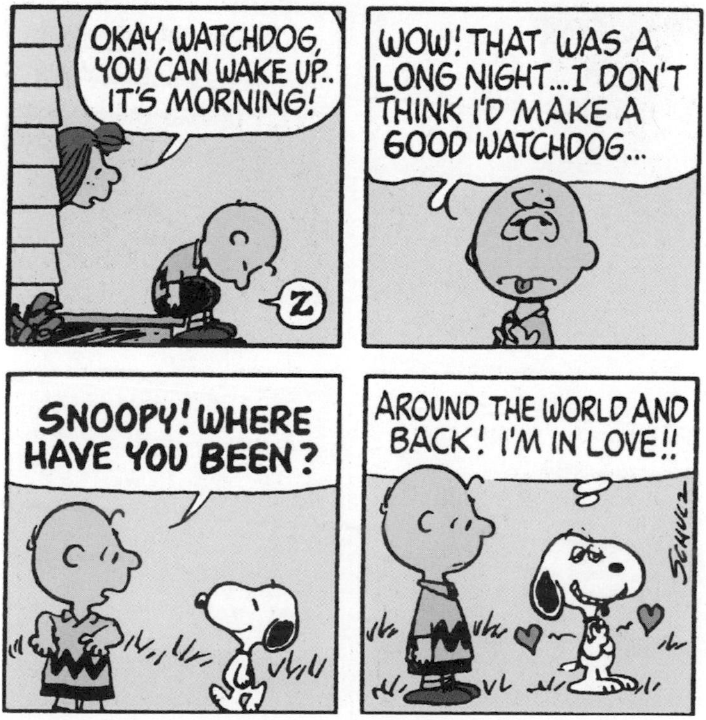
OKAY, WATCHDOG, YOU CAN WAKE UP.. IT'S MORNING!
Z
WOW! THAT WAS A LONG NIGHT...I DON'T THINK I'D MAKE A GOOD WATCHDOG...
SNOOPY! WHERE HAVE YOU BEEN?
AROUND THE WORLD AND BACK! I'M IN LOVE!!
SCHULZ

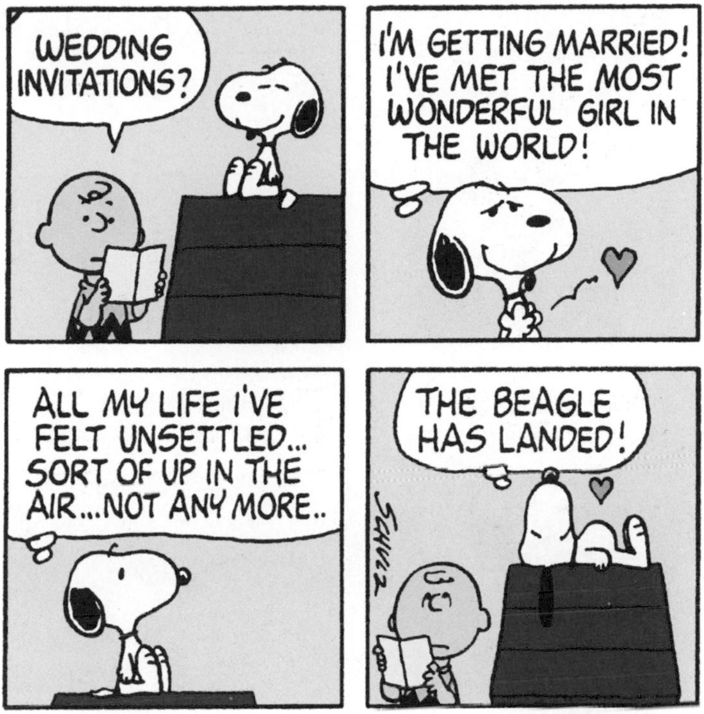
WEDDING INVITATIONS?
I'M GETTING MARRIED! I'VE MET THE MOST WONDERFUL GIRL IN THE WORLD!
ALL MY LIFE I'VE FELT UNSETTLED... SORT OF UP IN THE AIR...NOT ANY MORE..
THE BEAGLE HAS LANDED!

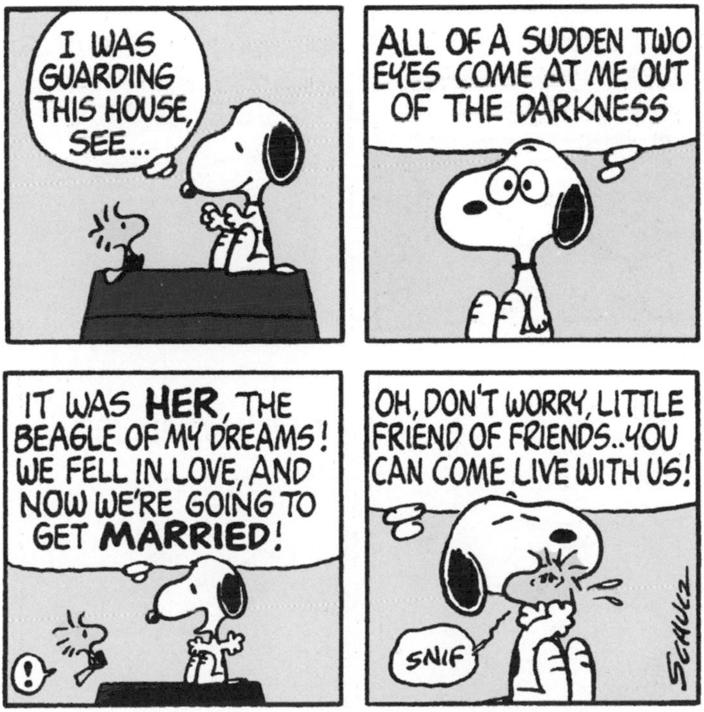
I WAS GUARDING THIS HOUSE, SEE...
ALL OF A SUDDEN TWO EYES COME AT ME OUT OF THE DARKNESS
IT WAS HER, THE BEAGLE OF MY DREAMS! WE FELL IN LOVE, AND NOW WE'RE GOING TO GET MARRIED!
!
OH, DON'T WORRY, LITTLE FRIEND OF FRIENDS..YOU CAN COME LIVE WITH US!
SNIF

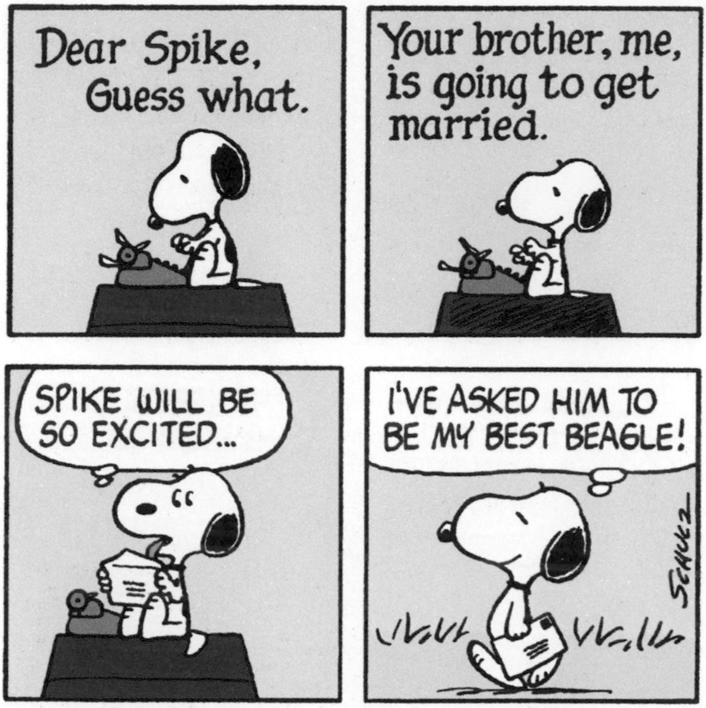
Dear Spike,
Guess what.
Your brother, me, is going to get married.
SPIKE WILL BE SO EXCITED...
I'VE ASKED HIM TO BE MY BEST BEAGLE!
SCHULZ

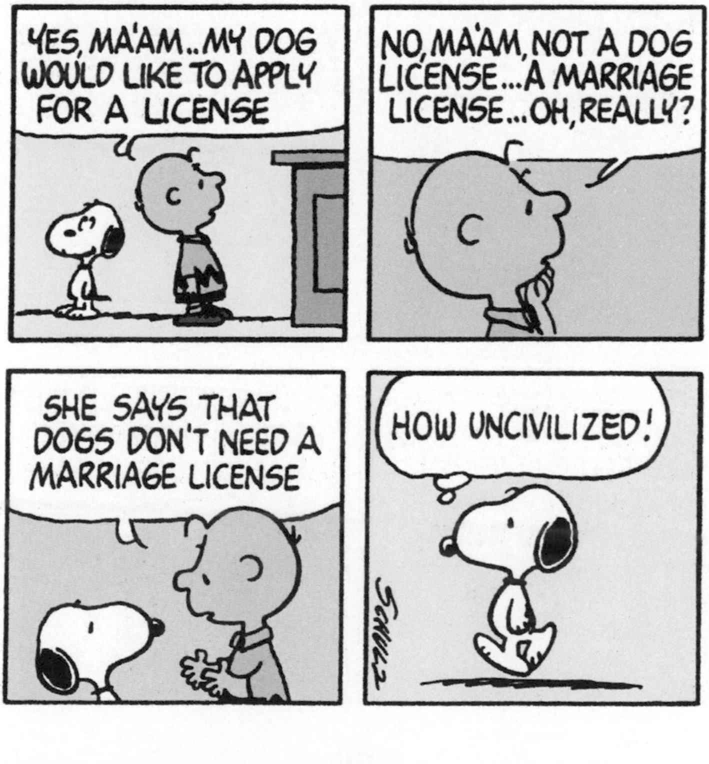
YES, MA'AM..MY DOG WOULD LIKE TO APPLY FOR A LICENSE
NO, MA'AM, NOT A DOG LICENSE...A MARRIAGE LICENSE...OH, REALLY?
SHE SAYS THAT DOGS DON'T NEED A MARRIAGE LICENSE
HOW UNCIVILIZED!
SCHULZ

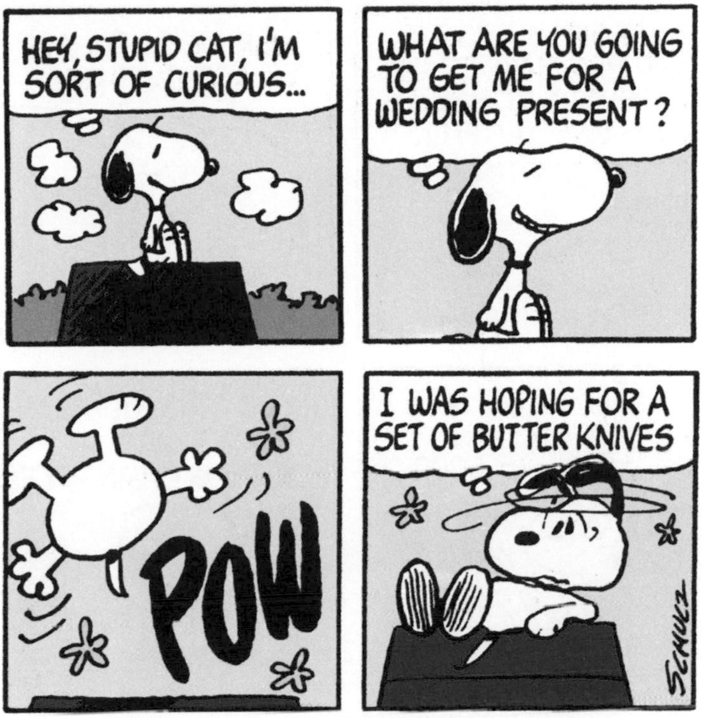
HEY, STUPID CAT, I'M SORT OF CURIOUS...
WHAT ARE YOU GOING TO GET ME FOR A WEDDING PRESENT?
POW
I WAS HOPING FOR A SET OF BUTTER KNIVES
SCHULZ

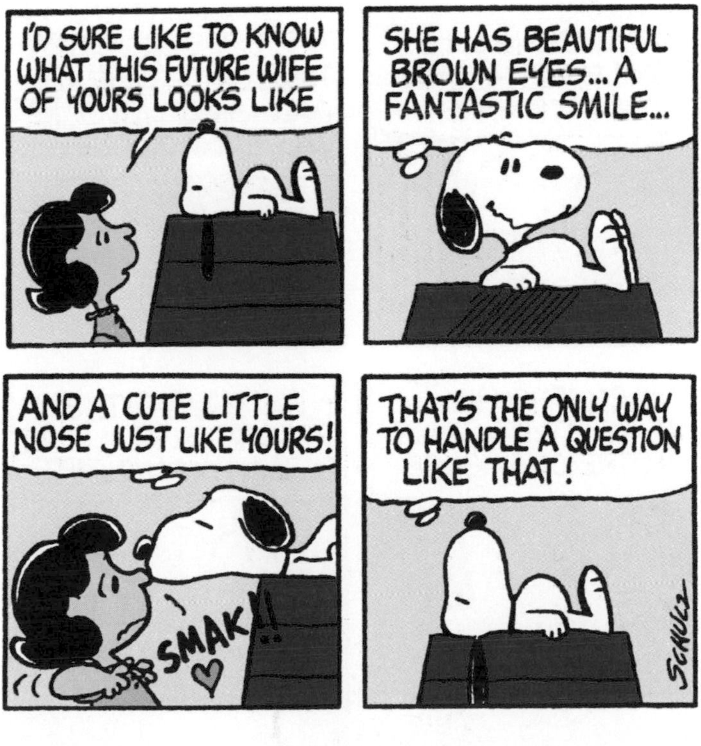
I'D SURE LIKE TO KNOW WHAT THIS FUTURE WIFE OF YOURS LOOKS LIKE
SHE HAS BEAUTIFUL BROWN EYES... A FANTASTIC SMILE...
AND A CUTE LITTLE NOSE JUST LIKE YOURS!
SMAK!
THAT'S THE ONLY WAY TO HANDLE A QUESTION LIKE THAT!
SCHULZ

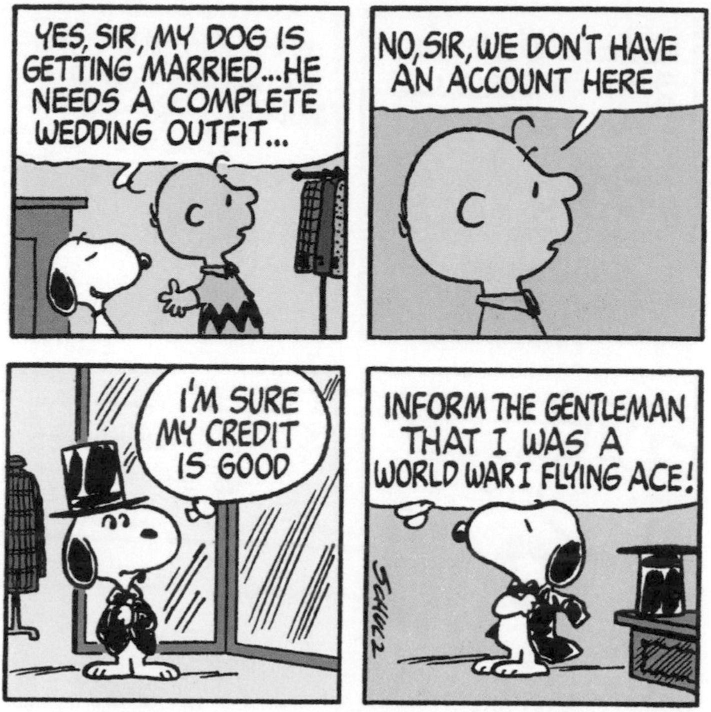
YES, SIR, MY DOG IS GETTING MARRIED...HE NEEDS A COMPLETE WEDDING OUTFIT...
NO, SIR, WE DON'T HAVE AN ACCOUNT HERE
I'M SURE MY CREDIT IS GOOD
INFORM THE GENTLEMAN THAT I WAS A WORLD WAR I FLYING ACE!
SCHULZ

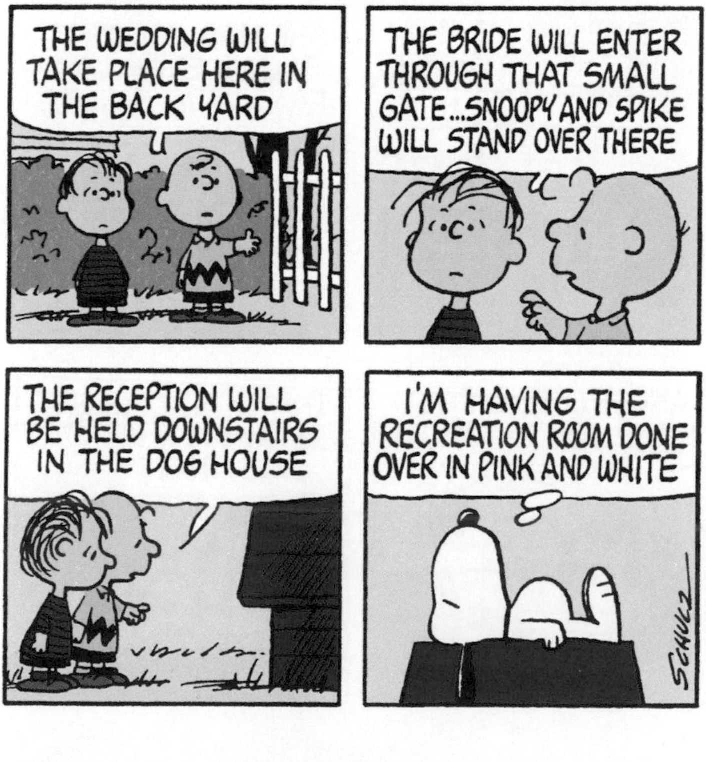
THE WEDDING WILL TAKE PLACE HERE IN THE BACK YARD
THE BRIDE WILL ENTER THROUGH THAT SMALL GATE...SNOOPY AND SPIKE WILL STAND OVER THERE
THE RECEPTION WILL BE HELD DOWNSTAIRS IN THE DOG HOUSE
I'M HAVING THE RECREATION ROOM DONE OVER IN PINK AND WHITE
SCHULZ

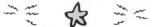

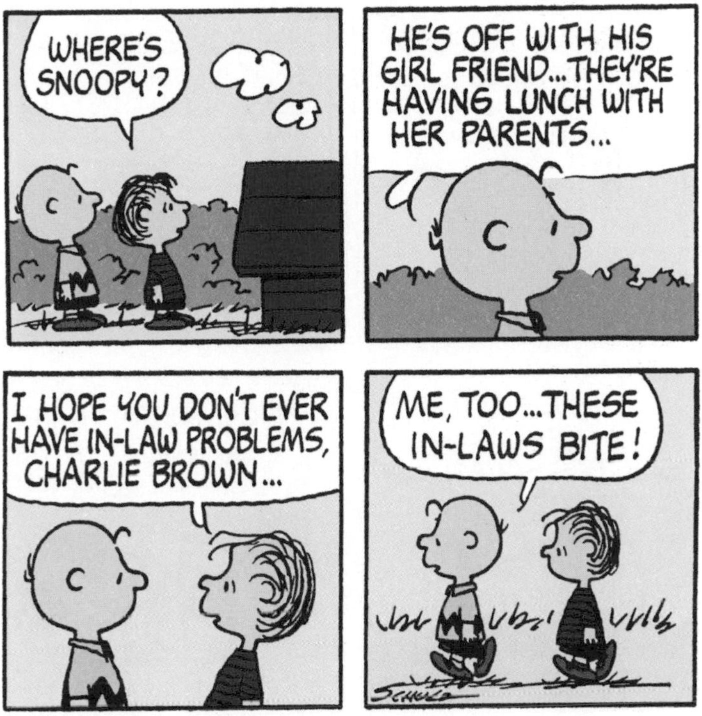
WHERE'S SNOOPY?
HE'S OFF WITH HIS GIRL FRIEND...THEY'RE HAVING LUNCH WITH HER PARENTS...
I HOPE YOU DON'T EVER HAVE IN-LAW PROBLEMS, CHARLIE BROWN...
ME, TOO...THESE IN-LAWS BITE!

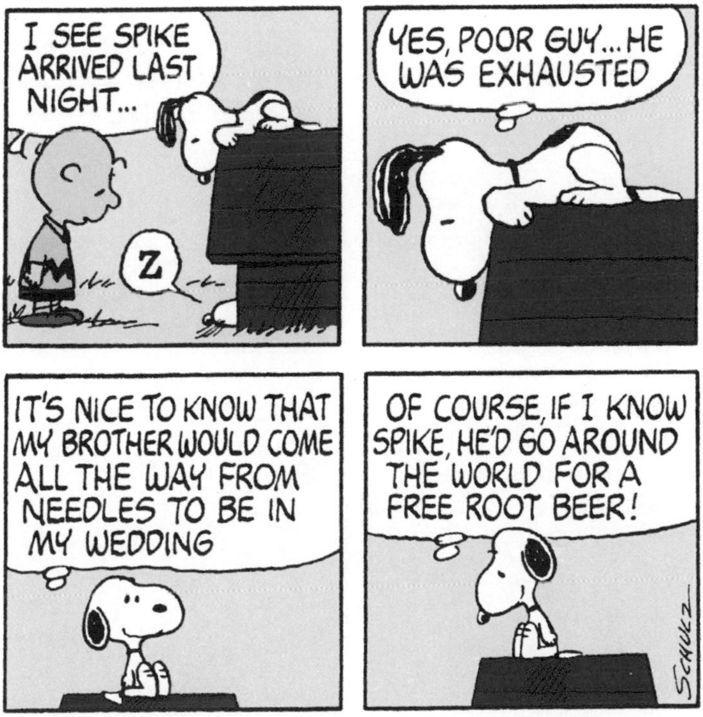
I SEE SPIKE ARRIVED LAST NIGHT...
Z
YES, POOR GUY...HE WAS EXHAUSTED
IT'S NICE TO KNOW THAT MY BROTHER WOULD COME ALL THE WAY FROM NEEDLES TO BE IN MY WEDDING
OF COURSE, IF I KNOW SPIKE, HE'D GO AROUND THE WORLD FOR A FREE ROOT BEER!
SCHULZ

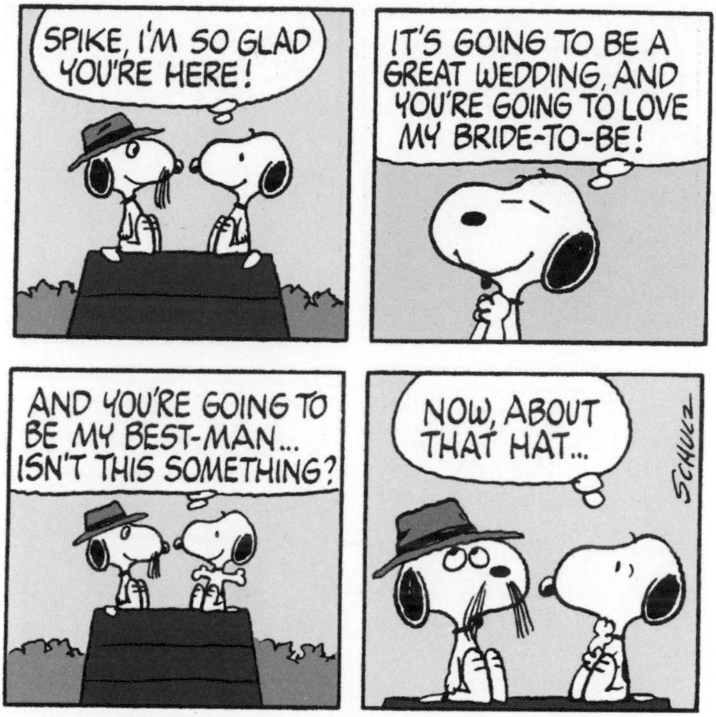
SPIKE, I'M SO GLAD YOU'RE HERE!
IT'S GOING TO BE A GREAT WEDDING, AND YOU'RE GOING TO LOVE MY BRIDE-TO-BE!
AND YOU'RE GOING TO BE MY BEST-MAN... ISN'T THIS SOMETHING?
NOW, ABOUT THAT HAT...
SCHULZ

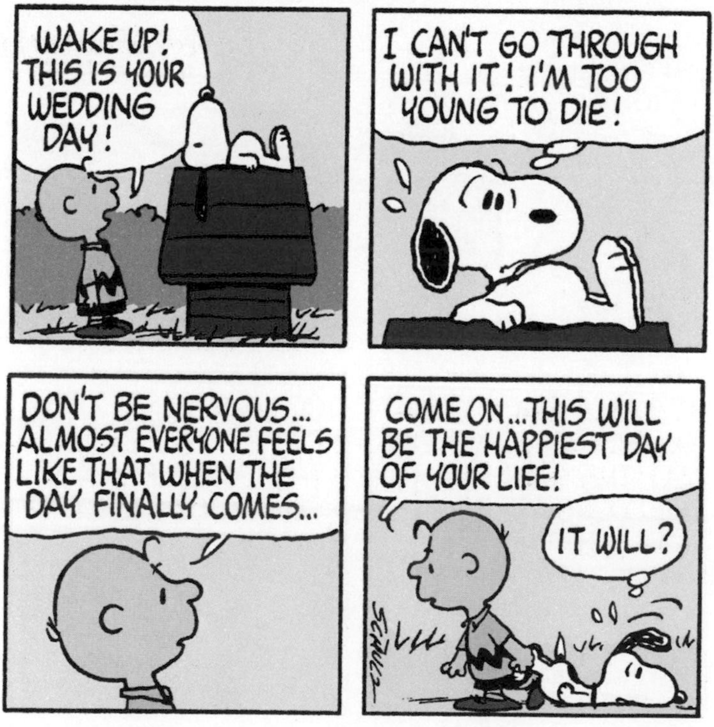
WAKE UP! THIS IS YOUR WEDDING DAY!
I CAN'T GO THROUGH WITH IT! I'M TOO YOUNG TO DIE!
DON'T BE NERVOUS... ALMOST EVERYONE FEELS LIKE THAT WHEN THE DAY FINALLY COMES...
COME ON...THIS WILL BE THE HAPPIEST DAY OF YOUR LIFE!
IT WILL?
SCHULZ

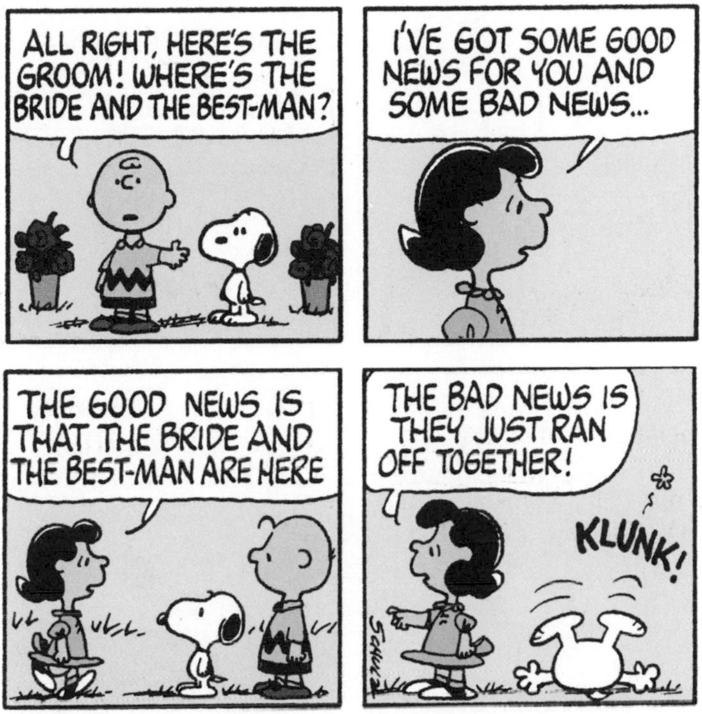
ALL RIGHT, HERE'S THE GROOM! WHERE'S THE BRIDE AND THE BEST-MAN?
I'VE GOT SOME GOOD NEWS FOR YOU AND SOME BAD NEWS...
THE GOOD NEWS IS THAT THE BRIDE AND THE BEST-MAN ARE HERE
THE BAD NEWS IS THEY JUST RAN OFF TOGETHER!
KLUNK!
SCHULZ

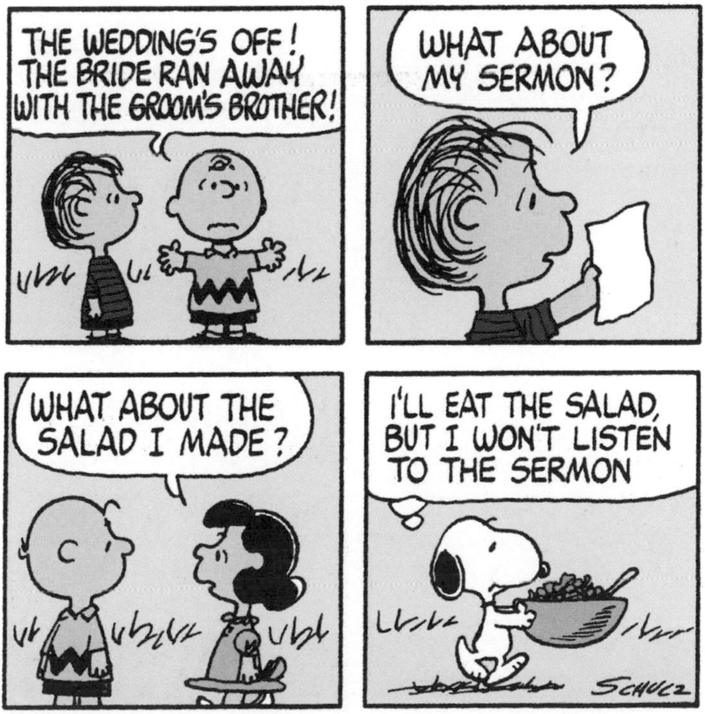
THE WEDDING'S OFF! THE BRIDE RAN AWAY WITH THE GROOM'S BROTHER!
WHAT ABOUT MY SERMON?
WHAT ABOUT THE SALAD I MADE?
I'LL EAT THE SALAD, BUT I WON'T LISTEN TO THE SERMON
SCHULZ

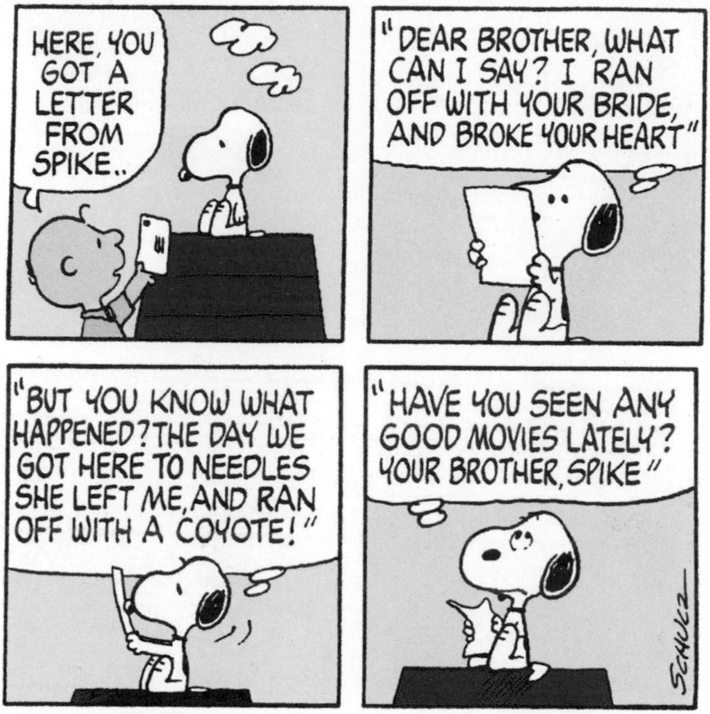
HERE, YOU GOT A LETTER FROM SPIKE..
"DEAR BROTHER, WHAT CAN I SAY? I RAN OFF WITH YOUR BRIDE, AND BROKE YOUR HEART"
"BUT YOU KNOW WHAT HAPPENED? THE DAY WE GOT HERE TO NEEDLES SHE LEFT ME, AND RAN OFF WITH A COYOTE!"
"HAVE YOU SEEN ANY GOOD MOVIES LATELY? YOUR BROTHER, SPIKE"
SCHULZ

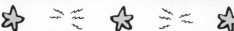

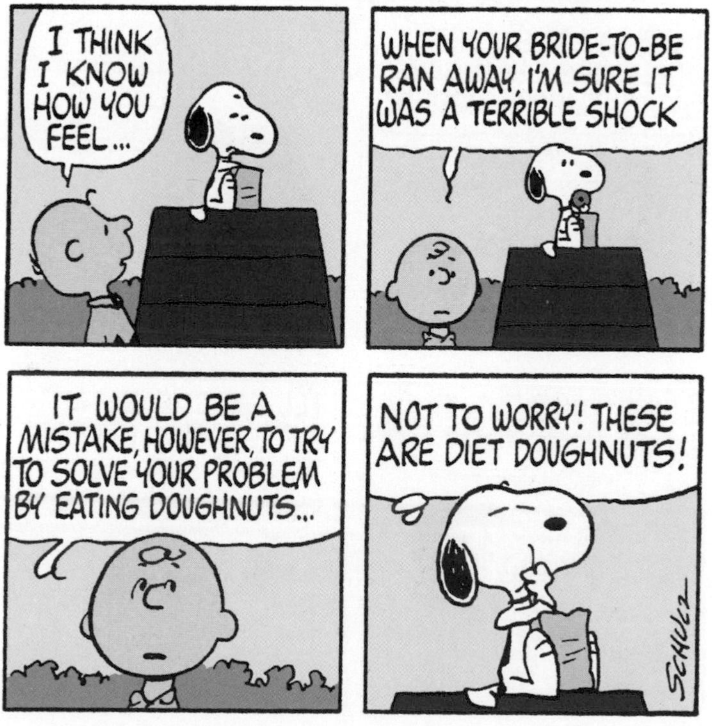
I THINK I KNOW HOW YOU FEEL...
WHEN YOUR BRIDE-TO-BE RAN AWAY, I'M SURE IT WAS A TERRIBLE SHOCK
IT WOULD BE A MISTAKE, HOWEVER, TO TRY TO SOLVE YOUR PROBLEM BY EATING DOUGHNUTS...
NOT TO WORRY! THESE ARE DIET DOUGHNUTS!
SCHULZ

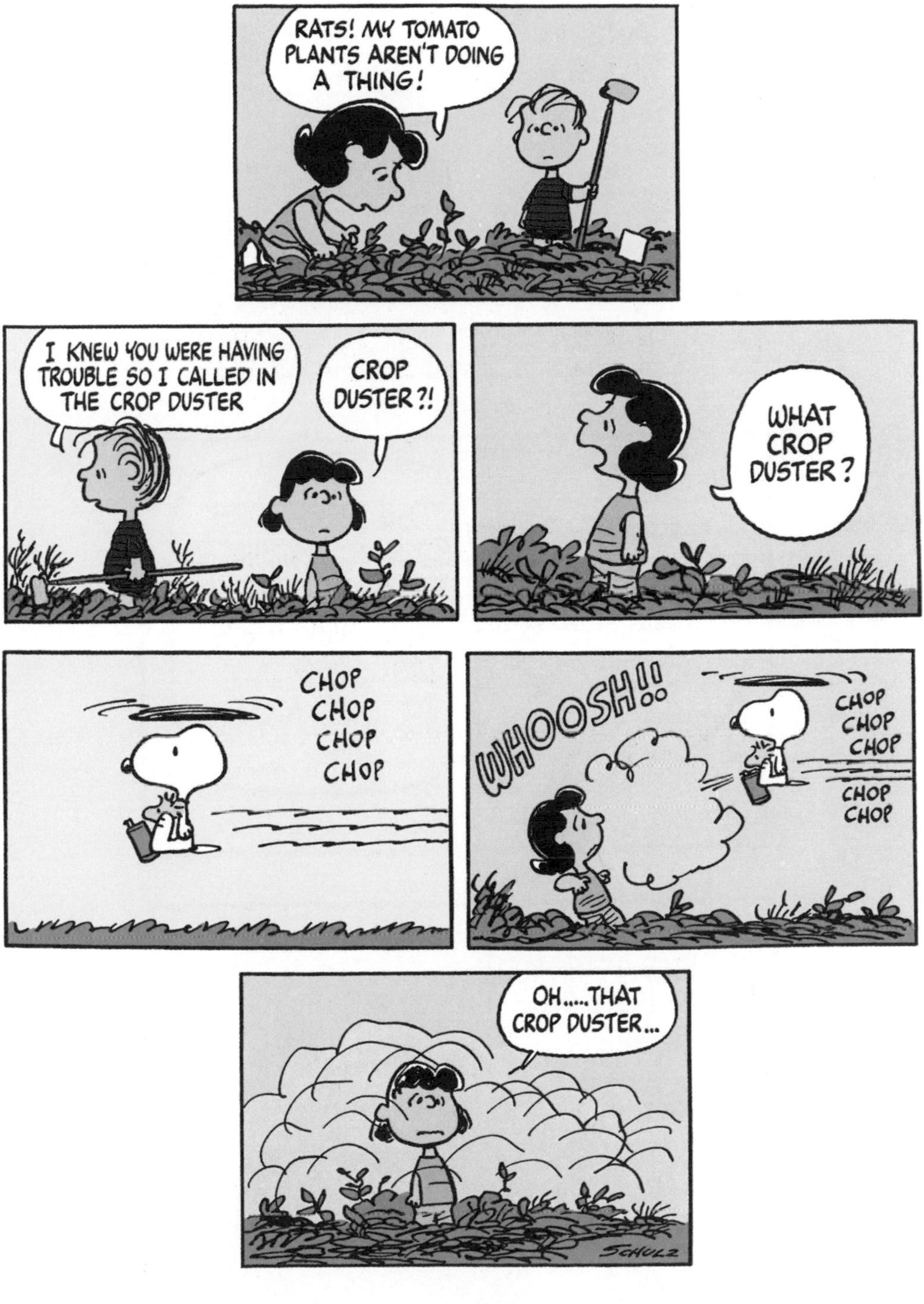
RATS! MY TOMATO PLANTS AREN'T DOING A THING!
I KNEW YOU WERE HAVING TROUBLE SO I CALLED IN THE CROP DUSTER
CROP DUSTER?!
WHAT CROP DUSTER?
CHOP CHOP CHOP CHOP
WHOOSH!!
CHOP CHOP CHOP
CHOP CHOP
OH.....THAT CROP DUSTER...
SCHULZ

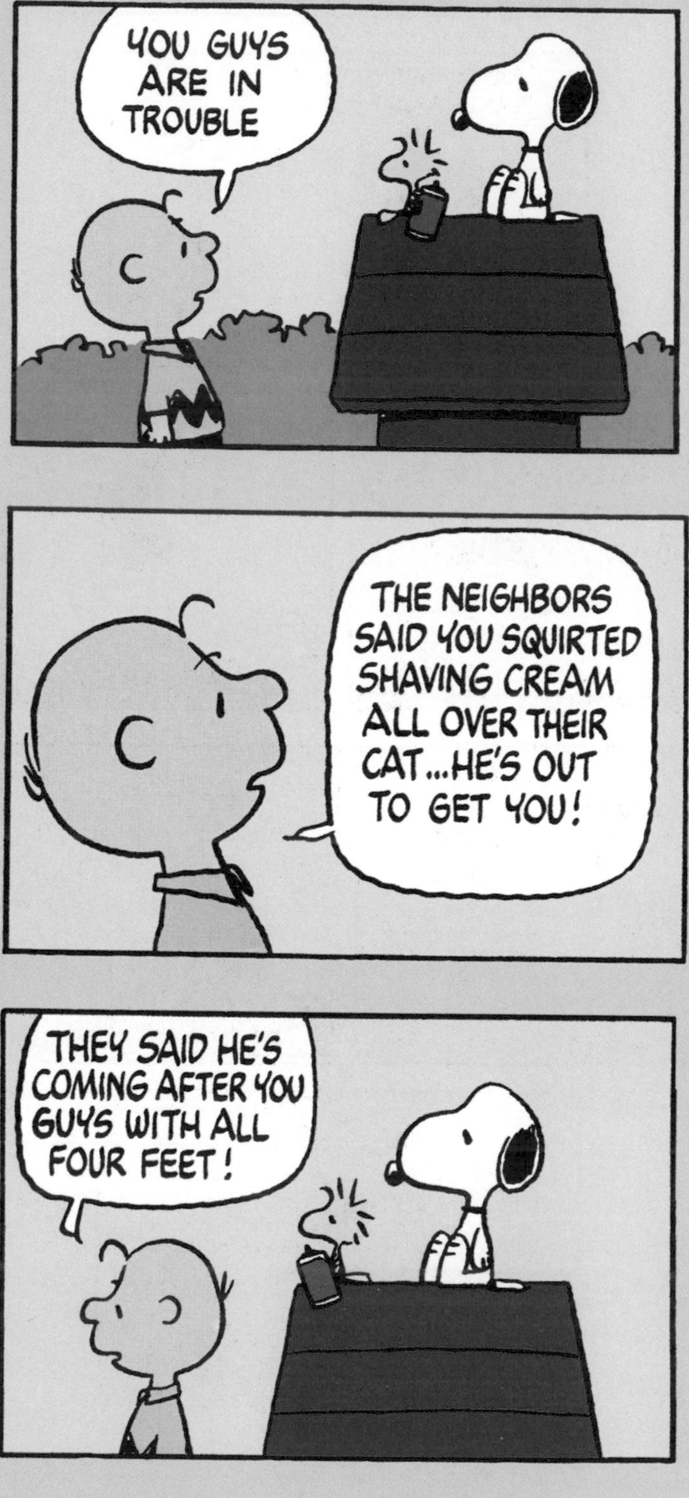
YOU GUYS ARE IN TROUBLE
THE NEIGHBORS SAID YOU SQUIRTED SHAVING CREAM ALL OVER THEIR CAT...HE'S OUT TO GET YOU!
THEY SAID HE'S COMING AFTER YOU GUYS WITH ALL FOUR FEET!

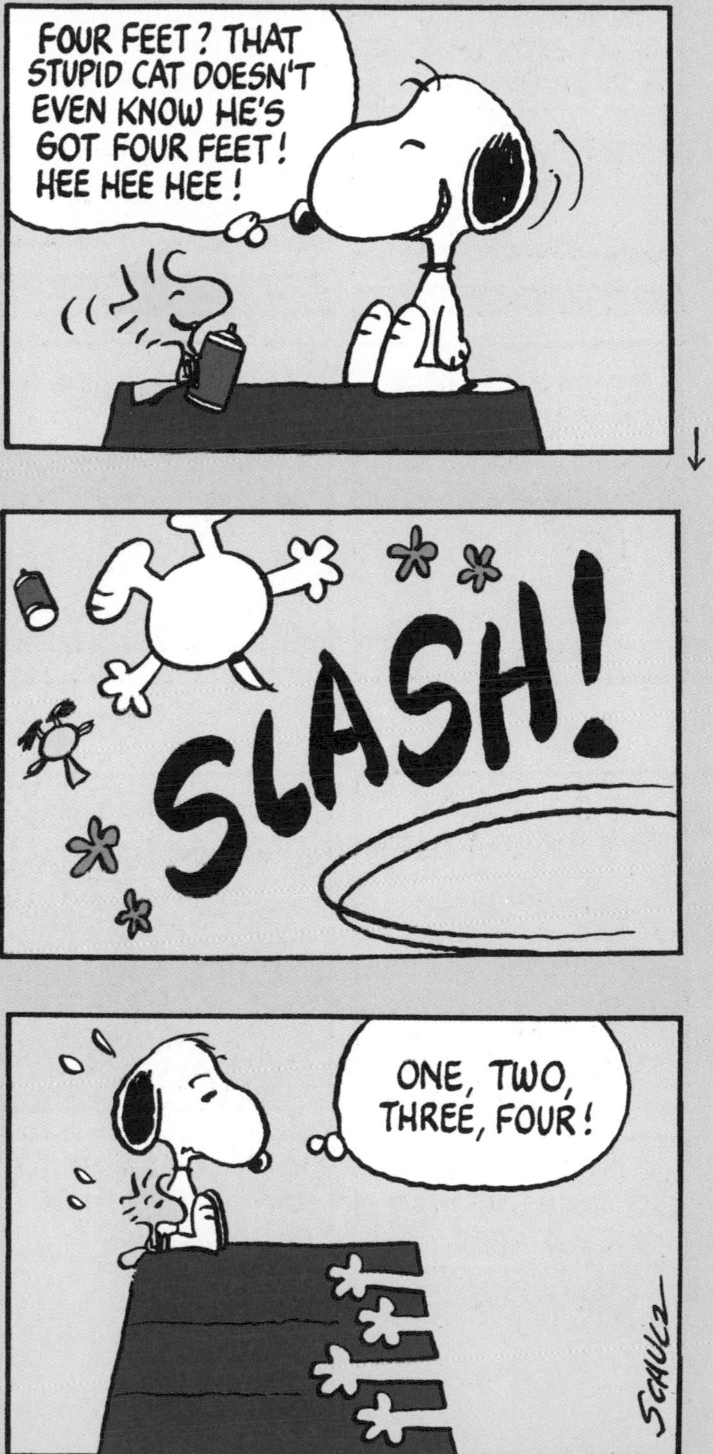
FOUR FEET? THAT STUPID CAT DOESN'T EVEN KNOW HE'S GOT FOUR FEET! HEE HEE HEE!
SLASH!
ONE, TWO, THREE, FOUR!
SCHULZ

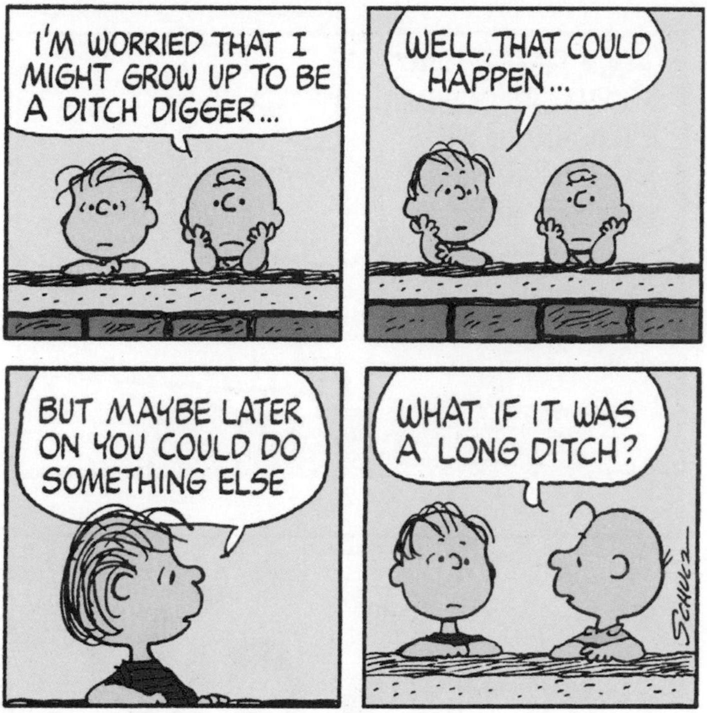
I'M WORRIED THAT I MIGHT GROW UP TO BE A DITCH DIGGER...
WELL, THAT COULD HAPPEN...
BUT MAYBE LATER ON YOU COULD DO SOMETHING ELSE
WHAT IF IT WAS A LONG DITCH?
SCHULZ

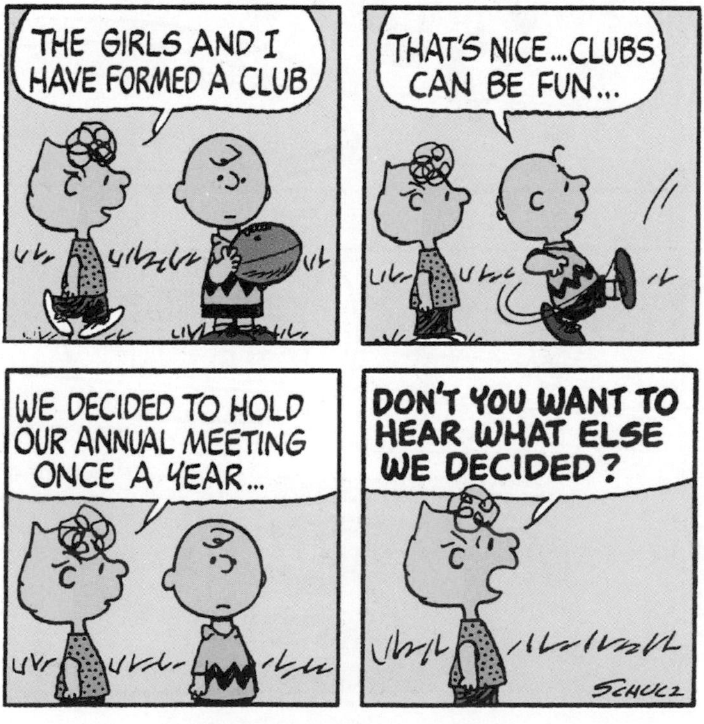
THE GIRLS AND I HAVE FORMED A CLUB
THAT'S NICE...CLUBS CAN BE FUN...
WE DECIDED TO HOLD OUR ANNUAL MEETING ONCE A YEAR...
DON'T YOU WANT TO HEAR WHAT ELSE WE DECIDED?
SCHULZ

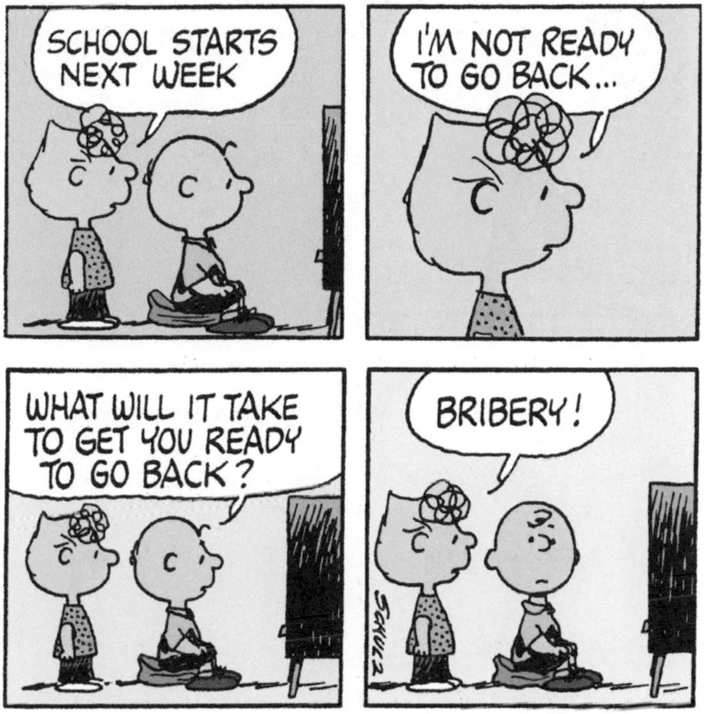
SCHOOL STARTS NEXT WEEK
I'M NOT READY TO GO BACK...
WHAT WILL IT TAKE TO GET YOU READY TO GO BACK?
BRIBERY!

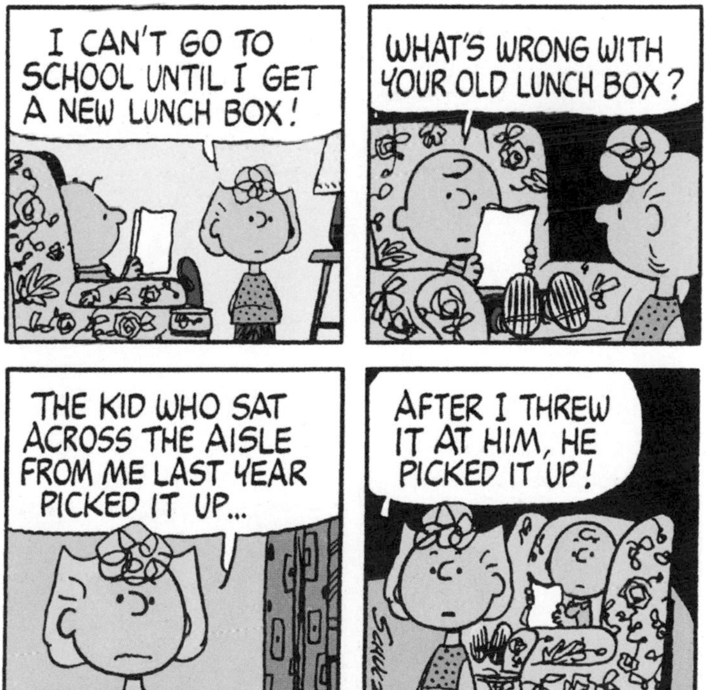
I CAN'T GO TO SCHOOL UNTIL I GET A NEW LUNCH BOX!
WHAT'S WRONG WITH YOUR OLD LUNCH BOX?
THE KID WHO SAT ACROSS THE AISLE FROM ME LAST YEAR PICKED IT UP...
AFTER I THREW IT AT HIM, HE PICKED IT UP!

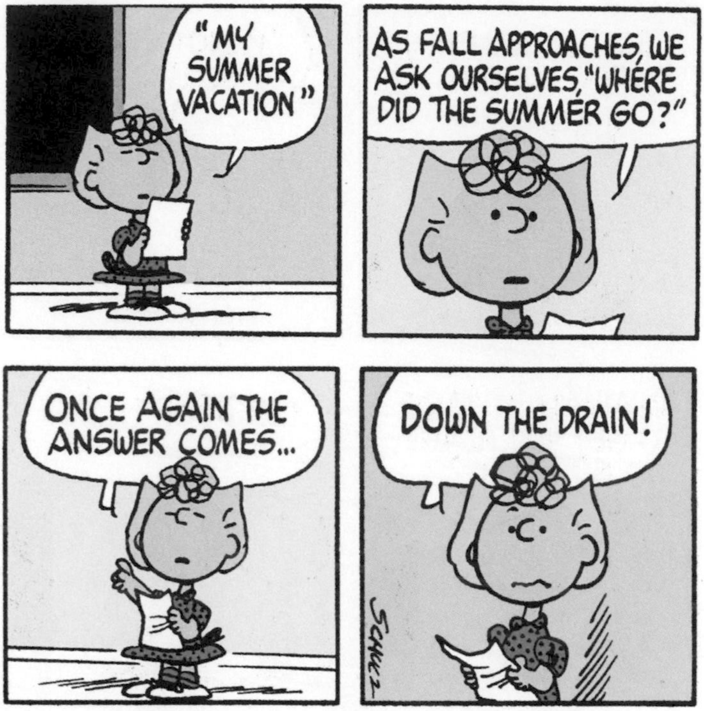
"MY SUMMER VACATION"
AS FALL APPROACHES, WE ASK OURSELVES, "WHERE DID THE SUMMER GO?"
ONCE AGAIN THE ANSWER COMES...
DOWN THE DRAIN!
SCHULZ

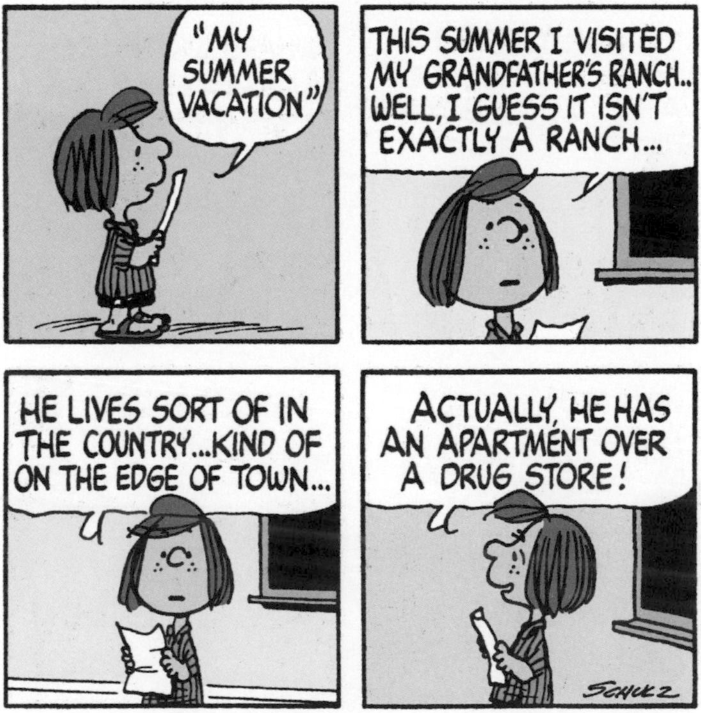
"MY SUMMER VACATION"
THIS SUMMER I VISITED MY GRANDFATHER'S RANCH.. WELL, I GUESS IT ISN'T EXACTLY A RANCH...
HE LIVES SORT OF IN THE COUNTRY...KIND OF ON THE EDGE OF TOWN...
ACTUALLY, HE HAS AN APARTMENT OVER A DRUG STORE!
SCHULZ

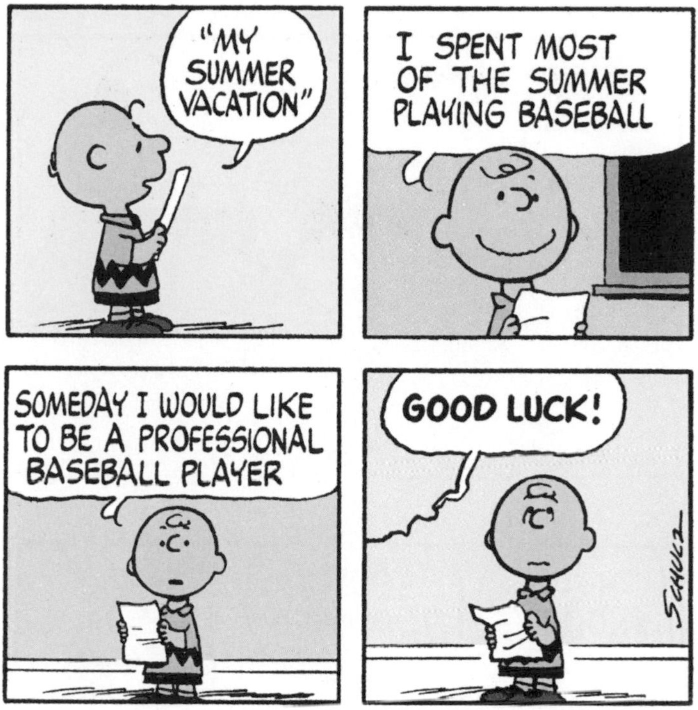
"MY SUMMER VACATION"
I SPENT MOST OF THE SUMMER PLAYING BASEBALL
SOMEDAY I WOULD LIKE TO BE A PROFESSIONAL BASEBALL PLAYER
GOOD LUCK!
SCHULZ

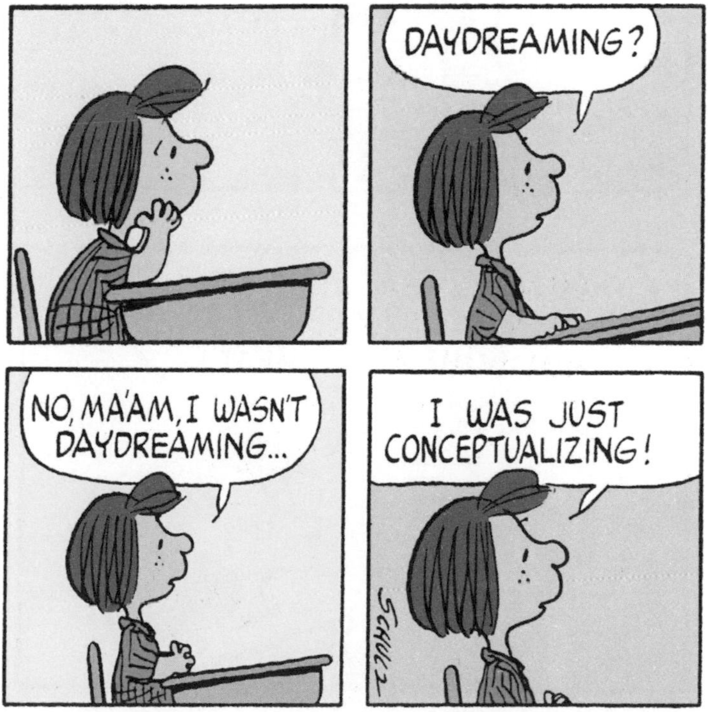
DAYDREAMING?
NO, MA'AM, I WASN'T DAYDREAMING...
I WAS JUST CONCEPTUALIZING!
SCHULZ

WHAT'S THIS?
THIS IS SNOOPY'S SUPPER
YOU'RE KIDDING!
YOU TAKE THAT RIGHT BACK, CHARLIE BROWN, AND YOU GIVE HIM SOME MORE MEAT!

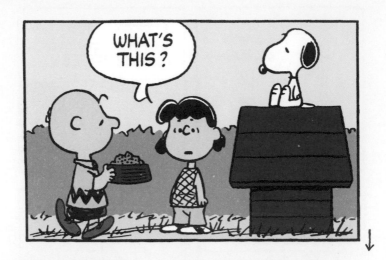

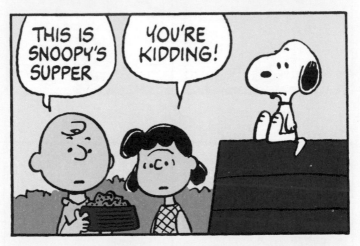

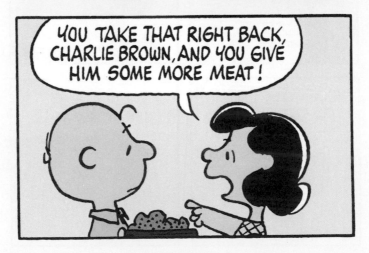

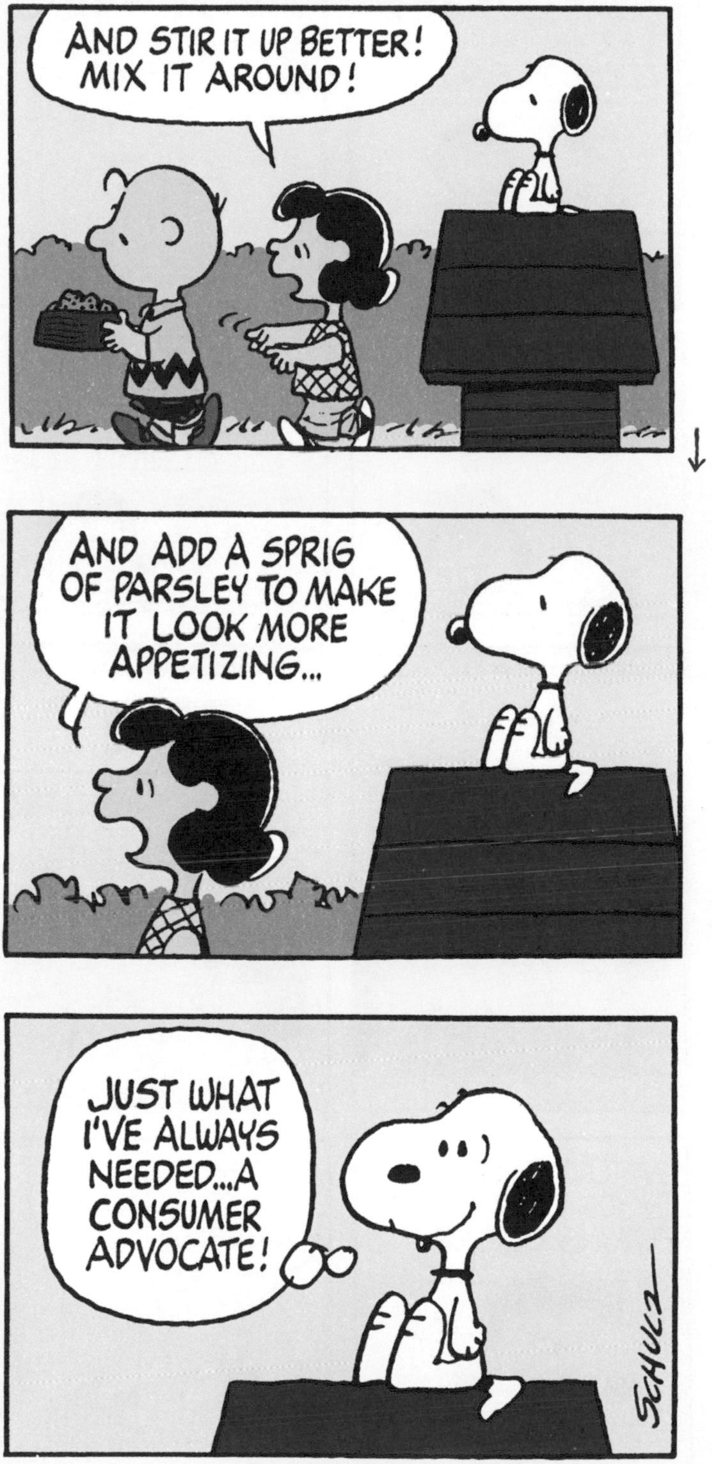
AND STIR IT UP BETTER! MIX IT AROUND!
AND ADD A SPRIG OF PARSLEY TO MAKE IT LOOK MORE APPETIZING...
JUST WHAT I'VE ALWAYS NEEDED...A CONSUMER ADVOCATE!
SCHULZ

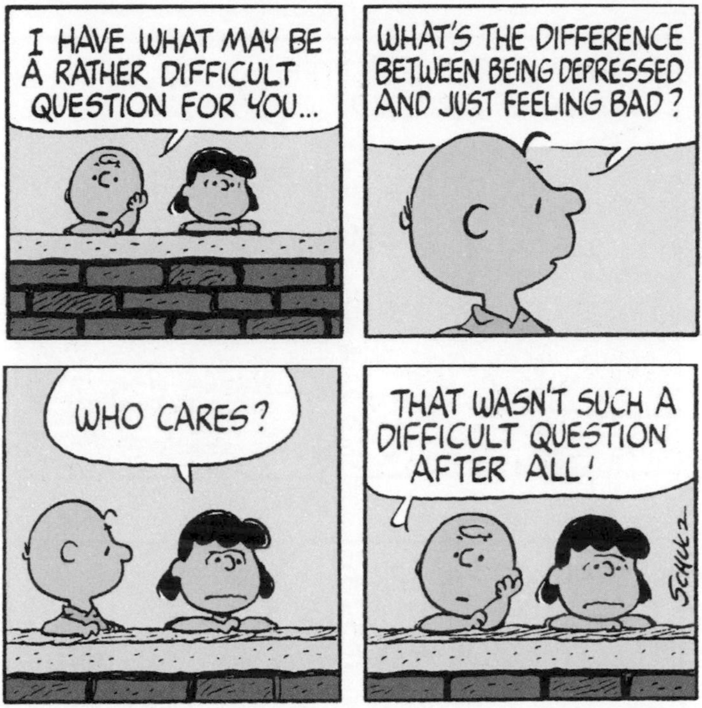
I HAVE WHAT MAY BE A RATHER DIFFICULT QUESTION FOR YOU...
WHAT'S THE DIFFERENCE BETWEEN BEING DEPRESSED AND JUST FEELING BAD?
WHO CARES?
THAT WASN'T SUCH A DIFFICULT QUESTION AFTER ALL!
SCHULZ

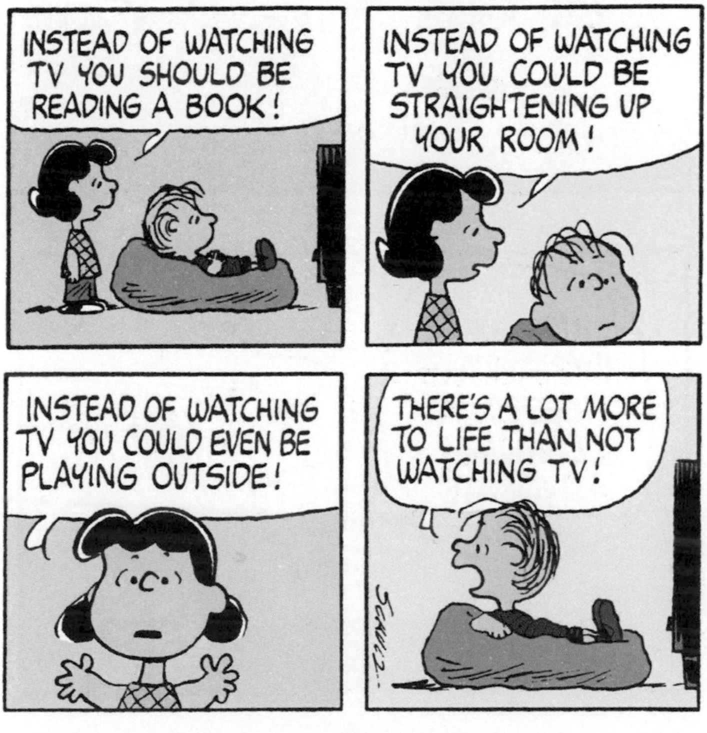
INSTEAD OF WATCHING TV YOU SHOULD BE READING A BOOK!
INSTEAD OF WATCHING TV YOU COULD BE STRAIGHTENING UP YOUR ROOM!
INSTEAD OF WATCHING TV YOU COULD EVEN BE PLAYING OUTSIDE!
THERE'S A LOT MORE TO LIFE THAN NOT WATCHING TV!
SCHULZ

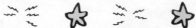

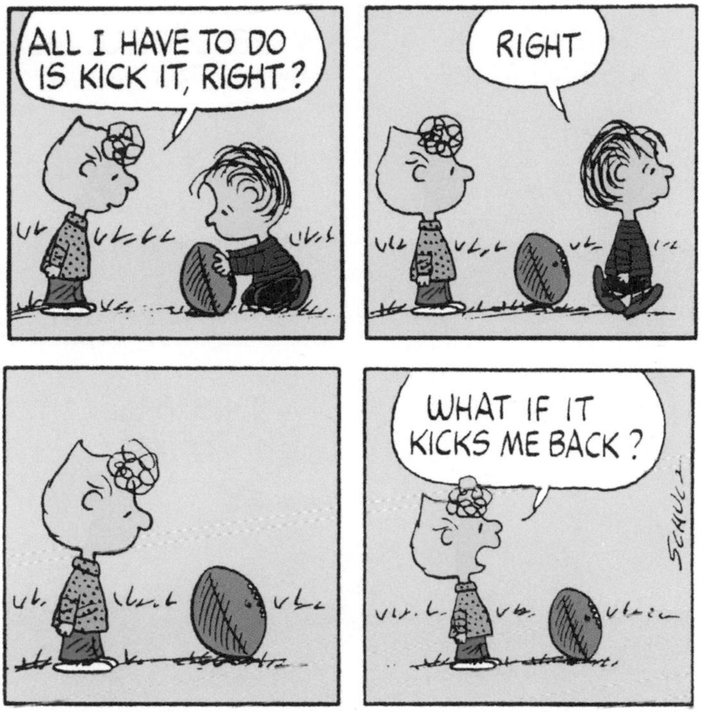
ALL I HAVE TO DO IS KICK IT, RIGHT?
RIGHT
WHAT IF IT KICKS ME BACK?
SCHULZ

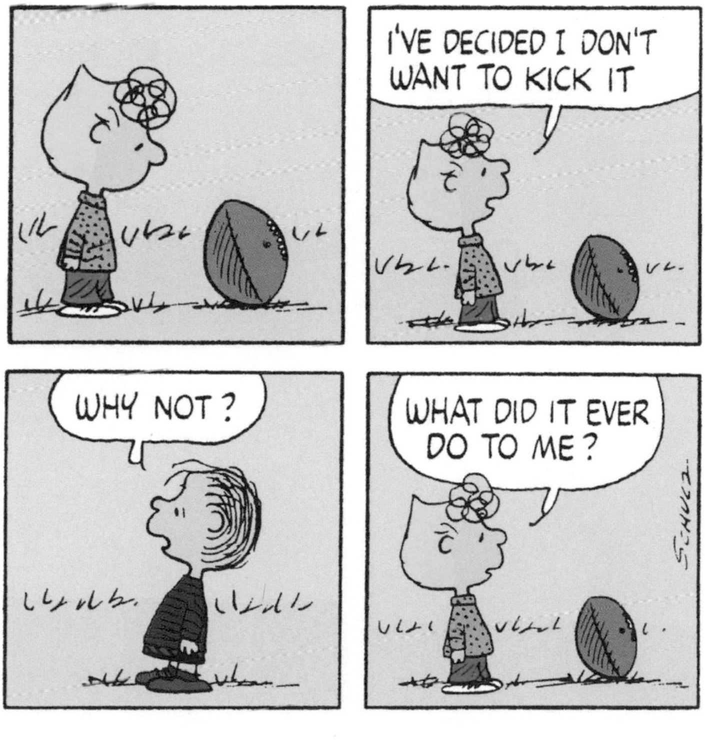
I'VE DECIDED I DON'T WANT TO KICK IT
WHY NOT?
WHAT DID IT EVER DO TO ME?
SCHULZ

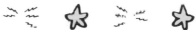

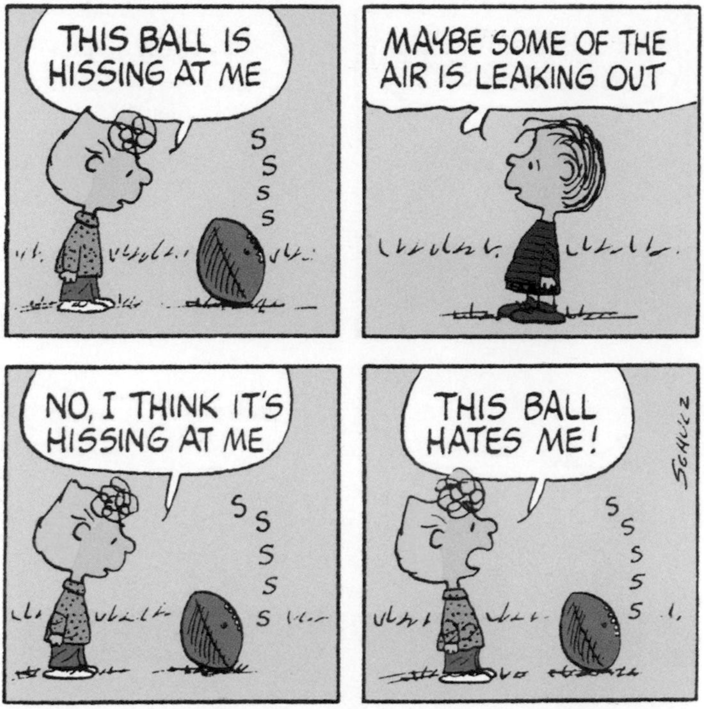
THIS BALL IS HISSING AT ME
MAYBE SOME OF THE AIR IS LEAKING OUT
NO, I THINK IT'S HISSING AT ME
THIS BALL HATES ME!

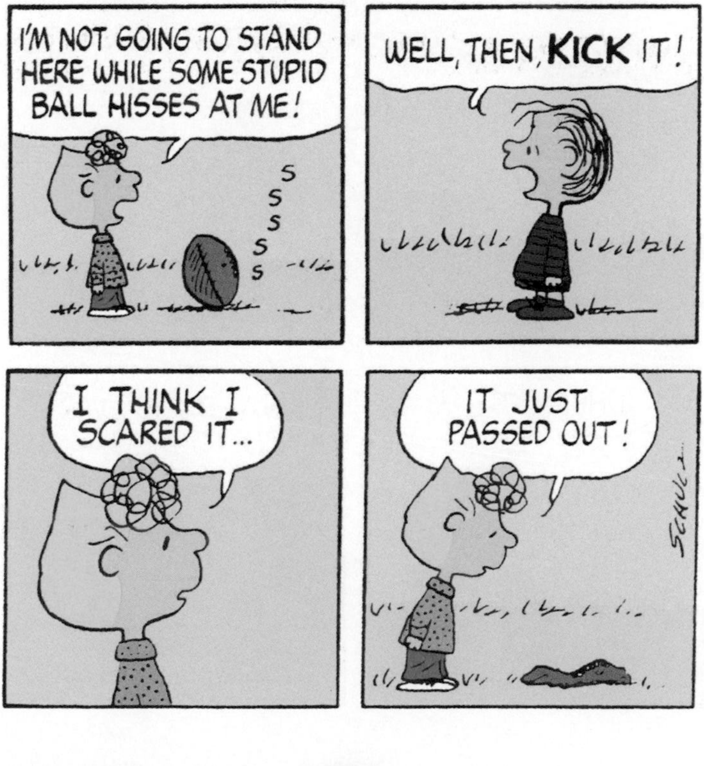
I'M NOT GOING TO STAND HERE WHILE SOME STUPID BALL HISSES AT ME!
WELL, THEN, KICK IT!
I THINK I SCARED IT...
IT JUST PASSED OUT!

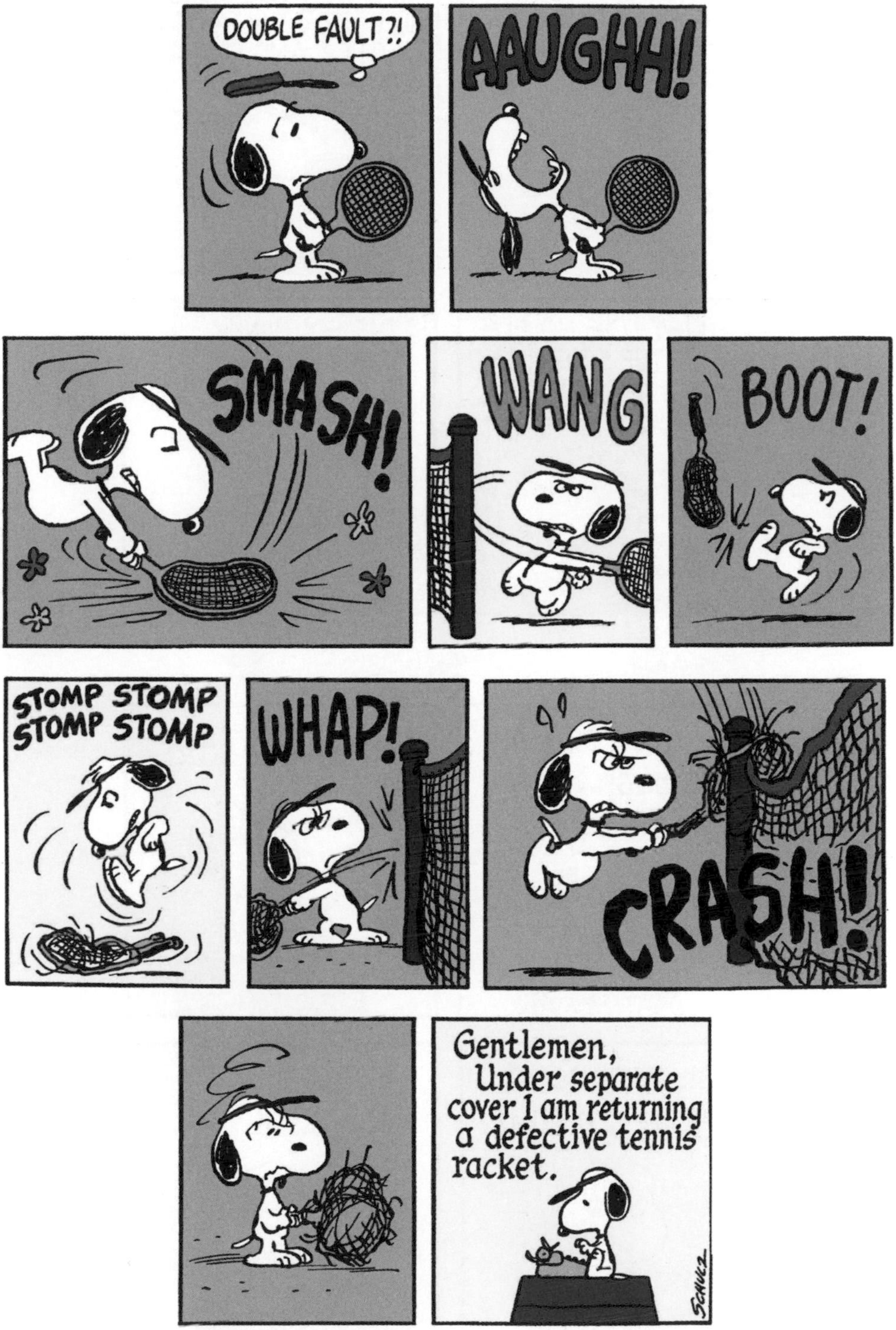
DOUBLE FAULT?!
AAUGHH!
SMASH!
WANG
BOOT!
STOMP STOMP
STOMP STOMP
WHAP!
CRASH!
Gentlemen,
Under separate cover I am returning a defective tennis racket.
SCHULZ

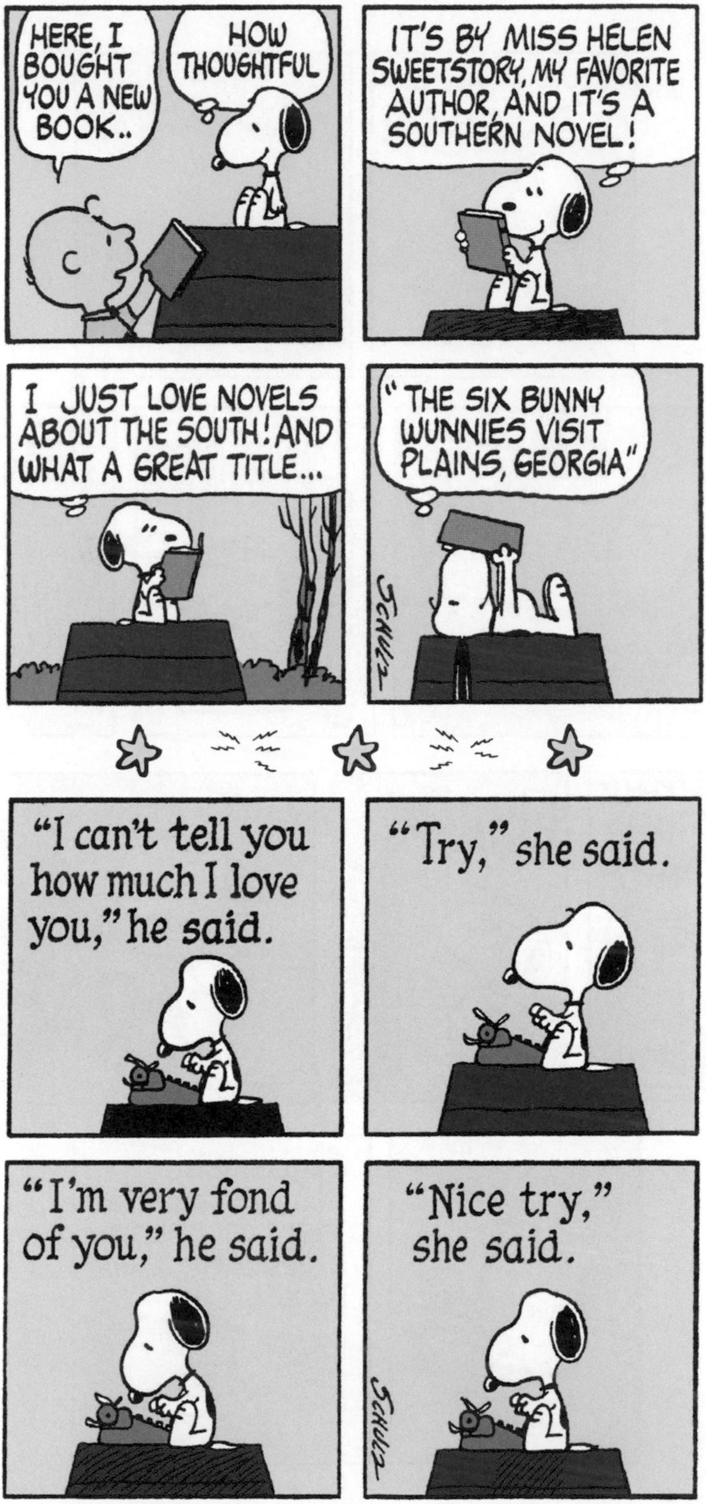
HERE, I BOUGHT YOU A NEW BOOK..
HOW THOUGHTFUL
IT'S BY MISS HELEN SWEETSTORY, MY FAVORITE AUTHOR, AND IT'S A SOUTHERN NOVEL!
I JUST LOVE NOVELS ABOUT THE SOUTH! AND WHAT A GREAT TITLE...
"THE SIX BUNNY WUNNIES VISIT PLAINS, GEORGIA"
SCHULZ
"I can't tell you how much I love you," he said.
"Try," she said.
"I'm very fond of you," he said.
"Nice try," she said.
SCHULZ

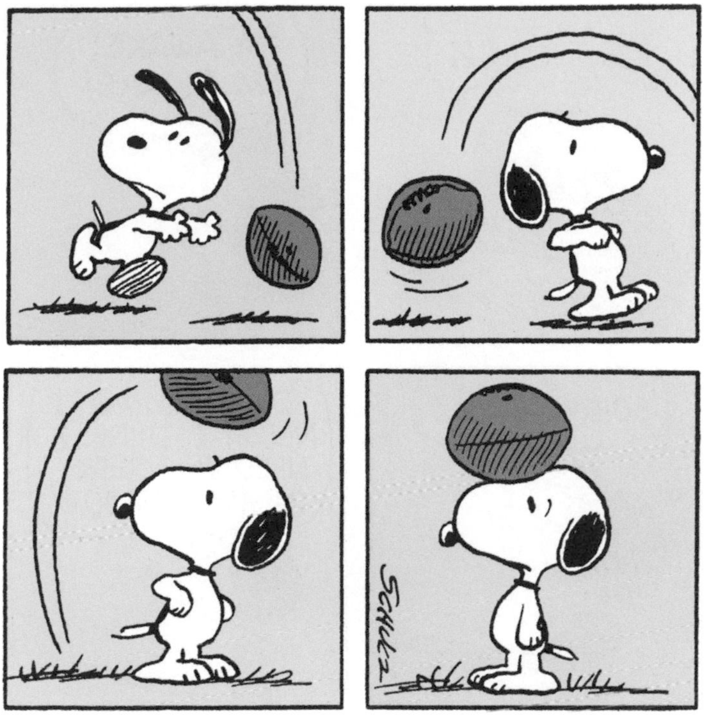
SCHULZ

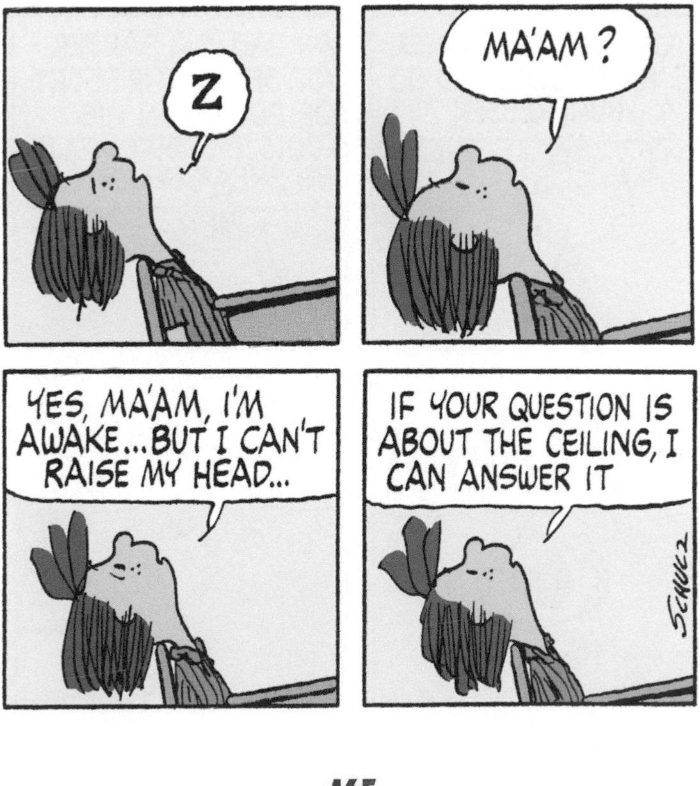
Z
MA'AM ?
YES, MA'AM, I'M AWAKE...BUT I CAN'T RAISE MY HEAD...
IF YOUR QUESTION IS ABOUT THE CEILING, I CAN ANSWER IT
SCHULZ

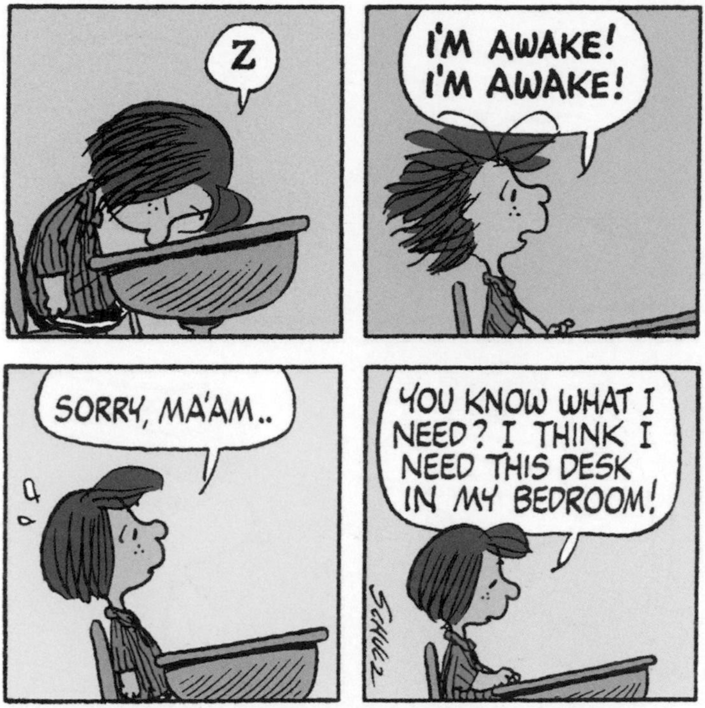
Z
I'M AWAKE! I'M AWAKE!
SORRY, MA'AM..
YOU KNOW WHAT I NEED? I THINK I NEED THIS DESK IN MY BEDROOM!
SCHULZ

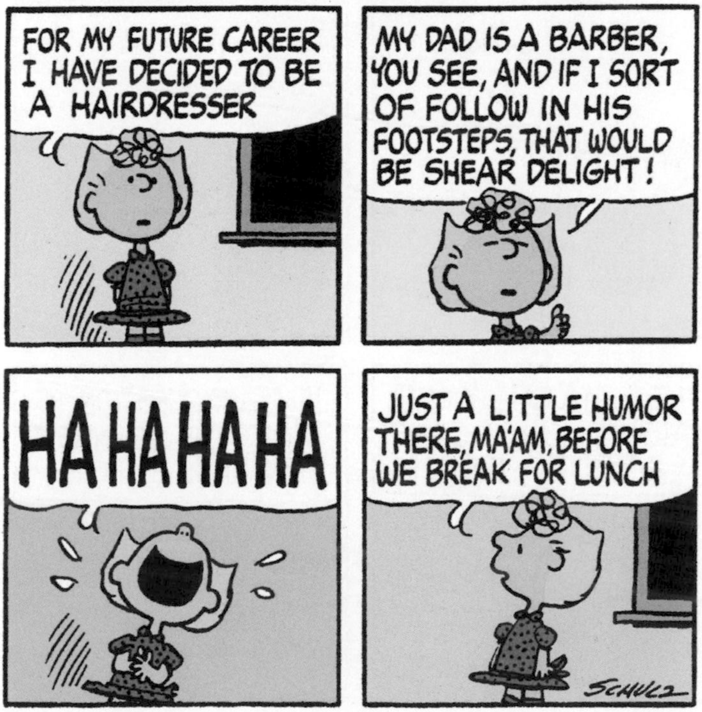
FOR MY FUTURE CAREER I HAVE DECIDED TO BE A HAIRDRESSER
MY DAD IS A BARBER, YOU SEE, AND IF I SORT OF FOLLOW IN HIS FOOTSTEPS, THAT WOULD BE SHEAR DELIGHT!
HA HA HA HA HA
JUST A LITTLE HUMOR THERE, MA'AM, BEFORE WE BREAK FOR LUNCH
SCHULZ

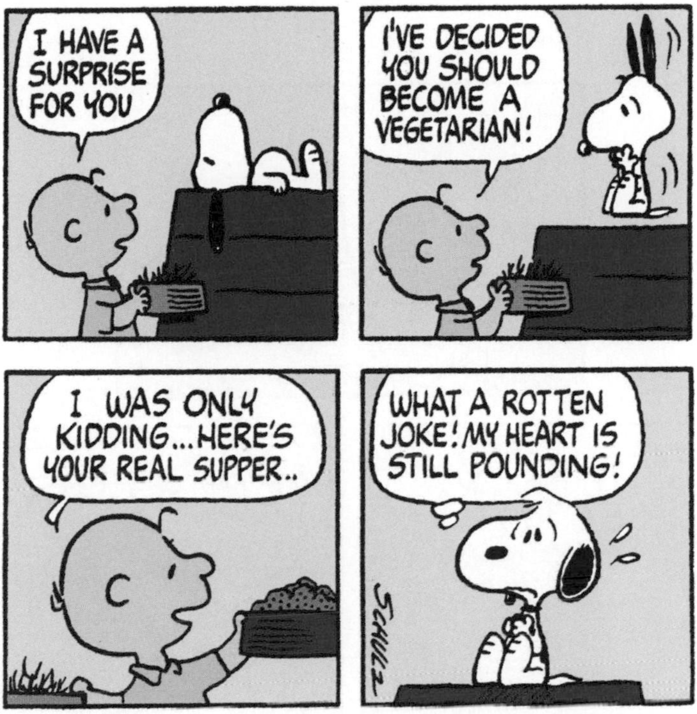
I HAVE A SURPRISE FOR YOU
I'VE DECIDED YOU SHOULD BECOME A VEGETARIAN!
I WAS ONLY KIDDING...HERE'S YOUR REAL SUPPER..
WHAT A ROTTEN JOKE! MY HEART IS STILL POUNDING!
SCHULZ

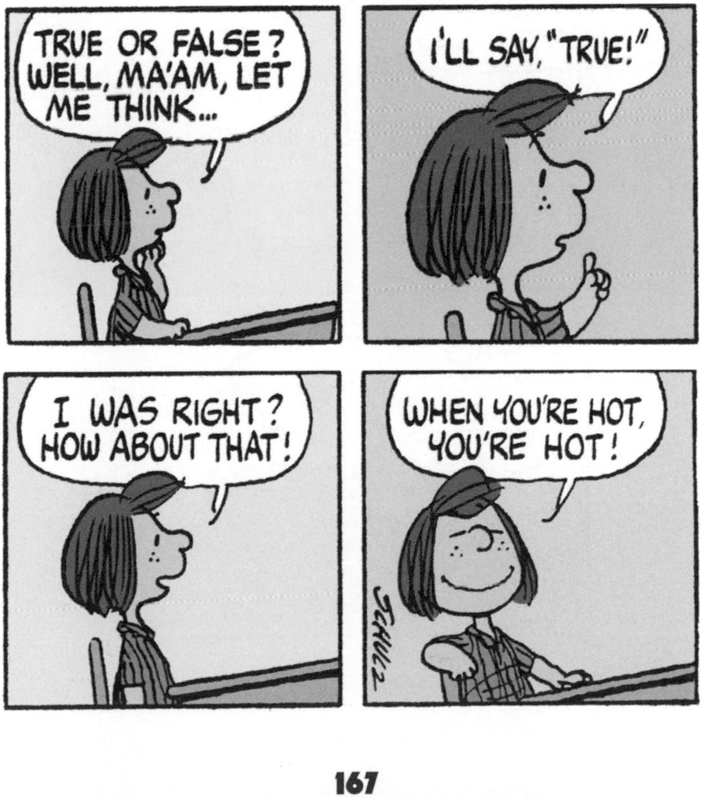
TRUE OR FALSE? WELL, MA'AM, LET ME THINK...
I'LL SAY, "TRUE!"
I WAS RIGHT? HOW ABOUT THAT!
WHEN YOU'RE HOT, YOU'RE HOT!
SCHULZ

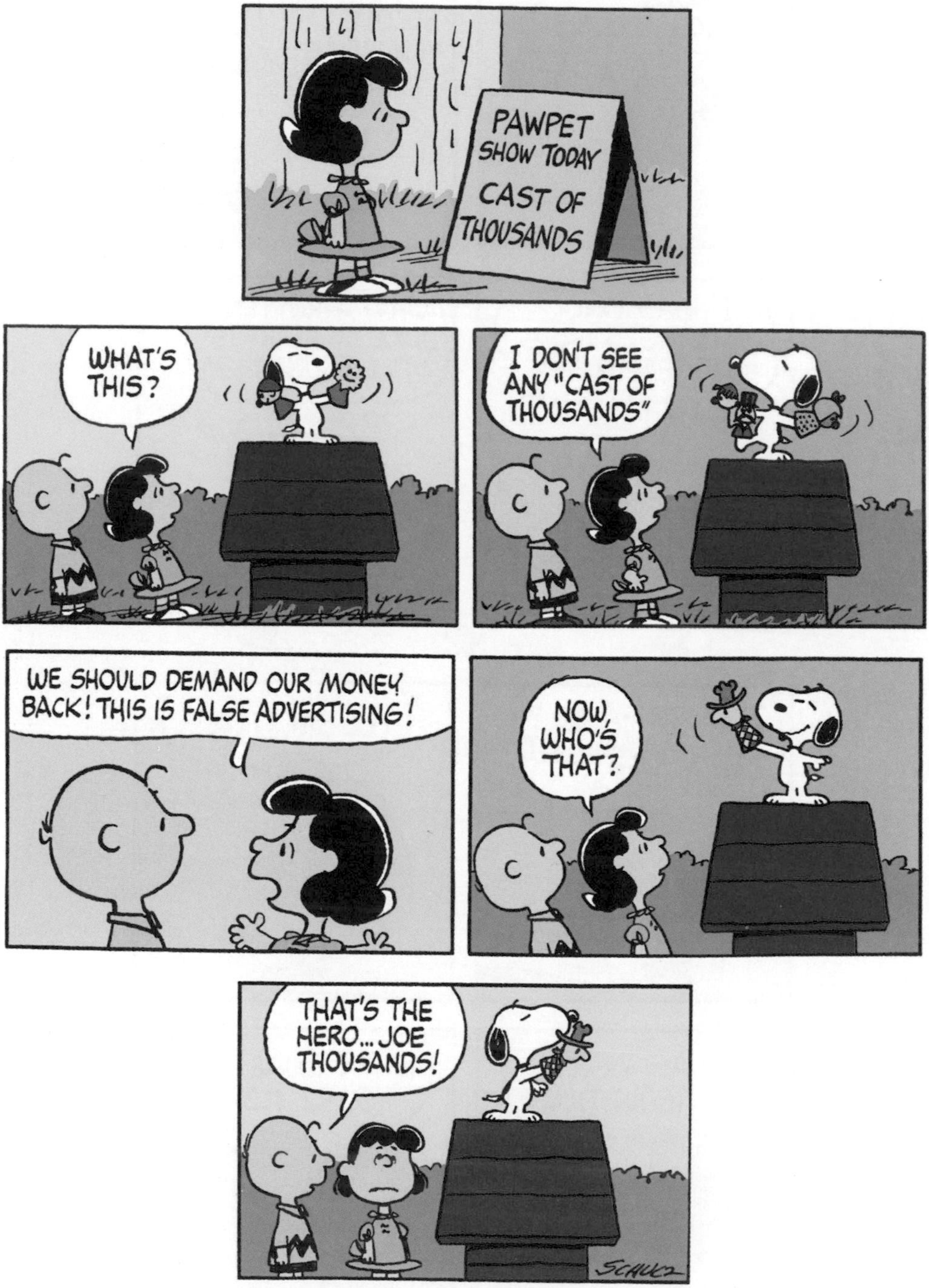
PAWPET
SHOW TODAY
CAST OF
THOUSANDS
WHAT'S THIS?
I DON'T SEE ANY "CAST OF THOUSANDS"
WE SHOULD DEMAND OUR MONEY BACK! THIS IS FALSE ADVERTISING!
NOW, WHO'S THAT?
THAT'S THE HERO... JOE THOUSANDS!
SCHULZ

MORE TO EXPLORE! Featuring cool activities and fun facts!

It's fun to see Snoopy being a helicopter, but of course a beagle can't really fly! And just like Snoopy saved Linus from the top of the barn, real helicopters are used to reach people in trouble and save them. They have other purposes, too.

Here's some fun information on what helicopters are and how they work.

Also, there are instructions for making your own origami paper helicopter!

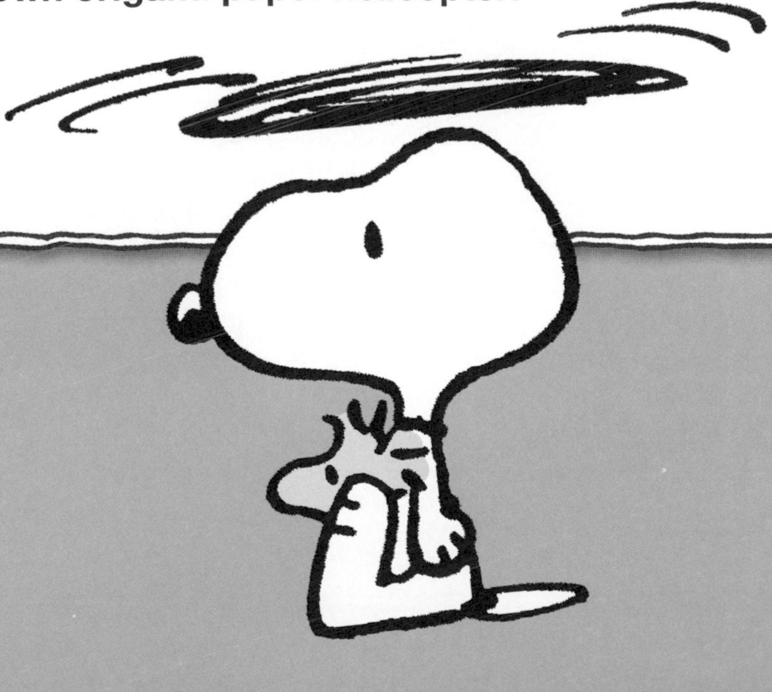

What Is a Helicopter?

A helicopter is a type of aircraft that uses rotating, or spinning, wings called blades to fly. Unlike an airplane or glider, a helicopter has wings that move. Unlike a balloon, a helicopter is heavier than air and uses an engine to fly. A helicopter's rotating blades, or a rotor, allow it to do things an airplane cannot.

How Does a Helicopter Work?

In order to fly, an object must have "lift," a force moving it upward. Lift is usually made by wings. Wings create lift because of a relationship called the Bernoulli Principle. The Bernoulli Principle describes how the speed of air and the pressure in the air are related. When the speed goes up, the pressure goes down and the opposite is also true.

Wings are curved on top and flatter on the bottom. This shape is called an airfoil. That shape makes air flow over the top faster than under the bottom. As a result, there is less air pressure on top of the wing; this causes suction and makes the wing move up. A helicopter's rotor blades are wings and create lift. An airplane must fly fast to move enough air over its wings to provide lift. A helicopter moves air over its rotor by spinning its blades.

What Can a Helicopter Do?

A helicopter's rotors allow it to do things an airplane cannot. Unlike an airplane, a helicopter does not have to move quickly through the air to have lift. That fact means it can move straight up or down. Most airplanes cannot do this. A helicopter can take off or land without a runway. It can turn in the air in ways airplanes cannot. Unlike an airplane, a helicopter can fly backwards or sideways. It also can hover in one spot in the air without moving. This makes helicopters ideal for things an airplane cannot do. For example, a helicopter can pick someone with a medical problem up where there is no runway. It can then land in a small area on top of a hospital.

What Are Uses of Helicopters?

Helicopters can be used for many things. They can be used as flying ambulances to carry patients. They can be loaded with water to fight large fires. Military forces use helicopters to attack targets on the ground and move troops. Helicopters are used to get supplies to ships. Helicopters can be used to transport large objects from place to place. Helicopters can rescue people in hard-to-reach places like mountains or in rough seas. Television and radio stations use helicopters to fly over cities and report on traffic. Helicopters are used by police and by people on vacation. These uses are just some of the many things that can be done with helicopters.

What Does NASA Do With Helicopters?

NASA conducts research on ways to make helicopters better. Crash tests help make helicopters safer. NASA studies how new materials can keep passengers safe if a helicopter crashes. Wind tunnel tests determine how to make helicopters quieter and more fuel-efficient. New ideas could help engineers create bigger, better and faster helicopters. Someday helicopters could carry 100 people on trips of 300 miles or more. NASA has even studied how helicopters could be flown on Mars!

NASA uses a model of a quad-rotor helicopter to test how the vehicle with four rotors can be remotely controlled. Credits: NASA

This NASA Skycrane helicopter can pick up and move very big things. It can even pick up and move a small house. Credits: NASA

NASA tested this rotor design in a wind tunnel to research ways to make helicopters quieter. Credits: NASA

This article is part of the *NASA Knows! (Grades 5-8) series*. "What Is a Helicopter," by David Hitt, edited by Sandra May. Published by NASA Educational Technology Services, 21 May 2014. www.nasa.gov

Make Your Own Helicopter!

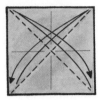 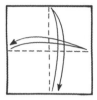

1. Fold diagonally, both directions. Flip over.

2. Fold both directions. Flip over.

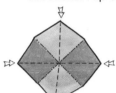 

3. Start to collapse.

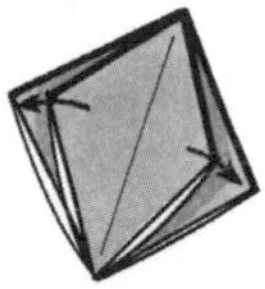

4. Collapse to sides.

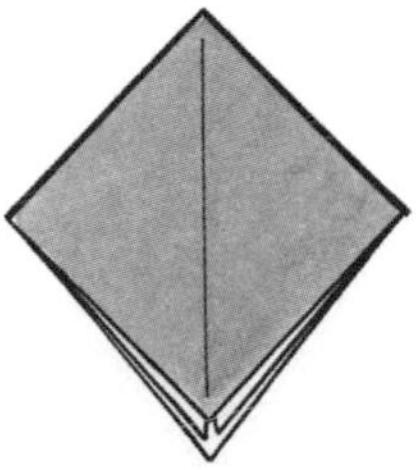

Square base.

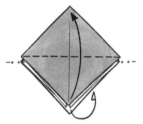 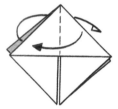

5. Fold front and back flaps of square base up.

6. Book fold the front and back.

7. Fold side points to the center. Repeat on back side.

8. Book fold the front and back.

Now throw your helicopter and watch it twirl!

(Instructions from *Easy Origami Fold-a-Day 2015 Calendar* by Jeff Coles, Andrews McMeel Publishing, 2014)

Make Your Own Halloween

Andrews McMeel Publishing
a division of Andrews McMeel Universal
1130 Walnut Street, Kansas City, Missouri 64106

www.andrewsmcmeel.com

www.peanuts.com

18 19 20 21 22 SDB 10 9 8 7 6 5 4 3 2 1

ISBN: 978-1-4494-8540-5

Library of Congress Control Number: 2017949865

Made by:
Shenzhen Donnelley Printing Company Ltd.
Address and location of manufacturer:
No. 47, Wuhe Nan Road, Bantian Ind. Zone,
Shenzhen China, 518129
1st Printing—12/18/17

ATTENTION: SCHOOLS AND BUSINESSES

Andrews McMeel books are available at quantity discounts with bulk purchase for educational, business, or sales promotional use. For information, please e-mail the Andrews McMeel Publishing Special Sales Department: specialsales@amuniversal.com.

Check out more *Peanuts* kids' collections from Andrews McMeel Publishing

SNOOPY
COWABUNGA!
A PEANUTS Collection

CHARLIE BROWN
AND FRIENDS
A PEANUTS Collection

POW!
A PEANUTS Collection

WOODSTOCK
MASTER OF DISGUISE
A PEANUTS Collection

SNOOPY
CONTACT!
A PEANUTS Collection

SNOOPY
PARTY ANIMAL
A PEANUTS Collection

CHARLIE BROWN
HERE WE GO AGAIN
PULL-OUT POSTER INSIDE
AAUGH
A PEANUTS Collection

SNOOPY
TO THE RESCUE
PULL-OUT POSTER INSIDE
A PEANUTS Collection

SNOOPY
WHAT'S WRONG WITH DOG LIPS?
A PEANUTS Collection

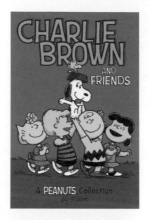

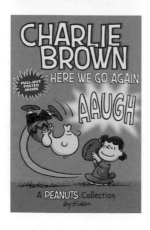

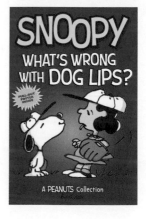